The new Zebra Re
is a photograph of an actual regency "tuzzy-muzzy." The fashionable regency lady often wore a tuzzy-muzzy tied with a satin or velvet riband around her wrist to carry a fragrant nosegay. Usually made of gold or silver, tuzzy-muzzies varied in design from the elegantly simple to the exquisitely ornate. The Zebra Regency Romance tuzzy-muzzy is made of alabaster with a silver filigree edging.

A MOST SCANDALOUS REQUEST

With great presence of mind, she dropped her parasol and wrapped both arms around Simon's waist. And just in case he still did not catch her meaning, she raised herself on tiptoe, opened her eyes, and—despite the blush that once more heated her face—squarely met his keen, probing gaze.

"Aren't you going to kiss me, Simon?"

A gentleman did not refuse a lady. His mouth covered hers before she had time to draw breath. But breathing mere air became unimportant when every fiber of her being came to life and breathed in the essence that was Simon.

He drew her closer, so close that they seemed to be touching skin against skin. She heard him groan, a deep sound that roused shivers of pleasure all over her body . . .

A Deceitful Heart

Karla Hocker

ZEBRA BOOKS
KENSINGTON PUBLISHING CORP.

ZEBRA BOOKS

are published by

Kensington Publishing Corp.
475 Park Avenue South
New York, NY 10016

First Printing: February, 1993

Printed in the United States of America

Chapter One

Aboard the frigate *Merry Maiden*,
sailing from Boston to Liverpool, March 1811.

A stiff breeze whipped her cloak and threatened to toss back her hood, but she paid no heed to the harsh elements of an alien northern climate or to the hoarse commands shouted at the seamen in the rigging and on deck. Her attention centered on the tall, stooped gentleman walking beside her.

"Papa, I can understand that you would wish to use your title when we reach London. But why must I be *Lady Caroline?* Why can I not be Jeannette in London as I was in New Orleans? All my life, I've been called Jeannette."

"And to me you'll always be Jeannette." Hugh Dundas, Marquis of Luxton looked at his daughter and smiled suddenly. "Though it should have been your mother who was called 'little Jeanne'. You're almost a head taller than she was."

Deep blue eyes shot him a look of reproof. Eyes, so much like his own but set in an oval face and framed by long raven curls that were a heritage from her Creole mother.

"Papa, don't sidetrack."

"England has been at war with France for a long time, Jeannette. You'll need a good English name, the name of your grandmother, to make your stay a success."

"My stay a success?" Her voice rose, high and clear above the bluster of the wind and the sharp slap of a sail.

"Papa, what are you talking about?" She stopped walking and waited until he faced her. "Are we not going to England for just a short visit? A visit of reconciliation with your family?"

"Your family, too."

Hugh Dundas was weary, more weary than he cared to admit even to himself. He wasn't a young man any more, and the long voyage up the Mississippi, then overland, had sapped his strength. A mere day out of Boston harbor, he was wishing the crossing at an end.

He turned up his coat collar. Why the devil hadn't he sailed straight from New Orleans instead of giving in to nostalgia and sailing from Boston, where he had arrived all those years ago!

And there was Jeannette with questions and arguments. Mayhap it would have been better after all to have this conversation in the cabin with a measure of the captain's best brandy warming his innards.

He looked at her again. He rarely addressed her in French. Somehow, though, it seemed fitting this time. Comforting, in view of the fact that she would not return to the Vieux Carré and her maternal relations.

"Jeannette . . . *ma fille.* We are going to London, where you will take your rightful place in society. You are the granddaughter of Frederick Dundas, Duke of Granby. And you will marry a gentleman of rank and fortune."

After a moment of incredulous silence, she gave a choke of laughter. "Marry? In England? *Quel plaisanterie!* Papa, you know I must return to the *boutique.*"

"You will not set foot in the shop again. Nounou and Marie do very well without your assistance."

"They do, but—" She gasped as a spray of salty water hit her face. Impatiently she wiped the cold drops with the back of her hand. "You've always supported me before. You said my work was important!"

"Indeed, I think it was admirable."

"Then, why—"

"Let me finish, *ma fille*. Opening a dressmaker's establishment and training young quadroons as *couturières* was excellent. I wholeheartedly supported your endeavors. But you became so involved in your crusade, you started to decline invitations. You rejected offers of marriage. Five, I believe."

She was silent. She had indeed turned down five proposals of marriage. And she had terminated the betrothal her father had arranged when she was fourteen.

"You turned nineteen this past September," said Hugh. "Your friends are married. Some already have a child. You don't even have a beau."

"Papa, I wish you had spoken of this before we left. I thought you understood that I am no longer interested in a beau. Or in marriage."

"So I finally realized."

He touched her elbow, steering her toward the steep ladder leading to the cabins below . . . to the brandy he felt sure he would need very soon.

Perhaps he should not have brought up the subject of rejected suitors. It was bound to remind her of that young fool, Raoul Fontenot. But it was time she opened her eyes and saw that not all men were cut from the same cloth.

Abruptly, he switched back to English. "I always believed I was a good father to you."

"You were! You are." She hugged his arm. "You're the best father in the world."

"I should have noticed sooner that you've made up your mind to become an old maid. Worse, I ignored a promise I made."

"What promise?"

"I swore to take you to England, Jeannette. And to find you a husband if you weren't married or, at least, betrothed by your eighteenth birthday."

Jeannette stopped at the ladder. She was suddenly very much aware of the wind, cold and moist against her face, of the creak of timber, of the ship's rolling first one way, then the other. And she remembered a night, seven years ago, aboard an old schooner. The rickety boat was filled to overflowing with planters and their families fleeing from Haiti, from Dessalines and his barbarous troops. On that schooner, her mother had died giving premature birth to a tiny boy, who survived her by a mere hour.

She felt a tingle of apprehension. The promise must have been made to *Maman*—a deathbed promise that could not be broken.

Hugh cleared his throat. "I may be late by more than a year, but I mean to keep my word, Jeannette."

London, April 1811

In the study of Dundas House in Grosvenor Square, Frederick Dundas, the Duke of Granby, sat behind his desk and stared at the note in his hand.

He was a fair young man of two-and-twenty, and the ducal responsibilities, assumed a scarce three months past, weighed heavily on his shoulders. Not that he walked with a stoop or sat hunched over, but since the death of his namesake, the fifth duke, young Frederick's brow was set in a perpetual frown, and a sharp crease along one side of his mouth marred the symmetry of his handsome face.

Imagining that the bold black scrawl on the ivory vellum mocked him, he tossed the missive onto the desk. Even if this was someone's misguised notion of a jest—and he was as certain as could be that it was—he did not feel like laughing. Not when the man who signed himself Hugh Dundas, Marquis of Luxton—a man dead and buried these thirty years or more—announced his intention to call at Dundas House that very afternoon.

Again Frederick stared at the bold scrawl. The message had to be the result of a cork-brained notion conceived by one of his Cambridge friends while in his cups.

But the sender had given his direction, an address in a less than fashionable neighborhood. George Street, north of Portman Square, brought to mind a down-at-the-heels adventurer hoping to dupe the present Duke of Granby, who wouldn't be a duke at all if the Marquis of Luxton were alive.

This was a dashed nuisance. A man bent on mischief could kick up quite a dust, and it certainly wouldn't do to tell the butler that he wasn't at home to anyone styling himself the Marquis of Luxton.

Frederick drummed his fingers on the desk top. He might be young, but he wasn't born yesterday. Neither was he one to lose his head. Let the scoundrel show his face. He'd tell him what was what!

Brave thoughts. Indeed, he was no coward. But he had a strong dislike of confrontations.

A deep voice in the foyer caught his attention. Footsteps, firm but unhurried, approached the study.

Frederick's brow cleared; the crease at the corner of his mouth smoothed. Snatching up the note, he pushed back his chair.

"Simon!" he shouted before the door had opened wide enough to reveal the visitor. "Just the man I want! You couldn't have come at a more opportune time."

The man who entered was the duke's senior by about six or seven years. He was as tall as Frederick but more powerfully built. A riding coat of fawn-colored corduroy showed off shoulders that required no padding. Leather breeches encased muscular thighs. Gleaming black boots completed the picture of a top-of-the-trees Corinthian.

Looking faintly amused, Simon Renshaw, solicitor, barrister, junior partner of the firm Renshaw and Renshaw, tossed gauntlets and crop onto the desk.

"Well, bantling? What scrape are you in that you greet your big, mean cousin with such unalloyed relief?"

"I could almost wish it were a scrape. But look at this note, Simon! I don't know what he wants, but he claims to be Hugh Dundas, Marquis of Luxton, and he will give himself the pleasure of calling on me."

Simon Renshaw's dark brows rose as he scanned the few carelessly scrawled lines.

"What do you think, Simon? If he goes about town saying he's Hugh Dundas, I could be in the devil of a fix, couldn't I?"

Simon put the note into a coat pocket. He picked up riding gauntlets and crop.

"Don't fret, bantling. I'll take care of the matter. That's what a solicitor is for."

"What will you do?"

"Call in George Street."

Chapter Two

"Lady Caroline—not so fast, if you please."

Short and plump, Mrs. Effington huffed after the tall, slender girl who swept from one room to the next, from one floor to the other of the terrace house that was to be their domicile for an undetermined period.

"Lady Caroline!"

"Forgive me." Belatedly, Jeannette responded to the desperate plea and slowed her step. How long would it take her to accept that she was Caroline? *Lady* Caroline.

In a vain effort to warm her bare arms, she tugged at the lacy shawl draped around her shoulders. "Never, as long as I live, shall I understand why English ladies must wear short-sleeved gowns made of muslin when long sleeves and wool would be ever so much more comfortable."

"It is the fashion, Lady Caroline."

"A ridiculous fashion, considering the expanse of goose bumps displayed."

"It is quite warm today."

Proving the point, Mrs. Effington snapped open the fan she always carried in her reticule next to a bottle of smelling salts and a rose-scented handkerchief. She fanned her pink face vigorously.

"And even if it were cold, a lady would not be

caught dead in long sleeves in April. Why, she'd be considered a dowd, Lady Caroline!"

"And that," Jeannette muttered under her breath, "would be a fate worse than death."

She and her father had arrived in London four days ago, and already, due to Mrs. Effington's exertions, she was well versed in the ways and manners of the *ton.* Not that life in the Vieux Carré had been so very different, but Jeannette was just a little too disgruntled to acknowledge any likeness.

She had not completely forgiven her father for keeping her in the dark about the purpose of the visit to England until it was quite too late to turn back. Neither was she reconciled to the switch of names. If Monsieur Dundas and Mademoiselle Jeannette were good enough in New Orleans, why, then, must they be Lord Luxton and Lady Caroline in London?

And on top of that she was always cold.

Jeannette looked into the drawing room and quickly shut the door again. How cramped everything was. All of the first floor was no larger than the salon of her spacious New Orleans home.

The leases of the beautiful large houses in fashionable Mayfair had been taken long before the onset of the Season, Lord Decimus Rowland, her father's old friend, had explained. Now that the Prince of Wales had finally been made Regent, every family, Tory and Whig alike, had come to town. If only Hugh and his daughter had arrived a month earlier! Or, at least, Hugh should have written and warned Decimus that he would be needing a house.

Jeannette's father had been perfectly willing to stay on at the hotel where he had bespoken rooms that first night. It wouldn't be for long, after all—only until he contacted his family, who would no doubt invite him and his daughter to Dundas House in Grosvenor Square.

But Lord Decimus had shaken his head, muttered something about a dashed embarrassing situation, and had drawn Hugh aside for a whispered conference. Jeannette still did not know whether it would be considered an embarrassment to live in a hotel, or whether there was some difficulty about getting invited to Dundas House. Neither her father nor Lord Decimus, or the gossip-loving Mrs. Effington, could be coaxed into an explanation.

Lord Decimus had offered this little house in George Street, which belonged to his niece Juliette Astley. Young Mrs. Astley was *enceinte* and had just a few days earlier allowed her concerned husband to carry her off into the country. Along with the house, Lord Decimus had produced Mrs. Effington, a chaperone for Lady Caroline.

After one glance at her charge's best New Orleans winter gown, Mrs. Effington had widened her rather sleepy eyes and instantly whisked Jeannette off to see a dressmaker and a milliner. Now, three shopping days later, they were installed in George Street. They had a cook and three maids. Mrs. Effington had her abigail, Lord Luxton his valet, and the domestic agency had promised two footmen, a coachman, and a groom by the morrow.

"Lady Caroline—"

This time, Jeannette responded instantly. Ascending the third flight of stairs, she looked over her shoulder at the matron lagging several steps behind.

"If you don't mind, Lady Caroline . . ." Mrs. Effington permitted herself several quick, shallow breaths and wished she had the figure of her charge, a figure that did not require the torture of stays.

"I'd like a little lie-down before luncheon. I'm not as young as I was, and these stairs—so steep and narrow. When I visited Miss Juliette—Mrs. Astley, I should say—I never ventured beyond the first floor."

"Of course you must lie down and rest. I do not expect you to be with me every moment of the day. And neither, I should think, does Papa."

"Thank you, my dear. So considerate of—"

The sound of the front door knocker cut off Mrs. Effington's words of appreciation. Her face registered consternation and disappointment. It seemed there would be no rest for her after all.

Jeannette gave her a quick smile. "It cannot be a caller, since no one knows we're here."

"Lord Decimus—"

"Papa is visiting him. They'd hardly knock if they had decided to join us for lunch."

Again, the knocker rang out. Three sharp, impatient raps.

"Go on up, Mrs. Effington." Jeannette squeezed past her chaperone. "It must be one of the tradesmen Cook sent for. Though why he won't use the areaway . . . but never mind. I'll take care of the matter."

"It's not fitting, Lady Caroline. Let one of the maids . . ."

Irresolute, Mrs. Effington watched as her charge ran lightly down the stairs. She shook her graying head. If she had told Lord Luxton once that they should have a footman or a butler first and foremost, she must have told him a dozen times. The maids in a fashionable household simply weren't used to answering the door. Not that they were precisely fashionable in George Street . . .

Mrs. Effington took one hesitant step downward.

Her feet hurt. She was still short of breath from the tour of inspection.

She sighed. Slowly, ponderously, she turned and moved upward—to her chamber and the bliss of kicking off her shoes and loosening her stays. Surely Lady Caroline could deal with the butcher or the grocer or whoever it was, knocking louder than ever.

Downstairs, Jeannette muttered, "Heaven grant me patience!", and with this heartfelt prayer, she swung the front door open while the last volley of raps still echoed through the narrow entrance hall. Knitting her brow in a repressive frown, she looked up at the gentleman outside. She was a tall girl and could not remember ever having to look up quite so high.

"Sir?" Her voice did not match her frown. It rather took the wind out of her sails to be facing a true English gentleman in riding dress when she had expected to see the butcher's lad in smock and apron. "Can I help you?"

For a fleeting moment she thought she must have encountered him before. The proud, aquiline nose, the square-cut chin touched a chord of memory. A second look proved the first impression wrong. There was nothing at all familiar about that lean, sharply etched face. And she was certain she would not readily have forgotten those keen gray-green eyes, blatantly admiring her from her long raven curls, tied with a ribbon, to the tips of her slippers.

Apparently, he had not found what he expected either. Beneath the gleam of admiration, she caught his look of puzzlement.

He swept off his hat. "You're no servant. Who are you?"

"Jeannette Dundas. But, more to the point, sir. Who are you?"

"I beg your pardon. Simon Renshaw, at your service." His voice was deep and smooth. "And you're Jeannette, you say? Miss Dundas?"

Belatedly, she remembered. "Caroline Jeannette Dundas. Lady Caroline."

"Ah! *Lady* Caroline. Your father neglected to mention you."

The voice was still deep and smooth, but it grated on her nevertheless. Admiration and puzzlement had given way to a look of derision.

It should not bother her, but it did. "My father, Mr. Renshaw?" she said stiffly. "Why should he have mentioned me to you?"

"May I come in?"

He did not wait for a reply but stepped past her, tossing hat, gloves, and riding crop on the hall table.

This was too much. Her bosom swelled. "Mr. Renshaw—"

"I have business with your father. Pray take me to him."

"My father is not at home." Look and voice were meant to wither. "State your business, and I shall see he gets the message."

He sketched a mocking bow. "Well done, my dear. The queen could not have spoken more crushingly. Great care has obviously been taken with your education and your training."

"Sir, you are impertinent!"

"In that case, I must beg your pardon."

Looking not at all contrite, he reached out and placed a long, blunt-tipped finger beneath her chin. "But, I fear, the impertinence is all on your part, *Lady* Caroline."

With a toss of her head, she shook off the offending

finger. "Is it the custom in England to accost a lady when her father is not there to protect her?"

She quaked beneath the quick flash of anger in his eyes but refused to budge.

"Well, sir? What have you to say for yourself?"

"A lady need not fear my touch. But beware the schemer and deceiver."

"You're mad." Now she did take a cautious step backward. "Utterly, totally mad."

"Not as mad as you and your father."

He *was* deranged. A person with an addled mind always believed that he was sane and the rest of the world afflicted with madness. Perhaps he was even dangerous?

She ventured another step backward. If she could reach the baize-covered door beneath the stairs, she might flee below to the kitchen and its arsenal of heavy pans, of rolling pins and meat cleavers.

"If he even is your father," said the madman. "Did he hire you from a traveling theater company? Perhaps he believes a daughter makes him look more respectable?"

Throwing caution to the wind, she turned and made a dash for the basement door.

"That's right, *Lady* Caroline," he mocked. "Run, lest I haul the pair of you before a magistrate!"

This brought her up short. To be threatened with the law was not what she expected from a madman. A hand within reach of the brass door knob, she spun.

"And what precisely do you mean by that?"

"Bravo!" He collected hat, riding gauntlets, and crop. "You play the outraged innocent as well as you did the queen snubbing her lowly subject."

Hard schooling by her grandmother, the formidable Madame Vireilles, had taught Jeannette the wisdom of keeping a tight rein on her temper. But Madame Vireilles was far away in New Orleans.

Jeannette flew across the narrow hall. Clutching her shawl, she barred his way to the front door.

"What do you mean, you'll haul me before a magistrate? Explain yourself, sir!"

He looked at her in silence for a long moment. Slowly, the harshness left his face.

"Could it be that your father has deceived you, too?"

"My father has deceived no one! We haven't been in town a week. We haven't met anyone save Lord Decimus Rowland and Mrs. Effington. We—"

"Lord Decimus?" he interrupted. "Well, well. At least, your father has done his homework."

"Oh, go away!" Exasperated, she shooed him toward the door. "Go quickly, before I have *you* hauled before a magistrate. I don't know why I thought I'd get a sensible word out of a man who ought to be locked up in—wherever it is you English lock up a lunatic!"

"In Bedlam. Remember it well, *Lady* Caroline."

Unhurried, he walked to the front door.

He turned briefly. "Tell your father that Hugh Dundas had a son who would now have been some thirty-odd years old—*if the son had lived.* But Dundas never had a daughter, especially not one as young as you, since he himself died in the winter of 1780."

Chapter Three

The snap of the door closing behind Simon Renshaw roused Jeannette from speechless confusion.

Indignation sharpened her voice. "The Marquis of Luxton's son, Mr. Renshaw, would have been *seven* years old if he had lived!"

But, of course, her protest came too late. The clatter of hooves on the cobbles told her that he was already riding away. Snatching the shawl off her shoulders, she flicked the lacy material as if it were a whip speeding him on.

"Nom de nom! Don't you think I know when my own brother was born—and when he died? And what do you mean, Mr. Madman Renshaw, that my father died in 1780?"

"He meant, my dear, that he believes you and me to be imposters."

"Papa, I've had more than enough time to figure that out for myself."

The shadows were lengthening when Lord Luxton, accompanied by his old friend, Lord Decimus Rowland, had finally returned to the house in George Street. By then, Jeannette's mind was in a turmoil. Not even the presence of her chaperone and Lord Decimus could delay her questions.

Keeping her eyes on her father, she paced between the fireplace and the drawing room door, a short distance that did nothing to soothe her agitation.

"Papa, if he isn't a madman, I wish you would tell me why he should believe something so nonsensical. Imposters! Pah!"

She pivoted at the door. "Granted, you have not written to your family. Granted, they may therefore believe you dead. But Mr. Renshaw named the *year* of your supposed death!"

"Indeed, that is strange." Mrs. Effington was seated on the sofa beneath the windows, as far as possible from the sluggish fire in the hearth. She lowered her embroidery frame and looked at Lord Decimus. "And it makes no sense, does it?"

"Of course it doesn't, since Hugh is obviously not dead." Decimus lovingly cradled a glass of brandy in his pudgy hand. "What we'll do is go to Dundas House tomorrow and straighten everything out."

Jeannette frowned at her chaperone, then at her father and his friend, ensconced in deep chairs near the fireplace. "You're not surprised? Angry? You all expected something like this to happen?"

Lord Luxton tugged at his collar. "Can't say I expected Simon Renshaw to show up here. Not when I'd sent word to Dundas House that I'd be calling."

"Papa, who the dickens is Simon Renshaw? What is his interest in your affairs?"

"He's the family solicitor. Also a cousin of sorts."

"Second cousin to the young duke," said Lord Decimus.

"The *young* duke?" Swiftly, Jeannette went to her father's side. "That means my grandfather is dead."

"Died this past January, just when I received confirmation from a cotton broker here in London that the old boy was sound and hale."

Jeannette was silent. She did not much wish to be in London, but she had looked forward to meeting her grandfather. Now she never would. The realization filled her with a sense of loss.

Suddenly, she missed her mother's large family in New Orleans—*Grandmère,* the aunts, uncles, and the flock of Creole cousins who never allowed her to feel the loneliness of an only child.

If her Grandfather Dundas was dead, and the young duke—

Her eyes widened. Kneeling on the hearth rug, she reached for her father's hand.

"Papa, who is this young duke? I am no authority on English laws of succession. But you—Papa, shouldn't *you* be the new Duke of Granby?"

"Whatever I should or shouldn't be makes no difference. 'Twas never my intention to step into the old gentleman's shoes. All I wanted was your grandfather's backing and one of your aunts to launch you into society."

"It would be pleasant to meet my English relatives," she admitted.

"You shall meet them. I'll see to it, my dear."

Before the illness that struck him in the fall and dragged on through the winter, Hugh Dundas had been a strong man with a physique belying his years. Now he was thin and stooped and weary, but he still possessed the force and determination that had made him a successful businessman in New

Orleans. His face might be haggard and pale, but the jut of his chin was as firm and pronounced as ever, and the fire in his eyes, as deep a blue as Jeannette's, was undiminished.

"You have four sisters, don't you, Papa? Do I have cousins?"

"Undoubtedly. But I confess I asked my broker only about the old duke. Said I was a distant relation and curious. Now I wish I had truly been curious and inquired about your cousins as well."

"You have ten cousins, Lady Caroline," said Mrs. Effington. "All but two are married and raising their own families. Your two youngest cousins, Lady Eleanor Hargrave and Miss Agnes Paine, are being launched this Season."

"Excellent." Hugh Dundas rubbed his hands. "My daughter can be launched with them."

"But if his grace and Mr. Renshaw don't acknowledge you, sir . . ." The dainty wisp of lace atop Mrs. Effington's elegant coiffure fluttered like butterfly wings as she shook her head. "It won't be easy to launch Lady Caroline if your sisters take their cue from Mr. Renshaw. Which, I expect, they will. They'll not permit Lady Caroline to join their daughters."

Jeannette's mouth tightened. A pox on Mr. Renshaw!

A new thought struck her. Suppressing excitement, she rose to her feet. "Papa, if you don't wish to be a duke, we can return to New Orleans. We wouldn't have to put up with the odious Mr. Renshaw, or—"

"What?" Lord Decimus choked on a mouthful of brandy. His round cherub's face reddened, but

whether from lack of breath or from outrage was difficult to tell. "Run away and *confirm* Renshaw's belief that you're imposters? Devil a bit, Hugh! You won't do it, will you?"

"Decimus, old boy, have you ever known a Dundas to run from anything?"

"Yes, I have." Lord Decimus scowled at his old friend. "You didn't fight very hard when your father arranged to have you shipped out of the country after the Rossiter affair."

For a moment, Hugh Dundas looked blank.

"That was a long time ago," he said finally. "I was too young to know better."

"Rossiter?" said Jeannette. "Is that the name of the man you fought in a duel?"

Hugh shifted in his chair. "Who told you about the duel? It isn't something a man's daughter needs to know. If it was Renshaw—"

"*Maman* told me."

"Oh. Hmm, well. In that case . . . what did she tell you?"

"That you fought a gentleman and injured him. That you had to leave the country. That the quarrel was over a lady."

"Rossiter's wife," said Mrs. Effington. She smiled at Jeannette. "Nothing to worry about, my dear. Evalina Rossiter was a very foolish woman. After your dear papa left, Rossiter fought three more duels before Evalina ran off with her groom."

Jeannette blinked. She could think of no reply, except a rather weak, "Gracious."

"Devil a bit! Who cares about that old tale?" Lord Decimus helped himself from the brandy decanter on the table at his elbow. "What I want to know is, will you stay and defend your name? Your honor, Hugh! Or will you run and let young Frederick and Renshaw say you're an imposter?"

Jeannette did not hold her breath. Truly, her father had no option but to stay. He must fight for his name, his rights. After all, young Frederick was usurping the title that was rightfully her father's.

Young Frederick! Bah! He was a usurper. Undoubtedly, he and his dastardly solicitor were scheming to keep her father from his birthright. They were cheats. Thieves. Gallows-bait.

"I'll do what I must," Hugh said quietly. "I'll not have my daughter cheated of what is hers."

Jeannette was about to protest that she wanted nothing from the Dundas family, but Mrs. Effington spoke first.

"Lord Luxton, I'm agog to know how your meeting with his grace went this afternoon. His father was a friend of yours, wasn't he?"

"The best, next to Decimus and Malcolm Renshaw, Simon's father. But I never got around to a visit with young Frederick. A private sale at Tattersall's . . ."

Hugh's gaze shifted to his daughter. "Bought some carriage horses. A team of matched bays, a sweet-stepping pair. Couldn't resist. Had to have that pair for you, my dear. Coats the same raven hue as your hair!"

"Papa!" Usurpers and scoundrelly solicitors forgotten, Jeannette dropped to her knees again and hugged her father. "You're going to let me drive my own carriage! Thank you! Thank you, best of fathers."

"Not a high-perch phaeton, mind you."

Noting the set of his jaw, she nodded meekly. "Just a plain, ordinary, very safe phaeton."

Mrs. Effington clucked. "I wish you had asked my advice, Lord Luxton. I cannot help but feel that, under the circumstances, Lady Caroline will invite unwelcome attention by driving herself."

"Why?" asked Jeannette. "While we were shopping, I saw several ladies driving themselves. You greeted them most civilly."

"Indeed. But, then, I am quite broad-minded. There are, however, those of a more straight-laced set, mothers of young ladies your age and, worse, mothers of eligible young gentlemen, who will consider you fast if you drive your own carriage in town. In the country it is different, of course."

Turning a reproachful eye on Hugh, Mrs. Effington added, "I would have advised you to purchase a nice little mare for Lady Caroline."

"Well, I did that, too. Pretty little chestnut filly. You'll like her, Jeannette. She's spirited and—"

"Lord Luxton!" cried Mrs. Effington while Jeannette kissed her father's cheek. "You told me your daughter is not used to being called Lady Caroline. How can you expect her to remember when you keep calling her Jeannette?"

"Only among friends." He bestowed a smile on Mrs. Effington that had the good lady scrambling for her fan to cool her face. "If you catch me saying Jeannette in company, you may rap my knuckles."

Lord Decimus had shown not the slightest interest in the finer points of distinction governing a lady's mode of conveyance or in the variances of Jeannette's name. He had risen and was prowling through the room. He had peered into corners and behind chairs and was approaching the sofa by the windows.

Still flustered by Lord Luxton's smile, Mrs. Effington gratefully turned her attention to the portly Lord Decimus.

"Have you lost something?"

"Eh? What? Oh, it's you, Mrs. Effington. I say, have you seen my Annie?"

Mrs. Effington's color rose. "For heaven's sake! Don't start on that subject unless you want to bring on my palpitations."

"Annie always comes to greet me," said Lord Decimus. "I've been here an hour or more. Where could she be?"

Exasperated, Mrs. Effington snapped her fan shut. "Perhaps Miss Juliette and her major took her into the country with them."

"Stewart's a lieutenant colonel. And, no, my niece would not have taken Annie off without telling me."

Jeannette joined them. "Who is Annie?"

"Annie Tuck," said Lord Decimus, his cherubic countenance wreathed in a smile. "Pretty little thing and dressed just the way I like it. Full skirts, frilly cap—none of your skimpy muslins for my Annie."

The description left Jeannette as unenlightened as before. The only full skirts she had seen were worn by her *grandmère* and other ladies of that generation.

"But *who* is she? Did Miss Juliette leave one of her staff behind?"

"Annie Tuck," Mrs. Effington said in tones of great disgust, "is a nursery maid Miss Juliette and

Lord Decimus brought from an old castle on the Sussex coast last winter. *Or so they say.*"

"You don't believe it?"

"Would you?" Mrs. Effington countered. "Lord Decimus insists Annie Tuck is as real as he and I. But Miss Juliette told me Annie is a ghost."

Chapter Four

A usurping cousin.

A scheming solicitor.

And now a ghost.

Brushing her hair the following morning, Jeannette reflected wryly that it was a good thing after all that her maid had balked at the very last moment and refused to board the frigate *Merry Maiden* for the Atlantic crossing. Mirabelle was a faint-hearted girl and would surely have indulged in an everlasting fit of hysterics at the thought of having to live and sleep in a haunted house.

Jeannette was not handicapped with cowardice. Thanks to Nounou, her old nurse, she had early on made the acquaintance of ghosts and spirits on Haiti. She would have enjoyed an encounter with an English ghost, one who had reportedly come from a medieval fortress on the Channel coast.

No ghostly footsteps or whisperings, not even the anticipation of such nocturnal disturbances, had disrupted Jeannette's sleep the previous night, but she had not given up hope. There was always another night.

Jeannette brushed her hair away from her face,

then pinned it in a loose knot at the crown of her head. Only a few long curls at the back were left to bounce untrammeled.

It did not look too bad, she decided, studying her reflection critically. Mirabelle would have been more precise in centering the knot, and, perhaps the pins would not have bitten quite so hard into her scalp if the maid had done the pinning.

But Mirabelle would be back in New Orleans by now, and despite a soothing letter of recommendation, would have to endure a number of formidable scolds from Nounou. Retribution for deserting her mistress. In the end, however, Nounou would permit Mirabelle to work at the *boutique* until she found a new post as lady's maid. It was, after all, the purpose of the dressmaker's shop to provide home and livelihood for free women of color.

Pulling one long curl forward to nestle against her throat, Jeannette was satisfied that she did not need the services of a lady's maid.

Not even to get ready for a confrontation with the abominable Simon Renshaw.

During the course of the previous evening, while Lord Decimus and Mrs. Effington had elaborated on the various members of the Dundas family, Simon Renshaw's name and that of his father, Malcolm, had cropped up more than once.

The Renshaws, it seemed, held the fate of the Dundas family firmly in their hands. They had far more power than would ordinarily be granted the family solicitors. But, then, the Renshaws were related to the Dundases—Simon's grandmother was cousin to the late fifth duke and great-aunt to the present duke, the usurper.

Lord Decimus's rambling way of talking had given Jeannette plenty of opportunity to relive her meeting with Simon Renshaw, to remember his derision when he learned that she was Lady Caroline, his threats to have her and her father taken up before a magistrate. She did not doubt that if there was a plot to cheat her father, it was Simon Renshaw who had been the instigator.

In a short while she would see him again, this man whose parting shot to her had been that the Marquis of Luxton had died over thirty years ago. She would see him and young Frederick at Dundas House, and the two gentlemen would have to face the living proof that their attempt to take over a dukedom had failed.

An hour later, at ten-thirty, a brand-new town carriage drawn by four splendid matched bays stopped at Lord Decimus Rowland's chambers in St. James's. The portly gentleman, who had personally arranged the meeting with the young duke, joined Hugh Dundas, Marquis of Luxton, and his daughter, Lady Caroline Jeannette, in the plush equipage. A scarce fifteen minutes later, they alighted at Dundas House in Grosvenor Square.

Jeannette furtively rubbed her arms below the short, puffed sleeves of her morning gown. April in London was no comparison to April in New Orleans.

Lord Decimus huffed up the wide sweep of steps, but Hugh stood for a moment gazing at the imposing stucco front.

"Memories, Papa?" Jeannette asked softly.

His stooped shoulders squared. Looking at her, he nodded. "Yes, indeed. Let us go inside, my dear."

A footman in crimson and white livery had thrown the double doors open. A second footman stood waiting to take the gentlemen's hats and gloves. An ancient butler, clad austerely in black coat and breeches, bowed stiffly.

His gaze flicked from Hugh Dundas to Jeannette. Etiquette demanded total impassivity from a butler, but the old man quite obviously labored under some strong emotion.

He finally fixed his attention on Lord Decimus. "Good morning, my lord. I hope I find you well?"

"A touch of the gout," Decimus said cheerfully. "But that's nothing new. Where's young Frederick? Got my message, didn't he?"

"Yes, my lord." Once more the butler's gaze moved to Hugh Dundas. "His Grace will see you in the study."

A sudden smile softened Hugh's gaunt features. "Demme, but if it isn't like old times! Ralston, how are you? I'd have thought you would have retired by now."

A gleam lit the butler's old eyes. His mouth worked soundlessly.

Don't tell me you didn't recognize me immediately, Ralston."

"Master Hugh! My lord!" the butler stammered. "We had heard—we never dreamed—my lord, you're alive!"

"Of course I'm alive. And this—"

Hugh looked around for Jeannette, who had stopped in the entrance for a better view of the white and gilt splendor of the vast foyer, the marble floor, the ornate pilasters, and the wide central stairway, dividing halfway to the first floor into two gracefully curving branches.

Taking her hand, Hugh drew her to his side. "And this, Ralston, is Lady Caroline, my little girl."

"How very affecting," a deep voice drawled as the butler bowed before Jeannette. "But not so little after all."

A door had opened far to their left, and Simon Renshaw came strolling toward them. Jeannette was flanked by her father and Lord Decimus, but to her confusion and annoyance Renshaw's hard stare singled her out.

Ralston beamed. "Mr. Simon, this is Lady Caroline. Doesn't she have a look of his grace, the late duke?"

"She has the blue eyes."

Renshaw's voice was noncommittal, but again, as on the previous day when she had introduced herself, Jeannette caught the derisive curl of his mouth.

"Very fetching," he drawled. "Startling, one might say. And quite unusual with black hair."

She met his stare haughtily. "Not when you have an English father and a Creole mother, whose ancestors are French and Spanish."

"I daresay."

He turned to acknowledge Lord Decimus with a nod, then, for the first time, looked fully at Hugh Dundas. And Jeannette knew the satisfaction of seeing his imperturbability crack. Astonishment, then disbelief, widened his eyes. But only briefly.

"If you'll follow me," he said calmly, "Frederick will see you now."

He strode off toward the door he had left open, a

door that was half again as high as a tall man, the white panel elaborately decorated with gilt scroll work. And he never looked back to make certain they did indeed follow.

Deliberately taking her time in the splendid foyer, Jeannette entered the study a few minutes after the men. In a glance, she took in the book-lined walls, upholstered chairs, two of which were occupied by her father and Lord Decimus. She saw an immense desk and a slim, fair young gentleman standing in front of the desk, his handsome face marred by a frown. She had the impression that the frown lightened upon her entrance, but her attention was caught by a painting high on the wall behind the desk.

It was the portrait of a gentleman, and the moment she saw it she understood Simon Renshaw's astonishment and disbelief when he faced her father.

Save for the look of robust health, the tie-wig, and the outdated style of his frilled shirt and velvet coat, the man in the painting might have been Hugh Dundas.

There! That should cook Simon Renshaw's goose! Matters couldn't have worked out better if the portrait had been of her contrivance.

She had time only for a quick look of triumph at Mr. Renshaw and to see him blandly raise a brow in reply before Lord Decimus rose and drew her toward the fair young gentleman.

"Permit me to present a connection of yours, Lady Caroline. Never did understand the intricacies of bloodlines, but he's a cousin of sorts, once or twice removed. Frederick Dundas." The man who had assumed the title of Sixth Duke of Granby, the title that should have been her father's.

She studied him curiously, wondering if she had imagined the frown she had glimpsed when she entered the study. He had such an open, friendly face. Impossible that he should be conspiring against her father. Or was it impossible?

He wasn't much older than she, young enough to blush when he bowed over her hand—young enough to be influenced by an unscrupulous solicitor.

"Charmed," Frederick murmured, then turned to Simon Renshaw in such a blatant appeal for help that Jeannette, despite her suspicions, could not suppress a smile.

"Are you afraid of me, Cousin Frederick? I promise you, even though the territory has not yet been granted statehood, we are quite civilized in New Orleans. Or did Lord Decimus not explain that Papa and I have come from America?"

"No. I mean, yes, he did. But I am not afraid of you. It's only—" Again, Frederick's gaze shifted to Simon before returning to Jeannette's face. "But we're not cousins, are we?"

"That is what we are here to determine." Smoothly, Simon Renshaw took over, seating them in a circle around a low table.

Simon looked straight at Hugh. "You claim to be Hugh Dundas, Marquis of Luxton. What proof can you offer, sir?"

"And how does a man prove he is who he is?" Hugh inquired mildly.

"I say he's Hugh Dundas." Lord Decimus looked as stern as his cheerful round face permitted. "That should be proof enough."

"You should have letters, sir—from the family." A tight groove appeared at the corner of Frederick's mouth. "And the signet ring worn by the Marquis of Luxton."

Hugh made no reply.

Jeannette frowned at her father's right hand, relaxed on the arm of his chair. The ring he usually wore was conspicuously absent.

She gave him a sharp look. He had never been a gregarious man, but this silence was carrying reticence too far. Why didn't he confirm that he possessed the ring his father had presented to him on his fifteenth birthday?

Again Simon Renshaw assumed control. "Possession of letters and a ring is not necessarily proof of identity. The items could have been taken from Hugh Dundas when he died."

"But he did not die!" Jeannette tried in vain to conquer impatience and indignation. "He's alive and well. And you, Mr. Renshaw, realized it when you saw Papa in the foyer."

She surged to her feet. Taking a few steps toward the desk, she pointed at the portrait. "Anyone but a blind man or an extremely stupid man can see that Papa is the living image of the fifth duke."

"Miss—" Frederick had risen politely. A faint flush mounted in his face when Jeannette turned to him. "Never mind. Simon will explain."

Simon Renshaw came to stand beside her. Again she realized how very tall he was, how very powerfully built. And again she was teased by that vague sense of recognition that had confused her when she first saw him on her doorstep.

It was the nose, that slightly hawkish nose and the

square-cut chin. Both her father and the gentleman in the portrait, and even Frederick in a vastly gentler version, were graced with those same distinct features. Dundas features.

"My dear Lady Caroline," Simon Renshaw said with just the slightest emphasis on Lady. "I fear you're laboring under a misapprehension."

She was about to set him straight when she realized that he was not denying his Dundas features but was referring to her comment on the portrait.

"Then why don't you explain, Mr. Renshaw?"

A glint of sudden laughter danced in his eyes. "Gladly. You see, Lady Caroline, the gentleman in the portrait is not the fifth duke, as you seem to believe."

She stared at the painting. "He's not? Then who the dickens is he?"

"He's the fourth duke."

"My great-grandfather?"

"Your great-great-grandfather." Hugh Dundas had not moved from his chair, and he did not bother to look at the portrait. "He was Augustus Hugh Dundas, and he outlived his son. Therefore, his grandson—your grandfather—succeeded him as the fifth duke."

Still looking faintly embarrassed, Frederick said, "The portrait was painted in 1746, when Augustus was sixty-five years old. A lively gentleman by all accounts."

"Very lively." Simon's tone was dry. "The family married him off at age nineteen, but, apparently, marriage did not settle him down. It is said he exercised his *droit de seigneur* until the day he died at the ripe age of eighty-five."

Jeannette heard Lord Decimus mutter something about "not fit for a lady's ears," and her father's assurance that she was not the missish type.

Indeed, she was not missish, and it was not embarrassment that kept her silent. She was stunned.

Droit de seigneur! Surely, Mr. Renshaw was not implying . . . Her mind boggled. The sheer brazenness, the affrontery it would take to make such a suggestion! Not even he who was conspiring with Frederick to cheat her father would be so outrageous.

She met his quizzing look and knew there was nothing he would not dare.

Chapter Five

An appreciative spectator, Simon watched her delectable mouth tighten. Unflinching, he bore the heat of her scornful look. He rather admired her, the self-styled Lady Caroline.

Contrary to what he had said the day before, he did not believe she was a professional actress, but her portrayal of innocence outraged was delightful. When her father's little game was finished—and, undoubtedly, the end was imminent—she should have no trouble finding employment on the stage.

With her nose in the air, she turned her back to him. She tugged at her father's sleeve, leaned close to the older man and whispered urgently.

Jeannette . . . a pretty name for an actress, and much more suitable than Caroline. Simon had been thinking of her as Jeannette—rather more often than was prudent.

He relaxed and waited. Save for the soft murmur of her voice the study was quiet. Frederick, shy and bashful in the presence of a lady, stared at his feet. Lord Decimus was holding his breath, or so his high color seemed to indicate. Probably knew by now that he had bungled when he accepted his dead friend's sudden resurrection and introduced him as Hugh Dundas at White's and Tattersall's.

Lady Caroline's whispers grew louder, more urgent. Agitated gestures accompanied her speech. She was speaking French, Simon realized, but he still could not make out the words.

Hugh touched her cheek. "Hush, child."

Rather to Simon's astonishment, she obeyed instantly. She even blushed.

"I apologize for my rudeness." She looked from Lord Decimus to Frederick and Simon. "Whispering, speaking French in your presence, it is unpardonable."

"Don't give it a thought," said Frederick. "You're distraught. My mother takes recourse to her vinaigrette whenever the fourth duke's name is mentioned."

Lady Caroline seemed about to argue, but her father shook his head, an almost imperceptible movement that stopped her as effectively as if he had commanded her silence. Simon could not help but acknowledge that she was a very well brought up young lady indeed.

Hugh rose. Running a frail hand through his thinning white hair, he smiled ruefully at Frederick. "No need to ask, I think, whether you're in agreement with your solicitor on the subject of my relationship to the Dundas family?"

"No, sir, you need not ask." Frederick drew himself to his full height. "You see, sir, we've been through this before. Well, not I, but the family. You're not the first of the fourth duke's illegitimate offspring claiming to be Hugh Dundas."

Simon saw Lady Caroline's eyes widen. Blue eyes and black hair—truly a captivating combination.

She caught him watching her, and the ire that

should have been directed at Frederick was launched toward him.

"Mr. Renshaw! You are the most despicable, the most—you *dare* suggest that my father is one of the fourth duke's by-blows?"

Although considerably startled by her choice of phrase, Simon did not suffer from mortification as did Frederick, betrayed once more by his easy blush. The thought crossed Simon's mind that Lady Caroline was truly innocent of deception. But that was impossible. It would mean that her father had planned this coup since her birth and had raised her as the granddaughter of a duke.

Impossible, he once more assured himself.

"I would have put it more delicately. But, yes, Lady Caroline. That is precisely what I am suggesting."

"It is outrageous! A dastardly plot to cheat my father. A vile fabrication of lies!"

Again Hugh silenced her with a gentle touch. "Renshaw, will you tell me when the earlier claim was made?"

"It was five years after America's independence. The imposter claimed to have come from Canada. My father dealt with him swiftly and competently."

"I've never known your father other than competent." Hugh met Simon's gaze. "Decimus told me that Malcolm is ailing. A stroke, I believe? I am very sorry. Illness can be a dashed nuisance."

Simon took in the other's parchment skin, the frail limbs and stooped shoulders. But this was not the time to show compassion.

"It was a very mild stroke. Father is recovering nicely and should be back in town before long.

Meanwhile, I shall guard the interests of the Dundas family just as competently as he would have done."

"Never doubted it, my boy. And when you're satisfied that I am entitled to the claims I'll bring forth, I shall be happy to place my interests in your capable hands."

Despite himself, Simon had to laugh. What a crafty rogue.

"Sir, I am honored. But since I'm determined to stop you from claiming the title—"

"Not so fast," Hugh interrupted. He looked tired, but his voice was firm. "I've made no demands so far, save for the very natural one to meet young Frederick. And, rest assured, I'll make no demands until you've had time to think the situation over."

He turned to Frederick. "My boy, if I were you, I'd have a look at the yellow sitting room in Granby Castle. On a marquetry table by the east window are two miniatures. At least, that's where they used to be when I was there last."

"I know the room, sir. But I don't remember any miniatures."

"What is your point?" Alert and wary, Simon studied the older man. "That you were inside Granby Castle once or twice? It hardly proves anything."

"One of the miniatures is a likeness of the fourth duke when he was eighteen or nineteen—the miniature he sent to his bride-to-be. And the other is of his great-grandson, Hugh Dundas, at the age of sixteen. Looking at them, you'll see that not only his by-blows are the image of the redoubtable Augustus, but he and his great-grandson were as two peas in a pod."

Simon inclined his head. "I'll check on the miniatures. But, tell me, sir. What do you hope to gain? Even if the likenesses exist, you'll still not have proven that you are Hugh Dundas."

"My father does not have to prove *anything!*"

Quite unprofessionally, Simon's eyes immediately turned to the angry young lady at Hugh's side. Jeannette. Lady Caroline. Or whatever her name might be.

The heavy knot of hair atop her head was slightly askew. Her cheeks were becomingly flushed. And if looks could kill, he'd be lying prostrate at her feet.

She was a charmer, all right. It was unfortunate that before long she'd be wasting away in Newgate prison.

A sobering thought.

"I fear, Lady Caroline," he said gently, "your father *will* have to present proof of his identity."

"Devil a bit!" Breaking his long silence, Lord Decimus lumbered to his feet. "I remember when word got out that Hugh was dead. 'Twas at the beginning of the '84 or '85 Season."

"April of 1784," said Simon.

"Aye. You'd know. 'Twas your father who brought the news from Philadelphia. Although, how you can remember a time when you must have been in leading strings . . ."

"I checked the records, Lord Decimus."

"Oh, aye. But that's beside the point, Renshaw. Dammit! What I want to know is what proof did your father have that Hugh's *dead?*"

"The word of the man who saw Hugh Dundas die."

In George Street, Annie Tuck had been moping since Miss Juliette left a little over a sennight ago, and that was the reason she had not greeted Lord Decimus the previous day. Neither had she paid much attention to the new lodgers—which did not mean, however, that she was wholly ignorant about them.

Sheer curiosity had driven Annie to take one little peek at Lord Luxton and his daughter, a peek that just happened to coincide with Lord Decimus's visit. And that was how she learned that, at least in one quarter of town, at Dundas House in Grosvenor Square, Lord Luxton and his daughter were regarded as imposters.

Annie knew Mrs. Effington. The lady had several times accompanied Lord Decimus when he visited Miss Juliette and Colonel Astley.

But all of that day and night Annie had remained hidden behind a shield of silence and invisibility. Now, that would change, at least as far as the young lady was concerned. Jeannette, she was called by her father. Lady Caroline, by Lord Decimus and Mrs. Effington.

Lady Caroline and her father were accompanied by Lord Decimus when they had returned from Dundas House earlier in the day, and Annie hadn't seen so much excitement or heard so many arguments in the cramped little George Street house since Miss Juliette confessed to her husband that she was *enceinte* and Colonel Astley said they must immediately remove to the country. That argument had lasted a full month.

The present argument, about the Dundas family, had lasted only until midnight, when Lord Decimus finally left for his own chambers. The portly gentleman had been in quite a pother about the existence of a letter from some American, a leader of a militia troop, who had confirmed that Hugh Dundas died in November of 1780, in a place called Savannah.

Apparently, his lordship had joined a band of American rebels in a futile effort to retake Savannah, which was in the hands of British forces. Imagine that! An Englishman, a marquis, the heir to a dukedom, joining rebels in a revolutionary war!

Annie was unfamiliar with the American Revolutionary War. It was a piece of history that had happened after Stenton Castle, where Annie then lived, was deserted by the Rowland family. For forty-one years, until Miss Juliette's cousin decided the previous December to open the old castle high on the chalk cliffs of Beachy Head for a Christmas gathering, Annie had flitted through empty rooms and silent halls. There had been no occasion for spying or eavesdropping, save on the old caretaker and an occasional smuggler.

In Annie's time—before the fire that took several lives and destroyed a wing of Stenton Castle in 1769—America had been a faithful colony of the crown, and that was all she knew. But she realized that in the year '80, at the height of the rebellion, four of her little brothers would have been old enough to enlist. They would have fought on the King's side. So what was the son of an English duke doing, fighting on the other side?

Lord Decimus had argued, or tried to argue, with Lord Luxton, who had been annoyingly reticent on the subject of the letter. Lady Caroline and Mrs. Effington, on the other hand, had more than made up for his lordship's silence. They had denounced the letter as a fake, denounced the new Duke of Granby as a usurper, and denounced the duke's solicitor as a scheming scoundrel.

However, the reason Annie was ready to give up her self-imposed silence and invisibility had nothing to do with the questionable letter or with the marquis who had died, yet was very much alive—and none knew better than Annie that he was *not* a ghost. No, Annie's downfall was a carriage delivered that afternoon in George Street.

A lady's phaeton, drawn by a pair of midnight-black horses. Lady Caroline's very own carriage.

One of the candles on the *escritoire* guttered. Jeannette did not bother to trim the wick, nor, when the flame died, did she relight it. The letter to *Grandmère* was finally finished.

She sanded the last of six sheets covered in the fine copperplate taught by the Ursuline nuns in New Orleans. Now all she had to do was find a ship to carry the package across the ocean.

The letter would give her grandmother quite a shock, but she was strong, the most formidable woman Jeannette knew. Madame Vireilles would be outraged that her son-in-law and her granddaughter had been dubbed imposters by the Dundas family. She would command Monsieur Dubois, the old family solicitor who had drawn up the marriage contract between Jeanne Vireilles and Hugh Dundas, Marquis of Luxton, to send one of his junior partners to London immediately.

Then they'd see how Simon Renshaw fared with

his fabricated evidence. A letter from some obscure militia commander saying that Hugh Dundas was fatally shot in an attempt to recapture Savannah!

Pshaw!

Yawning and stretching, Jeannette rose. The small sitting room on the first floor faced the street. Faintly, she heard the sing-song voice of a night watchman, announcing that it was three o'clock and all was well.

She yawned again. Nothing was well, if truth be told. But, gracious! She was too tired to think any more about the web of deceit closing around her father. And Papa not saying much and looking as if he were ill again. He always tired easily these days.

But she was young and strong. She hadn't wanted to come to England, but now she'd give her all to see that Papa was accepted, as was his due.

If only a letter to New Orleans would not take so very long. Blessed by favorable winds, the crossing from Boston to Liverpool had taken only seventeen days. But New Orleans? She very much feared she would have to wait three or four months for a response.

Jeannette extinguished the flame of a second candle, then picked up the third to light the way to her bedchamber two floors above.

"Lady Caroline."

It took her sleep-starved mind a few moments to respond.

"Mrs. Effington?" Caught halfway between the *escritoire* and the sitting room door, Jeannette raised her candle and peered into the darkness around her. "I thought you'd be fast asleep by now. Did I keep you awake?"

Even as she spoke, Jeannette knew that she hadn't kept Mrs. Effington awake, that it hadn't been the chaperone who called out to her.

Her heart pounded. "Who is there?"

"It's Annie. Annie Tuck. Lord Decimus told you about me."

The light of the candle in Jeannette's hand performed a macabre dance. It was one thing, hearing about a ghost and thinking that one would like to meet her; quite another to encounter her.

Jeannette did not doubt the existence of ghosts and spirits. She was born on Haiti, and Nounou, her nurse, had made certain she kept a proper distance from places where spirits were known to walk. Not the voodoo spirits, the *loa,* which were invoked by the *hungan* or the *mambo;* but the restless spirits of the dead.

There was the deserted Deschamp plantation, where at night the long-ago screams of tortured slaves could be heard, and where the ghost of Pierre Roulaux, the Deschamp's cruel overseer, pounced on any person of color who ventured too close to the overgrown shrubbery of the old plantation garden. It was a place of evil, and Nounou had not had any trouble keeping Jeannette away.

But Moon Lake, in the valley near her home, had drawn the young Jeannette with irresistible force. There dwelled the ghost of Jacques, a free man of color, who had tried to save a child from drowning. But Jacques could not swim, and they both had died. Now, Jacques's ghost patrolled the lake to watch over swimming children. Many a time had Jeannette felt the boost of his helping hand when she ventured farther than was prudent into the center of the lake or when an unexpected current tugged at her kicking feet.

Yes, she knew about the ghosts and spirits of her childhood home. But what sort of a ghost was this English ghost? Good or evil?

"Lady Caroline! Surely you must remember that Mrs. Effington and Lord Decimus told you about me!"

Instinctively Jeannette crossed herself. A ghost who spoke was quite different from a soundless, benevolent presence intent on helping her reach the lake shore safely.

"I'm tired." She spoke with rather more firmness than was necessary. "You're a figment of my imagination."

Annie chuckled. "The first time Miss Juliette heard me, she thought I was a wood beetle."

"A beetle?" Jeannette found herself wishing that someone were with her—her father, or even Mirabelle, who would undoubtedly have a fit of the vapors.

Even Simon Renshaw, in whose powerful presence no ghost would dare speak up.

"Rubbish!" she said. And that could apply to her wish for Simon Renshaw's presence as well as to Annie's ridiculous statement. "No one would mistake your voice for some pestilent insect."

"I wasn't speaking at the time, but never mind. I'll tell you that story some other time. Right now, I want to offer my help."

Jeannette's hand had stopped shaking. The light of the single candle shone as brightly and as steadily as a candle can shine. But it did not matter. She heard the voice yet saw no one. Was it truly Annie Tuck, a ghost, speaking to her?

"Where are you?"

"Right here, in the green plush chair closest to you."

Jeannette moved quickly. The flame of her candle flickered but did not go out. The glow fell on a slight form seated in the chair, a young woman in an old-fashioned striped cotton skirt with an over-dress of some dark-blue material. A huge mobcap all but hid a thin little face framed by wisps of dark curls.

"Annie?"

The mobcap nodded. "Aye, 'tis me."

Jeannette sank into the opposite chair. She blinked, and when she looked again, the girl in the huge mobcap was gone.

Or so she thought.

"Lady Caroline, I want to make a pact with you."

Jeannette blinked again. She even rubbed her eyes, but the figure did not reappear.

"What sort of a pact?"

"You and your father are in trouble, aren't you?"

"You cannot call it trouble, exactly." Again, Jeannette thought of Simon Renshaw. For sure, he'd clap her into Bedlam if he knew she was talking to someone she could not see. "It is the merest misunderstanding."

"You're in trouble." Annie's voice permitted no compromise. "If you're convicted as imposters, you'll end up in Newgate. Or mayhap you'll be deported."

Jeannette rose. Again, the candle flame danced wildly as she tried to pierce the darkness for a glimpse of the girl she had seen earlier.

"This is a trick! You're not a ghost at all. Mr. Renshaw put you up to this. He wants to frighten me."

"You don't believe that, do you, Lady Caroline?"

"Yes! Yes, I do. The only one who can be sent to prison as an imposter—or rather a usurper—is Frederick. And Simon Renshaw will hang as a cheat and a conspirator!"

"Humbug." Annie seemed to notice nothing incongruous in the discrepancy of punishment Jeannette wished on the two gentlemen. "Not when they have the letter from that militia man who says that Hugh Dundas died in some place called Savannah."

Jeannette knew that her best course of action would be to leave. Instead, she sat down again.

She remained silent for quite a while and merely stared at the chair across from her. Without a doubt, that was where the voice had come from. Not from some dark corner or from behind a piece of furniture. It had come from someone sitting in the chair.

Slowly, like a mist thickening and taking shape, the girl in the simple servant's gown of the previous century reappeared on the green plush seat.

It had to be Annie Tuck. The ghost.

Jeannette thought of Jacques, the ghost of Moon Lake. A good spirit. A helpful ghost.

She took a deep breath. Even if she was mistaken and allowed herself to be taken in by a trick, it wouldn't hurt to discover what Annie had to say.

"You spoke of a pact, Annie. What do you have in mind?"

"It's very simple, Lady Caroline. I'll help you, and you'll help me."

The figure in the green plush chair grew vague, turning into a shapeless gray mass.

Jeannette squinted at the foggy substance. "Why do you keep disappearing?"

"Oh, dear."

Jeannette heard a muttering and rustling as if skirts were being shaken vigorously. Then Annie was back.

"It's this house, Lady Caroline. I don't belong here, and my powers are growing weak. Colonel Astley, who heard me well enough at Stenton Castle, never could see or hear me in this house. He didn't believe either that Miss Juliette had brought me from Stenton. Whenever he caught her talking to me, he thought she was playing a joke on him."

"You were friends with Miss Juliette?"

"The best." Annie gave a little bounce on the chair. "But you will be an even better friend."

Jeannette was no longer tired; on the contrary, she was alert and keen to strike a bargain with this waif-like creature who said she'd help her. But Jeannette was also practical and cautious.

"Annie, I can certainly use help in fighting that odious Simon Renshaw. But before I accept your kind offer, perhaps you had better tell me what you expect of me. After all, if it isn't something outrageous you want me to do, why didn't your dear friend Miss Juliette help you?"

"She couldn't. Miss Juliette had no carriage."

"Oh."

Jeannette felt vaguely disappointed. She had expected . . . she knew not what. Perhaps a request to avenge a wrong?

"You want my phaeton, Annie? That's all?"

"I want you to take me with you whenever you drive out, Lady Caroline. Specifically, I want you to take me into the alleys and lanes around St. Paul's."

"Why?"

"I want to find my childhood home."

Chapter Six

Simon Renshaw, solicitor, was renowned for his competence and calm good sense. Simon Renshaw, barrister, had garnered the reputation of a brilliant, compassionate, infinitely patient counselor. He knew there was no point in calling at the house in George Street until his messenger had returned from Northumberland with word about the miniatures.

Not that the existence of a set of miniatures would convince him the gentleman from New Orleans was indeed Hugh Dundas, but it would show that the imposter was more familiar with the Dundas household than a by-blow of the fourth duke had any right to be. That possibly sometime, somewhere, he had met the real Hugh Dundas.

But for once, waiting was an almost unbearable strain. Twice he set out, once driving as far as Portman Square before he turned the curricle and proceeded to his offices in Lincoln's Inn Fields where a prospective client was awaiting his convenience.

Never had Simon wanted anything more than to rush to that narrow terrace house in quiet George Street. He wanted to stop the infernal masquerade of the man calling himself Hugh Dundas, Marquis of Luxton. He wanted to interrogate the rogue until he broke down and confessed to fraudulent intentions.

He was impatient for Frederick's sake. Or so Simon told himself—even when the face that came to mind in connection with the George Street house was the delicate oval of a young lady's face, dominated by a pair of deep blue eyes and framed by glossy raven hair.

Indeed, waiting was the hardest thing Simon had ever done.

Five days after leaving London, the exhausted messenger finally stumbled into Simon's private office at Dundas House.

"Harte! At last!" Simon pushed aside the brief on which he should have been working instead of staring into space and thinking about an adventuress from New Orleans. "Do you have the miniatures?"

"Only one. The fourth duke's likeness." The man brushed a shaking hand across his sweating, grime-streaked face. "No sign of a second one anywhere."

"What a buffoon I am, making you talk before you've caught your breath. Sit down, Harte." Simon reached for a glass and a decanter on the bookcase at his back. "Madeira? It'll take the shakes out of your hands and legs. You must have ridden day and night to get back so quickly."

"Thank you, sir." Harte downed the wine. He grinned, showing white, even teeth and a youthful dimple in his cheek. "Now I feel alive again."

"You finally look alive," Simon said dryly. "Less like a man with one foot in the grave. Tell me what you found out. Did anyone remember ever seeing a second miniature?"

"The housekeeper did, Mrs. Haggerty. Said she remembered both from her early days as a maid. But she hasn't seen the young Marquis of Luxton's likeness for twenty years. Not since the duchess's death. I asked her to search for it."

Simon pictured Granby Castle with its turrets and towers and dozens of wings, and suppressed a sigh.

Harte's thoughts ran along the same lines. "Might take months," he said gloomily. "That old place must have a hundred rooms or more."

"And many of them locked and forgotten. Since the duchess's death, the duke used only the south wing."

Simon refilled Harte's glass. "What about my father? Did he give you a letter for me?"

"No, sir. He read yours, but he only gave me messages for you."

Malcolm Renshaw was recuperating at his country home in Ainmouth, less than two miles from Granby Castle. Simon wondered if he should have kept the news of the appearance of Hugh Dundas from his father. But Malcolm would have heard about it eventually, and the quick flare of his temper when he learned that he had been kept in the dark would have wreaked more damage on his shaky constitution than the actual news of the imposter could do.

"Sir, your father says that the miniatures are unimportant."

"Does he remember seeing both?"

"He did not say. Just that they don't matter much. And he says, although he knows you've got a clear head on your shoulders and will handle the situation competently, he advises you not to jump to a conclusion about that man, Hugh Dundas."

"He does, does he?"

"And he also says that he feels fit as a fiddle and will be posting up to town very shortly."

Simon grinned. So much for Malcolm's trust in his son's clear head.

Drumming his fingers on the desk top, Simon considered the situation. If, heaven forbid, this matter should drag on, he needed information about the man who claimed to be Hugh Dundas. About his life these past thirty years. And he needed the right agent to carry out the investigation.

"How old are you, Harte?"

"Twenty, sir."

"A bit young, perhaps, to go abroad," Simon said absently. Harte had worked for Renshaw and Renshaw for six years. Difficult to remember that he was still so young.

"I've gone abroad for you before," Harte reminded him.

Simon frowned, then gave a shout of laughter. "You call Ireland abroad? Young cawker! I'm talking about America. New Orleans."

If a glass of Madeira had revived Harte, the mention of America and New Orleans electrified him.

"Sir! Do you mean it? New Orleans? I'm your man, sir! I've got family there. My mother's uncle. He was valet to the Vicomte Lefabre, and when the family left France during the Terror, he accompanied them."

"I had forgotten that your mother is French."

"Aye. She, too, stayed with her master and mistress when they fled, but she ended up in England. Which," Harte said cheerfully, "turned out dandy for me."

Simon gave him a pensive look. With a French mother, Harte was definitely his man. He only had to decide whether Harte would serve his purpose better in New Orleans or in George Street with Lady Caroline, who also had a French mother.

But George Street was his own domain.

"Do you speak French, Harte?"

"Bien sûr! Tout le temps je parle français avec ma mère."

"Very well. We'll talk about New Orleans again when you've rested."

He sent Harte to the housekeeper for a meal and, whistling softly, went in search of Frederick. He found the young duke in his chambers struggling with his cravat. At Simon's nod, Frederick's valet left.

"The *trône d'amour,* bantling?" Deftly, Simon arranged the intricate folds of the white muslin. "Are you seeing Eleanor?"

Frederick blushed. "I am driving her to Hampton Court."

"Then I shan't distract you with a request to go with me to George Street."

"Oh? Did you receive word about the miniatures?"

"Nothing definitive, unfortunately."

Frederick gave him an unexpectedly shrewd look. "Then, I suppose, your visit to George Street is prompted not so much by a desire to confront Hugh Dundas as by the wish to see his daughter. In which case, I'd be quite *de trop.*"

Simon laughed. "She's a charmer, isn't she?"

"I don't suppose she and her father could truly be who they say they are? I mean, it *could* be possible."

"Worried?"

"No. At least, I don't think I am." The frown that

came all too easily to one so young grooved Frederick's brow. "I admit, though, it wouldn't suit me at all if suddenly I were plain Frederick Dundas. Mind you, it isn't the title so much as—oh, I don't really know what I want to say."

"I understand, bantling. It's having been raised as the heir and groomed to the position. It would have been different if your father hadn't died so young. He'd have borne the brunt of the old duke's attention. He instead of you would have been schooled to shoulder the responsibilities that go with the title and the vast holdings. And you would now be happily engaged overturning a mail coach by day and toppling the watch at night."

A sudden grin lit Frederick's face. "Perhaps it would suit me after all if Hugh Dundas could prove he's the rightful heir."

"Don't count on it. Remember, it was my father who discovered that Hugh was killed."

"Aye." Frederick shrugged into his coat. "Next to you, Uncle Malcolm is the most painstakingly thorough man I know. I'm sure he checked every record minutely."

Simon nodded. But as he followed his cousin into the corridor and down the stairs, he reflected grimly on the possibility that during the upheaval of war a birth or a death might be recorded mistakenly.

Frederick's curricle was at the door. Taking the reins from the groom, he climbed in. "You're not driving, Simon? Shall I drop you off in George Street?"

"I should say yes and teach you a lesson."

Once more, a grin brightened Frederick's face. "Eleanor won't mind if I'm a bit late."

"Won't she! You have a lot to learn, my friend." Simon raised a hand in salute. "I'll walk."

"Simon!"

He had already turned away but, hearing the urgent note in Frederick's voice, he looked back.

"There's something about Hugh Dundas and Caroline, isn't there, Simon? Something very likable. Don't be too hard on them, will you?"

Simon could not deny the truth of Frederick's words. Yes, Hugh Dundas was a likable fellow. And Lady Caroline—no, Jeannette. That was how he thought of her. Not Lady Caroline, Not Miss or Mademoiselle Dundas.

Jeannette.

And he had more powerful adjectives for her than likable.

The closer Simon got to Portman Square and George Street, the faster he walked. Some very strange notions churned in his mind.

Steady now, he told himself. He had seen her only twice, and that five days ago. He could not possibly have made up his mind about the young lady.

As he turned into George Street and came within viewing distance of his destination, he saw two riders who had obviously just dismounted in front of the house. One was Lady Caroline. She was tugging at her gloves as she hurried up the narrow steps leading to the equally narrow front door. The other, a groom, gathered both horses' reins and led the animals toward Orchard Street.

Simon stopped when they passed him. He was no mean judge of horseflesh and recognized at a glance that the chestnut mare carrying the side saddle was worth a small fortune.

And what about the carriage and team of matched bays that had conveyed Hugh Dundas, his daughter, and Lord Decimus to Grosvenor Square? Simon was willing to wager his gown and wig that the equipage did not belong to Lord Decimus, who was known to squander his income at the gaming tables and on smuggled wine and brandy but not on horses or carriages.

Simon looked at the terrace house that certainly did not cost a fortune to rent. Undoubtedly, the lease was taken before Hugh realized just how powerful the name Dundas was.

Lady Caroline had disappeared inside, but as much as he wanted to rush after her, he took a moment to cool his rising ire. No easy feat when his mind, with a will of its own, was totting up the sums of money spent by Hugh Dundas on five horses, a carriage, and the expense of stabling the same.

Without a doubt, it was money borrowed against his expectations. False expectations.

Damn Lord Decimus! If the gullible old fool weren't running about town introducing his friend as Hugh Dundas, the Marquis of Luxton, no merchant would extend as much as a farthing's worth of credit to the imposter.

But now, when this business was settled, Frederick would find himself saddled with the debts incurred in the Dundas name.

Bloody hell! It was something he should have anticipated. He must put a notice in *The Times* and the *Gazette* that the Duke of Granby denounces all ties with the man calling himself Hugh Dundas.

But Simon did not immediately turn his steps to Fleet Street. Instead, he rapped sharply on Hugh Dundas's door. He was admitted by a footman.

A footman, by George! Why not a butler, too? Grimly, Simon added wages to the growing list of expenditure incurred by Hugh.

"I want to see your master. Immediately!"

Flustered by Simon's air of command, the young footman bowed.

"Yes, sir. Who may I say is calling?"

A door opened, just to the right of the entrance.

"Mr. Renshaw." Still in her riding habit but without the hat, Lady Caroline inclined her head the merest fraction. "I'm afraid my father is not at home."

She was lying. Wide-eyed and unblushing.

Not only a charmer, a brazen hussy as well.

He used his courtroom voice. Firm. Peremptory. "In that case, you will be good enough to give me a few moments of your time, Lady Caroline?"

He saw the small movement of her throat as she swallowed. A lovely throat, rising slim and graceful from the fall of lace at the neck of her crimson habit.

She turned abruptly and stepped back into the room from which she had come. He wondered if she would close the door in his face.

"Come in, Mr. Renshaw."

Handing hat and gloves to the footman, he followed with alacrity.

The room was dim, with barely enough light filtering through the drapes to show the chairs and tables, the sofas and what-nots crowded into the narrow space. The unwary might easily stub a toe or scrape a shin.

Lady Caroline stood at a marble-topped table supported by hideous carved crocodiles. She was fumbling with a tinder box.

She gave him an impatient look. "Please close the door."

The latch snapped into place.

"I had every intention of doing so, Lady Caroline. But wasn't it rather imprudent of you to suggest it?"

"Why? Are you planning to accost me again? Be warned, Mr. Renshaw, the bellpull is in good working order. One of the footmen would respond instantly."

Without a word he took the tinder box from her and lit the two lamps on the table. The soft glow disclosed the angry color on her face and a mouth tightly compressed.

"Lady Caroline, you cannot truly believe I would give you cause to summon help. So why are you angry?"

Her hands flew to her burning face, and just as quickly she snatched them away.

"Oh, pother! Why the dickens must you be so observant?"

He said nothing. And she, in startling contrast to her purely English exclamations, gave a shrug that was typically Gallic.

"To tell the truth, Mr. Renshaw, I am angry at myself. In fact, I am mortified. If there's one thing I dislike more than another it is being put in the wrong and knowing I am at fault."

He remembered her embarrassment at Dundas House when she was caught whispering in French to her father and, only a moment later, her unblushing reference to a by-blow. She certainly was an unusual blend of propriety and brazenness.

"But what was I supposed to do?" Raising her shoulders, she spread her hands in a gesture of helplessness. "If we must talk, I don't want the footman to overhear us. And if I send for my chaperone . . ."

A chaperone. Another expense to be chalked up against Hugh Dundas.

But Simon only said, "And I had the gall to point out the impropriety of the closed door."

"Precisely! No Creole gentleman would have been so insensitive."

He met her reproving gaze and in that instant knew for certain that he had indeed made up his mind how to deal with Hugh Dundas and his daughter.

Especially the daughter.

Chapter Seven

Jeannette turned abruptly. She did not understand herself. Speaking frankly with Simon Renshaw, as if he were an old and valued friend! It was his air of command, no doubt, the look of trustworthiness he presented to the world, that had momentarily deceived her into forgetting he was the foe.

"Sit down, Mr. Renshaw." She chose a straight-backed chair and sat stiffly on the edge of the seat. "I'm sure you've come here for a purpose, so we may as well come to the point."

After a skeptical look at the twin of her chair, he lowered himself onto a sofa to her right. Crossing his long legs, he looked utterly at home and comfortable—a sight that did nothing to soothe her irritation.

"Is your name truly Caroline Jeannette?"

"Yes, of course." If, earlier, she had been annoyed with herself, she could now, with good cause, direct her anger at him.

She turned to face him more fully. "Can you not get it into your head that Papa and I are *not* here under assumed names?"

"I have no problem with Jeannette. Are you named after your mother?"

"Yes. She was Jeanne. Jeanne Vireilles. At home,

I was called Jeannette, which, after all, is only natural in a French community."

"French? I was under the impression that New Orleans is American territory."

"Must you be so literal?"

He raised a quizzing brow. "Unlike a Creole gentleman?"

"A Creole gentleman would not at every turn try to put a lady in the wrong."

"I apologize. I can see that I must mend my manners if I want to make a good impression."

She gave him a sidelong look but could see nothing in his face warranting the suspicion that he was amused.

"Mr. Renshaw, I am well aware that the territory of New Orleans was purchased by the American government. I know, too, that our delegate to Congress, M. Julien Poydras, has proposed statehood for the territory."

"I'm sure you knew it before I did," he said soothingly.

She glared. "All I meant was that in New Orleans I lived in the French community. In the Vieux Carré. The Americans who moved south after the Louisiana purchase, live in Faubourg St. Marie—St. Mary, as they call it—and they have little traffic with Creole families. Thus, my first name, Caroline, was never of advantage."

"Until now."

"Caroline is appropriate here in England, since, as you should know, I was named after my grandmother, the Fifth Duchess of Granby."

"Yes, indeed, *Lady* Caroline. But may I call you Jeannette? It suits you, and it's how I think of you."

"It would be preferable to your calling me *Lady* Caroline, with that awful emphasis you put on the title," she burst out. "But I don't think Papa would like it."

"I'll do it only when we are alone."

"We shouldn't be alone," she snapped. "It's not proper. And calling me Jeannette is not proper either. It is not the same as addressing me as Lady Caroline."

"Certainly not."

"You're laughing at me! I can see it in your eyes. You believe I know nothing about the strict rules governing the *ton.* That a young lady does not permit a gentleman to make free of her first name! You want to use me in some underhanded scheme to make Papa look bad."

"No, Jeannette. You accuse me unjustly. If, as you claim, your father is Hugh Dundas, then there is a family connection. My grandmother was cousin to the late fifth duke, your grandfather. No impropriety attaches to our use of first names."

His voice was deep and smooth and convincing. But Jeannette would not be convinced. She knew only too well that he was behind the plot to defraud her father and could not be trusted.

A notion came to her, and she lowered her gaze. Mr. Renshaw wasn't the only one who could play an underhanded game. She had always scorned to take advantage of feminine wiles the way her cousin Félicie did. But that did not mean she didn't know how.

As Simon Renshaw would soon find out.

She flashed him a smile and hoped that it was the sort of smile one of her New Orleans suitors had likened to a dazzling sunrise.

"Very well. If you think it proper, you may call me Jeannette."

"Thank you. And I hope you will call me Simon." He paused. "When we're alone, if you wish."

Once again she saw the gleam of laughter in his eyes and vowed to herself she'd make dashed sure that no one ever caught her in a familiarity with the Dundas family solicitor.

"Now, tell me why you came here today, Mr. Ren—Simon. Have you found the miniatures?"

"Do you know how long it takes a man to ride to Northumberland and back?" he countered. "I came to ask your father one or two questions which might help settle the matter. But since he's not here . . ."

"Ask me. I, too, want to settle the matter, and I can tell you as much as Papa."

"Indeed?"

His tone was polite, but she could not like the sudden sharpness in those keen gray-green eyes. She regretted her rash words; retract them she would not.

"Jeannette, I wished to question your father about Savannah. He offered no explanation, nor did he dispute Colonel Adam's account of Hugh Dundas's death."

"No. He did not, did he?"

She busied herself with the short train of her riding habit. She should have expected this.

She did not understand her father's silence. When asked, he had patted her hand and told her not to worry. He would explain in good time.

Nom de nom! A good time would have been when Simon Renshaw first brought up the horrid letter.

She forced a smile. "No doubt my father has good

reason for his reticence. But I can tell you this much, Mr. Ren—Simon. Papa arrived in New Orleans on New Year's Day of 1781. He was badly injured and in a high fever, and if it hadn't been for my grandmother, he would have died."

"Your father told you this?"

"*Grandmère* did."

"Then you believe the letter from Colonel Adam is a fake?"

Jeannette hesitated. She remembered that Lord Decimus said it was Simon's father who had produced the letter confirming Hugh Dundas's death.

"Either that, or it is a fabrication of lies on the part of Colonel Adam."

"A fine distinction." For a moment, those keen eyes veiled as if she had given him pause to think.

But only for a very brief moment.

"Tell me, Jeannette. Were you born in New Orleans?"

"No. On Haiti." She relaxed her stiff posture. This was the kind of question she need not be leery of. "It was Saint Domingue then, and we—that is, *Grandpère*—had plantations there. I was born on the Plantation Vireilles and lived there twelve years."

He frowned. "The slave uprising—when was it? 1791, I think. Your parents did not leave?"

"It was impossible. The insurrection occurred in August. Papa was hurt, and *Maman* was expecting me. I was born on the twenty-fifth of September. By then the worst was over. We stayed on until—"

When she did not continue, he said, "I expect you stayed until news of Toussaint l'Ouverture's death in Paris reached Saint Domingue and caused another bloodbath on the island."

"Yes. We left in the winter of '03. Dessalines and his troops had taken over, and none of the French planters were safe any longer." Jeannette spoke brusquely. She wanted to get over that most horrid time of her life as quickly as possible and without awakening old pain.

"There weren't any ships when we got to Port-au-Prince. They had all left, except for a rickety old schooner. There were so many of us. Too many. But it couldn't be helped. Papa said no one must stay behind since there might not be another ship. The crossing was rough. So many storms. *Maman* died. And so did my baby brother, born prematurely aboard the schooner."

"I am sorry."

He deserted the comfortable sofa and sat down on the straight-backed chair beside her. His hand covered hers for just an instant, but the brief touch warmed her.

"Believe me," he said, "it was not my intention to stir sad memories."

"You had no way of knowing what my memories are. But now you will understand why I was rendered speechless when you told me that Hugh Dundas had a son who'd be some thirty-odd years old if he had survived. I am nineteen, and my brother would have been seven this past November."

Simon rose. He looked for a path suitable for pacing among the crowded furniture but gave up after a few steps.

He did not doubt what she had just told him, and he did not relish questioning her further. However, by denying a previous son, she had told him more than he ever hoped to learn that day. And if he let the occasion slip out of compassion, he ought to give up his profession.

He faced her. "Jeannette, did you not know, then, that Hugh Dundas married a Philadelphia girl in 1774 and had a son by her?"

"Married? In '74?" The blood drained from her face. "What are you saying? You cannot mean—are you accusing my father of bigamy?"

"The wife and child died in a freak accident during the British occupation of Philadelphia. A cartload of English gunpowder exploded. After the war, my father spoke with the girl's parents and several witnesses to the incident. There's no doubt at all. Hugh Dundas's wife and child are dead."

She had no time to feel relief. Or sadness at the waste of two young lives.

"But your father did not tell you that, did he, Jeannette? Or that it was after the tragic mishap that he decided to throw in his lot with the rebels?"

"No, but—"

"Your father most likely doesn't know about it himself," Simon cut in, forcing a display of harshness he was far from feeling.

Devil a bit! He must make her see reason.

"Jeannette, how can you go along with this charade?"

She pokered up immediately. "That's what it always comes down to, doesn't it? Your vile accusation that my father is an imposter!"

Jeannette swept to her feet, the use of feminine wiles forgotten. "For a while there, I thought you were asking questions because you had come to believe that Papa is telling the truth. But you're interested only in discovering what you can use to strengthen Frederick's position."

"It is impossible that your father is Hugh Dundas. I owe it to Frederick—to all of the Dundas family—to expose an imposter."

Snatching up the short train of her riding dress, Jeannette brushed past him. "I have no more time to waste on you, Mr. Renshaw. I must change."

"I'll call again at a more convenient time."

"Don't bother."

She made a hurried exit into the foyer. Simon followed slowly. He was in time to see her, at the foot of the narrow stairs, gesturing to her father who was descending from the first floor.

"Papa!" she whispered urgently. "Don't come down!"

"I'm looking for my spectacles, dear." Leisurely, Hugh continued his descent. "Must have left them in that cupboard of a bookroom which Decimus calls the library."

"Papa, please!"

"Caught in a lie, Lady Caroline?" Simon asked softly.

Jeannette spun on her heel, and the first thing she noted was the devilish gleam in his eye.

"Not at all, Mr. Renshaw. The excuse 'not at home' is always used when an unwelcome caller shows himself. But surely you are aware of that. This cannot be the first time it has happened to you."

"Baggage," he said without heat. "I wonder, though, how you can be familiar with this particular usage of the phrase. Or is it the same in Creole society?"

Joining them, Hugh Dundas said, "I have not been the only one speaking English with my daughter and talking to her about England. After the War of Independence, quite a few Tory widows from the north sought refuge in New Orleans."

"Over here," said Simon, "we call it the Revolutionary War."

Hugh Dundas ignored the interjection. "My mother-in-law took in a young English gentlewoman who had married a Virginia planter loyal to the Crown, and I had no trouble finding a lady born and bred in England when my daughter needed a governess."

Simon met Jeannette's look, a look that said, There! Try to find a way to use *that* against us.

Then she turned and fled upstairs.

Chapter Eight

Jeannette had no occasion for a private word with her father until late that night when Mrs. Effington excused herself shortly after the tea tray was carried into the drawing room by one of the footmen.

"Just a touch of the headache," the elderly lady replied to Jeannette's concerned question whether she was ailing. Refusing a second cup of tea, she said, "I have a cordial that'll help me sleep, and tomorrow I'll be as right as a trivet."

Jeannette watched the drawing room door close behind her chaperone, then joined her father by the log fire, which he savored as much as his daughter.

"Papa, do you suppose we're giving poor Mrs. Effington a headache by having a fire lit every night? She does not seem to feel the chill as we do."

Hugh shifted his gaze from the glowing embers. "What did you say, dear?"

Jeannette did not repeat the question but settled herself on the hearth rug at his feet.

"Papa, will you tell me about your first marriage?"

He sat quite still, looking at her. Yet she had the feeling that what he saw was not her face but something . . . *somebody* pictured in his mind.

"Papa?"

His gaze focused. "Ah, yes. My first marriage. I suppose Simon Renshaw brought up the subject?"

"He did." Jeannette hesitated. "Did *Maman* know?"

"Yes, of course she knew. And your grandparents Vireilles. A previous marriage is not something a man keeps from a wife or his in-laws."

"But why didn't you ever tell me?"

No lamp was lit near her father's chair, and in the fire's reddish glow his face looked more haggard than usual.

"My dear," he said. "In time, Jeanne and I would have told you. But when she died . . . and your brother, too, I simply—"

The hand resting on his black-clad knee clenched. "I'm sorry, Jeannette. I simply did not think of it."

Once more that day, she remembered the rickety old schooner, her mother's pale face contorted with pain, Nounou's frantic efforts to stem the flow of blood. The baby, so still, scarcely breathing. And then—

"Papa, *I* am sorry!" She covered his hand with hers. "Twice you lost a wife and son. I should have understood."

The hand beneath hers unclenched. He reached out with the other, cupping her chin.

"Don't apologize for asking, Jeannette. You have a right to know. Sarah—the girl in Philadelphia—died thirty years ago. So did the little boy. When Jeanne died and Baby Hugh, I did not think of Sarah and that other child. I only thanked the Lord that I still had you."

Tears blurred her eyes. A painful lump in her throat made speech impossible.

"You were ten minutes old when I first saw you," Hugh said softly. "And when you looked at me with those deep blue eyes which, contrary to Nounou's prediction, never changed, I lost my heart to you. Daughter, I love you."

Her throat was still tight with unshed tears. "Papa," she whispered, "I love you, too."

"And I'll do my best to see you properly established. As is your due."

Frowning, she shook her head. "What about *your* due Papa? To me it does not matter whether I am plain Jeannette or Lady Caroline."

"Of course it matters. And don't let anyone tell you differently." He gently pinched her cheek and said with an attempt at cheerfulness, "Seems to me, my dear, that next time Simon Renshaw comes calling, it had better be *you* who is 'not at home'."

"I can deal with Mr. Renshaw," she said fiercely.

"So can I, my dear." Hugh leaned back in his chair. Even in the fire's glow his skin had a grayish pallor. "So can I."

"I don't doubt it, Papa," she said, but in her heart she feared it was the Dundas family solicitor who knew how to deal with the unwelcome visitors from New Orleans.

Jeannette rose. She was troubled by her father's quickly flagging strength. And his earlier abstraction had been caused, no doubt, by worry. Without hesitation, she blamed exhaustion and worry on Simon Renshaw's visit.

"Did Mr. Renshaw stay long after I went upstairs?" she asked.

"Long enough to drink a glass of wine with me."

Hugh closed his eyes. "Forgive me, Jeannette. I'm

a little tired tonight. Will you ring for Perrier, please?"

"Odious man!" Jeannette closed the door to her chamber with unladylike force. "Insufferable scoundrel!"

She had left her father in the capable hands of Perrier, his valet. Annie Tuck, awaiting her in the third-floor bedchamber, did not, however, mistake the hurled epithets as anger directed at Hugh Dundas or at Perrier.

"Aye, he's a rotter all right, that Simon Renshaw," she said.

"Annie!" Jeannette whirled, tracing the voice to the four-poster bed, where the light of the bedside table lamp showed the ghostly waif perched on the carved headboard. "How you startled me!"

"Surely, after a week you should be used to having me around." Annie's face puckered. "Or am I being a nuisance?"

"Of course not. It's just that—Annie, you were in the drawing room, weren't you? When I asked Papa about his first marriage?"

She had asked but had learned nothing about her father's previous marriage that Simon Renshaw hadn't already told her, she realized belatedly.

The large mobcap on Annie's head nodded vigorously. "Aye, Lady Caroline. I was in the drawing room. And I was in the parlor when Mr. Renshaw came a-calling this morning."

"That's what I cannot get used to." Jeannette went to her dressing table and started to pull the pins from her hair. "Sometimes I can see you, and other times I don't even know you're there."

"I didn't want to be visible. Thought you might not want *him* to see me."

"Simon Renshaw?" Pensive, Jeannette stared into the mirror. Her eyes narrowed. "Not a bad notion. Might shake him up a bit. Is it something you do at will, Annie? Be visible or invisible? Audible or soundless?"

"Most of the time, yes. But like I told you before, my powers are not what they used to be at Stenton Castle. Sometimes, no matter how hard I try. . . ." Annie shrugged.

"Now, about Mr. Renshaw," she said, turning brisk. "Yes, indeed, you want to shake him up. But not with me. You need to employ different tactics, Lady Caroline."

"Feminine wiles," murmured Jeannette, cringing at the memory of her pitiful attempt that morning.

"Dazzle him." Annie bounced off the headboard. She danced across the bed and settled on a corner of the dressing table. "Make his head spin whenever he's with you so he can't keep his mind on American militia men who swear that your pa is dead."

Jeannette shook her head. The unpinned coils of hair slipped, covering her shoulders in a dark silken cloud.

"Annie, I'm afraid that plan won't work. I tried. But I forget all about smiles and eyelash fluttering when he makes me angry, and he always says something to make me absolutely furious. All I want to do is scratch his eyes out."

"But you mustn't! You must sweet-talk him, Lady Caroline. Ensnare him."

"For heaven's sake! *Ensnare?*"

The word conjured the unsettling vision of Simon

Renshaw caught in an unidentified female's arms. Scandalized and fascinated at the same time, Jeannette said rather weakly, "What an utterly rubbishing notion."

"It's the only way to turn his loyalty from the young duke," said Annie.

"Loyalty?" Now, that was a concept Jeannette could picture without blushing. "Why, Annie! You sound as if you believed loyalty is the reason he tries to expose Papa as an imposter. It's not, I tell you. Or, if it is, his loyalty should be directed at Papa. Simon Renshaw knows quite well that Papa is the Marquis of Luxton and should by rights be the new Duke of Granby."

Annie seemed absorbed in the contemplation of her buckled shoes. "I saw him this morning. Can't say he struck me as a scoundrel."

"You called him a rotter!"

"It wasn't because I think he hatched a plot with the young duke and is deliberately trying to cheat your pa."

"If he isn't trying to cheat, why does he deny what's obvious? You should have seen the portrait at Dundas House. It's of Augustus Hugh Dundas, my great-great-grandfather, and Papa looks enough like him to pass as his twin."

"Good. It proves your pa is a Dundas."

"Ha!" Jeannette flung a soft, woolen shawl around her shoulders. "On the wrong side of the blanket, says *loyal* Simon Renshaw."

"Gorblimey!" Annie finally tore her gaze away from her shoes. "I never heard the like!"

"Neither did I. But what was that exclamation? Gorblimey?"

Annie clapped a hand to her mouth. "Did I say that? I beg your pardon, Lady Caroline. It's the shock, I suppose. Miss Juliette would comb my hair with a fine-tooth comb if she'd heard me. She spent all this time since Christmas teaching me to speak and write like a lady."

Jeannette carefully tucked the word into a corner of her mind. *Gorblimey.* She liked the sound of it.

"Lady Caroline, you did say the gentleman in the portrait was your great-great-grandfather? That would make him your pa's great-grandfather, wouldn't it?"

"Yes, but Mr. Renshaw claims—"

"Don't you see?" Annie interrupted. "Mr. Renshaw cannot be thinking straight. Surely the old gentleman didn't . . . I mean he couldn't . . ."

Annie faltered. In her eighteen years of earthly life, she had never had a lover, but in the tenement where she lived as a child, it had been impossible not to know about the sexual act. Lady Caroline, on the other hand, would have been sheltered from such knowledge.

Annie picked her words with care. "I mean, wouldn't that Augustus Dundas have been too old to do whatever is necessary to father a child?"

"One would suppose so, but Papa later confirmed his great-grandfather's amorous tendencies. And, what's more to the point, he was aware of an illegitimate child born posthumously. Papa was ten or eleven at the time."

Annie cocked her head. "For a gently bred young lady, you speak very casually about these delicate matters," she said reprovingly. "Don't let anyone hear you."

Jeannette thought of the *boutique* she had opened with Nounou and Marie in New Orleans, and which was staffed by young women who would otherwise have fallen prey to such gentlemen as Augustus Hugh Dundas—gentlemen who had wives and children. Gentlemen who paid court and proposed marriage to young ladies like Jeannette and her cousins and, at the same time, looked for a mistress to set up in a house on Rampart Street.

Her mouth tightened, but she said nothing to Annie about Creole gentlemen and the pretty girls and beautiful women of color in New Orleans.

Annie slid off the dressing table. Arms akimbo, she said, "Well, Lady Caroline? Have you given some thought to my suggestion?"

Jeannette didn't pretend not to know what Annie was talking about. She might not want to admit it, but the notion of charming Simon Renshaw to her father's side had not been far from her mind. Which was strange, considering her preference to keep gentlemen at arm's length.

"It's the only way," Annie insisted.

Jeannette thought of the keen gray-green eyes that seemed to see so much more than was desirable.

"He won't be taken in," she said, half regretful, half relieved.

"Perhaps not. But with a little help, you can make him fall madly in love with you. Then he'd do anything you wished him to do."

"Anything?"

Jeannette tried to picture Simon Renshaw so bedazzled that he forgot his own schemes and admitted her father was indeed the Marquis of Luxton, the new Duke of Granby.

She laughed. "I'm afraid it would take more than a little help. It would take magic."

"Not magic. Just—"

Jeannette paid no heed. "Besides, why should I go to such lengths? Papa is the rightful new Duke of Granby. And he'll prove it."

"But when? *After* he's been convicted of fraud?"

"Don't talk nonsense, Annie. Even Simon Renshaw wouldn't dare drag this dispute into the courts."

"You don't know the worst. Why I called him a rotter."

The hollow sound of Annie's voice made Jeannette shiver despite the wool shawl draping her shoulders.

"Then you had better tell me, hadn't you?" she said with forced calm.

"This morning, Mr. Renshaw did not leave when you went upstairs to change out of your riding habit."

"Yes, I know. Papa invited him to take a glass of wine."

"But you don't know what Mr. Renshaw told your pa when they were alone."

"No, I don't." Jeannette's calm snapped. "And if you don't come to the point, I daresay I'll never know!"

"Mr. Renshaw says he has enough evidence to get your pa deported or clapped into gaol."

"Rubbish. How can he have evidence when there is none? You must have misheard."

"Listen to me, Lady Caroline! Mr. Renshaw is only waiting for his father to come to town. Then he'll bring suit against your pa."

"Dash it! Why didn't Papa tell me?"

Jeannette knew her father wasn't an imposter, but

the knowledge did nothing to ward off the cold touch of fear.

Her father dragged into court. His name smeared in the papers. It was unthinkable. He wasn't well.

She could not, would not let it happen.

"Annie." Her shoulders squared determinedly. "What must I do to ensnare Simon Renshaw?"

"Nothing much. We'll brew up a little concoction and you see to it that he drinks it."

Jeannette's eyes widened. "If I didn't know better I'd think you want to poison him."

"Gorblimey! Who says anything about poison? What we need is a *love* potion."

Chapter Nine

"So we need magic, after all."

"You sound disappointed, Lady Caroline."

Annie flitted to the fire screen where, despite the mild English spring, a white flannel gown was draped to toast before a small fire. She took the nightgown to Jeannette.

"Best get ready for bed. Everything will look brighter in the morning—even the use of magic."

"It's not that I doubt the power of herbs and barks and such. My nurse knew a great number of recipes for potions and charms. But, Annie! None of them worked *all the time.*"

"This love potion does. There was an old woman—some called her a witch—near Stenton Castle, where I lived. And old Marjory mixed a potion for Nancy, the second under-housemaid at Stenton. Nancy was wild for a young fisherman. She slipped the potion into his mug of ale the night before he was to wed another."

"And?" Jeannette prompted. "He did not marry the other girl?"

"He couldn't, could he? Ran off with our Nancy that night."

Still not quite convinced, Jeannette asked, "What is the recipe for the potion?"

"Honey and poppy, mistletoe and rose," Annie chanted, then abruptly switched the subject. "Lady Caroline, will you take me driving tomorrow?"

Three times, they had gone "driving" since Annie first made herself known to Jeannette. The outings could not be considered a success. Annie was drawn to the alleys and lanes east of St. Paul's Cathedral, where she lived as a child. It was a neighborhood which Archer, the sturdy groom employed by Hugh Dundas for Jeannette's protection, considered unsuitable for a young lady. And Archer did not hesitate to make his displeasure known.

Jeannette was always very conscious of Annie seated between her and the groom, although Archer apparently, neither saw nor heard Annie, despite the latter's incessant chatter. Unfortunately, he did hear when Jeannette forgot discretion and directed a remark to the little ghost. All in all, a drive with Annie was rather awkward.

"Annie, why does Archer not hear you when you speak to me?"

Annie cocked a brow. "Why does Lord Decimus hear and see me in such a way that no one can convince him I'm a ghost? Lady Caroline, I don't have all the answers. But I do know that there are people who simply will not hear or see things outside their understanding. Archer may be such a one. And then again, he may just be a slowtop and notice me by and by."

Jeannette nodded absently. Archer was a puzzle that might or might not be solved; Simon Renshaw was a threat that must be dealt with, immediately.

"Are we going driving, then, Lady Caroline?"

"Annie, I'm sorry, but I cannot take you to St.

Paul's tomorrow. I must find a ship sailing to New Orleans."

"I shan't ask if you're planning to run away, because I know you aren't. But why do you need a ship?"

"I wrote a letter the night you first spoke to me. A letter, asking my grandmother to help furnish the proof that Papa is Hugh Dundas, but I haven't had an opportunity to send it off. And now that I know what Simon Renshaw plans to do—oh, drat the man! But you see why, since I need Archer to accompany me to the docks, we cannot go to St. Paul's."

Annie sniffed. "A regular stick in the mud is Mr. Archer! Acts as if St. Paul's is situated in Seven Dials. But can you not let your pa take charge of posting the letter?"

"It's what I should have done. But Papa also wrote to *Grandmère*. A very civil note it was, telling her we arrived safely and that everything is fine and going just the way he had expected. And he had me add a few lines in the same vein."

"Closed-mouthed about the whole thing, isn't he, your pa?"

"Yes, and if I had asked him to send my letter—a thick package of six sheets!—he would have wanted to know what it was I found so newsworthy to impart to my grandmother. Annie, I cannot lie to Papa. I'll tell him about the letter when it is safely on the way, but if I told him now, I'm afraid he would not want me to send it."

Annie sighed but brightened again almost immediately. "Oh, well. You take care of the letter tomorrow. We'll go back to St. Paul's and to Cheapside and Watling Street the day after."

Jeannette nodded absently. If only it were that simple sending a letter to New Orleans. Alas, unlike her father, she did not have the advantage of knowing a cotton and sugar broker in town, someone who knew which ship was bound directly for New Orleans and not for some eastern seaboard port. But she'd manage. She had learned to be quite practical and resourceful since she started the *boutique.*

Then, when the letter was on its way, she needed only time. Time to wait for *Grandmère's* reply without the shadow of a lawsuit hanging over her father. Time which might be gained through the use of a magic potion.

"Annie, about the recipe you mentioned . . . rose and mistletoe make sense. Honey has many a good quality. But poppy? Dash it, Annie! All I know of poppy is that it induces sleep."

"Don't fret about the recipe." Annie assumed a lofty air. "I daresay after all these years I have forgotten an ingredient or two. But it'll all come back to me. You'll see."

Clutching the nightgown, which was no longer toasty warm, Jeannette frowned at the spot where, an instant earlier, Annie had stood.

The little ghost was gone.

In New Orleans, Jeannette had never ventured to the docks unless accompanied by her father or one of her male cousins. But there were times when a lady must overcome convention and do something that was not quite proper.

Expecting disapproval from her groom, even an outright refusal to fetch the phaeton from the livery stable, Jeannette did not disclose her destination early the next morning until they had passed St. Paul's and it became necessary to ask for directions to the docks.

Justifiably, Archer was incensed. Not so much because he felt Lady Caroline had no call to be visiting the docks, but because she should have taken the closed carriage. She should have had the coachman on the box up front and the groom riding behind. It might be proper for her to be driving herself in fashionable Mayfair or in the park, with the groom, arms folded, sitting beside her, but it wasn't anything but foolhardiness to be doing so on the waterfront.

In the end, since Jeannette absolutely refused to turn around, they compromised. Archer took the reins and Jeannette sat decorously beside him.

In silence, they continued eastward. Only when they crossed the top of Fish Street Hill and the massive towers and walls of the Tower of London loomed in the distance, Archer unbent sufficiently to inquire which of the docks she wanted to visit.

"There's the London Docks, my lady, which we'll get to first after passing the Tower. Then there's the West India Docks past Limehouse on the Isle of Dogs, the East India Docks at Blackwell, or the Surrey Commercial Docks south o' the river."

"Gracious! You sound like a guide book, Archer. Where would you look for a ship bound for New Orleans? The West India Docks?"

"I couldn't say, my lady."

Jeannette frowned. She wished she had paid more attention to her father's import-export business. If she had, she'd know whether he shipped his goods on vessels engaged in the West India trade.

On the other hand, she did not particularly wish to entrust her letter to a ship making half a dozen stops in the West Indies and, perhaps, the Floridas, before going to New Orleans. It would add weeks to an already long voyage—weeks she could not afford to lose, thanks to Mr. Simon Renshaw and his plans to drag her father into the courts!

Archer, softening further at the sight of her troubled face, said hesitantly, "Perhaps we should stop at Custom House. They know all about the ships coming in. Might know, too, about the ships leaving here."

"Archer, you are a treasure!"

The stocky groom was not so old that he was hardened against a young lady's dazzling smile, but he did his best to hide gratification behind a stern front.

"Just using me cockloft. For change! Know very well that what I *should* be doing is take ye straight home."

"But you won't, will you? Please, Archer. This is truly important."

"All I'm saying is, it's what I *should* be doing," he said severely.

Turning off Tower Street toward the river, he pointed the whip handle at a two-story building which looked as if it must be at least two hundred feet long.

"Custom House. Whatever ye do, my lady, promise me ye won't leave me side from now until we've left the waterfront."

Jeannette had no desire to leave his side. As they turned into the Custom House yard—or, perhaps, more appropriately the quay—she instinctively drew closer to the groom as her senses were assaulted by a jumble of smells and sounds.

What noise and bustle! Dock laborers, watermen, bargemen sweating and shouting as they unloaded barges, rolled heavy casks, or lugged wooden crates and packs wrapped in oilcloth; at the waterfront, the creak and rattle of the cranes' rusty winches; at the open warehouse doors, carters swearing at their teams as the wagons were loaded under the supervision of frock-coated merchants or spectacled, black-clothed clerks.

The air was moist and thick, a noxious blend of foul Thames water, spices, tar, rum, tobacco, rusting iron, and other, less easily definable odors. Jeannette's head started to throb before Archer had tied the reins to a convenient post.

Stopping a young man whose brass-buttoned coat proclaimed an official capacity, Archer inquired about ships leaving for New Orleans. Mr. Ludding, as the Custom House officer introduced himself with a bashful bow to Jeannette, did not know of any such ships but offered to take them to one of the customs commissioners, who surely could help.

Escorted by two strapping men, Jeannette knew no hesitation or trepidation as they wended their way across the cobbled yard, through the throng of rough-looking dock laborers. In fact, she was beginning to enjoy herself, and the throbbing in her head ceased miraculously. The quest for a suitable ship promised to turn into a fabulous adventure.

All of the Custom House ground floor consisted of warehouses, which Mr. Ludding bypassed without a glance. Reaching the central part of the building, he ushered them to the upper floor, to the Long Hall, where all customs business was executed.

If Jeannette had thought the quay crowded and busy, the Long Hall was even more so. It was teeming with officers, clerks, merchants, sea captains, and a great number of persons, male and female, young and old, who, Mr. Ludding said, were immigrants from the Netherlands.

Drawing a step or two ahead of Jeannette and Archer, Mr. Ludding addressed a harried-looking gentleman of ample girth. The commissioner, whose assistance he had promised.

"Yes, yes!" the commissioner replied testily to Mr. Ludding's query. "There's a ship bound for New Orleans. Chartered by French *émigrés* who decided they can't stomach England—after nigh on twenty years! But the captain's not taking any more passengers. So there's no point keeping me from my work with useless questions."

"Pardon me, sir." Jeannette produced her best smile and curtsy. "I do not wish to travel to New Orleans. I merely want to send a letter."

"Oh, in that case . . ." The commissioner thawed visibly under Jeannette's melting look. "Let me see what's to be done. They sail with the tide in less than an hour."

"If you give my groom the directions, I'm sure we shall have no trouble finding the ship."

"Directions are not so simple, miss. The docks are confusing, and we cannot take the risk of your getting lost. Especially," he added in an attempt at joviality, "if the letter is important to you."

"It is extremely important, sir."

"Ludding!" The commissioner passed a large, crumpled handkerchief over a shiny bald spot on his head. "You had best accompany the young lady. It's the *Caroline* you want. In London Docks. An American vessel out of Charleston. Captain's name is Wyllys."

"Aye, sir. He's the one our sailors dubbed the Flying Yank."

Jeannette beamed at the customs commissioner. "Thank you, sir! I call this a good omen. You see, my name is Caroline."

* * *

It was a rather tight squeeze in the phaeton for three people, even if none of them was corpulent. But Jeannette was not aware of discomfort. Her letter would leave London within the hour and, miracle of miracles, would go directly to New Orleans. On the *Caroline*. Surely the ship's name was a propitious sign!

In high good spirits, she allowed Mr. Ludding to help her down when they arrived at the basin where the *Caroline* lay at anchor. The ship he pointed out was not large and rode low in the water, which was not surprising since she must be loaded with baggage and furnishings and all the worldly goods the *émigrés* had collected during their stay in England. But she was a fleet ship, Mr. Ludding assured her, frigate-built and manned by an exceptionally competent master and crew.

Judging by the shouts and bustle on board and the looks of the two sailors hovering by a plank connecting quay to ship, the *Caroline* was about to cast off.

"Wait!" Jeannette clutched her reticule containing the precious letter. "Please wait!"

Without a thought for Archer or Mr. Ludding, she flew toward the plank and was halfway across before one of the sailors caught her by the arm.

"Here, miss! Ye can't go aboard now. We's about to sail."

"I know. That's why I am here. Please fetch your captain."

"Now, see here, miss!" said the sailor sternly, then abruptly let go of her arm.

His tone changed to resignation as he pointed to a bearded man in a dark, brass-buttoned coat climbing out of a hatch on mid-deck. "Looks like ye'll get yer wish after all, miss. There he be. Captain Wyllys.

Best pray he's not in one o' his moods."

Undeterred by whatever mood Captain Wyllys might suffer, Jeannette charged toward him and a young gentleman who had followed the captain out of the hatch.

Then a third man emerged from the ship's depths, and she came to an abrupt stop, which caused Mr. Ludding, who had finally caught up, to bump into her.

Jeannette neither felt Mr. Ludding's steadying hand nor heard his profuse apology. Her wide-eyed stare was fixed on the third gentleman.

Mr. Simon Renshaw.

For one wild, crazy instant she thought he might be sailing to New Orleans. And if he was in New Orleans, he could not bring suit against her father in London!

But Simon Renshaw was shaking the younger gentleman's hand. "A safe journey, Harte. And good luck."

Then he turned to follow Captain Wyllys—and saw Jeannette. Under different circumstances, his sudden smile might have encouraged her to start believing in the successful application of feminine wiles and Annie's magic potion. At the moment, however, she was distracted by Captain Wyllys and the thundercloud on his bushy brow. The *Caroline*'s master was indeed in "one o' his moods."

"Who the deuce let you aboard?" the captain bellowed. A true Yankee from one of the New England states. "I'll have the blathering fool keelhauled! And I'll thank you, miss, to turn about and get off my ship. On the double!"

Nom de nom! She'd never believe in propitious signs or omens again.

Chapter Ten

"Good morning, Captain Wyllys."

Trying to ignore Simon Renshaw and to reproduce the curtsy and smile that had won over the harassed customs commissioner, Jeannette tugged at the drawstring of her reticule. "I shan't delay you but a moment. I have a letter . . . Please, sir, won't you take it to New Orleans for me?"

But the master of the *Caroline* had turned from her and bent his glowering stare on Mr. Ludding.

"Customs!" he said with loathing. "What d'you want now? The *Caroline* was cleared when we unloaded. Is there a new law that says we must be searched before leaving? Perhaps you think my passengers are Bonapartist agents and I'm smuggling them back to France with all the secrets they've gathered here?"

While the young customs officer painstakingly explained his presence aboard, Simon Renshaw drew Jeannette aside.

"If you have a letter, give it to me quickly. As you can see, Captain Wyllys is not in the best of good humor. He wants to leave immediately. Made a wager that he'll best a five-week record from London Docks to New Orleans."

"How splendid!" Breathless with excitement, Jeannette pulled out the sealed package addressed to her grandmother. A journey of five weeks or less would be a sheer miracle. "I *want* him to win the wager. Very much so! But my letter—what will you do with it?"

He beckoned the young gentleman, still hovering near the hatch.

"Harte is going to New Orleans on my behalf. He'll see to the safe delivery of your letter."

"On . . . your behalf?" She clutched the precious package to her breast. "Because of Papa and me? You're having us *investigated?"*

"Mr. Renshaw!" Captain Wyllys's deep voice, although less irritated, boomed as loud as before. "Weren't you about to leave?"

"Indeed. And I'll take the young lady off your hands as well."

Simon offered his arm. "Come, Lady Caroline. Give your letter to Harte so the good captain won't miss a moment of the tide."

"Lady Caroline, eh?" Captain Wyllys stroked his beard and all of a sudden looked upon Jeannette with an expression bordering on the benevolent. "Why didn't you say so, miss? A namesake of my ship must always be welcome."

"Thank you, sir. Will you take my letter? It is for my grandmother, Madame Vireilles, in Royal Street in the Vieux—"

"I know where Royal Street is. And I'll take your letter, miss. But, to tell the truth, your grandmother will receive it two, perhaps three days sooner if you give it to Mr. Harte. I cannot leave the *Caroline,* or spare a man, until the unloading is seen to."

Jeannette hesitated to point out that there were messengers he could send. Insisting when he was so obviously reluctant would make her exactly the pushing sort of female she had always detested.

And then the opportunity to press her cause was gone when Mr. Harte addressed her.

"Lady Caroline, you can trust me to deliver your letter immediately upon arrival." The young man gave her a wide, ingenuous smile. "I must call on Madame Vireilles in any case, and what better introduction could I ask for than a letter from you?"

Captain Wyllys gave a curt nod, which could have been agreement with Harte or his way of taking leave. With a distinctly sinking feeling inside, Caroline watched the captain move off to join the helmsman, who apparently had trouble communicating with three gesticulating and very voluble Frenchmen.

Once more, she was aware of the bustle on deck and in the rigging. The *Caroline* herself, rolling gently, seemed to urge her to make up her mind.

Wishing she could read his thoughts, she stared at Mr. Harte. His gaze was clear, his smile appealing and infectious. And when she looked from him to Simon Renshaw and met the keen, watchful eyes of the solicitor, she was powerless to do anything other than hand the package to young Mr. Harte. The enemy's envoy.

Before she could reconsider or regret having so rashly placed her trust where caution should have prevailed, she was bustled ashore. Mr. Ludding, looking vastly relieved, followed hastily. The plank was pushed on deck. The two sailors leaped aboard, and before she could blink, the gap between quay and ship widened.

The *Caroline* was on her way.

"Where is your carriage, Jeannette?"

"Right over there. The phaeton."

She blew a kiss after the departing ship before turning to face Simon Renshaw.

"Thank you. If you hadn't called me Lady Caroline, Captain Wyllys would have personally set me ashore—with the letter still in my reticule."

"I doubt it. His bark is worse than his bite." A frown grooved Simon's high brow. "Where's your father, Jeannette? Don't tell me he permitted you to come to the waterfront alone."

Her chin went up. "I shan't tell you anything of the kind. I drove here accompanied by my groom. You must have seen him. He's holding the horses."

"Of course," he said silkily. "The company of a groom makes your presence on the docks quite unexceptionable."

"Yes, it does. So there's no need for sarcasm."

"Dash it, Jeannette! You told me you're well versed in the rules governing young ladies of the *ton*, but you did not study hard enough. A true lady does not—"

"Goodbye, Mr. Renshaw." She gave him a look, haughty, defiant, the look of a young lady who hated above all else to find herself put in the wrong. "I may be under some obligation to you, but that does not mean I must listen to you."

She would have walked off, but he gripped her wrist.

"I apologize. No insult was intended." His voice softened. "Jeannette, I wish I could convince you of the futility of this charade. Don't you see? The longer you and your father masquerade as Lady

Caroline and Lord Luxton, the worse it will go for you when you're exposed."

She tugged to free her wrist, but to no avail—which did not soothe her irritation.

"*You* will go to prison!" she cried, heedless of a score of dock laborers who had stopped work to watch the young lady engaged in a tug of war with a top-of-the-trees Corinthian whose driving coat sported no less than six shoulder capes.

"You'll be deported! Or hanged! And so will Frederick if he doesn't watch out. For conspiring to defraud my father."

Confounded, Simon looked at her. He and Frederick were conspiring? And how the devil could he get deported, unless—

"Sir! Lady Caroline!" Mr. Ludding cleared his throat, but it was obvious he didn't have anything else to say.

One of the dock laborers whistled, catching Caroline's attention. Warmth flooded her face when another cheered her on.

Then, suddenly, Archer was there. Fists doubled and raised suggestively, he stepped close to Simon Renshaw. But he did not have to demand the release of his mistress.

"Great Scot!" said Simon, finally mastering the astonishment that had held him speechless and, at the same time, dropping her wrist as if it burned him. "Your father must have marbles in his head if he believes he can bluff his way into a dukedom by bringing a countersuit."

"He is not bluffing!" Jeannette said fiercely and added for good measure, even though it would earn her a reprimand if it came to her father's ear, "If you insist on dragging Papa to court, of course he will bring suit against you."

Simon only looked at Jeannette and shook his head. Filial loyalty was one thing—in fact, he wouldn't want her to betray her father without a second thought—but this was sheer idiocy. He must make her see reason. Not, however, with two dozen or so onlookers hanging around.

"You!" he addressed the groom. "Take the customs officer back to Custom House before you return to George Street. I'll see Lady Caroline home. And don't let me catch you again in such parts of town where your mistress should not be seen without a chaperone or, preferably, a gentleman to accompany her."

Such was his tone, his air of command, that the groom instinctively pulled his forelock and turned to do his bidding.

"Archer!" Jeannette cried indignantly. "You're not going to leave me with this man! This bully!

Archer stopped, giving her a shamefaced look. "It's Mr. Renshaw, my lady—the Nonesuch. An' he's right. I should never have brought ye here."

Before Jeannette could fully take in the groom's desertion and utter a further protest, she was ushered willy-nilly to the curricle Simon had consigned into the care of a gangly youth. There was still time to refuse when he handed her into the carriage, but, strangely, she no longer wished to do so.

She did not speak for a while, and Simon made no attempt to break into her musings.

When they left the dock area behind and were approaching the Tower, she gave a deep sigh and finally turned to him.

"What did Archer mean? That you're the None-such?"

"It's an appellation bestowed on me by some of my less discriminating friends. I had no notion, however, that the name had spread among the grooms."

"Then you are a sporting gentleman of some note?"

"You might say so."

"But you're a solicitor!"

He gave her an amused look. "And a solicitor does not indulge in hunting, riding, shooting, fencing, boxing, or any of the pastimes enjoyed by a gentleman of leisure?"

"They are rather expensive diversions."

He made no reply but gave his full attention to the three chestnuts harnessed tandem style to the curricle, and to the dray pulled by four large, plodding horses which he was about to overtake.

Taking due note of his skillful handling of the reins while driving tandem, she waited until they were safely past the slower vehicle.

"You have expensive tastes." She kept her voice carefully casual. "The cut of your coats advertises the excellence and steep price of your tailor."

"Your gowns," he said, just as casual as she, "betray the hand of Madame Bertin, the dearest dressmaker in town."

"Your horses, the curricle—and likely you have a riding hack as well—must have cost a small fortune."

"My thoughts exactly when I saw your phaeton and the pair of blacks. By the way, an excellent match, the horses' coats and your hair. But it was an extravagant expense considering that your father had already purchased the bays, a town carriage, and the chestnut filly you rode the other day."

"Papa could buy a dozen horses and carriages and not feel pursepinched. But you—"

Hearing her voice tighten, she started over. "It does not seem likely that a solicitor can afford the extravagances you enjoy. Is that why you're supporting Frederick's claim? Did he promise you a share in the Dundas fortune?"

Except for slowing the horses to a sedate walk, Simon gave no sign that she had rattled him. He wanted to shake her for being such a pig-headed little fool. For carrying the charade beyond the point he was willing to tolerate.

She was watching him with a strangely troubled look in those startling blue eyes. It was a look that did not fit a scheming little baggage, an adventuress. It was a look that betrayed vulnerability. Was it so very strange to discover a frailer side of her character beneath the self-assurance she usually displayed? He had seen vulnerability, even innocence, in the eyes of a sixteen-year-old confessed murderess.

He was an old hand at dealing with lawbreakers, petty or otherwise. He would neither shake Jeannette because he was convinced she was guilty of scheming with her father, nor would he let the plans he had for her future beguile him into believing her fragile—or even innocent.

He would deal with her much as he dealt with clients who depended on him for his expertise as a barrister, which was to play along with whatever line they chose to take while Harte and his colleagues pursued their investigations.

The only problem was he did not want a confession forced by Harte's findings in New Orleans. He wanted her to admit to and give up the life of an adventuress before Harte returned.

Jeannette's voice, hesitant, even a little anxious, broke into his thoughts. "You do not answer, Mr. Renshaw. Did Frederick promise you a share in the Dundas fortune?"

"Why do you want to know? Do you think your father would double the offer?"

Jeannette flinched. It was foolish to feel hurt by the implied admission; despite her conviction that he was a scoundrel, she had hoped to hear an angry denial.

Determined not to let him see her hurt, she gave him a scathing look. "Papa would never stoop to such vile methods."

"I'd almost be willing to put it to the test," he murmured. Then, suddenly, he smiled at her. "For the present, shall we agree that whoever is the rightful sixth duke has no need to stoop to a bribe?"

Caught off guard by the smile that softened the sharp angles of nose and chin and lit a spark of warmth in his eyes, she nodded. He should smile more often, but perhaps not, if a transformation of stern features had the power to befuddle her mind. She should never have agreed with him. Surely, he still insisted that Frederick was the rightful heir?

Wishing to make up for her slip, she said fiercely, "And you may just as well admit that it is my father who has no need to buy favors."

Returning his attention to the business of driving, Simon reflected on the foolishness and contrariness of females.

They were near the Court of Old Bailey, and he was tempted to take her inside and make her watch one of the sessions. But it was early yet. Harte could not possibly return until late July with whatever incriminating evidence he'd dig up in New Orleans. Time aplenty before he must give her a scare. Time he would put to good use.

"Jeannette, did you ask your father about his first marriage?"

"I did."

Simon, who did not lose his calm with the most obstreperous of clients, fought a surge of exasperation.

"Surely you can be more forthcoming? You told me you were just as interested as I in establishing your father's identity. Have you changed your mind?"

She nudged his arm. "Mind where you're going. You missed that chairmender's cart by a whisker."

A gentleman did not swear in the presence of a lady, and Simon was above all a gentleman. But he wished he weren't. He wanted to spank her. But she wasn't a child. At nineteen, most young ladies were married and had started a family. At nineteen, Jeannette was old enough to know that deceit was a crime.

Silence stretched between them. Every now and then, he cast her a covert look. She should be embarrassed or, at least ill at ease after refusing to discuss her father's first marriage. Her posture, however, was relaxed, and presently, as if she were pursuing a most pleasant line of thought, a smile played at the corners of her mouth.

An enticing mouth. A mouth made for kissing.

Simon relaxed. No doubt about it, she was a scheming little baggage. But she was also utterly captivating and well worth a long, difficult pursuit.

They approached Covent Garden market, where the vendors were packing up after a busy morning. On impulse, he stopped the curricle and beckoned an old woman who carried one last posy of violets on her woven tray.

"Thank 'ee, good sir." The flower seller accepted his coin with a bob and a toothless grin. "An' may the posy please t' young lady's 'eart."

"I wonder if it will," he said, presenting the flowers to Jeannette.

"Thank you, Simon." She hid her face in the fragrant blooms, but not before he had seen that secretive smile deepen.

"I wish I could believe it was the posy that made you happy, but you were smiling long before I offered the flowers. What are you thinking, Jeannette?"

The smile deepened even more. "Isn't it rather early for violets? I thought they bloomed in May."

"I wouldn't know. But May is not far off, and it has been an extremely warm spring."

"Warm? I don't believe that you poor souls born and bred in England know the meaning of warm." A glow kindled in her eyes. "You should spend a spring in New Orleans! It's heavenly, Simon."

"You miss it very much, don't you?"

She nodded.

"I'm sorry."

His hand touched hers, briefly and very lightly.

"But I cannot be sorry that you've called me by my first name. Twice. And if it takes flowers to elicit a Simon from you, I'll present you with a posy every day."

Tucking the violets into the neckline of her spencer, she gave him a wondering look. "You are so different when we're not discussing my father. It surprises me every time it happens."

A young tulip of fashion who had drawn up his carriage behind them since the steady flow of vehicles leaving the market did not allow him to pass, gave an impatient shout. But Simon made no move to pick up the reins.

He kept his gaze on Jeannette. "I wish we could ignore your father, Frederick, and the question of who is the rightful duke. But we cannot, can we?"

There was something in his look that made her shy. This was very strange. Since the day she decided she had no use for admirers and suitors, she had never been shy with any man. But now her throat felt too tight to speak, and she merely shook her head.

Raising his whip to acknowledge the swelling chorus of shouts from behind, Simon flicked the reins. "I had better take you home before your father misses you. Am I correct you did not tell him you'd be venturing forth to the docks?"

"You are, but you should not make me admit it. A Creole gentleman—"

"Would never embarrass a lady so," he cut in. "But a Creole gentleman I'll never be. Dash it, Jeannette! From all I've heard, they put their ladies on a pedestal. Is that what you like?"

She thought of all the ladies she knew in New Orleans, high upon their pedestals of chastity, dignity, and loneliness, raised there by their gentleman beaux and husbands, who then went off gaily to seek the more earthy company of a mistress. And she thought of Raoul Fontenot and herself, and how narrowly she had escaped the fate of the ladies she pitied.

"Well, Jeannette? Do you want to be treated like a piece of rare, fragile glass?"

He was not surprised to see the sudden, fierce look he had observed on previous occasions.

"No!" she said. "I don't want that at all."

"That's all right, then. Now tell me why you smiled earlier. You reminded me of a cat who found a jug of cream."

She gave a reluctant laugh. "Do you never give up?"

"Never. Perseverance is my hallmark. Now tell me."

"Very well. It occurred to me that since you're going to the trouble and expense of sending Mr. Harte to New Orleans, you would not drag my father into court until the young man has returned."

Chapter Eleven

Simon's hands tightened on the reins as irritation with Hugh Dundas flared in his breast.

He said grimly, "So, after extracting my promise not to worry you with the possibility of a lawsuit, your father tells you himself! Does he always run to you with his problems?"

"He does not!" Jeannette gave him an indignant look. "And it wasn't Papa who told me about your threat. It was Annie!"

"Employing a maid to eavesdrop for you? Is that quite proper?"

"Annie isn't a maid. She's—"

"Yes, Jeannette? Who is Annie? Have you employed a female agent to spy on me?"

"Fudge! If you must know, Annie is a ghost."

Jeannette did not know what mischievous devil had prompted her to say that, but the look on Simon's face proved that even a moment of foolishness could reap a reward.

She watched as utter astonishment gradually gave way to amusement.

"Ah, yes. A ghost." Laughter danced in his eyes, but he kept his voice suitably grave. "I should have known you would not employ anyone as mundane as a maid or an agent."

"Yes, you should," she said, feeling virtuous because she had not lied, yet secure in the knowledge that he did not believe the truth.

He turned north on St. Martin's Lane, and with the turn, his mood changed abruptly. She saw his face only in profile, but the tight set of his mouth, the grim line running vertically from nose to chin, told their own tale.

Perhaps he was belatedly offended by her talk of a ghost. Papa had never liked it when she mentioned Jacques, the ghost of Moon Lake. He said it was utter nonsense.

Or, perhaps . . . her heart skipped a beat as she realized Simon had not confirmed that there would be no lawsuit until young Mr. Harte returned from New Orleans.

"Simon," she said, and at the same time he looked at her and spoke her name.

There was an awkward moment of silence, which, combined with his frown, filled her with foreboding.

Jeannette swallowed. "What is it?"

"I must warn you," he said grimly, "that filing suit does not entirely depend on Harte's return from New Orleans."

"Why? What do you mean?"

"My father will arrive in town within a week or two. He knew Hugh Dundas well as a youth. If he is satisfied that your father is an imposter—"

"Pish-tosh! Lord Decimus knew Papa just as well. And he is perfectly satisfied that Papa is who he says he is."

"Lord Decimus is a bumble-head. No court of law

would place the least dependence on his testimony."

"I don't give a straw about a court of law or some silly old judge's opinion!"

She clutched his arm, jolting the three horses into an uneasy canter. But they could have galloped and she would not have noticed.

Simon hastily slowed the confused animals, then, vowing to have the shafts altered to accommodate a pair before he took as volatile a young lady as Jeannette driving again, gingerly transferred the ribbons to one hand. He sincerely hoped no one would recognize him as the fool trying to drive tandem with one hand only.

"Simon!" She shook his arm for emphasis. "You absolutely *must* wait for Harte's return. What do a few weeks matter? After all, Frederick won't lose anything by waiting. On the contrary! He can remain at Dundas House, can even go on calling himself the Duke of Granby during that time."

"Jeannette—"

She was not to be interrupted. "I swear on my mother's memory Harte will bring proof positive that Papa is Hugh Dundas, son of the Fifth Duke of Granby."

"Jeannette, the 'few weeks' of Harte's absence encompass all of the Season and more. So far, despite Lord Decimus's efforts to the contrary, the *ton* has taken no notice of your father, but I'm afraid the quiet days are coming to an end and London will explode with the scandal of your father's claim. The matter must be settled as soon as possible."

"No, you're wrong. Papa wouldn't want a scandal. He and I will continue to live very quietly."

"Indeed? Your father made it very clear he plans

to launch you with your cousins Eleanor and Agnes. I don't call that quiet living. He might as well hold a torch to a stack of dry tinder."

"Nom de nom," whispered Jeannette, letting go of his arm.

She remembered all too well her father's delight when he learned that her cousins would be launched into society this spring. She also remembered the promise he had told her about when they were just a day out of Boston. The promise to see her wed—in England. If that was still his goal, then, naturally, he would insist on her participation in the social whirl.

And if there was an open dispute about her and her father's right to the Dundas name while she went about in society, the scandal would indeed scorch the whole Dundas family.

She sank against the squabs. As from a far distance, she heard Simon's voice.

"Eleanor's come-out ball is next Thursday, the second of May. Your father plans to introduce you to the family before then."

She did not answer. She wished only for the privacy of her narrow chamber on the third floor of the George Street house, where she could huddle beneath a quilt and devise a strategy to avert social disaster. Not so much for herself but for the sake of her two unknown cousins, who undoubtedly wished to attract the attention of eligible young gentlemen in that place Mrs. Effington called the marriage mart. Almack's, or something. Alas, steeped in a family scandal, Eleanor and Agnes would find themselves ostracized.

"Can we not go faster?" she complained. "I

swear those chestnuts of yours are the veriest slugs!"

"My dear, this is Oxford Street, not a racetrack."

It was a long drive home. She was convinced returning from the docks was taking ten times as long as the drive out had taken.

Jeannette's father was out when she finally arrived home. She breathed a sigh of relief, then immediately felt guilty. They had always been close, especially since her mother's death seven years ago. Never had she kept anything secret from him. Until now.

She had intended to tell him about the letter to *Grandmère* when it was safely on its way, but now she was no longer sure what she would do.

When, shortly after the termination of her betrothal, she had explained to her father about the *boutique* she wanted to open in New Orleans, he had pointed out the folly of flying in the face of convention, of setting up the backs of a great number of Creole gentlemen and possibly ladies as well. But he had also told her it was an admirable enterprise and had stood firmly by her side when the time came to confess to *Grandmère*.

Always had she been certain of his understanding and support—until now.

Until now, she had been his *confidante* as well. But he had told her nothing about the threatened lawsuit. He had not explained why he no longer wore his signet ring. Neither had he been as forthcoming about his first marriage as she would have wished, and about Savannah or his involvement in America's fight for independence he did not speak at all. Nor had he mentioned that she would meet her cousins within the week, or that he intended to go ahead with his scheme to launch her with Eleanor and Agnes.

She had not noticed until now—perhaps, she had not wanted to see—that gradually, subtly, their relationship had changed since their arrival in England. More precisely, since the visit to Dundas House.

Simon seemed to believe her father did not want her worried, but that was nonsense. Her father had never hesitated to talk to her when he had taken a huge risk in a business venture and odds were that he'd lose everything—his business and the two plantations he owned in the Bayou Teche—if the gamble didn't come off.

He had never denied that he was a gambler and an adventurer at heart; but he had never lost, either. Besides, claiming his rightful title was no gamble, no risk. And as far as she knew, he had not even made a claim.

Then why did he no longer confide in her?

The question kept nagging at her, especially when several days passed and he still had not mentioned a visit to his two youngest sisters, Louisa and Anne, their daughters Eleanor and Agnes, or the ball on the coming Thursday.

Despite his frail health, her father seemed to be constantly on the go, generally with Lord Decimus. When she saw him in the evenings, he was tired and had a feverish look. Yet when she reminded him that he mustn't tax his strength, he denied that he was exhausted.

She did not believe him. She wondered, however, whether it was something other than a fever that made him look flushed and ill. The jut of his chin and the look in his eyes reminded her of the determined, purposeful man in New Orleans before the illness. The man of whom it was said that he was shrewder and more persistent than a Yankee trader.

She asked bluntly what he planned to do. He told her to enjoy herself and not to worry. He was planning her future and had everything well in hand.

Jeannette was not satisfied, but neither was she in the habit of arguing with her father. For the present she would pester him no more. Undoubtedly, he wanted to surprise her with a visit to her cousins, never dreaming that now she dreaded meeting them.

She tried to keep worrisome thoughts at bay by staying busy. She rose early, when Hyde Park was still deserted, to exercise the chestnut mare, defiantly christened Princess of Granby the day after her drive with Simon. She stayed up late with Annie, arguing the respective merits of mistletoe, which had been Old Marjory's chief ingredient in a love potion, and powdered bark of cinnamon, which Nounou swore held powerful aphrodisiac qualities. Or they pored over a volume of medieval potions and elixirs Jeannette had discovered at the lending library.

Jeannette frequently accompanied Mrs. Effington to the lending library. Her chaperone, she learned, was an avid reader of poetry and novels. She usually found two or three volumes within a short space of time, while Jeannette's search for the right book proved more difficult. And since she was reluctant to confess to the helpful clerk that she was looking for love potions, Jeannette walked away empty-handed more often than not.

She also went with Mrs. Effington to call on the

older lady's numerous friends. Calling on elderly ladies would not ordinarily be considered a pastime to divert the mind from looming trouble, but Jeannette had benefitted from seven years of strict tutelage by her grandmother. Madame Vireilles had no use for young ladies who could scarcely hide their boredom behind a vapid smile. She had instilled in her granddaughter a deep respect for age which enabled Jeannette to pay full attention and never to lose interest even during the most rambling discourse.

Thus, she learned more than she ever wanted to know about the Prince of Wales, made Regent in January, his estranged wife and willful daughter.

She learned about her grandmother, Caroline Dundas, Fifth Duchess of Granby, after whom she was named. Frail and small of stature but with a mind as strong as that of her tall, powerful husband, her grace had been a force to be reckoned with.

Long before the evangelist, Hannah More, advocated the importance of schooling for the poor, the duchess had personally taught the tenants' children and the children living in nearby villages. She had commissioned the vicar of Ainsworth to tutor the brighter boys, then sent them as boarders to Rugby school in Warwickshire. She had purchased apprenticeships for countless boys and girls desirous of learning a trade. She had nursed the sick, assisted widows and orphans, and she had never turned her back on a girl or woman "in trouble".

The more Jeannette heard about her English grandmother the more she wished she could have known her. She wished her father had been more forthcoming about his family. He had indeed told her that her grandmother Caroline was the most generous woman he had ever known, but he had not drawn the vivid picture detailed by Mrs. Effington's friends.

Thus, Jeannette directed her questions to the elderly ladies, encouraging them to reminisce. They, in turn, were delighted with the well-behaved Lady Caroline and showed themselves disposed to support her and her father if and when they decided to enter society.

Only the dowager Lady Aldrich held back, pointing out that by supporting Lady Caroline they would, in effect, declare the young duke, dear Frederick, a usurper.

Jeannette had also been taught by her grandmother not to argue with her elders. She therefore smiled and assured the dowager that she quite understood.

And in a way, she did understand. As she was driving down Watling Street with Annie and Archer later that afternoon—Wednesday afternoon, the day before her cousin Eleanor's come-out ball, which her father still had not mentioned—she thought about Frederick and how difficult it was to believe that he would purposely scheme to defraud her father. Frederick seemed too diffident, too . . . nice. She had met him only once, but she believed him to be a very pleasant young man.

However, there was Simon Renshaw, the man who apparently ruled the Dundas family.

She had met Simon more than once, and she doubted he had known a single moment of shyness or hesitancy in his life. And he certainly wasn't what she considered "nice."

She remembered his smile, how it had softened the harsh features and charmed her into agreement with him when she didn't agree at all. She remembered the laughter dancing in his eyes when she tried to use feminine wiles on him and when she told him about Annie, the ghost. She remembered his smoothness of address that made her forget he was the enemy.

Yes, indeed. Simon Renshaw could be appealing. Dangerously so.

But he was not nice, even if he had been helpful with the letter. She must keep in mind the possibility that he had tricked her. And, definitely, a nice man did not scheme to cheat another out of his inheritance.

"Psst! Lady Caroline, listen!"

Annie's excited voice startled Jeannette. Deep in thought about Simon Renshaw, she had quite forgotten where she was and that she was not alone. Thank goodness it was Archer handling the ribbons this afternoon.

"Quick, Lady Caroline! Have Archer turn into that lane behind the bakery."

Jeannette instructed the groom accordingly. He obeyed, but not without grumbling.

"And how, I'd like to know, are we going to get out o' here if this is one o' them cooldeesacks? The lane's so narrow, we'll most likely scrape the paint off o' the wheels as it is."

"Don't fret, Archer." Jeannette gave him a mischievous look. "I know how to back a carriage if you don't."

As she had known he would, Archer pokered up and drove on in haughty silence.

Annie sniffed. "Stiff-rumped, aren't we, Mr. Archer?"

Naturally, the groom did not reply.

"Sometimes I wish he could see or, at least, hear me," said Annie. "Wouldn't that take the starch out of him!"

Out in the open, Jeannette could see only a hazy outline of the little ghost. But she heard her well enough, and it took willpower not to make a reply.

"Look, Lady Caroline! That building, the one that has the sign *Printer* over the doorway—I know it!"

Annie's voice had risen in volume and pitch, which made Jeannette cast an anxious look at Archer. The groom caught her look and asked grimly if she'd had enough of the filth and the screeching urchins tumbling in the lane.

"Keep driving," she said absently.

For the first time since they turned off Watling Street, Jeannette paid full attention to her surroundings. The unevenly cobbled lane winding in a northeasterly direction was indeed so narrow that, if she stretched, she might be able to touch the buildings they passed. Children screamed and scattered before the slow-moving phaeton, then stood silent and wide-eyed in doorways and watched the elegant carriage pass.

This was a poor neighborhood but not one of the ill-famed London slums. The houses had doors and windows. The children, though barefoot and ragged, were at least clothed.

"Archer, what is the name of this lane?"

"Beggars Alley, my lady."

"No!" cried Annie, who had been strangely silent after her excitement about the printer's shop. "It is

Basket Lane on account of the basket weavers living here."

Nowhere in the alley had Jeannette seen a signboard or shingle advertising baskets.

She gave Annie a hard stare, willing her to say what they should do next. Haggard women with infants in their arms and even several men were stepping out of narrow doorways to watch the progress of the phaeton-and-pair, and Jeannette did not like the avid, calculating looks directed at her. It seemed to her that the sharp-faced men and women judged to a nicety the price they could fetch at some musty old pawnbroker's shop for her earrings, her hat, her gown and spencer.

Perhaps Annie read her thoughts; perhaps she merely saw her discomfort. "Let's go home," she said. "I thought this was the lane where I was born and raised. I was sure when I saw the print shop. But here, where I expected to come upon the tenement where I lived, everything is different."

"Home, Archer." Jeannette tried to keep the eagerness out of her voice. "And if you can manage without running over someone, let's go a little faster."

Archer gave the horses rein.

"Wished I knew what's so danged special about these lanes to fetch us back day after day," he muttered. "No good coming of it that I can see."

Neither could Jeannette, but she said only, "Bear with me, Archer. A friend asked me to find the place where she was born and raised."

Shock and incredulity registered on his face. "A friend of yourn, my lady? Born *here?*"

"Starched-up old stick!" said Annie.

Chapter Twelve

Even though Simon suspected that his father might already be on the way to London, he dutifully posted a letter informing the senior partner of Renshaw and Renshaw that young Harte was off to New Orleans and that the man calling himself Hugh Dundas intended to present his daughter to the *ton*.

Feeling absolved from any further obligation to his unpredictable parent, Simon then spent several days trying to discover the extent of Hugh Dundas's debts. He'd had second thoughts about placing a notice in the *Gazette* and *The Times,* branding Hugh Dundas a swindler. Due to Lord Decimus's efforts, Hugh had already been introduced at Tattersall's and one or two of the gentlemen's clubs. A denunciation before Simon held firm proof of impersonation might give rise to knotty legal questions he deemed it best to sidestep for as long as possible, and, clearly, a public humiliation of her father would not endear Simon to Jeannette or help in any way to gain her trust.

Simon had conceived a better plan. He would make no effort to stop merchants from extending credit to Hugh Dundas; he would merely keep tabs on the self-styled marquis. Frederick would suffer no financial loss, for Simon could well afford to discharge Hugh Dundas's debts—which was precisely what he would do as soon as the old rascal admitted his knavery and agreed to sail back to New Orleans.

Without his daughter.

Simon was stunned when, one by one, Tattersall's, the coach builder in Long Acre, the tailors and bootmakers, the dressmakers and milliners, assured him that the Marquis of Luxton paid all bills promptly. And the livery stables in Orchard Street, where the two carriages and seven horses were stabled at great expense, had been paid several weeks in advance.

On Wednesday night, the night before Lady Eleanor Hargrave's come-out ball, Simon also learned at his club that Lord Decimus Rowland had spread the word his friend Hugh Dundas was willing to pay handsomely for the lease or purchase of a house in Mayfair.

It was incredible. When Jeannette assured him that her father could afford to buy a dozen horses and carriages and not feel pursepinched, Simon had taken it as another of her clever little ploys meant to strew sand in his eyes. But, bloody hell! She had apparently told no less than the plain truth.

Simon wasted no time speculating whether Hugh had borrowed from Lord Decimus. It was well known that Decimus barely managed to steer clear of River Tick.

Simon did, however, spend most of the night revising his judgment of Hugh Dundas. If Hugh was indeed wealthy, he would not be looking for a settlement in exchange for a discreet disappearance from England. Rather, Hugh's sight would be set on the position of social prominence he would hold as the Duke of Granby.

Reasoning thus, it was a simple step to conclude that Hugh Dundas's ambitions were not for himself but for his daughter. As Lady Caroline Dundas, Jeannette could look as high as she pleased for a husband—and this was not at all what Simon had in mind for the black-haired, blue-eyed minx from New Orleans.

At eleven o'clock on Thursday, the second day of May, Hugh Dundas sat behind the minuscule desk in the cramped ground-floor chamber ambitiously designated as the library by Decimus's niece and her husband.

Even if he did not admit it to Jeannette, Hugh was exhausted. The English climate and especially the soot-laden air of London did not agree with his constitution. His frail body longed for the warmth and humidity of New Orleans, for the scented air of his plantation home in the Bayou Teche. He felt boxed in, imprisoned, in the narrow chambers of the George Street terrace house.

It was time to make a push to get Jeannette established. A part of the past week had been spent with his sugar and cotton brokers, who reported yet more fees imposed by Parliament on American goods. He could well afford the fees, but they were a nuisance and an imposition. The devil fly away with those damned Orders in Council!

This afternoon, however, he'd forget about business. He'd introduce Jeannette to her cousins, the first step toward seeing her accepted as the late duke's granddaughter.

Absently fingering a stack of old, yellowed letters, Hugh wondered how his daughter felt. If she missed the spaciousness of their New Orleans home, she never said so. Jeannette was not a complainer. Even if she were homesick and longed for her *grandmère*, her cousins and friends, she would never tell him so.

Hugh sighed. It was just as well, for Jeannette would not return to New Orleans.

Donning his spectacles, Hugh spread open the topmost of the letters, the one dated September 21, 1791. Four days before Jeannette was born. The day he had promised to take the child—if it was a girl—to England when she turned eighteen and was neither married nor betrothed. And he had promised to see her suitably wed to an Englishman.

He was late—nineteen months late—in fulfilling the first part of the promise. But now that they were in London, he'd do his all to fulfill the second part.

A knock heralded a footman, announcing Mr. Simon Renshaw.

For a moment Hugh said nothing, merely gathered the letters, then locked them into a desk drawer where they rested beside the gold signet ring which had for generations been worn by every Marquis of Luxton.

He removed the spectacles. "Very well, James. Show Mr. Renshaw in."

When Simon entered, Hugh had secreted the key to the desk drawer in his coat pocket. The gentlemen shook hands; Hugh offered coffee and wine.

"Nothing, thank you." Simon drew a chair closer to the desk and sat down. "I shan't intrude on your time for very long."

"It's no intrusion. Malcolm's son must always be welcome. I only wish your father were here with you."

"You may see that wish fulfilled sooner than you think." Simon watched the older man closely. "I have been assured that Father is feeling as fit as a fiddle and will be posting down before long."

A spark lit in Hugh's tired eyes. "Excellent! We may then look forward to a speedy resolution of our little *contretemps.*"

This was not precisely the reaction Simon had expected, but he was not the man to betray that he was disconcerted.

"A *contretemps,* sir? Is that what you call your outrageous claim? One thing is certain—no one can accuse you of exaggeration."

"I am not aware that I have made any claim except that I am Hugh Dundas. Is that so outrageous?"

"It is. Because you cannot possibly be Hugh Dundas. He died in 1780, in Savannah."

"He did not. But, perhaps," Hugh said softly, "that is not even important."

"What do you mean, sir?"

Hugh shook his head. "Nothing, my boy. Pay no attention to the rambling of an old man. Tell me instead what brought you here."

"I wronged you, sir."

"Oh?" If Simon was a master at hiding astonishment, Hugh Dundas was no less of an expert. "Do you care to explain?"

"I believed you a down-at-the-heels adventurer when, in fact, you must be quite well-to-do."

"I am not a poor man," Hugh said complacently.

"I estimate my annual income somewhere in the neighborhood of seventy thousand pounds."

Simon did not blink. His own income, derived from agricultural and industrial properties inherited from his maternal grandfather, was well above a hundred thousand pounds, plus his share of revenues brought in by the law firm Renshaw and Renshaw.

"No doubt," said Simon, "my agent, when he returns from New Orleans, will confirm your estimate."

"No doubt at all. But I did not know you had sent someone to New Orleans to investigate me."

"Jeannette did not tell you?"

This did affect Hugh's composure. "Jeannette? What does she have to do with it?"

"Seeing off my agent, I encountered your daughter at London Docks. She was trying to send a letter to her grandmother."

"Devil a bit!" Hugh's sallow face suffused with irate color, but almost immediately his anger died. "I daresay she succeeded?"

"She did, indeed."

Hugh sighed. "For the most part, Jeannette is as complaisant as any well-bred Creole lady. But I should have remembered the odd kick in her gallop."

There was much that Simon wanted to say about Jeannette and her unpredictability, but he curbed his tongue and merely posed a question he knew was foolish but which, nevertheless, gave him no peace.

"Sir, does Jeannette truly believe she is Lady Caroline, the daughter of Hugh Dundas, Marquis of Luxton? What I mean—"

"I know what you mean. Since you're convinced I'm running a rig, posturing as Hugh Dundas, you wonder if my daughter could possibly be innocent of deception. I assure you, my boy, Jeannette *is* Lady Caroline Dundas."

Simon rose. He had the answer he wanted to hear. But he did not believe it.

He did not hide his exasperation. "The deuce you say! I warn you, sir, if you try to foist her upon society—and particularly on some unwary suitor—as the daughter of the Marquis of Luxton, you'll have me to deal with."

"Ah, the impulsiveness of youth." Hugh made no move to detain Simon when he strode to the door. "My boy, I can only warn you against the danger of jumping to a conclusion."

Simon stopped and turned. "Be assured, sir, that I am not the one in need of a warning."

Hugh smiled. "No doubt you feel that *I* stand in dire need?"

"So far," Simon said stiffly, "I saw no purpose in an investigation of your background beyond what can be learned in New Orleans. But I assure you, if I must I shall dig deeper and expose exactly which of the illegitimate offspring of the Fourth Duke of Granby you are."

"Good luck, my boy. I understand Augustus Hugh's bastards were legion."

"Not in his later years. I doubt there are more than two or three of your age."

Simon was about to stalk out when he heard a sound like a hiccough. Or, rather, like laughter hastily stifled. He swung around to face the library once more.

Hugh Dundas had leaned back in his chair, his eyelids and the corners of his mouth drooping wearily. He did not look like a man biting down laughter.

Besides, the sound had come from the direction of the fireplace, not the desk, and it had a feminine ring. Simon was willing to swear that someone was staring at him even now. Someone, hiding in the dim corner to the left of the mantel where he could just make out against the dark paneling a porcelain knob and a naked keyhole below the knob.

"Sir, is Jeannette at home?"

Hugh opened his eyes. Slowly he sat up. "I beg your pardon. Thought you'd left."

"Jeannette, sir. Could I have heard her just now?"

"She went out with Mrs. Effington before you arrived." Hugh drew a gold watch from his waistcoat pocket. He flicked open the lid and peered at the dials. "I shouldn't think they're back. It's not even noon."

Simon frowned at the dim corner. He was certain there was a door in the paneling, a door high enough to accommodate Jeannette if she ducked her head.

"Was there a particular reason you wished to see my daughter?" asked Hugh, suddenly alert and quite stern.

"No, sir."

Unconsciously, Simon's face softened. He did not need a reason for wanting to see Jeannette. And whether Hugh knew it or not, he'd see her in just a little over three hours.

He bowed to the older man. "Thank you for your time, sir."

* * *

At three o'clock in the afternoon of that same day, Thursday, the second of May, eight people had assembled in the stiffly formal drawing room on the first floor of the Earl and Countess of Upton's town residence in Curzon Street to await the arrival of Hugh Dundas and his daughter.

Lady Louisa, Countess of Upton, and her sister Lady Anne, wife of Sir Lewis Paine, were seated on straight-backed chairs, strategically placed in the center of the vast chamber to face the double-winged door through which must enter the brother they had believed dead. Or, rather, the man claiming to be their brother.

Lady Eleanor Hargrave, youngest child of the Earl and Countess of Upton, and her cousin, Miss Agnes Paine, perched on brocade covered benches in one of the window bays, from which vantage point they could not miss seeing Hugh Dundas and his daughter drive up.

The four gentlemen in the room, Robert Hargrave, Earl of Upton, Sir Lewis Paine, Frederick Dundas, Duke of Granby, and Simon Renshaw, had foregone the dubious comforts of stiff satin and brocade covered chairs and stood around a credenza laden with decanters and glasses.

"They are here!"

Agnes Paine's excited cry earned her a reproving look from her Aunt Louisa, but the young lady, having escaped from the rigors of the schoolroom a scarce month earlier, could not be repressed.

Agnes bounced to her feet. "And Caroline is just as pretty as Frederick said!"

"You could not possibly tell." Lady Eleanor rose in a much more ladylike fashion than Agnes. "She's wearing a hat and did not once look up."

"Come away from the window immediately," Lady Louisa said sternly. "Agnes, stand behind your mama. Eleanor, take your position behind me."

She turned to summon the gentlemen. Encountering Simon Renshaw's quizzing look, she hesitated. But only for an instant.

Lady Louisa's formidable chin jutted. "Robert! Lewis!"

Her husband and brother-in-law obediently set down their glasses and hurried to take their places. Lord Upton behind Lady Louisa, with Eleanor on his left. Sir Lewis Paine behind Lady Anne, with his daughter Agnes at his side.

It was an imposing tableau that faced the drawing room door. Louisa was almost satisfied. Almost. It needed the presence of the two younger gentlemen, their height and elegance strategically displayed behind the two girls, to perfect the picture.

But with Simon Renshaw's sardonic gaze resting on her, not even Lady Louisa dared make the suggestion. She wished, not for the first time, that Frederick were less dependent on Simon and had held his tongue about her summons to Hugh Dundas.

Downstairs in the marble-tiled foyer of Lady Louisa and Lord Upton's house, Jeannette and Hugh were received by a harassed butler, while all around them gardeners, footmen, and maids bustled about with potted palms and ferns, with garlands and baskets of roses, with trays of silverware, plates, punch cups, and champagne glasses.

Jeannette gave her father a reproachful look. This

was the day of Eleanor's come-out ball, and throughout the drive, she had tried to tell him that he could not have chosen a more inconvenient time to call on his sister.

Following the butler upstairs, Hugh assured her, not for the first time, "Believe me, my dear, it is at Louisa's express command that you're meeting Eleanor and Agnes here today. If I'd had my way, we would have called a week ago."

The butler threw open a double-winged door at the top of the stairs. "Lord Luxton and Lady Caroline."

Arrested by the tableau in the center of the vast chamber, Jeannette lingered just inside the doorway. Truly! *Grandmère* could not have staged a more imposing reception.

In front of two stoic, middle-aged gentlemen and two damsels wide-eyed with curiosity, sat a stern-faced matron who was talking to a somewhat younger lady beside her. It was obvious that the stern, unapproachable matron was determined to thoroughly snub the visitors before acknowledging them. The younger one, however, was staring at Hugh and looked as if she might jump up and cast herself into his arms.

Hugh had stopped also, surveying the group before him. A very reprehensible giggle rose in Jeannette's throat when the matron, who must be her Aunt Louisa, determinedly continued to ignore them. Jeannette suspected that this was how Caroline of Brunswick was treated when she was summoned to Windsor to account for herself to Queen Charlotte.

In an effort to control the bubbling laughter, Jeannette let her gaze roam along the window bays, the marble front of the fireplace against the far wall, the sideboard and credenza—

Her breath caught. Simon here.

In a blue coat of exquisite cut, dove-colored pantaloons, and shiny black Hessian boots, he looked magnificent. Not at all like a solicitor emerged from a musty old office.

And cousin Frederick was here as well, she saw belatedly. Then her father clasped her hand and drew her with him as he crossed the expanse of Aubusson carpet toward his sisters.

"Louisa, you haven't changed at all. Still a dragon, I see." He stopped in front of the stern-faced, beturbaned lady. "Meet Caroline, your niece."

"Indeed!" Lady Louisa's tone was glacial. "I believe, sir, that our relationship has yet to be determined, which is precisely why I summoned you."

But Hugh had turned to the second woman.

"Anne."

With a cry of delight, Lady Anne surged to her feet and cast herself upon the long-lost brother's frail bosom. Jeannette made certain her father did not crumble under the impact, then stood back to observe Lady Louisa's reaction.

"A clear victory for your father," Simon said in a low voice behind her.

She had not seen him move from the credenza at the back of the chamber and gave a little start. She turned slowly to face him, and saw in his eyes a reflection of her own amusement at the scene. He, too, had been watching Lady Louisa's chagrin and growing irritation at her sister's betrayal.

"Not, alas, a major victory," Simon continued.

"Lady Anne is the youngest of the fifth duke's children. Ten years younger than Louisa. She cannot have been more than three or four years old when Hugh was shipped out of the country. Hardly of an age to have spent much time in the company of a twenty-year-old brother, wouldn't you say?"

"But Aunt Anne seems genuinely pleased. You don't believe it is because she remembers Papa?"

"Do you, Jeannette?"

She thought of prevaricating but couldn't bring herself to do it.

"No. I daresay it's Papa's resemblance to the disreputable fourth duke," she answered.

"Thank you for your frankness."

A gleam lit in his eyes, but she could have sworn it wasn't a gleam of triumph at her defeat, but rather, the warmth of admiration.

This flustered her. It was as though she were transported back to that first morning in the George Street house when the lack of a footman had obliged her to answer the impatient knock on the front door. At Simon's first glimpse of her, before she told him she was Lady Caroline, a similar warmth had kindled in his eyes.

Struggling for composure, she said, "Since Papa seems to have forgotten about me, would you introduce me to the rest of the family?"

"With pleasure."

But he made no move to do so. Still looking at her he smiled in that special way that had once before quite befuddled her mind.

"You blush delightfully, Jeannette."

Chapter Thirteen

To her relief, Jeannette was spared the necessity of making a reply when Lady Anne swept toward her.

"My dearest niece," she murmured, engulfing Jeannette in a sweetly scented embrace.

The next instant, Lady Anne whirled back to Hugh.

Frederick, with Eleanor and Agnes in tow, joined Jeannette and Simon. With the grave air of a patriarch, an attitude Jeannette found as amusing as it was irritating, Frederick introduced her cousins.

Agnes, just turned seventeen, was a lively brunette who had not quite lost a childish plumpness. Lady Eleanor, eighteen, was as slim and tall as Jeannette. She had blue eyes like Jeannette, but her hair was the color of newly minted gold.

Eleanor was hesitant and cool in her approach to Jeannette. Agnes, on the other hand, showed an inclination to firmly attach herself to her new cousin.

Gray eyes shining, Agnes demanded, "You're coming to the ball tonight, aren't you, Caroline?"

"I don't know. Papa said this meeting would determine whether my aunt will extend an invitation."

"Oh, but you must come! I want you to see my gown. The most beautiful gown ever. It is silk! And it's pink!"

Eleanor frowned. "Not pink, Agnes. Pale rose."

"And the trim is dark rose, and I have ribbons to match for my hair." Agnes raised herself on tiptoe and whispered to Jeannette, "I'll tell you a secret, Caroline. Tradition or not, Mama says I mustn't wear white, for white makes me look sallow."

Jeannette smiled at the younger girl and whispered back, "I don't wear white either. For the same reason."

"Truly? Oh, I like you, Cousin Caroline. Please say you'll come to the ball tonight! And to my own later this month."

Lady Anne's and Agnes's impulsive acceptance of their relationship was a pleasant change from Lady Louisa's glacial demeanor and from the reception at Dundas House two weeks ago. Jeannette cast a look toward the credenza, where the older generation had gathered around the drink tray. Judging by Lady Louisa's tight-lipped mouth and the Earl of Upton's uncomfortable expression, no invitation to a ball would be forthcoming from that quarter.

Contradicting her thoughts, Frederick said, "I'm sure Lady Louisa will extend an invitation."

He looked at Eleanor, and Jeannette noticed that his earnest young face relaxed into a warm smile.

"Shall we ask her, Elly?"

Eleanor hesitated. "If you like."

Then, as if she realized she had been ungracious, she held out her hand. "You ask her, Freddy. Mama is more likely to say yes if the request comes from you."

"Because," Agnes said mischievously when, hand-in-hand, the two fair young people walked out of earshot, "Aunt Louisa very much wants Elly to be the Duchess of Granby."

"You're a brat." Simon had deliberately stayed in the background while the young ladies got acquainted, but now he tweaked one of Agnes's short curls. "Go fetch Caroline a glass of ratafia."

"No, thank you," Jeannette said hastily. She had tasted the sweet stuff and not found it to her liking at all. And ratafia was noticeably more potent than wine. "If my aunt does not offer tea, I'd as soon take a glass of sherry or Madeira."

Simon nodded approvingly. "Make it Madeira, Agnes. And a glass for me. There's a good girl."

Agnes shot him a rebellious look but departed readily enough when he said, "That way you can make certain Caroline will be invited for tonight."

"I didn't think you'd want me to get invited to the ball!" Jeannette blurted out.

"I don't."

For an instant, before long lashes veiled her eyes, he saw the hurt his curtness had inflicted.

His tone gentled. "Frederick means well, but I'm afraid it is most unwise to ask you and your father to attend. As I said last week, you might as well put a torch to a stack of dry tinder. But Frederick did not seek my opinion. And Lady Louisa—" Glancing toward the credenza, Simon shrugged. "I doubt she'll weigh the consequences in her eagerness to please Frederick."

Scandal, thought Jeannette. Ostracism. Simon was right. It could do no good if she attended the ball.

She banished the glum picture of Eleanor, Agnes, and herself, unsolicited by dance partners, doomed to spend the long night on the chaperone chairs.

"Is it true, then, what Agnes said? That Aunt Louisa would like to see a match between Eleanor and Frederick?"

"And she'll get her wish, too."

Simon narrowed his eyes as he once more looked toward the credenza where Lady Louisa, a somewhat pained smile on her face, was listening to Frederick. Perhaps the stiff-necked matron would not relent after all.

"In some ways, Aunt Louisa reminds me of *Grand-mère.*" A corner of Jeannette's mouth turned down in a rueful smile. "They're both forceful, both strong willed. I expect Aunt Louisa also always gets her way?"

"She does. But the match between Eleanor and Frederick will not be of Louisa's making. You need only look at Frederick to see that he's besotted."

"You don't sound pleased. Is it because Eleanor and Frederick are related?"

"Lord, no! Their connection is no closer than yours and mine. Or yours and Frederick's, for that matter. Second cousins, and removed at that. Frederick is simply too young to make a commitment."

Jeannette would have agreed had she paid attention to his last words, but she heard only the first.

"You admitted I am a Dundas!"

"How you do take one up." He kept his tone light. "I see I must carefully weigh every word I utter. But, to tell the truth, after meeting your father I wouldn't dare deny a relationship—however remote."

Head tilted at a proud angle, she challenged, "And however illegitimate?"

He said nothing for a moment, only looked at her. "I wish you hadn't said that, Jeannette."

By now, she wished it, too. But she knew it was what he thought, and somehow, when they discussed her father, Simon Renshaw aroused the worst in her—the pride, the defiance, the impulsiveness *Grandmère* had always deplored.

He said, "I truly don't wish to argue with you in Lady Louisa's drawing room. Just think how she'd delight in taking us to task. And you, I daresay, would take the brunt of her scold."

Lightning-quick, her temper rose. "Let her scold. I don't give a straw. But I wonder if you will ever get it through that thick head that my father is neither a by-blow nor an imposter!"

"I won't be difficult to convince if I am shown proof that Hugh did not die in Savannah," he said calmly.

"You'll have the proof when Mr. Harte returns from New Orleans. But even then, I wager, you'll fight Papa. By hook or by crook, you want Frederick to keep the title!"

His temper was as quick as hers. Pale with anger, he took a step toward her.

"Dash it, Jeannette! I'll not tolerate any more accusations. I am a lawyer and a gentleman. When you accuse me of taking a bribe from Frederick or of scheming to cheat your father, you go too far."

She was no longer certain what she believed of him, but neither would she back down without an attempt to make him see her side.

Steeling herself against the cold blaze in his eyes, she stared up at him defiantly.

"If you demand recognition of your honor as a gentleman, you ought to accord the same courtesy to Papa."

Simon was speechless. Exasperated. The workings of the female mind! There was just enough logic behind her reasoning to render him uncomfortable.

But his anger was dissipating.

He glanced toward the credenza to assure himself that the girls and Frederick were still there. They would be awhile, he judged. They were engaged in an argument with Louisa.

"Jeannette, I like your father. But as the family's solicitor I have certain obligations."

"Indeed," she said stiffly. "And I suppose it is *obligation* that compels you to brand one of the Dundas family a by-blow."

"You must admit that it is a distinct possibility."

"I admit nothing, and I find it reprehensible that you're willing to stir up heaven knows how many lives merely to satisfy yourself that an illegitimate son was indeed born to that loose screw, the fourth duke, at about—" Having run out of breath, she was forced to pause briefly. "At about the same time my father was born."

"What the dickens are you charging me with now? What lives—" An arrested look came into his eyes. "Or need I ask? Jeannette, are you, perchance, referring to my conversation with your father this morning?"

She faltered, then once more stared at him defiantly.

"Yes. You said you'd find out exactly which of the fourth duke's by-blows Papa is."

"And, I suppose, it was Annie who told you this? Your ghost was spying on me again?"

"Annie was not spying! She was—"

Jeannette's face grew warm. Annie had discovered

a volume on "Potions, Elixirs, and Decoctions" on the library shelves and had taken refuge with the book in the deep cupboard by the fireplace when Jeannette's father entered. She had still been there, trying to reconstruct the recipe of Old Marjory's love potion, when Simon was announced.

Noting the blush, Simon chuckled. "I am beginning to understand about Annie. Does she have dark hair?"

"As far as I can tell." Jeannette gave him a puzzled look. "Annie's hair is all but hidden beneath a mobcap."

"Very fetching, I don't doubt. Blue eyes?"

"I haven't noticed her eyes." By now, Jeannette was quite mystified. "Are you trying to tell me that you saw Annie this morning?"

"Not in person. But I saw the door in the paneling, where she was hiding while reportedly making calls with Mrs. Effington."

Jeannette blinked. *She* had been out with the chaperone. *She* had dark hair and blue eyes.

But he couldn't possibly believe—

A look at his face, the quizzingly raised brow, the laughter dancing in his eyes, confirmed he could indeed believe that she, Jeannette, was spying on him in the guise of Annie.

"My trick, I think?" he said, grinning impudently.

She should be offended, but it was an infectious grin, and besides, the whole situation was too ridiculous to be taken seriously.

Jeannette gave a peal of laughter. "Not merely your trick, Simon. I'll gladly cede the game to you."

* * *

When Jeannette drove home with her father, she was still thinking about Simon's assumption that she was playing ghost in order to spy on him. Her mouth curved in a smile. It was absurd, of course—and yet, from his standpoint, it was no doubt the only possible interpretation to put on her tale of Annie, the ghost.

Watching her, Hugh asked, "Happy you'll finally attend a ball again?"

"I don't know, Papa."

She remembered how abruptly Simon's face had hardened when Agnes bounced across the drawing room with the happy tidings that Lady Louisa had indeed extended an invitation to Eleanor's come-out ball.

Glancing out the carriage window, she said with assumed indifference, "Mr. Renshaw doesn't think it wise for us to appear at the ball."

"Does he not? But, then, there's nothing he can do about it, is there?"

"Papa, there's bound to be talk when we are introduced. Eleanor and Agnes are embarking on their first Season, and if the family is embroiled in a scandal, they may find themselves ostracized."

"Rubbish."

She turned. "It isn't rubbish. Unless—" Indignation swelled her breast. "Papa, shall we be introduced as some distant, impoverished relations?"

"Of course not."

"Then how can we possibly avoid a scandal?"

Hugh patted his daughter's hands, which were clenched around the drawstring of her reticule.

"I wish, my dear, you'd allow yourself to enjoy London. There's no need to fret about us, about the family, or about a scandal. You'll see, now that Louisa extended an invitation, you will be showered with requests to grace this ball and that soiree. Believe me, everything will work out fine and dandy. Only trust me, Jeannette."

Reassuring words. She was beginning to feel better about the ball.

"I do trust you, Papa. Still, a scandal—"

"Lud, child! This is not the first scandal the family has weathered. And it isn't the worst, either. Just think of the fourth duke!"

"I do. Far too often," she said wryly. She braced herself as the carriage turned sharply. "And I also remember that it was a scandal that made your father ship you out of the country."

"Aye." Hugh's haggard face showed the ghost of a smile. "And I doubt the family suffered. Louisa was about to make her come-out. And see whom she caught! Even for the daughter of a duke an earl is nothing to sneeze at."

He frowned. "Or was it Elizabeth, the second eldest, who was about to be launched?"

"It doesn't matter, Papa."

"No, it doesn't. It merely shows that there have always been scandals in the family. From Augustus Hugh and Cornelius—"

Hugh broke off, leaning back against the squabs.

"Who is Cornelius, Papa?"

He did not answer, and she prompted, "Another black sheep, apparently. Won't you tell me about him?"

Still, he made no reply. She reflected sadly that, truly, she was no longer his *confidante.*

Sensing her disappointment, Hugh roused himself.

Once more he reached for her hand.

"Cornelius was killed in a tavern brawl. That's all you need to know about him."

Hundreds of candles in eight chandeliers and many more in wall sconces set the ballroom ablaze with light, reflecting in tall windows on one side and in gilt-framed mirrors on the opposite side of the vast chamber. Red and white roses in urns and vases, in baskets, and woven into garlands mingled their scent with the perfume worn by the ladies—a heady mixture that stirred memories in Jeannette of her own come-out ball and the many balls she had attended in New Orleans.

This was London. So similar. So different. Instead of dancing with cousin Jean-Pierre or cousin Roland, she was performing the boulanger with young Frederick, who as yet denied any relationship.

For once, Jeannette did not miss the warmth of New Orleans. The heat generated by nearly a thousand lighted candles and almost as many guests made her feel quite comfortable. Eight hundred people were expected, Eleanor had told her proudly, for this was the first truly grand ball of the Season.

And a grand ball it was indeed, even though Jeannette's father had treacherously deserted her for the company of Lord Decimus and other similar-minded gentlemen who preferred the card tables to the dance floor.

Mrs. Effington, though, had proven a rare treasure. She and Agnes. They had introduced Jeannette to a number of young ladies and gentlemen. Speculative looks were cast her way, but no one had turned a cold shoulder on Lady Caroline Dundas. In fact, the dance program with its tiny, attached pencil dangling from her wrist was completely filled before the musicians struck up the first tune.

So much for her fears of scandal and ostracism!

So much for Simon Renshaw's warning!

Jeannette had been dancing for the better part of an hour, and just as Frederick claimed her hand for the boulanger, Lady Louisa, Lord Upton, and Eleanor had left their posts at the top of the red-carpeted stairs. But still more guests arrived.

For about the dozenth time Jeannette caught herself staring at the double doors opening into the ballroom and for about the dozenth time called herself sternly to order.

Why should she care that Simon Renshaw had yet to make an appearance!

Why should she care that there was not a single dance left on her program should Simon arrive late and ask her to stand up with him!

"You're frowning so ferociously," Frederick said shyly, "if you had not earlier assured me that you enjoy dancing, I'd think you detest it. Or have I stepped on your toes, Lady Caroline?"

"I beg your pardon." Jeannette tore her gaze from the doorway and turned it on her dance partner. "I assure you, the frown had nothing to do with the ball or with you. It is a splendid ball, and you are an excellent dancer."

They switched positions. A smile lit his serious young face, and she thought—as she had many times previously—how difficult it was to keep in mind that he was usurping her father's rightful position.

He said, "Anyone would qualify as excellent after your last partner. Poor Barnaby Herrington never did grasp the difference between right and left."

"Mr. Herrington made up for his lack in dancing skills, though. He kept me wonderfully entertained with tales of steeplechases and fox hunts."

"Most young ladies are bored with his sporting tales and never allow him to finish a single one. If you listened to him for the full duration of a dance, you've made a friend for life, Lady Caroline."

"Must you be so formal, Frederick? After all, I don't address you as your grace."

"But, then, you're contesting that I *am* the sixth duke."

Once more, the movements of the dance separated them briefly. When they joined hands again, she gave him a sidelong look.

"And you don't believe I am the granddaughter of the fifth duke. So why address me by my title?"

A frown creased his brow.

Before he could reply, the dance tune came to a startling, discordant finale. Heads turned in surprise and brows were raised at the musicians seated on a platform in a bower of garlands and bunting.

A buzz of excited whispers swept the room, for on the platform stood Lady Louisa.

Jeannette was close enough to see every haughty feature of her aunt's face. The cold eyes, the proud nose, the satisfied twist of her mouth when the whispers died to absolute silence.

"Dear friends," said Lady Louisa, "I have an announcement to make."

No one stirred. No one spoke.

Jeannette glanced at Frederick. An announcement

could mean that he and Eleanor had pledged their troth. But Frederick looked bewildered and curious. Even worried.

"Among us," said Lady Louisa, "is a man we all believed dead these past thirty years. Hugh Dundas. My brother. And with him is his daughter, Lady Caroline."

Heads nodded. Several people near Jeannette glanced her way, then at Frederick. Some smiled; others looked wary.

Jeannette saw her father, Lord Decimus, and Lady Louisa's husband wend their way toward the musician's platform. Neither Lord Decimus nor her father looked pleased. Lord Upton looked troubled and pushed through the crowd with a haste and vigor quite unsuited to the ballroom.

However, none of the three gentlemen could stop Lady Louisa's next words.

"I have welcomed Hugh Dundas as a brother," she said. "I embraced his daughter as a niece."

Fudge, thought Jeannette. You scarcely looked at me.

Although no one spoke, Lady Louisa raised a hand in a gesture as dramatic as it was regal.

"Alas, my friends! I have been informed that they are imposters."

Chapter Fourteen

Imposters.

It shouldn't have, but the word hit Jeannette with the force of a doubled fist. That her aunt would do this! Denounce them. Publicly.

Jeannette could not move. She could not breathe. She was aware of noise all around her but could not tell whether it was caused by the hum of voices or merely by the blood rushing to her head.

Louisa is a dragon, Papa had said.

A fire-breathing, poison-tongued dragon, Jeannette amended his judgment.

The droning sound in her ears swelled. She recognized it now as voices, high, sharp, excited, shredding the tidbit tossed out by Lady Louisa.

Scandal.

The dance floor, uncomfortably crowded a moment earlier, emptied quickly—at least around the spot where Jeannette stood, suddenly alone.

Ostracism.

She raised her chin, stiffened her back. Papa. She must go to him. He'd be devastated by his sister's perfidy.

She started toward the platform. Lady Louisa was

no longer there. Neither did Jeannette see Lord Upton, her father, or Lord Decimus.

"Caroline."

Someone touched her arm. Frederick. So he had not deserted her. And he had finally dropped formality.

"I am very sorry, Caroline. I had no notion—please! You must believe that I did not know what Lady Louisa's intentions were when she agreed to extend the invitation."

She stopped. "There's no need to apologize, Frederick. I did not for a moment believe you knew what my aunt planned to do."

"I should have been suspicious, though. Simon hinted that Lady Louisa cannot be trusted. I did not understand at the time. I believed it had to do with me and Elly."

"I daresay that is what Simon meant. He said something similar to me."

Frederick's troubled expression did not ease. "I don't think even Simon foresaw that Lady Louisa would denounce you publicly after having invited you."

"No," she murmured while her mind clamored, *And where is Simon? Why isn't he here?*

Frederick was still trying to reassure her. "Simon wanted above all to settle the matter quietly. Avoid all scandal and legal problems."

Jeannette was not interested in legal problems. She could not see her father anywhere. Only the faces of strangers, all of them turned toward her in avid curiosity or even hostility. Two or three older ladies, friends of Mrs. Effington, showed a trace of pity. Jeannette did not want pity.

Of Mrs. Effington herself, or of her father and Lord Decimus, Jeannette still saw no sign in the crowd. Surely, if her father had been taken ill, someone would have been sent to fetch her?

Frederick drew a deep breath. "Gad, how I wish Simon were here! He'd know what to do."

"Yes! Yes, indeed."

The heartfelt words had slipped out before she realized it. What was the matter with her? Wishing for the support of the man responsible for this whole sorry state of affairs!

"Frederick, I must find my father. He's not well. Do you know where—"

"Cousin Caroline!"

Short dusky curls bouncing, Agnes sped toward them, her eyes sparking indignation, her face flushed.

"Aunt Louisa is outrageous!" Breathless, Agnes skittered to a stop in front of them. "Mama is incensed. For the first time ever, she raked Aunt Louisa over the coals!"

"I am grateful to your mama," said Jeannette. "But, pray forgive me. I mustn't linger. My father—I do not see him anywhere, and he isn't well. Agnes, I must find him."

"Uncle Hugh is in fine fettle," Agnes said breezily. "No need to fret. You should have heard Eleanor and her father! They told Aunt Louisa—"

"Agnes!" Frederick interrupted with unusual sharpness. "All Caroline wants to know at the moment is *where* you saw her father."

"I was getting to that!" Agnes shot back, but her expression softened when she saw Jeannette's troubled face. "I'm sorry, Caroline. Your papa is in the blue salon. He truly is well. And Simon said I was to fetch you both."

Relief winged Jeannette's steps as she accompanied Agnes and Frederick to the blue salon on the first floor of Lord and Lady Upton's elegant town residence. Relief that her father was all right. Relief that she could turn her back on the eight hundred-odd pairs of prying eyes and ears in the ballroom.

And relief that Simon was present after all.

The next instant, anger rose. It was Simon's fault that she and Papa found themselves in this humiliating position. Simon's and Frederick's. They must be made to set matters right.

But she did not address Frederick. She rushed on toward the blue salon, toward Simon.

The blue salon, true to its name, was a vision of royal blue satin on chairs and sofas and draping four tall windows. It was a magnificent chamber, almost as large and twice as splendid as the drawing room where she and her father had been received earlier that day.

Hugh Dundas stood by the fireplace. Looking remarkably cheerful, he acknowledged his daughter's entrance with a nod but did not break off his conversation with Lady Anne's husband and a stranger, a tall, gray-haired gentleman leaning on a silver-knobbed cane.

After a quick, searching look at her father's face, Jeannette surveyed the rest of the assembled company. Lady Louisa, her husband and daughter were seated on one of two sofas flanking a low cherrywood table in the center of the room. Lord Upton rose politely and Eleanor smiled a greeting, but

Lady Louisa grimly ignored Jeannette's presence.

Lady Anne, as restless and energetic as Agnes, was pacing in front of the windows. She stopped, reluctantly, it seemed, when her daughter and Frederick joined her.

Simon Renshaw was conspicuously absent.

Jeannette's mouth tightened. He had sent Agnes to fetch her, and then he didn't have the courtesy to wait until she could give him a piece of her mind. Dash it! He would not escape her so easily.

She started across the room toward her father and had almost reached him when Lord Upton spoke to her.

"One moment, please, Caroline."

She turned to face him. Robert Hargrave, Earl of Upton, was a man of few words. She need not fear to be delayed for long.

"Lady Louisa is overset," he said. "In that condition, she neither weighs her words nor considers possible consequences of her actions. We will see to it that you and your father do not suffer unduly from my wife's impetuosity."

He bowed and returned to his wife and daughter before Jeannette could think of anything to say. Perhaps it was just as well since she was hardly in a frame of mind to thank him.

She did wonder, however, who was included in the "we" when he said, "We will see to it that you and your father do not suffer unduly."

Joining the three gentlemen by the fireplace, she begged pardon for interrupting, then turned to her father.

"Papa, where is Mr. Renshaw?"

Hugh did not seem to hear the grim note in her

voice or see the tension in her face. His eyes twinkled, a sight Jeannette had sorely missed these past weeks but found unsettling after the events in the ballroom.

"Which one, my dear?" he asked with a chuckle.

She faltered. Eyes widening, she looked at the gray-haired stranger with the cane.

He bowed. "Malcolm Renshaw, at your service, Lady Caroline."

Her first thought was that he and Simon did not share a family resemblance.

But then it struck her that there stood the man who would decide whether the Dundas family would go to court. Yet her father appeared quite unconcerned.

Hiding her confusion, she curtsied. For the present, at least, the matter of the lawsuit was not a priority. Confronting Simon was, she thought grimly.

"Very pleased to meet you, sir. Can you tell me where your son is?"

"Indeed, I can." His voice was dry. "The question is *should* I tell you?"

She revised her first impression that he and Simon were not alike. The look she encountered was just exactly the keen, sharp look his son had bent on her on more than one occasion.

"Why ever wouldn't you tell me, sir?"

A slight smile curved his mouth. "The way you scowled made me wonder how Simon would fare in a meeting. And, frankly, my dear, I am not up to taking over Simon's clients."

The tension drained from her. She found herself smiling back at him.

"I did not plan to run him through, sir."

"I'm relieved to hear it. May I ask what are your plans for my son?"

"I mean to—"

She did not know what suddenly caught her attention. Her back was to the door. She had not heard it open, and the thick Turkey rugs strewn on the parquet floor swallowed any footsteps. Yet she knew Simon had entered the room and was walking up behind her.

Slowly, she turned.

He was nearing the sofa where Lady Louisa sat with her husband and daughter, and the haughty matron beckoned him with an imperious hand.

"Later, if you please," Simon said curtly, striding past with firm, determined steps.

His expression was as determined as his stride. His eyes were fixed on Jeannette, and as he came closer she saw a muscle twitch at the corner of his mouth.

No misguided notion that he was trying to control a smile crossed her mind. Simon Renshaw was annoyed, and it was his temper he tried to control.

He stopped in front of her. "Don't say I did not warn you."

Her own temper flared. "You warned me of a possible scandal. Not of my aunt!"

No one noticed that Lady Anne's husband, Sir Lewis Paine, quietly walked off to join his wife and daughter, engaged in a low-voiced but animated conversation by the windows. Or that Eleanor and Frederick were now seated together on the sofa opposite Lady Louisa and Lord Upton.

Hugh Dundas said mildly, "You mustn't blame Simon, child. He could hardly have foreseen that Louisa would lose her head."

Jeannette glowered at Simon. "You are the family solicitor. You should have stopped Aunt Louisa."

"How could I have done so when I did not know what she planned to do?"

"You might have recognized her intentions if you had put in an appearance sooner."

"Allow me to point out," said Malcolm Renshaw, "that it never does any good to cry over spilled milk."

Hugh nodded. "Only thing to do is mop it up."

"Which," Simon said grimly, "is what I've been doing for the past half hour or more."

"You have?" Jeannette frowned. "I was sure I'd have a hard time convincing you that you must set matters straight. Could it be that your father has already confirmed Papa is indeed Hugh Dundas?"

"No, Lady Caroline. He has not."

Such was his tone and demeanor that she wondered if he had ever smiled at her or called her Jeannette.

She looked at the senior Renshaw and found that he, in turn, was watching her father.

"Sir, I know it was you who came to America and learned of Hugh Dundas's supposed death in Savannah. But now you've met Papa. You have spoken with him. Do you believe Papa is an imposter?"

Leaning on his cane, Malcolm Renshaw turned to face her.

"Your father and I were reminiscing before you joined us. I admit that he remembers much of what he should remember. I also admit that his looks are much as I would have expected Hugh Dundas to look after close to forty years."

"Then you did recognize Papa!"

Malcolm Renshaw glanced at Hugh before answering.

"My dear Lady Caroline, I am a cautious man. I will not commit myself one way or the other after one brief meeting."

Hugh Dundas and Jeannette did not return to the ballroom but, at Malcolm Renshaw's suggestion, left for George Street as soon as their carriage could be fetched. Jeannette protested that she would not run and hide from a parcel of gossip mongers, but Hugh firmly led her off.

Mrs. Effington stayed at the ball. At Simon Renshaw's request, she and Lord Decimus were circling among the guests, and had, in fact, been doing so since the fateful words left Lady Louisa's mouth.

Simon and his father had entered the ballroom in time to hear the denouncement and, after the briefest of consultations with Lord Upton and Hugh Dundas, had taken steps to avert total disaster. Whether Hugh was an imposter or not, Simon and Malcolm knew that an open dispute could bring about a Parliamentary inquiry. It would raise the question whether Frederick, until the matter was settled, should be barred from disbursing funds and managing the vast ducal estates and holdings. In short, an open dispute would have disastrous consequences for those depending on the Duke of Granby for their livelihood.

Both Renshaws agreed it was much better to assure the world that Frederick was willing to cede the title to Hugh if confirmation of his identity arrived from America. And that Hugh, should the title indeed fall to him, promised to honor any and all obligations entered into by the present duke in his management of the estates.

Mrs. Effington and Lord Decimus, with their multitude of friends, would drop a word in the right ear, and Messrs. Renshaw and Renshaw could be assured that in less than twenty-four hours the information would spread among the members of the *ton*.

Lord Upton, Sir Lewis, Frederick, Simon, and Malcolm would add their mite. Eleanor and Agnes, of course, must be seen to be enjoying themselves at the ball. And Lady Anne was assigned the post of Lady Louisa's keeper to ensure that no further slip occurred. These measures should avert an immediate inquiry into the state of affairs of the Dundas family.

It could not be said that Simon was overjoyed with this development. As he circled the ballroom, stopping to greet this person and that, he reflected grimly that, if Hugh had orchestrated the whole sorry affair, Lady Louisa could not have played more deftly into the rogue's hands. With a few ill-chosen words, she had gained for Hugh the status of contender to the title, a status Simon had been at pains to deny the gentleman from New Orleans.

Finally, in the wee hours of Friday, May the third, Frederick and the two Renshaws retired to Dundas House in Grosvenor Square. Simon had his own chambers in St. James's Square, but a room was always kept ready for him at Dundas House, and a suite of rooms had been at Malcolm's disposal since his wife passed away five years earlier.

Bidding Frederick a hearty but firm goodnight, Malcolm invited his son to join him for a glass of brandy in his sitting room. Leaning the silver-knobbed cane against the arm of a chair, the older man lowered himself onto the leather cushion.

"It's unfortunate Louisa had to be in town at this time," he said. "She was bound to kick up a dust."

"Was she, sir?" Simon's hand on the decanter tightened. Deliberately, he relaxed and poured.

Handing his father a glass, he said, "To tell the truth, I considered Lady Louisa too high a stickler to air the Dundas linen in public. My mistake, sir."

"You're touchy on the subject." Malcolm watched his son pace. "Let me assure you that I was in no way or manner implying you should have foreseen Louisa's extremely stupid 'announcement.' I would not have foreseen it either. She is proud, opinionated, and mulish. But she is not usually dimwitted."

Simon gave him a wry look. "Smoothing balm on the wound, sir?"

"Not at all. If you'll remember, I always left that up to your mother." Malcolm paused. "That little gal, Lady Caroline, got under your skin, didn't she?"

In reply, Simon tossed off his brandy. He refilled the glass, then took a seat opposite his father.

"That little gal, sir, is an adventuress. She is an actress *par excellence*. When she turns those guileless blue eyes on you, she can convince you that wrong is right. That she is the granddaughter of a duke, and her father is indeed the dead Hugh Dundas."

"And you took it to heart when she reproached you for not stopping Louisa."

Simon's expression softened. "Under the influence of blue eyes. Yes, I did. Whatever punishment she may deserve for this masquerade, I did not want her exposed to a public denouncement."

Malcolm raised his glass, swirling the contents under his nose.

He decided to warm the brandy awhile longer.

"Simon, you made it clear that you believe Hugh Dundas a crafty old rogue."

"Don't you agree, sir?"

"I do, indeed. But you've met him several times. I spoke with him only this once. Do you think he's wily enough to have set Louisa up?"

"Goading her into a denunciation to force the issue?" Simon frowned. "It's a notion that occurred to me also, for he's definitely wily enough. But he'd never expose his daughter to public humiliation."

"Yes, the daughter. She seems to be the key to this whole affair." *And not only from Hugh Dundas's point of view,* thought Malcolm. He raised his glass, this time drinking deeply.

"I keep asking myself," said Simon, "why Lady Louisa lost her head."

"I expect Anne's reception of Hugh Dundas rattled her. Louisa wants him to be an imposter. She's made up her mind to have a duke for a son-in-law."

"She'd get her wish even if Dundas turned out to be the fifth duke's son after all. Dundas has no son; thus Frederick would be his heir and Eleanor eventually a duchess."

"She wouldn't be a duchess immediately, though, and Louisa does not like her plans overset. Still, there must be something else." Snapping his fingers, Malcolm sat up. "Of course! The sapphires! She'd have to give the necklace to Lady Caroline."

Simon raised a brow. "Am I missing something? I understood the sapphires were the late duchess's personal property, hers to bequeath as she wished."

"Yes, indeed. But remember, Simon—no, of course you don't remember. You were but a boy when Caroline—the late duchess—passed away. She had drawn up a will when Hugh wrote of his marriage to a Philadelphia girl, and she bequeathed the set of sapphires to her daughter-in-law. Only in the event that both Hugh and his wife died, and there was no issue, would the sapphires be divided among her daughters."

"The necklace for Lady Louisa. The ring for Lady Anne. The bracelet for Lady Elizabeth. And the ear drops for Lady Mary," Simon listed.

"It's not as if giving up the sapphires would deprive them of every memento from their mother. Caroline had more jewelry than any woman I know—her private jewelry—and it all went to her four daughters."

Malcolm took another sip of brandy. "There's no denying the fact that Louisa is grasping. Once she has her hands on something, she does not like to let go."

"A sapphire necklace . . . and a ducal coronet for her daughter. No, I shouldn't think she'd want to let go." Simon rose. "I'll bid you good night, sir. It's been a long day for you."

"Aye, and I've never enjoyed traveling or attending balls. But don't start to mollycoddle me, son! Just because I was indisposed for a while doesn't mean I have a foot in the grave."

Simon smiled. "I wouldn't dream of mollycoddling you. If you remember, I also always left that to Mother."

"Then finish your brandy and leave me to seek my couch."

"Just one more question. Do you believe it at all

possible that the man you met tonight is Hugh Dundas?"

Malcolm grimaced. "Knew it was too much to hope you wouldn't ask."

Simon waited.

"No, son," Malcolm said slowly. "There's no possibility at all. He is not Hugh."

Chapter Fifteen

For a moment Simon said nothing.

His suspicion confirmed—Hugh an imposter. He should be gratified, but all he could think was *Jeannette, you little fool!*

He looked at his father. "Then, why the deuce didn't you say so to his face? Why didn't you say something when Jeannette—Lady Caroline asked you?"

Malcolm studied the dregs of brandy in his glass. "I have my reasons."

"And they are?"

Malcolm sighed. "I thought I had taught you patience."

"You also taught me perseverance."

"I'll say this much. I believe, given time, Hugh Dundas or, rather, the man calling himself Hugh Dundas, will confess and explain his deception. Meanwhile, it doesn't hurt to wait what information Harte will bring from New Orleans."

"Allow this to drag on all summer! Father, even if Harte—" Simon broke off. He thought of Jeannette, the time he had driven her home from London Docks and she had upset his horses by clutching his arm. She had asked what harm it would do to wait for Harte's return. And she had asked, nay, she had commanded him to postpone any action because Harte would bring back proof that her father was indeed Hugh Dundas, Marquis of Luxton.

Jeannette—the scheming little baggage.

More than ever, he wanted her to trust him and admit to the masquerade.

"It is too bad you did not recognize him as an imposter before we sent Lord Decimus and Mrs. Effington to—" Eyes narrowing, Simon looked at his father. "Or did you, sir?"

"Devil a bit!" Malcolm set his glass down with a snap. "You don't think I'd have worked so hard to prevent a Parliamentary inquiry if I'd known from the beginning!"

"No, sir. But I'm glad to see a spark of your old temper. I feared your illness had totally changed you."

"Impertinent jackanapes," muttered Malcolm but did not sound at all displeased. "Then it is agreed? We'll wait and see what move Dundas has planned next?"

"Unless the situation should prove intolerable for Frederick."

"Naturally. Frederick and the estate must always be my first consideration." Malcolm paused. "And yours."

They looked at each other, Malcolm's expression bland, Simon's wry.

"And mine," said Simon. "You always did read me much better than I ever understood you. As a youngster, I found it uncanny how you saw through me."

"But no longer?"

"Now I find it nothing short of marvelous, and I envy you your ability."

"It's not difficult. All you need to remember is that we feel and think very much alike."

"Do we, sir?"

"Definitely, I'd say, with regard to Lady Caroline."

Simon gave a bark of laughter. "Hardly."

"I stand corrected." The hint of a smile touched Malcolm's mouth. "No doubt, you'll explain your intentions toward Lady Caroline in your own good time."

"My intentions, sir, are to make her see the error of her ways."

"I wish you luck, my boy."

Simon started for the door but stopped and faced his father once more.

"Sir, you are certain about Hugh Dundas?"

"Quite certain."

"Will you tell me why?"

Groping for his cane, Malcolm rose.

"In the blue salon, he passed me a glass of wine. I saw the palm of his hand. Hugh Dundas, Marquis of Luxton, would have had a scar in his right palm. I should know. I put it there."

"The devil you say! How?"

"We were boys. Hugh was ten. I was twelve." Malcolm shrugged. "We fenced."

"The scar on your arm. Did Hugh give it to you?"

"Pinked me neatly. I tried to disarm him. Somehow, the point of my foil ripped open his palm."

"Great Scot! I hope you both received a thrashing."

"We did." Malcolm placed a hand on his son's shoulder. "Simon . . . if you deem it advantageous or necessary, you may drop a hint in Lady Caroline's ear."

Once more they exchanged looks.

Simon was grave. "If I think it necessary. Thank you, Father."

As Hugh Dundas had assured his daughter, this was not the first scandal the family had weathered, nor was it the worst. It was, however, quite out of the ordinary, and Hugh admitted that nothing short of Napoleon Bonaparte's defeat and capture would take people's minds off the Dundas family for some time to come.

Eleanor and Agnes did not suffer under the cloud of scandal. They were, after all, connected with the Dundas family only through the female line. No mother of an eligible young gentleman would snub Lady Eleanor Hargrave, youngest daughter of the wealthy Earl of Upton, or Miss Agnes Paine, only child of Sir Lewis Paine, whose vast estates equaled those of the Duke of Granby.

Neither did Frederick find himself at a disadvantage. The *ton* had known of him since he was six years old, when his father died and the fifth duke of Granby took a hand in the raising of young Frederick, the last male Dundas. When Frederick was eighteen, the old duke decided his heir must spend at least a part of the long vacation in town. Thus, in the late spring of '07, Frederick had posted from Cambridge to Dundas House in Grosvenor Square instead of traveling to Granby Castle in Northumberland and, under the aegis of the fifth duke and Simon Renshaw, made his bow to society.

His peers considered Frederick "a right 'un." Older gentlemen liked him for his sense of responsibility. And ladies, young and old alike, adored him for his handsome looks and unfailing good manners. They pitied him for having an indifferent mother, a chronic invalid, who resided year in, year out in Bath and had left him to the mercy of the old cantankerous duke.

It was not to be expected that anyone would turn against him—even if he lost the title—for Frederick was a very well-to-do young man in his own right.

Hugh Dundas also went on much as before, doing business with his broker, going about town with his friend, Lord Decimus Rowland. Some members of White's and Brooks's might cast him a wary look when he appeared at the clubs with Decimus, but since Hugh made no attempt to ingratiate himself or to force a recognition as the fifth duke's son, he was tolerated fairly well.

The only one to suffer in this uncertain situation was Jeannette. She was an unknown quantity. The *ton* did not know how to deal with the daughter of a man not proven to be one of them.

Unlike Eleanor and Agnes, Jeannette had not had a multitude of invitations already sitting on her desk when she first arrived in town, and she received no invitations after her introduction at Eleanor's ball—no invitations beside the one from Lady Anne for Agnes's ball on the twenty-fourth of May.

A week after Eleanor's come-out ball, Mrs. Effington said, "Don't worry, my dear, this won't last long. It only takes one hostess to include you in her guest list, and the others will follow."

Like sheep, Jeannette was tempted to say.

She and her chaperone were sitting down to luncheon, and the only missive delivered by post that day was a bill from the dressmaker, which Jeannette flung down at her father's empty place.

"I'd be lying if I told you I don't mind not receiving any invitations," she said. "I enjoy dancing and card parties and picnics—unless there's something more worthwhile to be done. But mostly, I mind for Papa. He had such high expectations. He wanted me to be *a success.*"

"And he wants you to make a good match."

Jeannette busied herself flaking the piece of poached salmon on her plate. Mention of a possible marriage had spoiled what little appetite she'd had.

She looked at the older woman. "Papa and I don't see eye to eye on that subject. He must have told you that I have no interest in a suitor?"

"He did." Mrs. Effington speared an asparagus tip. "I told him not to fret. That you'll change your mind before the Season is over."

Jeannette knew when it was futile to argue.

Instead, she asked, "Do you ever wonder about Papa? Whether he truly is the Marquis of Luxton?"

"La! Why should I? Lord Luxton is a gentleman. I do not question his word."

"Did you know Papa before he left England?"

"I knew of him. My sister, four years older than I, met him the year she came out. She said he was the most dashing young gentleman she ever encountered. And always charming, always polite. She was quite heartbroken when she heard he left the country."

Mrs. Effington sat for a moment in silence, her plump, rosy face pensive.

Abruptly, she switched the subject. "I know whom I shall approach about an invitation for you. Sophronia Aldrich. She does not entertain much, but she's bound to do something for her granddaughter this Season."

"Your friend, the Dowager Lady Aldrich? But she said she could not support Papa and me because of Frederick."

"That was before your Aunt Louisa made a cake of herself. Leave it to me, Lady Caroline. Sophronia may have married a mere baronet and dropped her own title—her father, you must know, was the Duke of Belmore—but she is still a power to be reckoned with. I promise you, within a week you'll be complaining you don't know which invitation to accept and which to reject."

Again, Jeannette did not argue. It did not matter if Mrs. Effington exaggerated. Anything would be better than now, when she still exercised her mare in the early mornings with only her groom in attendance. When she still drove around St. Paul's with only Archer and Annie to keep her company.

In fact, Jeannette had made Annie's quest her own. While waiting for Mr. Harte's return from New Orleans, she would search for the little ghost's childhood home, and she was determined to find it.

She had also looked forward to an outing with Frederick, Eleanor, and Agnes later that week, but the walk in Hyde Park at the fashionable hour of five turned into a less than pleasurable experience because of the curious and hostile glances cast her way.

Agnes comforted her, saying it was her exotic

looks—raven hair and blue eyes—that caused such a stir. Every gentleman wanted to get a closer look, which, the seventeen-year-old said with a great air of wisdom, naturally did not please the ladies and made them jealous and hostile. But Jeannette knew better.

Jeannette was also very much aware that she had not once seen Simon Renshaw during the past week.

A carefully offhand question put to Frederick while Eleanor and Agnes were speaking to a friend elicited the information that Simon expected to be occupied at the Court of Old Bailey for the better part of two weeks.

"He's at court?" Her voice rose embarrassingly, but she could not help it. She could think only that the Renshaws had decided after all to bring suit against her father. "What is he doing there?"

Frederick, his gaze on Eleanor, did not notice Jeannette's agitation.

He shrugged. "The usual. Simon's always pleading the case of some poor sod who was caught stealing. Or worse. And he always gets his clients a milder sentence than they would have dreamed possible in a month of Sundays."

"He's a barrister as well as a solicitor?"

"Hmm. A dashed good one, too."

"He could be your counsel if you decided to file suit against Papa?"

Frederick finally gave her his full attention.

"Of course he'd be my counsel. Didn't you know he is a barrister?"

She shook her head.

"Well, it doesn't matter," said Frederick, giving her one of his rare boyish grins. "You need not lose any sleep over it. Your father must have explained that we'll settle the matter out of court?"

Indeed, Papa had explained. It was nonetheless quite unsettling to know that Simon was a barrister, who could, if he so wished, plead a successful case on Frederick's behalf.

That night, when Mrs. Effington had retired, Jeannette rapped softly on the library door and entered.

"Papa? Can we talk awhile, or are you tired?"

Hugh was seated behind the desk. Removing his spectacles, he rubbed the bridge of his nose.

"I'm not at all tired," he lied valiantly. "Sit down and tell me how you spent your day."

"I went for a walk in Hyde Park."

He raised a brow. "Not alone, I presume?"

"Of course not." She perched on a corner of the desk, a posture frowned upon by her *grandmère* but tolerated by her father. "I was accompanied by Eleanor and Agnes. And Frederick was there as well."

Hugh nodded. "Agnes has taken a liking to you. What about Eleanor?"

"She's a bit reserved, but I believe she likes me, too. She certainly shows none of the animosity displayed by her mama."

"Good." Hugh paused, his gaze sharpening. "And Frederick?"

"I don't know, Papa. He is such a well-mannered young man, it is difficult to know how he feels. I am quite fond of him. But whether he reciprocates the feeling I cannot tell."

"Hmm," said Hugh. "Well, I'm glad you like him.

Very glad. He's a worthy young man. Can't think of a better successor to your grandfather's title and position."

"I can. Papa, *you* should be the sixth duke."

Hugh shook his head, a curt, impatient gesture. "Told you I've no intention of stepping in the old gentleman's shoes: I'm happy with my life in New Orleans."

"Then what are we doing here, Papa?"

Father and daughter looked at each other. And for the first time, it was Hugh who looked away first.

He picked up the port glass sitting on the blotter. Holding it up, he studied the dark red wine.

"We're here because I promised to see you settled in England, married to an Englishman."

"But I have no intention of marrying."

"Nonsense. Jeannette, you're in England now. I want you to forget about quadroon balls and the arrangements made there between Creole gentlemen and young ladies of color."

Jeannette's breath caught. Rarely had she known her father to speak so bluntly to her.

"How can I forget, Papa? How can I forget Cousin Félicie's unhappiness when her husband spends less time with her and the baby than with his mistress and child in Rampart Street?"

Her hands clenched. "And how can I forget Marie? She was sixteen when her mother took her to the quadroon ball and finalized an arrangement with Monsieur Bourrième. They lived together fifteen years, and Marie regarded him as her husband. She loved him. She was certain he loved her, too, and would never look at another woman. And then Monsieur Bourrième decided to marry."

Hugh shifted uncomfortably. "Bourrième settled the house on her. He told her he'd still visit her and the children."

"But don't you see, Papa? His marriage devastated Marie. She couldn't bear it!"

Jeannette closed her eyes, remembering the evening she had found the woman who was now in charge of the *boutique*. It had stormed all day, and when the rains finally ceased Jeannette had gone for a drive with Nounou. They followed the river, and on the high bank where a previous storm had cut a clearing among the cypress trees, Jeannette saw the tall, slender woman staring down into the churning water.

As if he had followed her thoughts, Hugh said, "I don't believe Marie would have killed herself. Three children are a strong bond tying a woman to life."

"She had sent the children to France with her mother," Jeannette said softly.

She looked at her father. "I don't know what Marie planned to do that night. All I know is that I *had* to stop the carriage. I *had* to climb that bank and speak to her. She looked so lonely. Lost."

Hugh, too, remembered the night Jeannette brought the beautiful quadroon to Royal Street. Jeannette had just a few months earlier terminated her betrothal to Raoul Fontenot, and he had been astonished but not displeased when she explained she wanted to invest the money inherited from her mother in a dressmaker's establishment to give employment to free women of color.

He said, "I've never doubted your compassion or your courage. But tell me, child. What does a seventeen-year-old girl say to a woman like Marie—especially when the girl suspects the older woman wants to end her life?"

"I simply asked her if she would like to come with me to light a candle for the Blessed Virgin."

He felt an unaccustomed tightness in his throat. "Bless you, child."

Jeannette smiled. "That's just what Marie said. And then Nounou was there and started scolding Marie that she wasn't wearing her turban, and if she planned to ride with us she had better put it back on and show herself off as the proud free woman of color she is."

"Trust Nounou to take charge in any situation."

Hugh sat up. Reaching across the desk, he clasped his daughter's hand.

"Jeannette, about marriage . . . I made a mistake when I pledged you to Raoul Fontenot. I knew he was not the right man for you, but—"

He looked at her uncertainly. They had not spoken of the unfortunate affair since the day she demanded, shaking with hurt and outrage, that he undo the betrothal.

"Poor Papa. Do you fear Raoul's name will cast me into the dismals?" Jeannette gave him a bright smile. "It won't. I promise. I have long since put Raoul behind me. And let me also assure you that I was well aware the engagement was *Grandmère's* wish more than yours. She spoke of the marriage between Raoul and me as a settled arrangement from the moment I arrived in New Orleans."

"That soon? She did not mention it to me until you were fourteen." Reassured by the smile and the lightness of her tone, Hugh cocked a brow. "At that time, I must admit, I had the impression you were not opposed to the union."

She grimaced ruefully. "Your impression was correct. I was ecstatic. Raoul was handsome. He was considerate, always treating me like something rare and fragile. And I was a romantic young fool, dreaming of a marriage like yours with *Maman.*"

"*He* was the fool," said Hugh. "If he hadn't been young enough to be my son or even my grandson, I would have called him out. Attending the quadroon ball on the night you made your very first appearance at the Mardi Gras balls! Devil a bit! He must have known you'd be looking for him. Must have known, too, that his sisters would find out about his assignation and talk!"

"Thank goodness, they talked. All I had to do was ask you to terminate the betrothal. If I had already been married to him—"

A gleam lit in her eyes. "Think of it, Papa! If Raoul and I had been married, *I* would have felt compelled to call him out. And I was always a better shot than he."

He chuckled but immediately turned serious again. "Don't try to get me off the subject, daughter."

"I am not aware that I tried," she retorted, looking demure. "The subject was my marriage."

"Your future marriage. Jeannette, surely here in London you can find a young man to whom you can give your trust. Your affection."

Lightning quick, Simon Renshaw's keen, assertive face and powerful figure flashed through her mind.

Startled, she dismissed the image. As if she could ever look upon the Dundas family solicitor with trust and affection!

She became aware of her father's expectant look. She hated to disappoint him, so she said only, "Perhaps, Papa. If I can find someone who will love me as dearly as you loved *Maman.*"

A shadow crossed his thin face. "Yes, I loved your mother with all my heart. But looking back, thinking of the odds stacked against my ever meeting Jeanne . . . it was a miracle, child."

"But then, you've always been fortunate when the odds were against you. Even *Grandmère* admits you're the most successful gambler she ever met."

"A gambler. Yes, I am that." He frowned and shook his head as if to rid himself of a troublesome thought. "Don't gamble with your life, Jeannette. If you fall in love and find someone who loves you deeply, that will be splendid. But remember! Mutual affection, respect, and suitability are a sound basis for a happy marriage."

She nodded absently, her eyes on the hand still clasping hers.

"Papa, why have you stopped wearing your signet ring?"

Slowly, he pulled his hand away.

"I've turned into skin and bones these past months. I'd hate to lose an heirloom."

"Take it to a jeweler. He can tighten the band. I know Simon Renshaw said that possession of the ring does not prove your identity, but Simon doesn't even know you have it! I wish you'd wear it for him and everyone to see."

Hugh rubbed his finger where a pale mark still indicated that a ring had been worn for many years. "In good time, daughter. All in good time."

Chapter Sixteen

Yet another week later, Hugh sat once more at the narrow desk in the library where he frequently took refuge when not going about town with his friend Decimus. The drawer containing the signet ring and the bundle of old letters gaped open.

He looked at the ring and thought of Jeannette's suggestion to have it tightened.

Slowly he shook his head. The ring would stay as it was until the next Marquis of Luxton was old enough to wear it.

He looked at the letters but did not take them out. He knew every one by heart. Every one was addressed to Lord Decimus Rowland. The dates ranged from April, 1781, in New Orleans, to September, 1791, on Haiti.

Every one of the letters was signed by Hugh Dundas, Marquis of Luxton.

None had ever been posted.

Soon, he knew, he would have to produce the letters. Unlike young Frederick, he could not afford to wait for Simon's agent to return from New Orleans. He wanted to see Jeannette settled before the end of the Season.

Devil a bit! He had counted on Malcolm Renshaw.

Malcolm should have recognized him. But he claimed he could not yet commit himself. Perhaps this shouldn't have come as a surprise. Malcolm Renshaw had always said and done the unexpected.

Hugh was tempted to nudge Malcolm's memory, but three incidents heartened his resolve to play a waiting game. News had gone out from Carlton House that the Prince Regent was planning a *fête* in early June—news which should ease the attention centered on him and Jeannette. Then there was Jeannette's admission that she was fond of young Frederick. And two invitations had finally arrived in the post.

One of the gilt-edged cards had come from the Dowager Lady Aldrich for a Venetian Breakfast on the twenty-seventh of May, and one from a Mrs. Herrington. A dinner and dance on the eighteenth, two days hence.

The invitations were addressed to Hugh Dundas, Esquire, and Miss Caroline Jeannette Dundas. The omission of their titles did not matter. Hugh was not one to stand on ceremony.

Jeannette would have her title in the end. And she would have the social position that was hers by right. That was what counted for him.

Nervous and at the same time elated, Jeannette got ready for the dinner and informal dance given by Mr. and Mrs. Herrington, the parents of young Barnaby Herrington, who had regaled her with stories of fox hunts and steeplechases at Eleanor's ball.

She knew her aunts and cousins would be there as well. Malcolm Renshaw had sent a note, reminding her and her father that a show of cordiality toward all members of the family was of the utmost importance.

Be cordial to Aunt Louisa?

For the second time, the hairbrush slipped from her fingers.

"Why don't you get a maid?" asked Annie from the bed, where she sat surrounded by half a dozen thick tomes.

"I don't want a maid. I've come to like taking care of myself."

Resolving to avoid her Aunt Louisa whenever possible, Jeannette finished dressing her hair. She clipped a rosette of pearls into the cluster of curls pinned at the crown of her head, then stepped back from the mirror.

Annie clapped her hands, a light, muffled sound like a bird's wings flapping.

"Oh, Lady Caroline! You look ever so lovely."

Jeannette dipped into a curtsy. "Thank you," she smiled back.

As she gathered long white gloves and a dainty, pearl-encrusted reticule from the bed, her gaze fell on the books.

"Why don't you give up, Annie? After all, it is no longer important to find a recipe for a love potion. Messrs. Renshaw and Renshaw have agreed to do nothing until that young man returns from New Orleans."

Annie raised her brows until they all but disappeared beneath the frill of her mobcap. "And who says you wouldn't use the love potion, except to help your pa?"

"What other reason would I have to catch Simon Renshaw's fancy?"

"Don't you like him?"

Jeannette smoothed the gloves over her hands and arms.

Finally, she looked at Annie. "I like him well enough when we're not at loggerheads over Papa. But those occasions have been few and far between."

"Do you like him better than other gentlemen you know?"

No," Jeannette said unhesitatingly. "I like Frederick better. And there were several young men in New Orleans more likeable than Simon Renshaw. To tell the truth, most of the time I find Mr. Renshaw utterly exasperating."

Annie stared at her. Then, with a little sniff, gave her attention to a volume dedicated to the magical powers of herbs, roots, and barks.

Jeannette turned to leave. "Goodbye, Annie."

"Enjoy the party," said Annie. "And if Mr. Renshaw is there, take a good look at him and remember that your pa wants to see you married to an Englishman."

Jeannette did not look back. "I have no desire to marry, and so I told Papa on the ship carrying us over here."

But Annie had the last word.

"And what was it you told your pa only a week ago, in the library? You told him you'd consider marriage if you found a man to love you as well as he had loved your ma!"

Mrs. Herrington had not been pleased when her oldest son demanded that Hugh Dundas and his daughter be invited to the dinner and dance so carefully planned for his sister. But after a look at Barnaby's glowing face Mrs. Herrington had wisely swallowed her objections.

It wasn't the first time that Barnaby had succumbed

to female charm. And, Mrs. Herrington hoped, it wouldn't be the last time either. Barny was too young to fix his interest. She did not want to encourage his dangling after Lady Caroline but knew from experience that opposition at this point would only set up his back. Unfortunately, there was no denying the sad fact that Barnaby, since his younger brother's departure to Portugal, had turned into a very ornery young man.

Thus, the invitation was sent out, and Mrs. Herrington comforted herself with the thought that, if the young lady was indeed the granddaughter of the late Duke of Granby, no harm was done. Lady Caroline Dundas would not be interested in plain Mr. Barnaby Herrington. And if she was an imposter, she'd be shipped back to New York—or whatever outlandish place she had sprung from—before the end of the summer.

However, complacency was short-lived. One glance at the seating arrangements for the dinner table cast her into deep despondency. No rule of etiquette told her in what order to seat the young Duke of Granby and Hugh Dundas, who *should* be the Duke of Granby if he truly was the late duke's son.

And what about Lady Caroline? If her father was indeed the rightful duke, she would take precedence over . . .

Mrs. Herrington groaned, certain that long before the end of her little party her hair would turn pure gray. But it was too late to change the invitation and make it out for the dance only.

So great was her distress that she ventured to disrupt her spouse's perusal of *The Times* on the morning after she had posted the invitation.

Mr. Herrington did not put the paper down while

she recited her woes, but he nodded now and again to show that he was listening. She ended with a plea to seek counsel from the Renshaws, who were also invited to the dinner and dance.

This made Mr. Herrington fold the paper with a snap.

"Margaret," he said severely, "you must have windmills in your head. Why the devil should I seek counsel? This is not an affair of state."

She gave him a reproachful look. "No, indeed, sir. It is only the dinner and dance that will launch your daughter."

Mr. Herrington rose. He had not had his customary third cup of tea, and he no longer desired it.

"If you don't know how to seat them," he said, stalking to the door, "for heaven's sake, get a round table."

A round table. Mr. Herrington might have spoken in exasperation, but his wife latched on to his words as if they were a lifeline. On the morning of her party a huge round table was assembled in her dining room, and that night the female half of the twenty-six dinner guests expressed their delight at the novelty. They were certain Mrs. Herrington had set a new trend.

"It is cozy," admitted Hugh Dundas, seated between his sister, Lady Anne, and Mrs. Effington.

Malcolm Renshaw, beside the tight-lipped Lady Louisa, raised a brow but said nothing.

Jeannette sat between Barnaby Herrington and Frederick, an arrangement that suited her—until she realized that Simon Renshaw's place was almost directly opposite.

To her annoyance, Jeannette instantly remembered Annie's admonition. *Enjoy the party,* the little ghost had said. *And if Mr. Renshaw is there, take a good look at him and remember that your pa wants to see you married to an Englishman."*

Neither of Jeannette's dinner partners was a demanding conversationalist. Barnaby preferred to do the talking himself, as usual about his prowess on the hunting field, and Frederick was too polite or perhaps too shy, to reprimand her when her attention wandered. Thus, Jeannette had ample opportunity to follow Annie's instructions.

If she wished to do so.

Which she definitely did not.

And yet, between murmurs of appreciation directed at Barnaby Herrington at appropriate intervals, her gaze turned to Simon time and again.

She watched his smile, the spark of laughter in his eyes—directed not at her but at Agnes on his right. She watched as he turned to his left and deftly set at ease Barnaby's sister, Miss Vivian Herrington in whose honor the dinner and dance were held.

She could find no fault with his sharply-hewn features, the proud, aquiline nose and square-cut chin. His dark hair was thick and straight, and she thought he would have looked splendid in an age when gentlemen still wore their hair tied back in a queue or a club.

But she wished Annie hadn't mentioned the love potion and the possibility of using it even if her father was safe now that Simon and Malcolm Renshaw had agreed to wait for Mr. Harte's return.

She had not thought of Simon in terms of a prospective suitor—she refused to think of that brief flash of imagination when her father suggested that she find a young Englishman to whom she could give her trust and affection. She had not thought of any gentleman as a suitor since the blinders had abruptly been torn from her unworldly eyes during that Mardi Gras season when she was sixteen years old and betrothed to Raoul Fontenot, and she had no intention of looking for a suitor now—even if Papa had given a solemn oath to take her to England and to see her married to an Englishman.

Her father's responsibility was fulfilled by bringing her to England. The marriage part was *her* responsibility. *She* would have to live with the burden of knowing that the promise to *Maman* had been kept in part only.

She reached for her wine glass, for her mouth was uncomfortably dry. Dash it! With a resolve as firm as hers, the mention of a love potion and the sight of Simon Renshaw across the table should not make her breath grow short. As she had told Annie, there were times when she found him utterly exasperating. Times when he made her so furious that she wanted only to scratch his eyes out.

She once more turned to Frederick. So far she had not tasted a bite of the undoubtedly delicious dinner, and she looked to Frederick to keep her mind off the distracting and disquieting matter of the love potion and her father's wish to see her married.

At ten o'clock, those guests not invited to the dinner started to arrive, and by ten-thirty, the dancing was well under way.

This time, Jeannette's dance card did not fill as quickly as it had at Eleanor's ball, despite her cousins' and Vivian Herrington's efforts to introduce her to all the young gentlemen she had not previously met.

By one o'clock, she had danced with three young men whose only purpose had been to discover her father's finances, one brash youth who told her his mother had forbidden him to dance with her, and a fifth, who turned out to be Barnaby Herrington's best friend and looked as if he had been threatened with the rack if he did not stand up with Lady Caroline.

She had danced twice with Frederick and twice with Barnaby, gratifyingly eager to solicit her hand again and again. But two dances was all she would grant him, even if denying Barnaby meant sitting with the chaperones and matrons. Rules were rules, the same in London as they were in New Orleans.

It was a novel experience for Jeannette to sit out several dances. It was a novel experience, too, to find herself treated with reserve by other young ladies. Her father had told her that the prospect of a ball at Carlton House would work in their favor, but for once he was wrong. Talk of the ball and who might or might not be invited, only helped to make her feel excluded from the laughing, chattering company at Vivian Herrington's dance.

When the musicians struck up the last dance before supper, Jeannette joined Mrs. Effington in a quiet corner. She wished she had the fan her chaperone plied so vigorously. She had pride and composure. She knew her face showed nothing of the chagrin she suffered at not having a partner for the supper dance. But a fan would give her hands something to do, might even release the tension building in her.

"My dear," said Mrs. Effington, "have you seen your father?"

"He and Mr. Renshaw—Mr. Malcolm Renshaw—went off somewhere. That was about an hour ago." Calling herself a coward, Jeannette cast her chaperone a hopeful look. "Are you tired, ma'am? Would you like to go home?"

"No, dear. It is just that . . ." Mrs. Effington's rosy face turned a shade darker, and the fan fluttered more forcefully than ever. "Your papa suggested that he should take me in to supper."

"In that case, he'll be here as soon as the music stops. Papa never forgets an assignation with a lady."

Looking more flustered than before, Mrs. Effington searched her reticule for her smelling salts.

"An assignation! It is nothing of the sort, I assure you, Lady Caroline. Your father is a kind and thoughtful man. He was merely being polite."

Jeannette gave her chaperone a quick hug. "And he'll have a wonderful time being kind and thoughtful and polite. Dear Mrs. Effington, I am a naughty girl, and you mustn't let me tease you."

"I quite agree," said a deep voice behind Jeannette.

A voice, she realized with a strange flutter inside, she had been waiting all evening to address her.

"Good evening, Mr. Renshaw." Slowly, she faced him. "To what do you agree? That I am a naughty girl or that Mrs. Effington mustn't allow me to tease her?"

She was smiling, and for a moment Simon let his gaze linger on the enticing curve of her mouth. But her eyes, he noted, showed signs of strain. They had never looked as deep a blue as this evening. They were the color of sapphires—the color of her silk gown.

Did she know about the sapphires that would have been hers had she truly been the late duchess's granddaughter? Or would she care?

The pearls she wore in her raven hair and around her slender neck were worth a fortune. No doubt, if she asked, her father would shower her with all the sapphires and diamonds her heart desired.

And so, Simon acknowledged wryly, would he.

If only she would finally admit her deception.

Instead of answering her question he asked one of his own. "Will you sup with me, Lady Caroline?"

"Yes."

Terse and to the point. Without a doubt, she was on edge. He wished he knew her well enough to judge whether tension would drive her into a confession or whether it would merely stiffen her resolve to see this game through to the end.

He turned to Mrs. Effington. "With your permission, ma'am?"

Clutching her fan in one hand and the smelling salts in the other, Mrs. Effington gave him a stern look.

"It is high time you took an interest in Lady Caroline. Merely telling people that Lady Louisa didn't mean what she said hasn't helped Lady Caroline one little bit."

"I don't need—" Jeannette started, but Mrs. Effington stopped her with uncharacteristic firmness.

"I beg your pardon, Lady Caroline. But you don't have the first notion about what you need. That young man, Mr. Harte, cannot possibly return from New Orleans before the end of the summer. Do you want to be ogled for the rest of the Season by every loose screw and fortune hunter in town?"

"Mrs. Effington," said Simon. "I can assure you that from now on I shall take the greatest interest in Lady Caroline. No fortune hunter will get close enough to ogle her."

Nor, he thought grimly, would he permit the self-styled Lady Caroline to cast out lures to susceptible young gentlemen of respectable stock.

Chapter Seventeen

Jeannette was still pondering that little scene at Vivian Herrington's dance when she drove out with Archer and Annie the following afternoon. One moment Simon had sounded almost like a gallant, promising to take an interest in her. Not that she wanted him to turn into a gallant—quite the contrary! But it was baffling that the very next moment his face turned harsh.

True to his word, he had stayed close to her for the rest of the night. Every time she was approached by a gentleman, she had felt his eyes on her. Watchful. Intent. And when Barnaby Herrington tried once more to coax a third dance from her, Simon ruthlessly dispatched the young man as if she couldn't have done it on her own—and in a politer and less offensive manner than he.

Wondering what Simon Renshaw was scheming, Jeannette gently pulled on the reins and guided the horses off Watling Street into Beggars Alley. During the past two weeks she had driven Annie so often, she could find the way in her sleep. But once they entered the narrow lane, always dark and cheerless with the high, close buildings blocking the light, she must pay attention to her surroundings lest she wanted to have the reins snatched from her by Archer.

The groom sat stiffly beside her. Until they passed St. Paul's Cathedral, he had kept his arms crossed in front of his chest. But now, in Beggars Alley, he displayed powerful fists resting on his thighs, even though such a show of force was hardly necessary. No longer did the clatter of hooves and the rattle of wheels draw sharp-faced men and women to the doorways. Only the children of Beggars Alley remained unflaggingly curious, scattering before the carriage, then goggling and whispering and pointing.

Jeannette glanced at Annie, huddled between her and Archer. She could hardly see the little ghost, very still and quiet in contrast to earlier visits. If there was such a thing as an ailing ghost, then Annie was it. She said her powers were waning. Jeannette believed it was disappointment that turned Annie into a mere shadow of herself.

They had explored every lane and alley in the area east of St. Paul's, but nowhere had Annie felt the stab of recognition that had pierced her at the sight of the print shop in Beggars Alley, which she still insisted was Basket Lane. And always, as soon as they rounded the bend past the print shop, all sense of recognition fled and Annie quietly asked to be taken back to George Street.

This time, Jeannette had decided to take matters into her own hands. Before Archer realized what she was about, she pulled up in front of the grimy, four-story building with the creaking sign board *Printer* on the ground floor and pressed the reins into the groom's hands.

"I shan't be long, Archer. No need to walk them."

"My lady!"

Horrified but helpless to stop her, he watched as she stepped down onto the filthy cobbles.

"Lady Caroline!" cried Annie, roused from whatever dark thoughts had kept her silent. "Wait for me!"

"Don't let the children come near the horses," Jeannette admonished the groom. "They're still fresh, and I wouldn't want anyone hurt."

Raising the hem of her skirts, she covered the few steps separating her from the print shop's door. The wood was gray with age but fitted tightly into the frame, and the lock was new and shiny.

She pushed down the handle. The door opened silently on oiled hinges, but the tinny clang of a bell heralded her entry into the surprisingly clean and well-lit shop furnished with shelves and several slant-topped counters.

"You're early, Bess." The woman seated at a massive knee-hole desk at the back of the shop did not turn around or stop writing in her ledger. "I told you it would take till evening to print a thousand copies."

"Good afternoon, ma'am." Again the bell's tinny peal rang out as Jeannette closed the door. "I'm afraid I'm not Bess."

"No, indeed." Unhurried, the woman rose. Tall and slender, she moved gracefully despite a limp. Graying blond hair pulled into a tight knot at the base of her neck made no concession to vanity, yet there was beauty in the high forehead and the angle of cheekbone and chin.

"My mistake. I heard a woman's step and made an assumption." Pale eyes measured Jeannette guardedly. "I am Mrs. Hunter, the proprietress. How may I serve you, miss?"

"I wondered if you could tell me about the neighborhood."

Mrs. Hunter's face took on a closed look. "I am a business woman, miss. Not a gossip."

"I'm sorry. I expressed myself badly."

Jeannette stepped farther into the shop. The floor beneath her feet seemed to hum and vibrate. She looked down. "Gracious! What is that?"

"The printing presses are in the basement, miss. You don't hear them because the floor is thick, but you can feel them. Now, if you don't have a print order, you must excuse me, please. We're very busy."

"Ma'am, I promise I won't keep you long. I only have a question or two. And perhaps I can purchase some of your prints. I see you have drawings."

As Jeannette moved closer to one of the slant-topped counters displaying a variety of printed materials, she saw a sheet of paper lifted off the counter by an unseen hand.

Annie! The little ghost would plunge them into a bumble-broth if she didn't watch out.

Quickly, Jeannette grasped the floating paper. She glanced at Mrs. Hunter, but the woman stood half turned away, drumming her fingers on a neighboring counter.

Annie tugged, whispering, "Let go, Lady Caroline. You shouldn't be looking at this."

Not unnaturally, this piqued Jeannette's curiosity. She took a good look—and hastily let go of the sheet. Annie, apparently, let go at the same time. The paper fluttered back onto the countertop and slid until it came to rest against the raised bottom edge.

Face flaming, Jeannette turned away. But the boldly drawn characters were indelibly etched into her mind. Three people. On a four-poster bed canopied with a huge crown. One male, two females draped across him suggestively. *En déshabillé.*

She had not read the lampoon beneath the drawing, only the caption, "Mrs. Fitzherbert and Lady Hertford wooing the Prince Regent." But she expected that the short verse was as lewd and cruel as the illustration.

"Miss." The drumming of Mrs. Hunter's fingers became more forceful, more impatient. "If you'll kindly ask your questions, I'll answer as best I can."

Jeannette walked away from the cartoon. "My groom says this is Beggars Alley, but a friend believes it's properly called Basket Lane. There are no street signs—"

"No," Mrs. Hunter cut in. "They're torn down as soon as they're put up. None of the residents likes the name Beggars Alley. I'm new here. Took over the print shop only two years ago, but I do know that the name Basket Lane hasn't been in use for forty or fifty years."

Jeannette heard Annie's sigh and the soft whisper, "Why don't I recognize anything past the print shop?"

"Mrs. Hunter, do you know of any changes, any reconstruction in this street since the name was changed?"

"No, miss." The woman walked toward the street door, her limp more noticeable because of her haste. "And now, if you'll excuse me?"

Before she could reach the door, it was thrust open from the outside with a jarring peal of the bell. In strode a gentleman, a Corinthian in a coat of brown superfine, his champagne-colored pantaloons tucked into gleaming black Hessian boots.

A pair of keen, gray-green eyes looked straight at Jeannette. Eyes that showed not the least sign of pleasure at their encounter.

"I thought I recognized your phaeton and your groom," Simon Renshaw said coldly. "What the devil are you doing here?"

Jeannette's chin went up.

Predictably so, thought Simon. He had never known a female roused to defiance as quickly as Jeannette, especially when she knew she was in the wrong.

Her voice matched his in coldness. "I hardly think I owe you an explanation for my visit to a print shop."

Mrs. Hunter said quietly, "Good afternoon, Mr. Renshaw. The young lady has come to no harm in my shop."

"Hasn't she, Amelia?"

He did not take his eyes off Jeannette. He could not had he wanted to, and it was damned hard to keep up a severe and disapproving front. Against the drab gray and dun colors of the shop she looked like an exotic flower in her cherry-striped gown and bright red spencer, her long raven curls spilling from beneath a wide-brimmed straw hat tied with cherry-colored ribbons under one ear.

And she was blushing. He'd wager that she had seen some of Amelia's more bawdy prints. But, of course, Amelia would see no harm in that.

Jeannette looked adorable. He wanted to snatch her up in his arms and kiss her until she was breathless. Or until she confessed to her deception. But even more he wanted her to turn to him without coaxing or coercion and admit that she was a scheming little baggage.

Jeannette was looking curiously from Simon to Amelia Hunter. "You know each other? Are you a customer of the print shop, Mr. Renshaw?"

"Mrs. Hunter was a client," he said curtly. "And now, young lady, let's get you out of here."

He firmly clasped her wrist, a high-handed act, reminding Jeannette vividly of a similar encounter at London Docks.

A muffled exclamation came from the back of the shop, then a voice, soft, but clearly audible. "Gorblimey! Will you look at this!"

Amelia Hunter swung around, her eyes darting from one corner of the shop to the other. "You brought someone with you, miss? Your maid?"

"No, ma'am."

Holding her breath, Jeannette watched three sheets of paper lift off Mrs. Hunter's desk, then settle back onto the open ledger. Mrs. Hunter, thank goodness, hadn't been looking that way. She was staring at a counter near the back door. And Simon? Jeannette darted a quick look at his face and just as quickly looked away. He was watching her! And he was clutching her wrist as though he feared she'd escape.

"I don't like illiterates fingering my samples," muttered Amelia Hunter. Once more she scanned the shop. She shook her head. "I could have sworn I heard someone."

"You did," said Simon. "Bess, most likely. She ran down the area steps just as I walked up to the door."

"Bess!"

Amelia swung around to face Simon.

"Is that why you came?" She did not sound pleased. "To speak with Bess?"

"That was my intention." Simon's grip on Jeannette's wrist tightened. "However, I had best see to this young lady first."

"You're hurting me." Jeannette gave him a reproachful look, which made him loosen his grip immediately. But he did not let go.

She scowled. "And you may as well do what you

came to do. I'm quite familiar with the route home."

Ignoring her, he addressed Mrs. Hunter. "I'll be back by seven. Make sure the girl is here."

"Bess has her own mind."

"Then don't try to change it for her, Amelia."

"Isn't that what you are doing?"

Jeannette watched their eyes lock. She was sure a message was exchanged. A warning, perhaps? One thing was certain, the message was not a pleasantry, and yet there was mutual respect in their attitudes.

Very puzzling, indeed.

Chapter Eighteen

"Come along now." Transferring his grip to Jeannette's elbow, Simon steered her toward the door.

She did not resist. There was no point, since she had no notion whom to approach next for information about the history of Beggars Alley or Basket Lane.

Once more the bell emitted its tinny clang, then she was outside the shop. She looked for Annie but saw no sign of the little ghost.

"Up you go." Clasping her waist, Simon swung her effortlessly into the phaeton.

It was not the first time that a gentleman had clasped her waist and lifted her—into a swing or carriage, or off a horse—but it was the first time that a man's touch took her breath away and made her wish he hadn't let go quite so promptly.

She even wished their contact had been closer, warmer. She wondered what it would feel like to be embraced by him.

Nom de nom! Was this what Nounou referred to as a woman's secret yearnings?

Or, perhaps, it was because—despite her resolve to have nothing to do with a husband and marriage—she still had the talk with her father on her mind. And Annie's association of the love potion with Simon Renshaw and the English husband her father wanted her to take.

Her face flamed, and she did not dare look at Simon. Determinedly, she looked at Archer standing at the horses' heads. Beside the groom hovered a bent old woman, wizened and toothless, bundled in a multitude of scarves and shawls. Squinting at Jeannette, she hobbled closer.

"Yer groom says ye want ter know 'bout Basket Lane?"

"Yes, indeed. Glad to give her thoughts a new direction, Jeannette eagerly leaned toward the old woman. "What can you tell me? Is this truly Basket Lane?"

"Used ter be. They try ter tell us different now."

Jeannette fumbled in her reticule for a coin. Have you lived here long?"

"All me life, dearie."

Just as Jeannette's fingers closed around a half crown, Simon pressed a coin into the woman's mittened hand.

"I'm sorry, Selina, but we cannot linger." He climbed up beside Jeannette. "The young lady is in a hurry."

Indignation drove the last vestige of shyness from her mind. Eyes flashing, she faced him. "I am not!"

The old woman chuckled and started to hobble off. "Young 'uns! They's always in a hurry."

"Wait!" cried Jeannette.

"Don't ye fret, dearie." The woman turned her shawl-wrapped head. "Old Selina's in no hurry. I'll be here when ye get back."

Jeannette rounded on Simon. "Just because you seem to know everyone in Basket Lane gives you no right to—"

She broke off when Archer handed Simon the reins and started to walk away.

"Archer!" she said sharply. "Where are you going?"

The groom looked over his shoulder. "Mr. Renshaw said I was to walk home, my lady."

"Nonsense! You take your orders from me, not from Mr. Renshaw. Stand up behind, Archer."

She turned back to Simon. "How dare you! Twice now you've forced me to go with you. I can do nothing about that, since physically you're stronger than I. But I will not permit you to order my groom about."

"At London Docks, I warned Archer not to take you into neighborhoods where a young lady should not be seen."

"But it is none of your concern!"

"You're wrong. Since you claim to be Lady Caroline Dundas, anything you do is very much my concern."

For a moment, she was speechless. Perhaps he had a point. And yet . . . Trying to think of a suitable retort, Jeannette scarcely noticed that Annie settled herself between them.

Simon nodded to Archer, who doffed his cap and walked off.

"Any further arguments, Lady Caroline?" Simon raised a quizzing brow. "Or shall we remove ourselves from the curious eyes and ears of all these urchins?"

"Aye," said Annie, grumpy with disappointment at the mission's lack of success. "Do let's remove ourselves."

Ignoring Annie, Jeannette glanced at the children huddled around the area railing of the next building. Round eyed and utterly silent, which was why she had not noticed them sooner, they stared at Simon.

"I haven't seen them quiet in a long time. They're frightened of you." She gave Simon an accusing look. "Did you rake them over the coals, too? Perhaps you don't like that they're playing in the street, Mr. Renshaw?"

"Those imps frightened? Hardly." He smiled suddenly. "Or, let us say, it wouldn't suit my pride if they're frightened. I prefer to think it's awe that's keeping them quiet. They know I'm trying to save one of their neighbors from the gallows."

"The *gallows*," muttered Annie. "In my day, Basket Lane was a respectable neighborhood."

Jeannette, however, was once more bereft of words. If only she had thought before turning on him. Dash it! She should have remembered what Frederick told her about Simon and some poor fellow he represented at the Court of Old Bailey.

She felt the familiar surge of irritation at having been put in the wrong. Irritation that was directed at herself, yet made her flare up at everyone but her father and grandmother, from whom she had always accepted rebuke, implied or direct. This time, under Simon's look, half quizzical, half rueful, she took a deep breath.

Holding out her hand, she said quietly, "May I have the ribbons? This is my phaeton and I think it's only right that I drive."

"But of course."

Taking the reins, she smartly set the carriage in motion.

She gave Simon a covert look. What was it about him that made her react with such a vast range of emotions in so short a span of time? *Grandmère* had drummed into her head that a lady must be cool and composed at all times. It had seemed a reasonable dictum—until she met Simon Renshaw.

For the present, she had regained composure. Yet how long would it last? The phaeton caught up with old Selina, who gave Jeannette a toothless grin and a wave.

Jeannette waved back. She would have liked to stop and ask the woman's direction but thought it prudent to continue. She would come back. Surely every child in Basket Lane would know where Selina lived.

"Who was that?" asked Annie, who had still been in the print shop when Jeannette spoke with the old woman.

Simon, like Archer, apparently could not hear the ghost—even though both he and Mrs. Hunter had heard the exclamation in the print shop. He sat with his arms crossed, but unlike Archer he was quite relaxed, lounging back against the squabs.

Jeannette could not help but wonder what would happen to his theory that she was playing ghost if she started a conversation with Annie. It was a tempting notion, but perhaps one to be saved for another day.

"There's Archer," said Annie, pointing to the groom striding along briskly some distance ahead. "Why's he walking? Dash it, Lady Caroline! It seems there's lots you'll have to explain when we get home."

And you, too, thought Jeannette. You almost landed us in the basket at the print shop.

To put an end to Annie's distracting chatter, she addressed Simon. "Where is your curricle? Perhaps you should have asked Archer to drive it back for you."

"I never drive when I come here." He looked at her, and his harsh features softened. "Believe me, Jeannette. Your groom will take no harm from the walk."

"I know he won't. But you should not punish him for obeying my orders."

"Then, perhaps, the next time you will think twice before issuing an order?"

Slowing the horses to a crawl, she rounded the last bend in the narrow, twisting alleyway before it turned straight as an arrow pointed toward Cheapside. She reined in sharply. As she had feared, children were playing in the middle of the lane.

Watching the youngsters scramble for the safety of a stoop, she said, "You may be the Dundas family solicitor, Simon. But what I do or don't do is for me and my father to decide."

She flicked the reins. The horses, sensing the greater freedom of a wider thoroughfare nearby, pulled ahead eagerly.

Simon turned on the seat to get a better look at her.

"And does your father know where you're exercising your horses? Did you tell him you were planning a stop at a print shop of the shadiest reputation? And what about your chaperone?"

"Ha!" said Annie.

Jeannette's face stung. Mrs. Effington always rested after luncheon, the time Jeannette had chosen for her drives with Annie. Her father, if he was not out with Lord Decimus, was closeted in the library. Resting, she always told herself and virtuously tiptoed past the closed door.

And she didn't dare think of the print shop with the "shady reputation." That bawdy drawing! But the worst part was that Simon *knew.*

"Oh, pother! Why must you always be so aggravatingly perceptive?"

She heard his soft chuckle, then the deep voice that could, at times, sound like a caress.

"To see you blush so delightfully."

For just an instant she took her eyes off the road to catch a glimpse of the smile which she felt sure accompanied the words. And in that short span of time, a scream from somewhere inside a house pierced the air, startling the horse on the off side. It reared and bucked, jolting the carriage, then came down with one hind foot over the traces.

She acted instinctively, shortening the reins and pulling with all her might.

A second scream shrilled out, louder than before. A woman hurtled from a doorway on the left and darted into the lane directly in front of the phaeton.

"Gorblimey," whispered Annie.

One moment the woman was running, the next she lay in a crumpled heap on the cobbles. Jeannette did not know whether she stumbled and fell or whether one of the flaying hooves struck her, but she did know she could not hold the horses much longer.

And then Simon's hands were in front of hers on the reins. She felt the strength of his arms against hers, the powerful muscles of his shoulder as he leaned close.

"Slowly let go," he said.

She obeyed gratefully and before the phaeton had stopped rocking, jumped down into the street. She ran to the woman's side. Annie was already there, clucking in distress.

"Her head's bleeding," said Annie.

The young woman, scarcely older than Jeannette, lay alarmingly still. The part of her face that could be seen was chalky white and streaked with blood. The back of her gown was torn from the neck down, exposing several lacerations.

Jeannette knelt on the cobbles and gently wiped the girl's face with her handkerchief. The cut did not seem very deep. What worried her more was the closeness of the horses, calmer now, but still snorting and stamping restlessly despite Simon's efforts to quiet them with a steady flow of soothing words. Some horses, she knew, were driven wild by the smell of blood.

She looked for Archer, but the groom must have turned into Cheapside before the commotion in Beggars Alley started.

A few women with toddlers clinging to their skirts gathered nearby.

"Please keep the children away," said Jeannette, rising. "But I'd appreciate the help of one of you. I must get this poor girl out of the street."

"They don't look like they'll be much help," said Annie. "They don't look strong enough to carry their own little nippers."

After a whispered consultation, two women came forward.

"We'll carry 'er," said the taller, sturdier of the two. "If you'll tell us where, miss."

The other, small and pitifully thin, pointed her chin at the house from which the injured girl had run. "Heard 'er scream, I did. Don't think she'd want ter find 'erself back in there."

One of the horses nudged Jeannette's back, and she reached out to stroke the soft neck while she looked at the house in question.

A woman stood in the open doorway. A statuesque woman in a low-cut black gown. Her face was painted, her hennaed hair elaborately curled and styled. From behind the woman came the sound of laughter. Female voices, high and shrill, mingling with the deeper, sonorous voices of gentlemen.

"Jeannette!" Simon called from the phaeton's perch. "Why the deuce don't you move that girl?"

The girl chose that moment to stir and moan. Instantly, Jeannette and the two women knelt down to help her into a sitting position. She cried out once, then opened her eyes.

"Bloody hell," she said, darting quick looks around her. "Didn't get far, did I?"

Chapter Nineteen

"Come now, luv." The sturdier of Jeannette's assistants placed her hands beneath the girl's armpits. "Let's see if ye can stand as well as talk."

But whatever burst of willpower or energy had made her speak up now deserted the girl. Like a puppet, she allowed them to shift and move her until she stood, supported by three pairs of hands.

"Can you help me get her into the carriage?" asked Jeannette.

The women nodded. Half lifting the girl, they slowly approached the side of the phaeton. At the same time the red-haired woman left the doorway. Followed by two strapping men in leather breeches and black waistcoats over homespun linen shirts, she stalked toward them.

"And now we're in the suds," said Annie.

"Miss!" The woman's mouth was an angry red slash in a white-powdered face. "How dare you steal my girl! Isabella! You come here this instant."

The injured girl darted a scared look at the woman and the two silent, beef-faced men behind her. She started to shake.

"Isabella!"

Suddenly, Jeannette alone was supporting the girl.

Her assistants had melted away and stood with a handful of spectators at a safe distance.

"Jeannette." Simon's voice was as firm as his grip on the reins. "Let the girl go."

"I beg your pardon?" Brow puckering, she looked up at him. "What did you say?"

"Let her go."

"I most certainly will not!"

She tightened her hold on the girl's waist. "Isabella? Is that your name? Put a foot on the step. I'll help you into the carriage."

But the girl did not move.

"Twice in the suds," muttered Annie. "Lady Caroline, there's no telling what will happen if you interfere with that woman and her henchmen. Perhaps you had better listen to Mr. Renshaw just this once."

"No!" said Jeannette, forgetting that most likely no one else had heard the ghost.

Simon frowned, but she could not tell whether the frown was directed at her or at the woman in the low-cut black gown who stopped, arms akimbo, directly in front of her and Isabella.

"That's kidnapping." The woman's formidable bosom heaved. "I'll set the law on you."

"Very well, do so. But perhaps I had better warn you that I am Lady Caroline Dundas, cousin of the Duke of Granby. The gentleman in the phaeton is Mr. Renshaw, the duke's solicitor. He's also a barrister, well known at the Court of Old Bailey, and he's taking note of everything you say."

Simon groaned. But the woman, kohl-rimmed eyes widening, took a step backward.

"Don't think you can frighten me with talk of dukes and barristers and the Old Bailey! I'm not the one stealing a girl. And I have a very good lawyer of my own, I tell you." With a toss of her head, she indicated the two men behind her. "And friends, willing to help a lady when someone's trying to take advantage."

"Lady Caroline," said Simon, at his most reasonable, "you're not helping the girl."

He did not feel reasonable, though. Only impatient to have Jeannette safely in the phaeton. If he were alone, he would not fear a confrontation with the madam and her bruisers. He'd even get Isabella away.

But he could not let go of the reins, and he must extract the bloody horse from the traces before he could take Jeannette out of Beggars Alley, where she had no business being in the first place. And where, most particularly, the bothersome chit had no business setting herself up as the champion of a member of the muslin company.

"You're only creating more problems for Miss Isabella," he said. "Let her go. Now."

"He's right." Isabella trembled like an aspen leaf. "If I don't go back to her now, no matter where I hide, Mrs. Pelham will send her thugs after me. And next time they'll kill me."

Mrs. Pelham shot Isabella a furious look. "I don't know what you're talking about, gal. But I do know that my patience is running out."

"And if that ain't a threat," said Annie, flitting about as if preparing to thrust herself between Jeannette and Mrs. Pelham if necessary, "my name's Princess Charlotte."

Keeping a wary eye on Mrs. Pelham's brawny escorts as they inched closer, Simon reached out with one arm in an attempt to drag Jeannette into the phaeton. But his fingertips barely brushed the top of her shoulder.

She turned her head, giving him a questioning look.

"Jeannette," he said softly. "You heard me tell Amelia

Hunter that I'll be back tonight. Let the girl go. I promise I'll check up on her later."

Jeannette held the girl more tightly. "You don't want to go back, do you?"

"What does it matter what I want?" Isabella gave the slightest of shrugs. "It never made no difference before."

"That settles it." Jeannette faced Simon. "She's not going back. Don't you know what that woman—that Mrs. Pelham is?"

Simon stared at her. Did he *know?* Devil a bit! It was Jeannette who should know nothing about Mrs. Pelham and women like her.

"She is an abbess, Simon! And I am not speaking of the superior of a convent." Outrage sharpened Jeannette's voice. "This woman is running a house of prostitution."

"Miss!" sputtered Mrs. Pelham. "I'll thank you to watch your language. I'm a respectable woman, I'll have you know."

Neither Jeannette nor Simon paid her the slightest heed.

"So, you see, Simon?" Jeannette turned wide, trusting eyes on him. "We simply cannot send poor Isabella back. Why, it would be the shabbiest thing when it was my fault that she did not succeed in running away!"

He knew he was defeated. Merely by looking at him she had stifled every argument he might have used to impress upon her the foolishness of interfering between a madam and one of her girls.

"Get in, then. And, for goodness' sake, hold the horses steady while I disentangle them from the traces."

Simon stood up in the phaeton, showing off his height and the width of his shoulders to the two bruisers.

"It's kidnapping!" screeched Mrs. Pelham.

But she was a shrewd woman, and she was not prepared to tangle with a duke's cousin and a gentleman with the build of a pugilist. Isabella, after all, was easily replaced. Not so her two trusted henchmen if they ended up with broken bones or bashed heads. Barrister or not, that Mr. Renshaw looked ready to fight with a vengeance if her men took a step too close to that Lady Caroline.

Head high, Mrs. Pelham stalked off, followed with obvious reluctance by the bruisers.

Isabella's story as she told it during the drive to George Street was not uncommon. The only one of six children surviving infancy, she had been respectably brought up by parents who owned a greengrocer's shop in Aldersgate Street.

She had attended school as a day boarder at an establishment run by two genteel spinsters in Kensington. When she left the girls academy at the age of seventeen, it was with the understanding that within a year she would marry the son of the fishmonger next door, thereby uniting the two businesses. Tragically, a week before the wedding, an influenza epidemic swept the neighborhood.

Isabella had been spared, but her parents and her betrothed fell victim to the epidemic. When she returned from the joint funerals, a hurried affair because the attending cleric had many more such burials on his agenda, she found that the physician's services, the night nurse's and mortician's fees had swallowed her inheritance.

She did not understand how her parents' brief but violent illness could have cost so much. But the bills were there and had to be paid, even if it meant selling home and store.

Eighteen years old, devastated by the loss of parents and betrothed, without a roof over her head, uncertain how to put her knowledge of reading, writing, and arithmetic to use in a world where clerks were male and governesses had a pedigree as long as that of her employers, Isabella was easy prey for Mrs. Pelham.

The woman, saying she ran a domestic agency, combed the sickness-riddled streets and alleys north of Cheapside for girls who had lost home and family. She offered board and lodging until the girls could be placed in a suitable position. She asked no payment, only the girls' promise to undergo a certain amount of training for their future employment.

But the "training" Mrs. Pelham offered was not to Isabella's liking. She'd had a dream of marriage and children and was reluctant to give it up. When she protested that she'd rather keep books than "keep company" with lecherous gentlemen, Mrs. Pelham told her not to be silly. This was the position she offered, and Isabella had better conform.

Isabella packed her meager belongings, placed two of the thirteen shillings she owned on the pillow shared with another girl from Aldersgate Street as payment for supper and one night's sleep, and walked out of Mrs. Pelham's house. She had not reached the corner of Cheapside when Mrs. Pelham's bruisers caught up with her.

That had been the first of more than a dozen attempts to run away. Each time, Isabella was caught. Each time, punishment was more severe than the time before, until she had all but given up.

"Don't know what made me try again this day," said Isabella, looking over her shoulder as if she expected a hot-footed pursuit of the phaeton. "Christmas was the last time I ran away, and they almost killed me. I swore then I wouldn't ever try again."

"Can't blame her," said Annie, standing up behind the seat. "Those welts on her back don't look like hoof scratches to me."

Jeannette had given her spencer to Isabella to cover the torn back of her gown. She, too, wondered about the lacerations and, remembering the screams, concluded that someone had beaten the girl.

"Well, I'm glad you ran away again," she said. "And I promise I'll find you a safe place, even if it has to be outside London."

She adjusted the makeshift bandage around Isabella's head—Jeannette's folded handkerchief tied in place with Simon's cravat—then put her arm around the girl's waist to brace her against the jolting of the carriage.

Simon kept his eyes on the crush of carriages and wagons as he guided the phaeton along busy Cheapside toward Oxford Street. He had heard stories like Isabella's before, and they never failed to rouse pity and a deep-seated anger at a society in which the vulnerable had no protection against vultures like Mrs. Pelham.

Isabella's tale held no surprise for him. What did astonish him was Jeannette's concern for the girl. Most ladies would have turned up their noses at someone in Isabella's position.

"Did no one warn you against the woman?" he asked. "Your friends? The neighbors who would have been your in-laws?"

"No, sir. Though I don't doubt they would have, if they had known. But there was so much sickness. Everyone was mourning the dead or nursing the sick. No one had time to worry about anyone else."

"Relatives? Was there no one who might have given you shelter?"

"Only my mother's parents. They live in Lancaster. Thirteen shillings did not pay for a stagecoach ticket."

"Would you like to go to Lancaster?" asked Jeannette.

Isabella did not reply but cast a wary look at Simon on her right.

He caught the look. "No need to be leery of me, Isabella. It had nothing to do with you personally that I did not want Lady Caroline to take you up. I merely didn't want her to fall afoul of Mrs. Pelham and her bruisers."

The girl nodded. "And, I suppose, you also thought I'd change my mind in a day or so, and all Lady Caroline's trouble would be for nothing."

"Nonsense," said Jeannette. "Girls in your position only change their minds if they do not find alternative employment."

Simon gave her a startled look. Once more she had astonished him.

"How the deuce did you learn so much about girls in Isabella's position?"

"It is not difficult to learn about people."

"But most ladies—" Encountering Jeannette's fierce stare, he said hastily, "I'm not implying you're *not* a lady. But, devil a bit! Most ladies *don't* know about . . . girls like Isabella."

"I think you're wrong. Ladies are aware of street girls and bawdy houses," said Jeannette, uninhibited by the scruples that did not allow Simon to use plain language.

For once, he didn't know what to say, which was probably for the best, since Jeannette had not finished.

"And they're aware of the discreet little houses in discreet neighborhoods where the more fortunate girls are set up by wealthy protectors. The truth is, some ladies do not want to admit—even to themselves—what they see and know. Because if they did, they might feel compelled to do something about it. And others pretend they don't know because ignorance is expected of them."

Confounded, Simon kept his eyes on the road.

"There!" said Annie. "Now you've gone and done it. You've utterly shocked Mr. Renshaw. Didn't I warn you not to speak so plainly of delicate matters?"

Jeannette wanted to tell Annie that she didn't give a straw she had shocked Simon. But she couldn't even convince herself. Not with disappointment at his silence gnawing at her.

She squared her shoulders. Too bad, but there was yet another shock in store for him.

"Isabella, I want to help you. Before I came to London I lived in New Orleans, and there—about three years ago—I set up a dressmaker's shop. It is staffed by girls who don't want to work in a house of prostitution or be a man's mistress. I've decided to do something similar here. Would you like to work as a dressmaker or a milliner?"

Isabella, who had been leaning heavily against Jeannette, drooped even more. But Jeannette scarcely noticed. She was watching Simon.

He was approaching the turn into Orchard Street but gave her one quick look. It was not a shocked look. She saw interest and something else. The warmth of admiration.

"Watch out!" cried Annie. "The girl's about to swoon. Don't let her tumble off."

With a guilty start, Jeannette secured her hold on Isabella.

Simon, having just pointed the horses into the turn, reached out with one hand and clasped Isabella's shoulder.

"Great Scot, Jeannette! I won't let her tumble off, but you ought to know better than to set up a screech in the middle of a turn."

She sat dumbfounded. He had heard Annie.

"This pair is quite a handful," he said. "I plan to have a talk with your father. It is my opinion that the horses are too frisky for you to handle."

Recovering quickly, she gave him an indignant look.

"They're not too frisky for me! But if they're too much for you, best keep both hands on the reins."

He said nothing, merely urged the blacks to greater speed. Portman Square flashed by. Then came the turn into George Street.

"I must talk to you," said Simon as he pulled up in front of her home. "In private. I don't doubt that for the rest of the afternoon you'll have your hands full looking after Isabella. And tonight, as you know, I must get back to Beggars Alley."

"Basket Lane," Annie muttered.

Simon frowned. "I beg your pardon?"

"I did not say anything." Jeannette gave Annie a quelling look.

The front door opened and the footmen rushed out.

Jeannette directed one to take Isabella up to the small chamber next to her own and to fetch the housekeeper and a maid, and told the other to take the phaeton and fetch a physician.

"But, my lady!" The young footman looked aghast. "I don't know how to handle a pair. I can only lead them."

"Then take the carriage to the mews." Relieved of Isabella's weight, she stepped down from the phaeton. "If Archer is there, send him. If he's not yet back, you'll have to walk because I want a physician immediately."

"Yes, my lady." Meekly, he accepted the reins from Simon and led the horses away.

Jeannette turned to Simon. "You said you wished to speak with me. Very well. I exercise my mare every morning at seven. You may meet me in Hyde Park. Rotten Row."

He raised a brow. "I shall do nothing of the kind. I'll call for you *here*. At seven."

Chapter Twenty

Alas, the unpredictable English weather put paid to any and all outings planned for the following day. A heavy thunderstorm accompanied by torrential rains broke in the middle of the night. Thunder and lightning eventually abated, but the rain kept pouring down. A keen wind blew from the northeast, and the temperatures plummeted.

Awakened at six by dagger-sharp raps against the window panes, Jeannette scrambled out of bed. Incredulous, she blinked at sheets of ice falling from the sky and glazing the cobbles below. Shimmering icicles hung from the eaves of the opposite houses. It was unbelievable.

In contrast to previous mornings the street was deserted. No milkman with his cart. No baker's boy with his baskets. No maids scrubbing front steps and areaways.

Her spirits sank. No ride in the park.

She opened the window and cautiously stuck out a hand only to pull it back in a hurry when she felt the needle pricks of ice.

"Gorblimey," she muttered, borrowing Annie's favorite exclamation. "I don't believe this."

One exceptionally cold January morning she had seen ice and a few snowflakes in New Orleans. But May? She could not imagine what England must be like in winter, if ice could form in mid-May.

And Papa expected her to marry and live in this country.

By eleven, ice rain had changed to plain, ordinary rain. But the feeling of heaviness that had settled over Jeannette did not ease. She could not remember a single day in her life when she had felt quite so glum and listless and yet strangely restless. Not even when she learned of Raoul Fontenot's visit to the quadroon ball had she been quite as blue-deviled as on this dark, cold day.

At eleven-thirty, a messenger delivered a note from Simon Renshaw and a flower wrapped in layers of tissue.

It was a white camellia.

Shivering in the long-sleeved wool gown she had dragged from the back of her closet, Jeannette cradled the delicate bloom in her hands.

Simon couldn't possibly have known how much she liked camellias. But she had told him when he drove her home from the docks that she missed springtime in New Orleans.

And he had remembered. His note said, *Apologies for the weather and a ride postponed. I cannot give you a spring as you knew it in New Orleans, but I can give you this camellia and hope it will bring memories that will see you through an English spring.*

Foolishly, a tear gathered in her eye. She had not believed it possible that he could be so thoughtful.

So why was she turning into a watering pot? The flower should have made her feel better, but she could think only of the missed ride. Touching the camellia to her cheek, she blinked away the treacherous moisture.

"The fire smokes atrociously today," said Mrs. Effington, her gaze resting pensively on Jeannette.

"Yes, it does." Jeannette snatched at the excuse for watering eyes. "I wonder if it is because we're using coal in this room?"

They were sitting in the small front parlor, and on this day even Mrs. Effington had pulled a chair close to the fireplace.

"Wood or coal, it makes no difference on a wet day," she said. "Somehow, there never seems to be enough draft to draw the smoke up the chimney. Is that flower from Mr. Renshaw?"

"Yes, in apology for the weather. Where on earth could he have found it? I didn't think camellias grew anywhere in England."

"Is that a camellia? I always wondered what they looked like." Setting aside her embroidery, Mrs. Effington leaned forward for a better look.

Politely, Jeannette handed her the short wooden stem with its glossy dark leaves and large white bloom. How foolish to feel such reluctance to let go.

"Camellias do well in parts of Cornwall," said Mrs. Effington. "Sophronia Aldrich told me she planted them around the terrace of her St. Ives home. But Mr. Renshaw, I daresay, knows someone who grows them in a forcinghouse."

She gave the flower back to Jeannette. "Very pretty. And a very pretty gesture from Mr. Renshaw. One might think he's courting you."

"Fudge!" Jeannette's voice was sharp. Too sharp.

Moderating her tone, she changed the subject. "I'm worried about Isabella. I know Dr. Moore assured us she's not seriously hurt, but she was still asleep when I looked in on her at ten. And she must be asleep now, else the maid would have come to fetch me. Surely that is not normal?"

"Did she seem feverish?"

"She did not look flushed, and her forehead was cool to the touch."

"Then I shouldn't worry." Mrs. Effington resumed her embroidery, a tablecloth for her niece's trousseau. "Sleep is a powerful healer, and not necessarily of physical ailments alone."

Jeannette nodded. She trusted Mrs. Effington's judgment. The chaperone had accepted Isabella's arrival with amazing calm. She had helped undress the girl and clucked over the welts on her back. She had received Dr. Moore and assisted him in dressing Isabella's wounds. And she had not uttered one word of condemnation when Jeannette later explained where Isabella had spent the past eighteen months.

"What will you do with her when she's recovered?" Mrs. Effington peered at the needle she was trying to thread. "If you simply let her go, she'll end up with that Mrs. Fulham again. Or worse."

"Mrs. Pelham," Jeannette corrected absently.

She placed the camellia in a slender crystal vase the footman had carried in along with the flower.

"Mrs. Effington, did Papa tell you about the dressmaker's establishment I own in New Orleans?"

"No. Should he?"

The plump, elderly lady frowned suddenly. "A dressmaker's establishment? Lady Caroline, if that is where you had your gowns made, you ought to send some fashion plates to New Orleans. Everything you brought with you is horribly outmoded!"

Jeannette's mood lightened. Dear Mrs. Effington. No raised brow at the news that her charge was the proprietress of a dressmaker's shop. Only a prosaic recommendation to send fashion plates.

"An excellent notion," she said. "But listen now while I tell you about the *boutique* and the women who run it."

Long before Jeannette finished, Mrs. Effington had set aside her embroidery. Her rather sleepy eyes opened wide when she heard about the young women of color, many of whom spent several years in France—an arrangement paid for by their Creole fathers—and returned to New Orleans as well or better educated than Creole ladies.

Mrs. Effington's mouth pursed when Jeannette told about the "placement" arranged by the girls' mothers, a contract of concubinage with a Creole gentleman. Then, and it was often at a quadroon ball, the girl and the prospective protector met for the first time and the arrangements were finalized.

"Some of these relationships last for years," said Jeannette. "When they break up, the young woman may keep the house she lives in, and a fund is set up for the education of her children. It all depends on the terms of the contract negotiated by the mother—well before the girl ever met her protector."

"And then?" asked Mrs. Effington, fascinated. "Does the woman look for another protector when the relationship breaks up?"

"Rarely. Some of the women eventually marry a free man of color. Others, if they have the resources, start a business."

Jeannette took a deep breath. "And still others simply . . . exist. Even though they should have known better, they convinced themselves that their relationship was different, permanent. They're devastated when they're cast off."

Absently running her fingers along the camellia

petals, Jeannette said, "Some now work in the *boutique*. Their embroidery and needlework are exquisite. And they're wonderfully patient with the very young girls who have come to the shop because they'd do anything rather than be "placed" and live in one of those pretty little houses near the ramparts. Even during the years they're pampered and showered with gifts by their protector, it's a lonely life. And when the gentleman marries . . ."

"Yes, I see," said Mrs. Effington. "But wouldn't the younger girls rather marry one of the free men of color than become a seamstress?"

Jeannette shrugged. "Not many of the marriages turn out well. It's the difference in upbringing, I suppose. The quadroons are raised and educated as ladies. Free men of color are artisans, mostly."

"Still, a seamstress—"

"At the *boutique* they're independent of any man's whim," Jeannette cut in. "That, I believe, is what draws them most. They're devout Catholics, and there has been talk of a convent for free women of color. But it is only talk so far."

Mrs. Effington opened her mouth and immediately closed it again tightly.

But Jeannette had seen.

"You were about to say that entering a convent is a drastic step, weren't you?" She smiled at her chaperone. "The Mother Superior of the Ursuline Convent would agree with you. She has been a staunch supporter of my little enterprise because she believes that very few women are cut out to be a nun."

"Yes, indeed." Mrs. Effington snapped open the fan which was never far from her reach and fanned herself briskly.

"Am I correct, then, that you want to start a dressmaker's shop here in London for girls who want to escape the streets and the fleshpots?"

Jeannette had no trouble understanding the term fleshpot. She did, however, blink at hearing it from her chaperone's mouth.

"Yes. That is my intention."

"Good. I'll help you. Just tell me this: Do any of the Creole ladies come to the *boutique* to order their gowns or do they avoid the place?"

"Of course they order their gowns at Marie's. You may think our styles outmoded, but I assure you we are quite the best establishment in New Orleans."

"You call it Marie's?"

"After my first employee. Marie is the manageress and top *couturière*. Nounou, my old nurse, is in charge of the girls' residence above the shop."

"And do the quadroons also go to Marie's for their gowns?"

"They do." Jeannette met her chaperone's gaze squarely. "We have a separate entrance and fitting rooms—just as some London dressmakers have a separate entrance and fitting rooms for courtesans."

Mrs. Effington nodded. "A clever arrangement. And now, my dear, I have only one more question. Your papa does not object to your enterprise?"

"Not at all. I was not quite seventeen when I opened the *boutique*. Without Papa's help I wouldn't have known how to go about it."

"Good. Then we need only consider what your future husband might think about your scheme."

"My future—"

Suddenly it was impossible to sit still any longer. Jeannette rose. She snatched up the poker and stabbed at the glowing coal.

The act of aggression calmed her. She restored the poker to its stand and faced her chaperone.

"Mrs. Effington, I have no intention of marrying."

"Nonsense. Lord Luxton told me distinctly that your marriage to an Englishman was the purpose of your visit."

Jeannette did not argue. Instead, she asked a question that had hovered at the back of her mind for some time.

"Do English gentlemen habitually take a mistress?"

The older woman hesitated. She dug out her vinaigrette and, after a fortifying whiff of the aromatic salts, looked up at Jeannette.

"My dear, since you have no mama to tell you the facts of life, will you permit me to speak frankly?"

"By all means."

"Very well. English gentlemen do take mistresses, but any woman worth her salt will see to it that the gentleman of her choice does not continue to see his *chère amie* after marriage."

"How?"

"By not behaving like a shrinking violet in the marriage bed."

Jeannette's mouth formed a silent "oh."

"More often than not these days, a marriage is founded on mutual affection. Young ladies 'fall in love,' and the gentlemen confess themselves 'head over heels.' In my day, a young lady was told that falling in love is vulgar, that showing enthusiasm in the marriage bed is a sign of wantonness. I say, fudge!"

Jeannette almost jumped, so forceful was her chaperone's tone.

Mrs. Effington continued. "In New Orleans you have the quadroon balls. Here we have the balls of the fashionable impures—although I doubt the two are comparable. From all you've told me, I gather that a quadroon ball is a pattern plate of decorum. A ball of the fashionable impures is a masquerade, a disgraceful romp. But it serves the same purpose. Gentlemen attend to find a high-flyer to take under their protection. What a young bride must do is see to it that her husband has no hankering for an opera dancer or a west-end comet. Do you follow me, Lady Caroline?"

"Yes, ma'am," said Jeannette, overwhelmed.

"Then we'll have no more talk of not wishing to get married. What happened to you in New Orleans is best forgotten—and I do hope, Lady Caroline, you understand that your papa had your best interest at heart when he mentioned the broken betrothal to me."

Again Jeannette could say only, "Yes, ma'am."

"I don't mean to set myself up as a matchmaker, Lady Caroline. However, I cannot help but think that Mr. Renshaw, once he gets over this ridiculous notion that your father is an imposter, would make an admirable husband."

Jeannette swallowed. First Annie, then Mrs. Effington pointed to Simon as a prospective husband. Now she needed only her father to single out Simon Renshaw as the Englishman she was to marry.

"He's eligible," said the chaperone. "Unless you're looking for rank and title?"

"No, indeed. I—"

"He's wealthy."

Jeannette's eyes widened. "He is?"

"Inherited his grandfather's estates and factories. If Simon Renshaw is not as rich as Croesus, he comes awfully close."

Jeannette no longer shivered. Her face flamed, and she felt hot all over. Perhaps she stood too close to the fire.

Moving away from the heat did not help, she found. After taking refuge behind a tall screen, she still burned. Not only had she taxed Simon with expensive habits and taste in sports, carriages, and clothing, but she had accused him of conspiring with Frederick for a share of the Dundas fortune. She should have known better.

"He may not be as good looking as the young duke," said Mrs. Effington. "But in my younger days I always preferred a dark, rugged kind of man to a blond Adonis. Don't you agree, Lady Caroline, that Mr. Renshaw's looks are quite appealing?"

Didn't she! Jeannette had never denied Simon's appeal. But admit it, she would not.

Mrs. Effington did not need confirmation. After a look at Jeannette's face, she nodded wisely.

"Simon Renshaw is a man upon whom a young lady may unhesitatingly bestow her trust—and her affection."

"Trust, perhaps," murmured Jeannette.

She remembered the many occasions she had trusted Simon. At times against her better judgment, and other times—as in Beggars Alley when she trusted him to help Isabella—quite spontaneously.

"But don't you see, Mrs. Effington? Because he refuses to believe Papa and me, I could never hold him in affection, let alone marry him!"

Mrs. Effington, however, was listening to something other than Jeannette's protest.

"It's quiet outside," she said. "The wind is no longer blowing. Do you think the rain has stopped as well?"

Jeannette flew to the window. She flung the drapes wide.

"Yes, indeed! The rain has stopped. It looks as though the sun wants to come out."

Again that strange, unfamiliar restlessness assailed her. This time, she knew why.

The ride with Simon. He said he wanted to speak with her. In private.

"Mrs. Effington, how long do you think it will take for the park to dry out?"

Chapter Twenty-one

Jeannette had been overly optimistic. The sun, if it did want to come out, did not try very hard to break through the cloud cover. The rain, when it stopped, started up again after scarcely five minutes. It was damp and cold, though not freezing, and Jeannette kept wearing her New Orleans winter gowns.

For days she stayed in the house, dividing her time between Annie, Isabella, Mrs. Effington, and her father. And that was how she made a discovery that at first startled her, then made her chuckle appreciatively. Her father and Mrs. Effington were not, as she had assumed, resting after luncheon. They met instead in the small sitting room on the first floor to play piquet. The chaperone, it turned out, was quite as fond of cards as was Hugh Dundas.

Annie, after hearing about old Selina, was eager to return to Basket Lane and chafed under the delay imposed by the weather. The little ghost was mopish, spending most of her time in Jeannette's bedchamber, and only once showed a spark of her old bubbling nature.

It was late at night, and Jeannette's eyes were just

about to close when a screech from Annie brought her wide awake.

"I've got it, Lady Caroline! The recipe for the love potion!"

Jeannette sat up. The bedside table lamp, which she remembered dimming before she climbed into bed, shone brightly and in its glow there was no mistaking Annie's wildly dancing shape.

"Annie, we don't need the love potion any longer."

"Yes, we do. Your pa wants you to marry an Englishman. So you might as well marry one you can fancy."

"I don't fancy Mr. Renshaw."

Annie looked sly. "Who said anything about Mr. Renshaw? But he seems to be on your mind, so I'm willing to lay my money on him."

Jeannette threw a pillow, which, of course, went right through Annie.

"If Mr. Renshaw is on my mind, it's because you and Mrs. Effington won't allow me to forget about him."

"Here." Annie thrust a tablet of paper and a pencil at Jeannette. "Write down the ingredients we don't have in the house. Tomorrow morning one of the maids must go to the apothecary's."

Annie's eagerness, the air of vitality surrounding her, stopped any further protest from Jeannette. If it would keep her from moping, the little ghost could brew as many potions as she liked.

Jeannette wrote down mistletoe—specifically, mistletoe taken off an oak. Then, syrup of cinnamon, powdered pomegranate, essence of rose and lime tree blossoms, and sweet woodruff.

She refused to add syrup of poppy to the list.

"That is opium, Annie. It not only induces sleep, it is quite addictive besides. I'll not have such horrid stuff in the house."

Annie argued that she would use only a drop or two, that the recipe wouldn't be the same without it, then, abruptly, gave in.

"Very well. Just see to it, please, that I have everything else first thing in the morning."

Jeannette gave her a sharp look, but Annie seemed so happy and content that Jeannette dismissed any suspicion over the sudden capitulation, and the following morning, when she tried to capture Isabella's interest with talk of the dressmaker's shop she planned to open, syrup of poppy was the last thing on her mind.

Isabella was not mopish like Annie, but she was quiet and did not want to leave the tiny room which had been an airing closet before the shelves were removed and a cot and window installed.

"I wouldn't feel right joining you and that nice lady, Mrs. Effington, in the drawing room." Isabella's gaze strayed to a pile of books Jeannette had brought up from the library. "And I've never had the leisure to do much reading. I'd just as soon stay here, if you don't mind, until you've decided what to do with me."

"But I want you to help make the decision. If you like, you may go to your grandparents in Lancaster. Or, if you prefer, you may learn dressmaking."

"I'm not a good seamstress, Lady Caroline."

Something in the girl's tone caught Jeannette's attention.

"Isabella, is it that you do not like sewing?"

"I'm sorry." The girl hung her head. "I don't want to be any trouble after all you've done for me."

"It's no trouble. I want to do what's right for you. What about Lancaster, then?"

"I'd like to see my grandparents. Only . . . I'm a little scared, Lady Caroline."

"But why? Are they not kind?"

"I don't know. You see, I've never met them. All I know is that they weren't too happy when my mother decided to leave and try her luck in London."

Daunted but not defeated, Jeannette said, "Perhaps, at first, you could go for just a visit."

"Perhaps. But in the meantime, while I'm here, isn't there something I can do for you? I'm very good at accounts if the housekeeper will let me have the books."

"At present, I'd rather you rested," said Jeannette, who doubted that the housekeeper would welcome anyone's assistance with the household accounts.

As she went downstairs to join her father and Mrs. Effington for a game of three-handed whist, she remembered Isabella saying after her rescue that she would rather keep books than "keep company" with lecherous gentlemen. Perhaps, if she could find a position as clerk for Isabella, all would be well.

She'd ask Simon what he thought of the notion.

It did not occur to her until later, when she had lost a small fortune to her father and Mrs. Effington, that wanting to ask Simon's opinion rather than her father's was, to say the least, a startling development.

During that rainy week she spent more time with her father than she had done in the five weeks since their arrival in London. They would sit in front of a roaring fire in the library, Hugh with a rug wrapped around his legs and Jeannette in her winter gown. She soon learned to thoroughly rout her father at chess. When it came to card games, however, he could not be beaten.

"I am a gambler," he said, a gleam lighting in his eyes. "There are no stakes in chess. You either win or lose. That is quite uninteresting. The excitement of a game is measured by the stakes you put up."

She cast a wry look at the scraps of paper she had lost

to him at piquet. "Even if they are imaginary stakes?"

"Even then." He riffled through the paper scraps, counting quickly.

Shaking his head, he said, "You had best never play for real stakes. In less than an hour, you lost thirty-five thousand pounds."

"Poor Papa. I must be a severe disappointment to you."

"Indeed. A daughter with no head for cards. Truly a severe punishment for a father."

They looked at each other across the card table—Jeannette's eyes as deep a blue as her father's, and Hugh's as bright and warm with loving affection as his daughter's.

Hugh threw off the rug and stood. "I want you to read something, Jeannette."

He went to the desk, his gait stiff after the long rest in the chair. He unlocked the drawer holding the stack of old, yellowed letters and the signet ring.

For a moment, he looked at the letters. Then, carefully setting aside the topmost, he lifted out the others. He locked the drawer and returned to the card table by the fireplace.

"I am aware I've not answered your questions about the past as fully as I should have. But I am an old man now—"

"You're not!"

He continued as if Jeannette had not interrupted. "And it is difficult to recall or retell what drove a young man to do the things he did."

He handed the letters to Jeannette. "These, perhaps, will help you understand."

"They're addressed to Lord Decimus." Jeannette unfolded one of the letters, glanced at the signature and at the date.

She gave her father a look in which excitement struggled with confusion and uncertainty.

"*Your* letters to Lord Decimus. This one is dated April of 1781. *Solid proof* that you did not die in 1780, in Savannah. Papa, when did Lord Decimus give you these letters? And why have you not shown them to Simon?"

"Child, Decimus does not know they exist. The letters were never posted."

"Still, they're proof." Excitement gave way to uncertainty. "Aren't they?"

"For Malcolm they should be."

Hugh gently touched Jeannette's cheek. "I'll leave you now. Read the letters, daughter. And as soon as this infernal rain lets up we'll take them to Dundas House."

Hugh Dundas had written the first letter to his friend Decimus Rowland in April of 1781. The bloody fight between America and England still raged and Hugh did not know when he could send the letter off.

He wrote of the injuries he had received in Savannah the previous November, a bayonet cut in the thigh and a ball in the shoulder, above the heart. He would have died had it not been for a trader, a Frenchman, who took him into his home. But as Nathaniel Greene and his Patriot troops pushed southward, the British occupying Savannah became more vigilant and conducted house-to-house searches for hidden rebels. This, Hugh wrote, was the reason he did not address the letter to his parents. Hugh Dundas, Marquis of Luxton, had turned rebel after the death of his wife Sarah and his young son in occupied Philadelphia.

He had tried to stay politically neutral, a difficult undertaking in Philadelphia, the rebel capital. He had been torn between an inherent loyalty to King and country and a deep sympathy for the American cause. But it was English gunpowder that killed his wife and son and several others when a whole cartload exploded, and in his anguish Hugh devoted himself to the struggle for independence.

Hugh did not know how his father would take the news of a rebel son—his mother, he felt certain, would understand. He wanted Decimus to break the facts personally to the fifth duke.

When the Frenchman, Jean Lenoir, could no longer keep Hugh safely hidden in his house, he smuggled the wounded rebel out of Savannah in a wagon piled with trading goods. Lenoir had friends in New Orleans, where Hugh would be safe. The journey took a month, and the rattling and jolting almost accomplished what the bayonet and the gun had failed to do. When Hugh arrived in New Orleans on New Year's Day of 1781, he lay at death's door.

Hugh wrote that he had no recollection of the last week of travel or of the first two weeks with the Vireilles family in Royal Street. But he recovered, thanks to Madame Vireilles's efforts and the untiring care of Nounou, a formidable woman with skin as dark as ebony and a smile as warm as the New Orleans sun. And now, in April, he was finally strong enough to wield a pen.

The next letter, a year later, told of Hugh's growing awareness of Jeanne Vireilles, his hosts' youngest daughter. Hugh wrote of Jeanne's beauty, her raven hair, her soft laughter and gentle disposition. He wrote of Jeanne's unquestioning compliance with her parents' arrangements for her future, the longstanding betrothal to a Creole gentleman, who, until Jeanne was old enough to marry him, was passing the time in the arms of a beautiful quadroon he had installed in a cozy little house near the ramparts.

Hugh wrote of Jeanne's parents—Monsieur Vireilles, jovial, easy-going, and quite content to let Hugh take over more and more responsibilities in his flourishing import-export business; and Madame Vireilles, a Spanish Creole, very strict and watchful in her chaperonage of Jeanne.

The third letter was dated the twenty-third of June, 1783. It was a letter of triumph and happiness. Hugh's love was reciprocated. Jeanne Vireilles had fallen as deeply and irrevocably in love with him as he had fallen in love with her over a year ago. And for the first time in her life, Jeanne had stood up to her parents and insisted that her betrothal to Pierre Fontenot be terminated.

It had been a difficult time for his dearest Jeanne, wrote Hugh, but she had stood firm, and finally even the strong-willed Madame Vireilles had given in. On June twentieth, at the age of thirty-three, Hugh had married seventeen-year-old Jeanne Vireilles, and he need not even feel guilty about having snatched his bride from the cradle. It was done all the time in New Orleans. Jeanne's former betrothed was thirty-five!

There was gossip, of course, over the sudden switch in bridegrooms, but Monsieur Vireilles had offered Hugh the management of his plantations on Saint Domingue, where the young couple would not live under a cloud of scandal. Accompanied by Nounou, Jeanne's former nurse, they planned to leave New Orleans in mid-July, when the bride visits would finally be over and done with.

Three letters, each spaced two or three years apart, told of Hugh and Jeanne's happiness and of plantation life on Saint Domingue. There was no mention why the letters had not been posted when King George and his government finally acknowledged the independence of the United States of America and ships resumed regular traffic between the two countries.

Then the last, a brief, terse note, dated October of 1790. Hugh wrote: Jeanne miscarried. But for Nounou, she would have died. We shouldn't have any children, says Nounou. Jeanne won't hear of it. She's determined to give me both, a son and a daughter.

Slowly, Jeannette refolded the letters and stacked them neatly. She was glad her father had shared these sketches from his past, that he had allowed her to see her mother, her grandparents, and Nounou through his eyes as a young man.

She had known of the miscarriage. Nounou had told her after her mother's and the infant's death aboard the schooner.

But she had not known that *Maman* had been betrothed to Monsieur Pierre, Raoul's father, before she married Papa. How ironic. It certainly explained why *Grandmère,* who did not usually show her feelings, had smashed a lovely Chinese figurine, then cried, when Jeannette broke her betrothal to Raoul Fontenot.

Jeannette unfolded the last note once more. Poor Papa.

But it was strange that he should have written no more. Even the earliest memories she had were of the deep love in her father's eyes when he carried her in his arms, his pride in her every accomplishment. Surely, after committing so much to paper, after the anguish in that brief notation of the miscarriage, he would have written about the birth of his daughter?

Telling herself she was merely feeling piqued at the

omission of her birth, she laid the letter atop the others, then put them on her father's desk.

Suddenly, elation surged. Simon would read the letters, soon. And Papa would show him the signet ring. Then Simon would have to admit that his distrust and suspicion of her and her father were unfounded.

She was aware of a deep, soothing relief, and of impatience. She wanted that time to be soon, the time she and Simon would no longer be antagonists.

Chapter Twenty-two

That evening, Hugh Dundas sent his valet to the drawing room where Jeannette was keeping Mrs. Effington company while the older lady enjoyed a glass of sherry before dinner.

"Lady Caroline, my lord asked me to fetch the letters he gave you this afternoon," Perrier said in his precise, stilted English.

"I left them on the desk in the library. Is Papa not coming down to dinner?"

"My lord begs pardon, but he is not feeling up to par."

"Lord Luxton looked pale when we played cards this afternoon," said Mrs. Effington. "Though when I asked him if he was unwell, he assured me he was in fine fettle."

The valet hovered in the doorway as if uncertain what to do next.

Jeannette rose. "I'll take the letters up myself, Perrier. Tell Papa I'll be with him in a moment."

"I beg your pardon, Lady Caroline. But my lord particularly wished not to be disturbed."

The unwelcome thought crossed her mind that he was avoiding her, that, for some reason, he had changed his mind about taking the letters to Dundas House and did not want her to question him.

But Perrier's next words drove any such notion from her mind.

"Mademoiselle Jeannette," said Perrier, betraying by the old, familiar address how very perturbed he was. "My lord said you must not be worried. But me, I think it is high time to worry. I think the doctor must be asked to see him. My lord, I believe, has a fever. And I have heard him cough once or twice."

Mrs. Effington clucked. "Why did he not tell me about the cough? A mustard plaster applied to the chest and the juice of hoar-strange taken in a glass of wine this afternoon would have put him to rights by now."

Jeannette, who had every reason to be alarmed since her father's previous illness had started with just the same symptoms, forced herself to remain calm.

"Take the letters to him, Perrier, and try to make him comfortable. You know how. I'll send James to fetch Dr. Moore immediately."

"But my lord said—"

"Tell my lord that *I* said he either sees the physician or he sees *me*."

"Yes, Lady Caroline."

Looking vastly relieved, the valet bowed himself out of the chamber.

Jeannette rang for the footman.

"My dear, I understand your concern," said Mrs. Effington. "But is it wise to summon Dr. Moore against your father's wishes?"

"Perhaps not wise," Jeannette said rather grimly, ". . . but prudent. Papa was very ill this past winter. Pleurisy-pneumonia the physician called it, and he warned me that it could recur."

* * *

Even though Dr. Moore ruled out any form of pleurisy or pneumonia and assured Jeannette that her father suffered nothing worse than a chest cold, she could not be easy about his condition until she was finally admitted into the sickroom two days later, and even then her concern was not laid to rest. She was shocked to see him more haggard than before he had taken to his bed.

"Gracious, Papa!" Forcing a smile and a bantering tone, she approached the four-poster bed where he lay propped against a mountain of pillows. "What a tyrant you are. It is more difficult to get permission to see you than to wrangle an invitation to the Prince Regent's ball."

Hugh allowed her to kiss his cheek, then waved her to a chair.

"What is this about wrangling invitations? I understood the guest list was drawn up. Fifteen hundred people, most of them Members of Parliament. And, going by Hanovarian court custom, Prinny excluded all women lower in rank than the daughter of an earl."

"And that is precisely what set off such a hue and cry that a great many more invitations have been sent out, and now the Prince Regent says he cannot possibly have Carlton House ready on time for the great event. As a result, the ball has been postponed to the nineteenth of June. At least that is what Mrs. Effington told me this morning."

Hugh stirred restlessly. "You should have been invited."

"I have no interest in such flimflammery, Papa. Bowing and scraping to a man of loose morals. Oohing and aahing at the waste of money on the new furnishings at Carlton House, money that could have been spent on parish schools or hospitals."

Hugh gave her a weak grin. "Little reformer."

Jeannette did not bother to defend herself. He might still refer to the Prince Regent with the affectionate "Prinny" he undoubtedly used in his youth, but at heart her father agreed with her on the prince's extravagance.

She moved her chair closer to the bed. "But *you* should have been invited, Papa. Not Frederick."

Hugh's smile faded. "Understand this, Jeannette. I made up my mind years ago not to claim the title or the estates of the Duke of Granby. I am happy with life in New Orleans. The only thing I want is for you to have what is yours by right of birth."

"If you can deny your birthright, I can do the same."

He raised himself higher against the pillows. The thin hands on the bedcover clenched and unclenched. "Jeannette, I promised to see you settled. Don't, I beg you, make me break that vow!"

Alarmed by his agitation, she rose. "I'll have Perrier bring you a posset, and then you must rest. My future does not have to be settled this very instant."

"But soon. Very soon."

"We'll talk about it when you're well."

A cough shook his thin frame but subsided quickly. "Yes," he muttered, as if to himself. "I must get well. Too much is at stake to try and make the push while I'm as weak as a newborn kitten."

As Jeannette moved off, he said, "It's little Agnes's ball tonight, isn't it? Ask your Aunt Anne about the miniatures. Malcolm told me they found one, the likeness of the disreputable Augustus. But the second miniature is missing."

The miniatures had quite slipped her mind. She had half decided not to attend the ball but now, instantly, made up her mind to go.

"I will, Papa." She gave him a severe look. "If you promise not to send your dinner back to the kitchen untouched."

"I promise. Jeannette . . . you read the letters?"

"Indeed, and I thank you for sharing them with me. But I wondered, when I read that last note, why you stopped writing Lord Decimus so abruptly. You wrote about *Maman,* your happiness, even about the miscarriage, and I thought—"

"What did you think?" he prompted.

"That you would have written about me later on. That terse note about the miscarriage, about *Maman*'s determination to give you children despite Nounou's warning, left a feeling of . . . incompleteness. Of something, another letter, missing."

His breath caught, throwing him into a paroxysm of coughing.

Instantly, she was at his side, supporting his frail body in her arms. On the bedside table she saw the bottle of cough drops prescribed by Dr. Moore. She should have made him take the medicine when he coughed the first time.

The attack ceased as suddenly as it had come on, and Hugh pushed her from him.

"Devil a bit," he said weakly. "What a nuisance I am."

Jeannette picked up a spoon and counted the prescribed twenty-five drops from the small brown bottle.

"Here, Papa." Anxiety tightened her voice. "No one told me your cough was so severe."

"It isn't." He swallowed the medicine. "You took me by surprise with your talk of a missing letter. I choked."

"I did not mean to distress you."

"I know you didn't." He patted her hand. "I am a bit on edge, that's all. We've been in town six weeks and I've accomplished nothing."

"Why don't you let me take the letters to Mr. Renshaw? Malcolm Renshaw," she added hastily, even though her father could not possibly know that it was Simon the name Renshaw brought to mind. "Then you need do nothing but relax until Mr. Harte returns from New Orleans and confirms everything."

Hugh shook his head. "I'll see you settled long before that young man even arrives in New Orleans."

"Hardly. If the *Caroline* made as good a time as the captain expected, she should be docking any day now."

"In that case, I had better hurry and get well, hadn't I?" He patted her hand. "Run along, child. Those dratted cough drops always make me sleepy. And you'll want to get ready for the ball."

"There's plenty of time. About the letters, Papa. Shall I take them to Mr. Renshaw?"

"No. That is something I must do myself."

On that first dry evening in over a week, the *ton* appeared in full force at Sir Lewis Paine's house in Upper Brook Street, rendering Agnes's ball an unqualified success.

Perhaps as a result of the improving weather, which had put everyone in high spirits, Jeannette did not lack dance partners, and the ladies greeted her more warmly than at Vivian Herrington's dance. But her pleasure was dimmed by her father's illness and nothing could sway her from the conviction that the night would be a dull one.

And it was, except for the two dances she had given to Barnaby Herrington. Dancing with Barny could never be dull, since the young man with the two left feet approached the exercise with the vigor and forcefulness he applied to a hunt or steeplechase.

The second dance with him, a country dance, had been particularly challenging for Jeannette. While the musicians rested, she retired behind an arrangement of potted hibiscus plants to survey the damage to her dancing slippers.

She wrinkled her nose at the sight of several smudges on the rose silk.

The buzz of laughter and conversation swallowed the whisper of silk skirts and soft footsteps, and Jeannette was unaware of Lady Anne's approach until she heard her aunt's voice.

"Mementoes of Barny Herrington?" Smiling, Lady Anne peeked around one of the large plants. With her was Malcolm Renshaw.

"Good evening, Lady Caroline." Malcolm used the silver top of his cane to shift a hibiscus branch touching his satin knee breeches. "Lady Anne mentioned that Hugh is unwell. I hope nothing serious?"

Stepping out from behind the plants, Jeannette dipped into a curtsy. "The physician assured me it is nothing worse than a chest cold, sir."

"Hugh's no longer used to our damp and cold, I expect. Tell him to drink a glass of grog morning, noon, and night. That'll soon put him to rights."

Laughter danced in Jeannette's eyes. "The prescription will certainly ensure plenty of rest. Hot rum in the morning!"

"I'll look in on dear Hugh tomorrow," said Lady Anne. "What he needs is some restorative pork jelly. I'll bring several jars."

"Thank you, Aunt Anne. I know Papa will be glad of your company," Jeannette said politely although she knew nothing of the kind. In his present state, her father's desire for company was unpredictable. And he certainly would not take pork jelly, restorative or not.

"Aunt Anne, Papa bade me ask you something."

"What is it, dear?"

With the slightest inflection of her head, Lady Anne directed a passing footman to serve them with champagne. When the man had moved on, she asked, "Would you like to come to my sitting room, where we can converse in private?"

"Oh, no. I wouldn't dream of taking you away from your guests at this time."

Malcolm bowed. "I'll be happy to withdraw and leave you ladies to your privacy, if you wish."

"Please don't. If Papa's question were at all private, I wouldn't have mentioned it in your presence."

He gave her one of his sharp looks, so disconcertingly like Simon's, then nodded. "I don't believe you would have. And I'm curious. Hence, I'll stay and eavesdrop."

Jeannette turned back to her aunt. "Papa wondered if you knew what became of the second miniature that used to be in the yellow sitting room at Granby Castle. One, a likeness of the fourth duke, is still there."

"It was there," said Malcolm. "I brought it with me."

"Oh. Thank you, sir," said Jeannette without taking

her eyes off her aunt. "But no one, apparently, has seen the other, which is a likeness of—"

"The second likeness is of Hugh," Lady Anne interrupted. "Of course I know what became of it. It is upstairs in my bedchamber."

"I should have known," said Malcolm. A sharp tap of his walking stick on the floor accentuated the disgruntled tone of his voice.

Jeannette took a deep breath. The letters, the signet ring, and the miniature. Surely that was enough to prove her father's identity. She raised her glass as if in a toast and sipped her champagne.

Lady Anne gave Malcolm Renshaw a puzzled look. "Did I do wrong? Are you annoyed with me for taking the likeness?"

"Not at all. I'm annoyed with myself. I should have realized that you would have the miniature. You were the only one of Hugh's sisters who never got tired of listening to your mother talk about him or of gazing at his likeness with her."

Lady Anne made some reply, but Jeannette was no longer listening to her companions. As had happened once before, by some strange process of alchemy, she was suddenly aware of Simon's presence somewhere nearby.

She looked at the noisy, crowded ballroom, the throng of people, standing or promenading, talking, laughing, waving to each other. Slowly, irresistibly, her gaze was drawn to the right.

He was still thirty paces or more from the potted hibiscus where she stood, but the distance shrank to nothing when their eyes met. It was only for an instant, until three giggling young ladies and their escorts came between them. But in that brief moment

Jeannette knew that the evening would not be a dull one after all.

The musicians struck up the next tune. The young ladies and their escorts hurried off toward the dance floor. Once again Jeannette had a clear view of Simon as he strode toward her.

A man of the dark, rugged kind, as Mrs. Effington had described him.

A man you can fancy, had been Annie's words.

Only about ten paces separated them when her mouth, with a will of its own, curved in a welcoming-smile.

Perhaps it wouldn't be so horrid after all if she were courted by an Englishman.

If the Englishman were Simon Renshaw.

Chapter Twenty-three

Simon had gone to the ball filled with resolve to have a much-needed talk with Jeannette. But resolve had lagged behind when his stride lengthened the moment he spied her across the ballroom with his father and Lady Anne. And resolve had been utterly lost in the crowd when he came within ten paces of her and saw her smile.

When she smiled at him like that, he saw no need to warn her against setting her cap at a young sprig like Barnaby Herrington or any other fool who might fall prey to the appeal of blue eyes and propose marriage to the self-styled Lady Caroline.

When she smiled like that, he saw no need to tell her that he could never permit her to marry into a respectable English family while she persisted in deception. That there was only one man she would be permitted to marry.

He had planned to warn her that the game was up. If necessary, he would have told her about the scar Hugh Dundas had in the palm of his hand and which was so conspicuously absent in her father's hand. His goal had been to make her confess to the masquerade she and her father perpetrated on the *ton*.

But under the influence of her smile, he revised his strategy. He would teach her the error of her ways in a manner that must not only be more pleasant for both of them but more persuasive to one as stubborn as Jeannette.

Thus, on the spur of the moment, Simon made up his mind to wait no longer but to make use of the few remaining weeks of the Season and woo the little adventuress from New Orleans.

At nine-and-twenty, he was not inexperienced in the art of wooing. But never before had he pursued the art with confession as the first goal. And never before had he wooed a young lady like Jeannette.

Any preconceived notions about charming her with compliments on her gown, a deep rose satin that made her skin glow like a rare pearl, had to be dismissed as soon as he was within speaking distance.

"Simon," she said, "I was hoping to see you tonight. Did you save your client from the gallows?"

He should have known. Not for Jeannette the polite topics of weather, the Prince's fête, or the dowager Lady Aldrich's upcoming Venetian Breakfast.

He bowed to Lady Anne and acknowledged his father's presence with a nod before allowing his gaze to be drawn by a pair of deep blue eyes.

"I'm afraid not yet. The poor fellow is in the infirmary. Gaol fever."

Her smile faded. "I am sorry. Gaol fever is fatal, isn't it?"

"In many cases."

"He may not need saving from the gallows, then."

"We shall see. I made sure that a physician attends the sick at the Old Bailey. Would you care to dance, Lady Caroline?"

"I'd like to, very much. But—" She took a deep breath. "To tell the truth, I'd rather hear more about your work in court, and it's difficult to converse when you have to turn and dip and part constantly. So, would you mind terribly if we did not dance but talked instead?"

"Caroline!" cried Lady Anne. "You cannot be serious. No lady would wish to know about those filthy thieves and murderers Simon defends. They are the dregs of society, found in the most horrible stews and slums."

Jeannette's chin assumed a mulish tilt. "But I do want to know."

Aware of his father's interested gaze moving from him to Jeannette, Simon offered his arm to the troublesome young lady.

"Let us go for a stroll. But I warn you, there isn't anything to tell about my work that's worth listening to."

"There must be." She fell into step beside him. "Frederick said that all the time you represent some poor fellow or other. Why?"

"Because I happen to believe that a fourteen-year-old girl caught stealing an apple for a hungry little brother should not be deported. And that a father protecting his daughter should not hang because he is a crossing sweep and the man he attacked is of the nobility—even if that nobleman dies from his injuries."

"No, indeed. But it is rare that someone not of the lower classes holds that opinion. What opened your eyes to the needs of these people?"

To Simon's astonishment, Jeannette did not grow bored listening to him. Perhaps her interest should not have come as a surprise. After all, he had seen her with Isabella.

Explaining his work to a young lady and answering her countless questions was a novel experience, one he wasn't sure he enjoyed or approved of until he realized that they had promenaded along the periphery of the dance floor for the better part of an hour and that somewhere along the way self-consciousness and unease had disappeared.

Much like his earlier resolve to wring a confession from her.

He admitted that he had never spent a more stimulating hour at a ball and that the resentful looks from gentlemen who wished to claim promised dances from Jeannette only added spice to the situation. He admitted he did not want their tête-à-tête to end, but, of course, it must. He started to apologize for keeping her from dancing for so long.

She interrupted firmly.

"Please don't apologize, Simon, or you'll make me feel guilty for monopolizing your time."

She stopped walking. Her hand still resting on his arm, she gave him a frank look.

"I have never minded missing a few dances for something worthwhile. And getting to know you, talking with you without coming to cuffs over Papa, has been very much worth my while."

"And mine."

He did something he had never done before because it had always seemed old-fashioned and exaggerated. He took her hand and raised it to his lips.

Her eyes widened, and when his mouth brushed against the thin silk of her glove, a faint blush rose to her face.

Simon had pierced her composure, but her grandmother's training proved stronger than the momentary desire to hide her burning cheeks. Unhurried, she withdrew her hand from his clasp.

Once more she met his gaze squarely. "But now, I think, it is time to part lest we set the gossips' tongues wagging."

He feared they must already have done so, since he was not in the habit of devoting the better part of an hour to one young lady exclusively. But, wisely, he did not point this out and let her go with her composure once more restored.

Annie was sitting cross-legged on the bed, waiting to hear about the ball, when Jeannette entered her chamber. Annie was given a ruthlessly edited account. So ruthlessly edited that the complete absence of Simon's name made the little ghost suspicious.

Pushing back her mobcap, she cocked a brow at Jeannette. "And was Mr. Renshaw not at the ball? Mr. Simon Renshaw?"

"Yes, he was. Did I not mention him?"

"No, you didn't." Annie assumed the same airy tone Jeannette had used. "But it's not as if his presence would make a difference, is it?"

Jeannette gave a reluctant laugh. "Is there nothing I can keep secret from you?"

"Too much. I used to be very good at reading

minds, but even that is getting harder and harder. All I know is that you're . . . different. A little perturbed, I think. And excited. And Simon Renshaw is the cause."

Jeannette looked at her hand, the hand Simon had kissed.

"I'm not sure I understand what is happening. To me. To Simon." She shrugged. "Nothing has changed. He still believes I'm an imposter, but not once did he allude to it."

"So you didn't come to dagger drawing?"

"Not at all." Jeannette removed her wrap and laid it on the bed. "Perhaps because I said nothing objectionable? But I confess, I'm rather looking forward to seeing him again."

Once again, Annie cocked a brow. "Is he coming to call on you?"

"He did not say."

No, Simon had said nothing about calling or seeing her again. Suddenly deflated and tired, Jeannette turned to the dressing table and started to unpin her hair.

"I had best get some sleep, Annie. If it stays dry, we'll want to drive to Basket Lane in the morning."

To her astonishment, Annie shook her head.

"Basket Lane and old Selina can wait until I've perfected the potion. It tastes rather strong, and we want to be sure it cannot be detected if we mix it with Madeira. Can you get me a bottle of Madeira tomorrow?"

"Madeira?"

"Yes," Annie said impatiently. "That's what Mr. Renshaw chose when your pa invited him to take a glass of wine the morning you and he came to cuffs in the front parlor. We want to be sure we're ready when he comes to call on you again."

Jeannette was about to point out that Simon might never call again when he had seen her father's letters. And that, if he should indeed call, she would hope a love potion was not required.

But for some reason she said nothing.

Annie bounced off the bed. "If you must gad about in the morning, take Isabella to get measured for some gowns."

Jeannette gave an absent-minded nod. Yes, she'd see to Isabella's needs. That would take her mind off Simon.

Until she could see him again.

Jeannette and Simon met three days later at the Venetian Breakfast the dowager Lady Aldrich was giving for her granddaughter. The event took place in St. James's Park, and Lady Aldrich had ordered several large octagonal tents erected in which guests and musicians could shelter from either rain or sunshine.

The day was sunny. The tents' side panels were rolled up so that the ladies might enjoy the warm air and yet have their delicate complexions protected from the destructive rays of the sun. The food, the champagne, the tunes produced by the string quartet were excellent. The mood should have been festive, and those present tried their best to appear cheerful. But every now and then a hush would fall over the company.

Word had arrived from the Peninsula about a battle at some obscure Spanish village called Albuera. A British victory. But the casualty lists accompanying the news of victory held close to four thousand names. Several families invited to the Venetian Breakfast, including the Herringtons, had sent their apologies to Lady Aldrich that very morning.

"Barnaby's younger brother, Vivian's twin, was injured," explained Simon when he and Jeannette joined the throng of young people leaving the tents after a scrumptious repast. "A cornet. Eighteen years old. A leg amputated. If he survives the voyage, he'll be home in a week or two."

"How sad for the young man, for the whole family. I did not even know Barnaby and Vivian had a brother. Barnaby never mentioned him."

"Barnaby was the one mad for a pair of colors, but as the elder he was expected to stay home. And he resented it."

"And so he talked about his sporting exploits rather than the brother who went off to fight Napoleon Bonaparte? How very sad."

Simon steered her down a path the others had bypassed. Jeannette did not miss the maneuver. Her sense of propriety screamed a warning, but for once she closed her ears and mind to every stricture her grandmother had drummed into her head.

This was St. James's Park. It was early afternoon. And a great number of couples were taking a stroll nearby.

Still, she was a little self-conscious walking with Simon and kept her gaze on some iris in full bloom beside the path. The flowers did not seem to have suffered from the ice rain the previous week, but the leaves on several rose bushes drooped sadly.

She became aware of Simon's eyes on her.

Twirling her parasol, she asked, "Did you long for a pair of colors when you were Barny's age?"

"I still do, occasionally." He gave her a wry look. "I'm not so old yet that my blood cannot be roused by Bonaparte's cockiness."

He watched for the faint blush that never failed to delight him, and was not disappointed.

"That is not what I meant, Simon. But you're an only son, aren't you?"

"Yes. I have two sisters, both married. You'd like them and their brood of children."

Her mind was still on explaining herself. "It is just that I cannot picture you resenting the responsibilities of an only son. You seem always to be in control of yourself and any situation in which you find yourself."

"What an erroneous picture you have of me," he said, reflecting how little in control he was when dealing with her. He gave her a wry look. "I assure you that I was quite as resentful as Barnaby Herrington when my mother lectured me on filial duty. Father would not have stopped me, but then the late duke summoned me to Dundas House."

"My grandfather? But, surely, he had no say in your decision?"

Simon gave a bark of laughter. "He certainly felt he did. Told me that it was my duty to keep myself alive. That since he and my father were a pair of decrepit old men with one foot in the grave—his words!—Frederick was *my* responsibility. I must guide my young cousin past the pitfalls awaiting him at Cambridge. I must bear-lead him once he was old enough to spend the Season in town."

"You did your duty well. My grandfather must have been satisfied. How easily Frederick could have turned into a rude, high-nosed, stiff-rumped, overbearing jackanapes, expecting everyone to bow and scrape to him."

"Yes," said Simon, pride in his voice. "He did turn out rather well."

Jeannette nodded. That pride in Frederick, the responsibility he felt for the younger man, explained much of Simon's attitude when she and her father appeared so unexpectedly.

She closed her parasol as they entered a patch of shade cast by tall oaks and beeches flanking one side of the path. She wanted to warn Simon of what was in store for Frederick when her father got well. But she could not.

For some reason, her father had kept quiet about the letters and his signet ring. Now that he had decided to produce them, she could not take matters into her own hands.

But there was something she must and would do.

"Simon, I owe you an apology. Two apologies."

He stopped walking and faced her, his gaze quizzing.

"Only two?"

"Don't tease, Simon. This is serious. I wronged you when I accused you of conspiring with Frederick in return for a share of the Dundas fortune. I'm sorry. I should have known better."

He remembered his own apology to Hugh Dundas when he realized the old rogue wasn't sponging off the Dundas name after all. But Jeannette, the imposter's daughter, knew all along that he and Frederick were not conspiring. So what the dickens was she scheming now, the little baggage, with her apology?

"And I was a mean-spirited shrew when I said you'd fight Papa even when you hold the proof of his identity in your hands."

He looked at her for a long moment. Slowly, a smile lit in his eyes.

"Never a shrew. A fighter and a brazen hussy."

Placing a finger beneath her chin, he tilted her face up. "And, I'd say, you're the only brazen hussy who blushes."

A brazen hussy. She should be offended. But the smile in his eyes, the touch of his finger moving slowly and feather-light from chin to throat and along the sensitive skin of her neck made it impossible to concentrate on rebuke.

Instead, brazen hussy made her think of the secret yearnings Nounou had warned about.

Yearnings Jeannette no longer denied. Yearnings, a hussy would surely explore.

How very fortunate that they happened to be on a secluded path. But Simon, though close, stood too far away and did not seem to see the need to step closer.

She thought of her Cousin Félicie and the feminine wiles employed by the enterprising damsel before her marriage. Surely, she could do as well?

Of course she could.

Jeannette gave the whisper of a sigh, closed her eyes, and swayed—toward Simon.

And Simon, always a gentleman, instantly caught her in his arms.

With great presence of mind, Jeannette dropped her parasol and wrapped both arms around Simon's waist. And just in case he still did not catch on, she raised herself on tiptoe, opened her eyes, and, despite the blush that once more heated her face, squarely met his keen, probing gaze.

"Aren't you going to kiss me, Simon?"

Chapter Twenty-four

A gentleman did not refuse a lady, but rarely had a gentleman complied with such speed and willingness as Simon complied with Jeannette's wish.

His mouth covered hers before she had time to draw breath. But breathing mere air became unimportant when every fiber of her body came to life and breathed in the essence that was Simon. When every nerve tingled under the touch of his hands caressing her back, her hips, then moving upward until they rested against her breasts, and with the gentlest of strokes awakened them to pleasure.

Unbidden, she opened her mouth to deepen the kiss. She slid her hands up his back until she felt the strong column of his neck, the thick, straight hair that was surprisingly silky to the touch.

"Jeannette."

The name was but a breath, the brush of his lips against hers before he claimed her mouth again in irresistible demand.

He drew her closer, so close that they seemed to be touching skin against skin. She heard him groan, a deep sound that roused shivers of pleasure all over her body.

Then, suddenly, Simon was pulling away. Cupping

her face in his hands, he stilled her instinctive protest with a quick, feather light kiss.

"I'm sorry to cut this short." His voice was low, tender. "But we won't have privacy much longer."

As her breathing steadied and the clamor of her body calmed, she heard the sounds of company approaching through the trees. Agnes's voice, high and excited as usual. Eleanor's, soft, decorous. And Frederick's, calm and soothing.

"I saw them disappear this way," Frederick was saying. "I tell you, we'll find them."

"And, then, perhaps you won't." Simon scooped up the parasol. "Can you run, Jeannette?"

She took his proffered hand. The smile she gave him was a little strained, but her tone was firm.

"As a Yankee would say, you bet your bottom dollar, Mr. Renshaw."

Jeannette was at first inclined to reproach herself for giving in to a quite improper impulse, but the inclination lasted only until she realized that her reproaches were half-hearted, mere lip service to the conventions she had been taught to observe.

Kissing Simon had been wonderful, exhilarating, and being held in his arms had not felt the slightest bit improper; only right and fabulously exciting. The way he caressed her had made her feel beautiful, desirable, everything a woman secretly wished she were.

A woman.

That was the key. She had felt a woman, not a girl.

And it was not the success of a dressmaker's establishment that had achieved the transformation into womanhood. It was a man's embrace. Simon's embrace and kiss.

Since Mrs. Effington's prediction of more invitations was coming true, Jeannette met Simon at several functions during the following two weeks. She did not suffer embarrassment when he greeted her. If she blushed, it was for the pleasure of seeing him and the warmth that kindled in his eyes whenever they rested on her.

There was no repeat of the kiss, nor did either of them allude to the experience, but she knew, when the time was right, she would once again feel his arms around her. She would know once more the response of her body to his caress, feel the fire she could ignite in him with her touch.

The awakening of her body had shaken her, and though it did not frighten her, she was, for the present, content merely to be with Simon once in a while. To see him at a party, to ride with him in Hyde Park, Archer following at a discreet distance, to question him about his work, about the progress of the man who might survive gaol fever only to face trial for murder.

She talked to him about Isabella and the girl's strange preference for doing accounts rather than needlework, and she answered Simon's questions about the *boutique* and the women who staffed it.

She had never before discussed that aspect of her life with a man—save for her father. Somehow, she had come to believe that no man—again, save for her father—would understand. She should have known better.

"Simon is as much, or more so, a reformer than I

am," she told Hugh one night when, upon her return from a card party she saw the light still showing beneath his bedroom door and went in to bid him goodnight.

Hugh raised a brow. "And that changed your mind about him, eh? No longer is he a scheming villain?"

She drew a hassock toward the arm chair where her father sat, still fully dressed, a book and his spectacles resting on his knees.

"Papa, I was never more wrong than when I accused Simon of scheming with Frederick to cheat you. Simon is truly convinced that Hugh Dundas died in that rebel skirmish on occupied Savannah. He is only doing his duty as he perceives it."

"Aye. And I've never blamed him for protecting Frederick's interests."

"No, but I have. Papa, don't you think it is time that you showed Simon and Malcolm Renshaw your ring, the letters, and the miniature Aunt Anne brought you? It is not right to let Frederick go on believing he is the sixth duke when he isn't."

Hugh's gaze sharpened. "Feel sorry for the boy, do you?"

"I have reason to believe that he's trying to fix his interest with a young lady. But how can he propose marriage when he cannot be certain of his position?"

Frowning, Hugh stared at the book on his knees.

"Papa, you're better, aren't you? You've been out once or twice and took no harm. Couldn't we go to Dundas House tomorrow?"

He looked up. "Aye. We'll go."

* * *

Simon paced back and forth between desk and door of the study at Dundas House.

They were late. Two-thirty, Hugh Dundas said in his note. Now it was three o'clock.

Simon looked at Frederick, seated behind the desk, an open ledger before him. A frown marred Frederick's brow and he stared at the entries as if in deep concentration. But the ink on his pen had been dry for some time and not a single figure written.

Simon had assured his cousin that there was no need to worry about the unexpected meeting called by Hugh Dundas, but, obviously, Frederick needed more than reassurance.

What the devil was keeping Hugh? If he had finally decided to put an end to the masquerade, he could at least be on time.

Pacing faster, Simon cast a look at his father, reading in a deep leather chair. When Hugh's note arrived, Malcolm had given a satisfied nod and said, "The next move. Knew we wouldn't have to wait for Harte's return."

Simon frowned. It was all very well for his father to be satisfied and sit at his ease, whiling away the time with Robert Burns's poems. Malcolm was content to let Hugh Dundas end the game in his own time, but Simon was no longer willing to wait.

Not after he had held Jeannette in his arms and tasted the sweetness of her kiss. A kiss he had wanted to claim for a long time.

It was now the middle of June. For two months he had watched her get deeper and deeper entangled in her father's schemes. The role of Lady Caroline was now a natural one for her. No more hesitation when she was addressed by that name. No more slips as on the day he had asked her name and she replied, "Jeannette Dundas," then corrected herself, "Caroline Jeannette Dundas. Lady Caroline."

She was, indeed, living her role, referring to the late fifth duke quite naturally as her grandfather, to Eleanor and Agnes as her cousins, and addressing Lady Anne as "Aunt." The only person she did not address at all was Lady Louisa. And there again, in her role as Lady Caroline, that was only natural.

But all this must stop. Now. If Hugh had decided to make a clean breast of it today, then Simon would be satisfied. But if Hugh planned to add yet another twist to his scheme—

Devil a bit! Simon's patience was at an end. He had wanted to gain Jeannette's trust, had waited for her to ask his help in disentangling her from the web of deceit. But he would wait no more.

Not after that kiss in the park, the promise of passion and delight. Not after their talks, which had shown their minds in tune.

Sensing his father's eyes on him, Simon stopped his pacing and turned to face the older man.

"What do you say, sir? Shall we go to George Street?"

"Only if you *don't* wish to hear what Hugh has to say. I daresay you were too preoccupied to notice the knocker."

At that moment, the study door opened and the butler announced Lord Luxton and Lady Caroline.

Jeannette's eyes were grave when they met Simon's across the room. He took it as a good sign. She and her father had come to end the charade.

Then he saw the slim black leather satchel Hugh

carried, the kind of satchel Simon used at times to carry papers to court.

Hugh apologized for their tardiness. "Took Mrs. Effington to West India Docks this morning. Should have been back in plenty of time to get here by two-thirty, except that one of the horses cast a shoe on Tower Hill and not a smithy anywhere close."

"That's quite all right, sir," Frederick said politely. "We didn't mind waiting."

He stepped around the desk. Unlike during the first meeting with Hugh and Jeannette, he asserted himself as host and ushered them to chairs near Malcolm Renshaw's.

"Why the docks?" asked Malcolm, setting the volume of Burns poems onto the low table around which the chairs were grouped. "Has your chaperone deserted you for a sea voyage, Lady Caroline?"

"No, sir." Jeannette shook her head, and Simon noticed that just like on her first visit to Dundas House, the heavy knot of curls atop her head was slightly askew. "Mrs. Effington was merely curious. She had never been aboard a ship."

An awkward silence fell. Simon was burning to get to the point of the meeting requested by Hugh but knew better than to betray impatience. "When you lose patience, you lose control," his father had told him when he joined the law firm as a junior partner.

He looked at Jeannette, but her eyes were on Hugh, who was unbuckling the satchel.

"Here's the second miniature," said Hugh, setting the silver-framed oval down beside the volume of poetry. "I realize it proves nothing, save that I looked like the disreputable Augustus when I was but a sprig of sixteen or seventeen. I'm touched that Anne should have taken it with her when she left Granby as a bride."

Next, Hugh took a small cloth pouch from the satchel. He opened it and shook out a ring. It came to rest beside the miniature.

"Do you recognize the ring, Malcolm?"

The senior Renshaw picked it up.

Simon did not need his father's confirmation to know that he was looking at the signet ring of the Marquis of Luxton. From handling the estate papers, he knew the description by heart—a ring of heavy gold, set with black onyx in the shape of a strawberry leaf, and engraved with the initial L.

Again, he looked across the low table at Jeannette. This time, as if she felt his gaze, she faced him and returned his look gravely. She did not speak. Neither did anyone else after Malcolm identified the ring.

Into the silence, Hugh addressed Frederick.

"You said when I first came here that I should have letters. You meant, of course, letters from the family sent to me in Philadelphia. I have none of those, my boy. But I have letters written between 1781 and '90. Letters written as a catharsis you might say, for they were never posted. They are addressed to my friend Decimus Rowland. Again, I think, Malcolm will confirm their authenticity, that the handwriting is indeed that of Hugh Dundas."

Hugh withdrew a slim stack of folded yellowed vellum from the satchel.

He placed the letters on the table beside the ring and the miniature, but when Simon reached for them, he laid a protective hand over the letters.

"Allow me to speak first. There'll be plenty of time later to study these."

Simon could have easily displaced the frail hand barring him from the startling, new evidence. But he leaned back in his chair.

Across the table, he saw Jeannette relax.

Frederick was staring at the yellowed paper beneath Hugh's hand.

"1781? But that means—" Frederick rose abruptly and walked to the desk, where he stood with his back to the others.

"You're quite correct, my boy," Hugh said genially. "It means that the report of Hugh Dundas's death in 1780 was false."

"Nothing is proven yet." Simon's face was tight, every muscle in his body tense.

He shot a look at his father, who had brought the report from America. But if Malcolm was perturbed, he did not show it. His expression conveyed nothing but mild curiosity as he sat with his arms folded across his chest and his eyes on Hugh Dundas.

Hugh slowly got to his feet. He started toward Frederick but stopped after a step or two.

"I came to London to see my daughter take her proper place in society," he said. "To see her married and comfortably established. Those were my intentions, and for that purpose I wanted her grandfather's backing. I did not know then that he was dead."

Again, Simon's gaze sought Jeannette's. So his guess had been correct. The thrust of Hugh's scheme was to find Jeannette a husband of rank.

He saw her blush, but this time the delicate rose

of her cheeks failed to delight him. She should never have agreed to the old rogue's plan.

But, devil a bit! If the letters should turn out to be authentic . . .

Was his father wrong about the scar?

"Papa, please!" Jeannette's voice was low, trembling with embarrassment. "My affairs can hardly be of interest to the gentlemen. It is to establish proof of your identity that we have come here."

Hugh said, "Aye, my identity. That was the one thing I didn't consider. That anyone would doubt who I am, and therefore deny my daughter the right to her name and title."

"What about *your* rights?" Malcolm asked. "You do not plan to claim those?"

"It was never my intention to claim the title or the estates. Simon and Frederick will bear me out. Since I've come to London I have not made a single demand, save on my daughter's behalf. Caroline Jeannette's future is my sole concern. I am suited well in New Orleans, and I plan to return as soon as my daughter is settled."

Simon saw Jeannette's eyes widen as if her father's words had taken her by surprise.

"Frederick." Hugh advanced slowly on the young man who stood quite still at the desk, his back stiff, his face turned to the fourth duke's portrait on the wall behind the desk. "Caroline's grandfather can no longer help establish her in a marriage suitable to her position. But you can."

Frederick turned. He was pale, his face tightly set.

"Sir, it appears I have wronged you. The ring, these letters—damn it, sir! I am usurping your position."

"No, no, my boy. Told you I don't want the title. It's yours. You were raised to it."

"Sir, I don't understand why you refuse what is yours by right. But if it is your wish to return to New Orleans, I will do anything in my power to see Caroline established. Just tell me what you want me to do."

"Marry her, my boy."

Chapter Twenty-five

"The devil you say!" Simon jumped to his feet. "I won't allow it."

Jeannette flew across the room. She shook her father's arm. "Papa, what are you doing? I don't want Frederick to marry me!"

Frederick, blushing to the roots of his hair, stammered, "Sir, I'm sorry. I'm afraid—you see, sir, I've already asked someone."

The conversation turned incomprehensible when Jeannette and Frederick spoke simultaneously and Hugh tried to answer and soothe them both.

With a scowl at the vociferous trio by the desk, Simon snatched the letters off the table and scanned them quickly. He handed them to Malcolm, the only one who had neither stirred nor spoken since Hugh's demand that Frederick marry Jeannette.

"Do you know the handwriting, sir?"

"Hugh Dundas's," Malcolm said without hesitation. "But, of course, we'll compare the writing with the letters Hugh sent his mother from Philadelphia. Anne has those."

"And with the note *this* Hugh sent Frederick

in April. I have it in my office here. I'll get it."

Malcolm put out a restraining hand. "There's time, son."

Simon looked at his father, whose judgment he valued and respected above any man's.

"Sir, you heard Frederick. He hasn't even looked at the letters, but already he's convinced he's usurping the title. You said you had reasons for not pressing Hugh when you first confirmed that he is an imposter. I must ask you to share those reasons with me or to let me confront the rogue with the evidence *we* have."

Their eyes locked, and after a moment, Malcolm nodded.

"Give me the opportunity to warn him. Then, if he has not explained himself within a week, I'll tell you what I know, and yours will be the decision what to do about him." Malcolm paused. "Also, if you'll remember, you have my leave to drop a hint in Caroline's ear, thus, perhaps, forcing Hugh's hand."

This was what Simon had firmly intended to do—until she smiled at him. Until she kissed him.

Glancing toward the others, he nodded. He had no choice but to agree. There was no time for argument. Hugh, his hands thrown up as if in defeat, turned away from Jeannette and Frederick and was coming toward him and his father.

Frederick hurried from the room, and Jeannette, left standing by herself, raised her chin and squared her shoulders before following Hugh.

She looked calm and self-possessed, yet, for a moment, while she stood by herself, Simon could have sworn she was as bewildered by her father's actions as he was by his father's reluctance to end the charade.

Hugh sat down opposite Malcolm, and Jeannette went to stand behind his chair.

Simon still stood at Malcolm's side.

Battle lines drawn, positions chosen. An unwelcome thought, but one Simon could not banish.

"Knew you were a gambler, Hugh." Malcolm's brows rose a fraction. "But I never expected you to play for high stakes when you knew you held a losing hand."

A spark lit in Hugh's tired eyes. "Fate forced my hand to play this game when I arrived and found Frederick installed as the sixth duke. I'll double the stakes if I must."

Malcolm's gaze flicked to Jeannette, then back to Hugh. "I can only guess at the game you're playing, and I'm beginning to wonder if my guess is as good as I thought."

He leaned forward suddenly, his voice sharpening. "Damn it, Hugh! Neither one of us is playing fair with our children. So far I've not shared my knowledge of the past and the family with Simon. But I will not risk losing his respect. Neither will I allow Frederick to feel guilty."

Pushing heavily against the arms of his chair, Hugh rose. "And I will not risk losing my daughter or her love."

Above their father's heads, Simon and Jeannette exchanged a look, hers puzzled, Simon's grave. Simon had never felt so helpless, so ignorant. Thanks to his father and to Hugh Dundas, he did not know whether to comfort or to shake the woman he longed to hold in his arms.

Again, Malcolm's glance flicked to Jeannette. "I wonder. Perhaps you underestimate your daughter's love for you."

Jeannette's eyes flashed. "Papa knows I love him. And I wish you'd stop talking in riddles! Both of you. Games! Stakes! I'm beginning to think I've strayed into a gambling hell."

Unexpectedly, Malcolm chuckled. "You sound just like your Grandmother Caroline. She could never abide it when, as boys, Hugh and I tried to talk over her head."

Turning serious, he said to Hugh, "Perhaps I should warn you that Anne is having second thoughts as well. It was the miniature, I believe, that stirred her memory."

Simon bit down an expletive. Jeannette might believe herself in a gaming hell; *he* felt as though he had strayed into Bedlam. One moment, his father talked as if the late duchess were in fact Jeannette's grandmother, and next he issued another warning to Hugh.

Exasperated beyond endurance, he did not notice that Hugh and Jeannette were leaving until they had reached the study door.

"Jeannette!" He covered the distance in a few long strides. "I shall call on you tomorrow morning. Is nine o'clock too early?"

A smile lit her face. "Nine o'clock will be perfect."

Silence as dense as the maroon velvet covers on the seats hung between Jeannette and her father as the town carriage rattled toward George Street.

Twice, Hugh had cleared his throat preparatory to speaking. Twice, a look at his daughter's closed face had stopped him. But he could bear the silence no longer.

"Jeannette . . . would it be so very awful to marry Frederick?"

"Yes." She turned her head to look at him. "I don't love Frederick. And he's in love with Eleanor."

"It would have been perfect. Frederick and Caroline. Just like your grandparents."

With an impatient hand gesture, Jeannette swept aside such mawkish sentiments.

"Papa, why didn't you *tell* me? Did you not realize how very awkward I would feel? *My father* offering a title and estates to a young man so that he'll take me off your hands!"

"I did not!" He was indignant. "Only a fool would have tried to bribe young Frederick. He's far too proper. That's why I made it absolutely clear I want nothing to do with either title or estates *before* I suggested the marriage."

"Well, I won't marry Frederick."

Folding her arms across her chest, she leaned back against the squabs.

"There's nothing more to be said, then?" Hugh pressed.

"Nothing."

"After Prinny's ball, everyone will be fleeing to the country. How, then, am I to find you a husband?"

"Perhaps you could let me find my own husband?"

The carriage rocked, and Hugh reached for the strap to steady himself.

Surprised but eager, he asked, "Is there someone you're interested in?"

She evaded the question. "Papa, will you truly return to New Orleans and leave me here?"

"It will be the hardest, most difficult thing I have ever done. But we both knew from the start of the journey that you would be married here."

"At the start, I assumed I would return with you."

Jeannette turned her face to the window. Marriage was no longer a word to raise her hackles. On the contrary, it was a promise of warmth and sharing, of such delights as she could not possibly imagine. Yet.

But, foolishly, she had not considered that marriage would part her from her father.

"Papa, what did you mean when you told Malcolm Renshaw you would not risk losing me or my love?" She faced him. "You must know that I'll love you always."

"Daughter, you are everything to me." He touched her cheek in a gentle caress, the way he had done when she was a child. "And I'll not let Malcolm or his son or Frederick stop me from giving you what is yours."

He had not answered her question. And she did not want what he was determined to give her. She cared nothing for a title or position. But the set of his jaw, his look of feverish determination, decided her against argument.

For a while, they sat in silence. Outside the carriage window, the tall, elegant houses of Portman Square slid past.

"Jeannette, do you know why young Renshaw wants to call on you tomorrow?"

She heard the tired note in his voice. The drive to West India Docks and the meeting at Dundas House immediately afterward had been too much for him.

"No, Papa. I don't know."

And she did not know. She could only dream and

hope that Simon's angry protest against a marriage between her and Frederick was a betrayal of his own desires. That he would call to make his intentions known.

They were turning into George Street.

"Papa, what did Malcolm Renshaw mean, that you're playing for high stakes with a losing hand?"

"I don't think he himself knows what he means. I certainly don't."

Jeannette subsided, but she could not forget Malcolm Renshaw's strange utterances. They pursued her even in her sleep.

That night Hugh sat at his desk in the library. In his hands he held the last yellowed letter, the letter he had set aside when he gave the others to Jeannette.

How the deuce had he come to this pass? He had crossed an ocean to fulfill a promise. To see his daughter creditably established—as was her due. But he was thwarted at every turn.

He had wanted only to introduce Jeannette to her grandfather, to assure the old gentleman that, after all these years, he had no intention of disrupting anyone's life. That he merely wanted to see his daughter suitably married. Then he would have withdrawn and returned to New Orleans.

What damnably poor timing of the old gentleman to die just when his granddaughter needed his backing! Or, if at least Malcolm had been in town when he and Jeannette arrived. They'd have had a quiet talk, and everything would have been settled.

Still, despite Simon's aggression, despite Louisa's

animosity, he had tried to follow the original plan. He had not made a claim for the title—hell, that had never been his intention. But he wanted Jeannette acknowledged, and if that meant he must prove his identity as Hugh Dundas, he would damn well do so.

He had done it. With the letters and the ring he had established himself. Malcolm's veiled warnings had come too late. In any case, they were bluster. There was nothing Malcolm could do, even though the letters, instead of helping, had apparently raised more doubts.

Bloody hell! Why the doubts? Even after forty years, Malcolm must have recognized the handwriting.

Donning his spectacles, Hugh scanned the last letter. The letter he had not given to Jeannette to read. If he took it to Malcolm, chances were that Jeannette would be welcomed into the bosom of the family.

But, of a certainty, he would lose her.

He must not lose Jeannette, the daughter of his heart, who had become even more dear to him since he lost Jeanne and the infant boy.

Losing Jeannette to marriage was different from losing her altogether . . . irrevocably. Losing her forever was what he had fought to avoid. That's why he had gambled and taken risks.

His fingers tightened on the letter. He should preserve it for Jeannette. To read . . . perhaps after his death.

But Malcolm's son would be calling in the morning. He had a hunch that Simon would try to turn Jeannette against him. And then Jeannette would start asking questions, and she would ask once more why there was no letter announcing the happy event of her birth.

And he would feel honor bound to show her the letter.

Unless it disappeared.

Stiffly, Hugh rose and approached the hearth where the remnants of several logs still smoldered.

Once more, he glanced at the letter, seven pages covered in a bold scrawl, the black ink faded to gray.

He was a gambler. Until his return to England, he had never engaged in cardsharping. But fate had dealt him a damnably poor hand.

In fact, fate had dealt him one trick after another, starting back in November of 1780 when the rebels left Hugh Dundas for dead in a muddy lane leading to Savannah's town hall. And the twinge of conscience when he recovered from his illness this past winter and realized that Jeannette had passed her nineteenth birthday and he had yet to fulfill his solemn oath to take her to England was not the last trick, either.

But he, too, had a card up his sleeve. If he could bring himself to play it.

He thought of Simon's agent, who might already be in New Orleans. Harte would find Madame Vireilles and dozens of witnesses to testify that Hugh Dundas had married Jeanne Vireilles, that he returned from Saint Domingue in 1803 with a daughter, Jeannette.

Only if Harte went to the *boutique* . . .

Hugh took a deep breath. That was a hurdle he'd take in due course.

One more deep breath to steady his hand. Slowly,

he stooped until the letter was above the grate and he felt the heat of the glowing embers.

Even more slowly, he let go.

"No!"

A blast of turbulent air stirred around him. The letter, every single page, with scarcely a corner scorched, blew onto the hearth rug.

He could not move. His heart raced, and his mouth was dry.

He did not understand what happened, did not know where the draft had come from, did not even know whether he had imagined the shouted "No!"

But he did know that fate had once more intervened.

Fate dealt the cards, and whether he liked it or not, it was the hand he must play.

And, after all, Jeannette should read the letter. Some day.

He bent and picked up the scattered pages. He put them in order, folded them, and returned them to the drawer in his desk.

Annie wiped her brow. What a close call!

She waited until Hugh had locked the drawer and pocketed the key. Then she flitted up to the third floor.

Annie had not read the letter—she had not come into the room until Hugh rose to toss it into the fire—but she had observed him often enough on previous occasions to know that the yellowed pages belonged with the set of letters he had earlier given Lady Caroline to read.

And she had seen him hesitate when he stood by the fireplace. She had sensed his conflict.

It was pure instinct that made her swoop down and snatch the sheets before they caught fire. Instinct that had paid off. His lordship had looked relieved when he picked up the scattered pages and put them back in the desk.

But, perhaps it wouldn't hurt to let Lady Caroline know that there was one more old, yellowed letter she had not yet read.

Chapter Twenty-six

Simon walked to George Street. He had not slept during the past night, and he needed the exercise to clear his head.

The letters dated 1781 to 1790 were authentic. There was no doubt at all. The handwriting was the same as that in the letters written earlier by Hugh Dundas from Philadelphia, which a messenger had fetched from Lady Anne as soon as Hugh and Jeannette left Dundas House.

Thus, it was certain that Hugh Dundas, Marquis of Luxton, had not died in November of 1780. It was certain that he had lived a full and happy life until, at least, October of 1790.

But it was also certain that the man who had presented the letters written in New Orleans and Saint Domingue was not the Marquis of Luxton.

The most difficult part had been to convince Frederick that he was truly and rightfully the Sixth Duke of Granby, but Malcolm and Simon had finally succeeded. And then Frederick had voiced aloud the questions Simon had tried to keep buried in the deepest recess of his mind.

"What happened to the real Hugh? And how and when did Hugh—the imposter, I mean—get a hold of the letters and the signet ring?" Frederick paled. "Great Scot, Simon! You don't suppose—no, of course not! That would be too outrageous. But did he go to Haiti—or Saint Domingue, or whatever the dratted island was called—to meet Hugh Dundas? And how did he know where Hugh was when no one else did?"

Simon had not been required to answer, and if he had, he could have said only that he did not know. But Frederick, turning to Malcolm, asked yet another question.

"Who is he, sir? Surely *you* must know which of the fourth duke's illegitimate sons was raised and educated as a gentleman."

"He's not one of the fourth duke's butterprints," said Malcolm.

Leaning heavily on his cane, the older Renshaw had excused himself abruptly and retired to his rooms, leaving his son to deal with any further questions from Frederick, preoccupied with the puzzle of the imposter's identity.

"We cannot deny his looks, Simon. But if he was not fathered by the fourth duke in the old lecher's last years of raking . . . Dash it! That leaves my namesake, the fifth duke, in which case Caroline's father would be a half-brother of the real Hugh Dundas."

"Certainly a motivation for what he has done."

"But there was also my grandfather and his brother, Cornelius, who could have fathered Hugh—the imposter. Though Cornelius died young, didn't he? In a tavern brawl?"

"Perhaps we should leave all questions to solve themselves."

"But will they?" Frederick's brow grooved. "The

way matters stand, Hugh Dundas only has to sit mum. We cannot *do* anything about him, can we? And, somehow, I don't believe your man Harte will find anything useful in New Orleans."

"I'm afraid you may be correct, but we shall see. I'll lay you odds, though, that my father knows who he is." Simon rose and stretched. "And now, bantling, I'm off to bed."

Frederick had nodded and accompanied his cousin to the study door. He had asked one last question.

"Tell me, Simon. Should I marry Caroline so Hugh will go back to New Orleans and we can forget about this whole sorry mess?"

It was no wonder that Simon had spent a sleepless night.

What about Caroline? Jeannette. She was her father's daughter. Brazen. Deceitful.

And he loved her.

Frederick's noble sacrifice would not be necessary. He'd see to it. With pleasure.

But it would give him no pleasure at all if he must use Jeannette to force her father's hand. Unfortunately, it might be the only way to get the self-styled Hugh Dundas to acknowledge defeat.

The imposter, and possibly worse.

As he walked toward the small terrace house in George Street, Simon grimly faced the possibility Frederick had dismissed as too outrageous. The possibility that Jeannette's father had killed the man he impersonated.

Jeannette received him in the crowded little downstairs parlor where she had told him about her childhood on Saint Domingue, about her mother's and infant brother's death aboard the schooner carrying the French planters and their families to safety in the fall of 1803.

She came toward him with a smile and both hands outstretched. "As you see, I am being improper again, receiving you without a chaperone. But I hope you won't read me a lecture on the behavior of a lady."

Taking her hands, he looked at her without speaking. Her smile was warm, her voice light and teasing, and he wanted nothing more than to take her into his arms and kiss her. But he hardened his heart against such ill-timed desire and searched her face for signs of unease and a guilty conscience.

The signs were there. No smile could hide them. The pallor of her cheeks, the bruised look of the delicate skin beneath her eyes. She, too, had spent a sleepless night. As well she should.

His grip tightened. "Jeannette, the game is finished. Please make your father see that he has lost."

"Simon!"

Eyes wide and disbelieving, she stepped back from him. "How can you still refuse to acknowledge Papa! The letters, the ring—"

"They are authentic. No one denies that."

"Then, what—" Her voice rose. *"Nom de nom de nom!* Now you believe he stole them!"

"I don't know how your father came into possession of the letters and the signet ring. I do know he is not Hugh Dundas."

Her breath caught at the harshness of his tone. When Simon stepped into the room she had felt as if he had brought the sunshine into the house with him. The graveness of his expression had made her heart beat faster; she believed that he had come to tell her he would not allow her to marry Frederick or anyone else because *he* wanted to marry her.

Now, she knew better. The implacable tone of his voice, the set face, the hard look in his eyes, had a meaning that drove a chill down her spine. She could not have felt colder if it had started to freeze again.

She clasped her hands to keep them from trembling. What a fool she had been! A silly, romantic fool.

"Jeannette, you *must* convince your father to give up. He made it clear yesterday that he will stop at nothing to see you married to a man of rank and fortune. Surely you know that I could never permit this?"

Her eyes flew to his face, so grim and stern. No doubt, she was a fool again, but the flicker of hope in her breast could not be denied.

"Why could you not permit it, Simon?"

"You need to ask?"

He started to pace, knocked against a chair in the crowded space, and flung around to face her again.

"Your father may be lost to all decency and think nothing of it if he blackmails Frederick into marriage or, failing that, foists you as Lady Caroline Dundas on some unsuspecting sprig of the nobility. But you cannot expect me to stand by and allow such treachery under the guise of the Dundas name."

She was too shocked to feel anything but numb.

"Mr. Renshaw, I think it is best if you leave. Immediately."

"The deuce I will!" Gentlemanly conduct forgotten, he grabbed her shoulders. "You will never be the Duchess of Granby or the Countess of who-knows-what. If you must marry an English fool, you'll have to make do with me."

She stood stock still. He had said it. Said that she mustn't marry anyone but him. And her heart was breaking. Surely it was. Why else would her chest hurt with every breath she drew?

"Goodbye, Mr. Renshaw." She swallowed. How difficult it was to preserve composure while struggling with humiliation and tears. "And don't bother to call again. Neither my father nor I shall be at home to you."

"Stop it, Jeannette!" He gave her a shake but dropped his hands when he felt her flinch. "Do you want to end up in Newgate Prison? Ask Amelia Hunter how a woman convicted of fraud fares in Newgate."

She turned as pale as the parlor walls.

Hating himself but knowing that he must press his point, he kept his voice harsh.

"You're a pampered young lady. You would not survive prison. Only a woman accustomed to harshness can survive, or preserve her dignity and start a new life when she is released. Only a strong woman can live with the memories, the nightmares. Only a strong woman can daily face the mementoes of prison, the prematurely gray hair, a stiff ankle."

In a sudden surge, color returned to her face.

"And I daresay *you* will see to it that I am convicted! And then, Simon? Will your conscience nag at you? Will you bribe the warden to bring me a mattress and decent food? Or do you have no conscience?"

"Damn it, Jeannette! Both you and your father ought to have known we would compare the handwriting of the letters not only with that of earlier letters written by Hugh from Philadelphia, but also with the note your father sent to Frederick in April.

Your father's writing may be similar to Hugh's, but it is not the same."

She hadn't meant to dignify such nonsense with an answer but could not stop herself.

"A person's handwriting changes over the years. *Anyone* knows that."

"Not significantly. Hugh Dundas used to dot an 'i' with a circle; your father uses a slash."

How well she knew the bold, slanted mark above every "i," half the size of the letter itself. Chicken scratches she had called them as a child.

Strangely, she could not recall whether circles or slashes dotted the "i's" in the letters she had read. But she did recall Annie's late visit the previous night, her baffling tale of yet another letter, one her father had almost burned.

For some reason, the thought of that letter, a letter her father apparently had not wanted her to see, made her feel even colder than Simon's harshness had done. And angry. Angrier than the threat of prison had made her.

A pox on Simon for making her want to take a second look at the handwriting in the letters.

"Your father's loops come to a point," Simon went on relentlessly. "Hugh's are more rounded."

"I *know* my father's handwriting. You need not describe it. I read the letters he gave you, and I tell you I did not notice any difference in the writing."

He heard the anger in her voice, saw her tightly clasped hands, her rigid stance, but in her eyes, he caught a bewildered look. And dawning apprehension.

His breath caught as if he had received a punch in the stomach. He knew, suddenly and as certainly as if he could see into her heart, that she was not playing a role.

He did not understand how it could be possible, but she had truly believed—still believed—her father to be Hugh Dundas, the Marquis of Luxton.

But he had just planted the first seed of doubt.

Great Scot! What was he to do now? It was one thing to press her when he believed her to be a partner in her father's game of deception, quite another when he knew she was as much a victim of Hugh's schemes as Frederick.

But neither could he allow her to continue in ignorance or she would let that rogue of a father marry her off under a false name. Then, she'd truly be in the basket.

"Jeannette." His voice gentled. "Did you look for a difference in writing?"

"There's nothing wrong with my eyes," she said coldly. "I'm sure I would have noticed."

"You did not expect to see anything but your father's handwriting. As I said, it is similar to Hugh's—the bold strokes, the slant of the letters. And, of course, the ink has faded, making the differences less noticeable."

She might begin to have doubts, but she would not admit them.

"I read the letters with an unbiased mind. *You* were looking for something—*anything*—to prove that my father is an imposter. Simon, I don't believe you!"

"Forget the letters. Do you believe that Hugh Dundas and my father grew up together? That they shared a tutor, a fencing master, and many a boyish exploit?"

"I know our fathers were friends. And Frederick's

father and Lord Decimus as well. Papa told me."

"When Hugh Dundas was about ten and my father twelve, they fought a mock duel. With rapiers. Hugh pinked my father's arm. A slight cut, but the scar still shows. My father foolishly tried to disarm Hugh. He may even have succeeded, for Hugh let go of the rapier, and the point of my father's blade slashed the palm of Hugh's right hand. Yet *your father* does not bear a scar."

Jeannette took a step backward. And another, until she was stopped by a chair.

Abruptly, she sat down. Her heart beat hard and fast, and the feeling of chill penetrated to the very core of her being.

None of this made sense. Nothing had made sense from the moment she understood that Simon still did not believe her father.

Once, in anger, she had flung at him that he would fight for Frederick even when he held the proof of her father's identity in his hands. She had apologized, and now, ironically, her accusation had come true.

Only, Simon wasn't fighting her father out of spite or for gain. He was fighting out of conviction.

That was what made her feel cold, desolate . . . and afraid.

"Jeannette, do you believe me now?"

She gave a start. Believing him, meant—

"No! No, I don't! You said yourself the letters are authentic. Thus, my mother did marry Hugh Dundas. My grandparents knew him well. He lived in their home for almost two years before he and my mother left for Saint Domingue. Do you think my grandparents would have accepted an imposter when he returned with me in 1803?"

"In his letters, Hugh Dundas mentions a woman, Nounou, who cared for him when he was ill. She went to Saint Domingue with the young couple. Do you know her?"

"But of course! She was my nurse. And *Maman's* before that. She was there when *Maman* died, and the poor little baby. Now, she's helping Marie look after the *boutique*. I told you about the dressmaker's shop. I must have told you about Nounou."

"I don't recall."

And it did not matter. It only mattered that he had not known about Nounou when Harte left.

"And what about *Maman?*" Jeannette made a sound that might have been a sob or a choke of laughter, and probably was a bit of both. She rose to face him. "Do you think my mother would have lived with an imposter for twelve years or more? Do you think she would have borne him a child? Two children?"

Chapter Twenty-seven

The feeling of having scored a victory over Simon lasted only until the door closed behind him.

A moment earlier, Jeannette had paid scarce attention to his parting words, a warning that Malcolm Renshaw would wait no longer than a sennight before confronting her father again. But as soon as Simon was gone, the prospect of a meeting between Malcolm and her father began to haunt her.

A circle to dot the "i" and a scar in the palm of his right hand. Those were the marks distinguishing Hugh Dundas, Marquis of Luxton.

Rather shakily, she climbed the narrow stairs to the second floor where her father had his chambers. The father who dotted an "i" with a slash and whose palm was unmarred.

She knew he was waiting to hear about Simon's visit, and as she approached the second floor landing her steps quickened. But she did not turn into the corridor. Instead, she raced to the next floor.

Opening Isabella's door, she said, "Hurry, we're going to call on the modistes and milliners who have furnished my wardrobe for the Season. There must be some business woman in town who needs help with her accounts."

It was the act of a coward. She knew it, but she

could not face her father with Simon's voice—harsh, implacable—fresh in her mind.

I do know he is not Hugh Dundas. I do know he is not . . . Over and over, the words repeated themselves.

She could not face her father while the questions she wanted to ask were born of doubt.

If she doubted anyone, it should be Simon. She assured herself that she did not believe a word he had said, and yet she could not dismiss a gnawing apprehension.

For several days, Jeannette made certain she saw her father only in Mrs. Effington's company. And even then she felt uncomfortable, guilty, when she caught herself staring at his hand. She felt guilty about not passing on Simon's warning.

Yet if she warned her father, she would be admitting that something was wrong, wouldn't she?

For several days, she concentrated on finding Isabella a position, without success. She quarreled with Annie when the little ghost still refused to abandon the love potion in favor of a visit to old Selina. And she snapped at Mrs. Effington when she asked why they weren't seeing Simon any more after seeing him with such encouraging frequency during the previous weeks.

Jeannette did not want to think about Simon. When she did, she remembered his harsh words, that he would marry her rather than have an imposter besmirch the Dundas name in a marriage with someone else. And a deep, painful cold invaded her body, a cold that had nothing to do with climate.

And thinking of the shared warmth of their talks during the past weeks, the fire of their kiss, only strengthened the feeling that she was slowly freezing to death.

The Prince Regent's fête passed. Eleanor and Agnes, who had both attended the ball, were in raptures over the splendor of Carlton House. Mrs. Effington, whose friend Lady Aldrich had been one of the lucky ones invited to the dinner preceding the ball, reported such questionable delights as goldfish swimming and dying in a miniature stream that had run the length of the Prince's dining table. But Jeannette listened with only half an ear.

She was preoccupied with that terse note written on Saint Domingue in October of 1790. The notation of her mother's miscarriage and Jeanne's insistence on giving her husband a son and a daughter, despite Nounou's warning that she should never bear a child at all.

What if there had been no more children? That would explain why her father had written nothing after the miscarriage.

But where would that leave her, Caroline Jeannette Dundas?

What if Jeanne Vireilles was not her mother?

Impossible.

And there was that other letter. The letter that would have been burned if Annie had not interfered.

What if—what if Simon was correct and her father was not Hugh Dundas?

Then, who was he?

Who was *she?*

Despising herself for her doubts and questions but unable to ignore them any longer, she braced herself for a talk with her father six days after Simon's visit. If she waited another day, she might be forestalled by Malcolm Renshaw.

She knocked on the library door and entered,

coming face to face with Mrs. Effington, who was about to leave.

"Good morning, Lady Caroline." Mrs. Effington's plump, rosy face dissolved in a smile. "And wasn't I just assuring your dear papa that you'd be looking in on him? The poor man is afraid you're still angry with him over his suggestion to marry the young duke."

That embarrassing moment at Dundas House seemed so far in the past and so insignificant that Jeannette could say with complete honesty, "I am not angry. In fact, I had quite forgotten about it."

"I'll be running along, then. Sophronia Aldrich asked me to luncheon. She's leaving for St. Ives tomorrow. Now that the Prince's fête is past and more than half forgotten, everybody is leaving town."

The door closed softly behind Mrs. Effington.

"Louisa's gone, too," said Hugh from his chair at the desk. "Upton took her to one of his estates in Ireland. They left Eleanor with Anne and Agnes."

"Perhaps that is for the best, Papa."

Jeannette approached the desk. Did she imagine it, or did her father look better? He had deep circles under his eyes as if he hadn't slept well for some time, but he sat up straight, his skin had lost the grayish tinge, and he looked younger, more sprightly than she had seen him in a while.

She perched on a corner of the desk. Busying herself with the careful disposition of her skirts, she said, "Perhaps I should have told you earlier, but I believe Malcolm Renshaw will be calling on you tomorrow."

"I know. He sent a note. I agreed to the meeting but told him we'd be calling at Dundas House." A corner of Hugh's mouth twisted in a disparaging curl. "No room here would accommodate eight people."

She gave him a startled look. "Eight! It is not, then, a meeting about . . . a meeting to establish who we are?"

"It is, indeed. But your Aunt Anne will be present, and I have asked Decimus and Mrs. Effington to be there." He looked straight at her. "This time, we'll get it sorted out. I promise you, Jeannette."

She saw the love in his eyes—and sadness, as if he knew about her doubts this past week.

Her throat tightened. How could she ever have entertained doubts about him, about his identity? He was her father. He had showered her with love since the day of her birth. She should have had more faith.

Deeply ashamed, she lowered her gaze. She loved him, and yet she had wondered about him. Because another man insisted her father could not be who he said he was.

Another man. Simon.

And, heaven help her, she loved Simon, too.

Her breath caught.

Simon. She loved him!

When it had happened, she did not know. But what a time she had chosen to make the discovery. Or was it, in truth, not so much a discovery as a long overdue acknowledgement?

"Jeannette."

Very much aware of the warmth stealing into her cheeks, she faced her father.

"My dear, there is something you must know before we go to Dundas House. Malcolm suggested last week that, perhaps, I am underestimating your love. Today, Mrs. Effington said very much the same."

"Papa, I love you. There can never be a question about it. But what does it have to do with Malcolm Renshaw? Or Mrs. Effington?"

He pushed back his chair, as if, thought Jeannette, he wanted to distance himself from her.

"I was unsure what to do. Mrs. Effington is a sensible woman. This morning, I asked her advice about a matter regarding you."

Jeannette's heart beat in her throat. That awful feeling of apprehension was back.

"And what was Mrs. Effington's advice?"

"To make a clean breast of my misdeeds."

She wanted to protest that he couldn't have done anything wrong, but her throat was too tight for speech.

Her father took a key from his pocket. He looked at it as if he expected it to tell him what to do or say next.

Stiffly, he leaned forward and unlocked a desk drawer. He took out several sheets of yellowed vellum.

The letter Annie had told her about. It had to be! The letter her father wanted to burn.

"You wondered why, among the letters I gave you to read, there wasn't one announcing your birth. Here it is."

He handed her the sheets.

"Take your time reading it, Jeannette. I'll be in the sitting room upstairs, waiting to answer your questions."

"No! Please stay, Papa."

In the act of rising, he gave her a questioning look.

"I don't want to be alone." Her hands shook, and she tightened her grip on the stiff pages for fear of dropping them. "I'd like you to be with me while I read."

He sank back into the chair. "Go ahead. I'll wait right here."

She slid off the desk and walked over to the fireplace which, finally, at the end of June, was swept clean of ashes and held instead of logs a brass container filled with daisies and roses.

Settled on the hearth rug, Jeannette read the letter, dated September 21, 1791. Four days before she was born.

She saw the slashes dotting every "i," but she would not doubt her father again. Simon had made a mistake when he compared the letters written from Philadelphia with those written on Saint Domingue.

Or her father's handwriting had changed.

Like the very first letter to Decimus Rowland from New Orleans, dated April of 1781, this one was a lengthy epistle, conversational in tone. Hugh Dundas wrote that a slave uprising had swept Saint Domingue in August, but that now the worst of the bloody revolt was over. A free man of color, Toussaint l'Ouverture, had taken control and was doing his best to protect the French planters with his troops.

Hugh admitted that he had been tempted to leave the island at the first whisper of an uprising, but that his wife's condition had made flight impossible. Any day now, Jeanne expected to give birth to their child.

At present, I find myself an invalid once more. Nothing serious, just a minor head wound received when I helped a neighbor, whose home was attacked. I'm well on the mend and should be able to ride out and inspect the property by next week. Those of my people who ran away at the outbreak of the uprising are now returning to work. And just in time! We're nearing the end of the rainy season, and the cane fields and coffee plantations have been badly neglected.

Decimus, old friend, I'll wager a pony that you won't guess in a month of Sundays who arrived here at the Plantation Vireilles three weeks ago, at the height of the insurrection.

Hugo.

Yes, indeed. My Cousin Cornelius's offspring.

Hugo arrived on horseback, escorted by some of Toussaint l'Ouverture's men from Port-au-Prince, just as I was carried home on a stretcher, my bleeding head all wrapped up in rags.

You probably know that Hugo came to America to buy land. He had explored the Carolinas and traveled south to Florida. From Cape Sable he crossed to New Orleans, and as luck would have it he literally ran into my father-in-law on the docks. Barely saved the old gentleman from toppling over. Monsieur Vireilles mistook him for me, and even Jeanne, my beloved wife of eight blissful years, was briefly confused and did not know whether it was her husband lying on the stretcher or sitting proudly on the horse when she first saw us together.

Hugo has been a great help to me while I was laid up, and a comfort to Jeanne. Nothing can intimidate Hugo. He's still the intrepid, enterprising boy I remember—only now, of course, he is a man.

It is difficult to perceive that the scrawny youngster who followed me about whenever I stayed at Granby has turned into such a splendid example of manhood.

Service in the dragoons did that, I suppose. My mother must have been proud of him. She always believed that Hugo inherited only the strengths of his Dundas forbears and none of the weaknesses. And, indeed, I would trust Hugo with my life and family—even though he fought for the King during America's struggle for independence.

He told me that Mother died and that the family believe I was killed in Savannah. Father, apparently, has accepted Cousin William's son as his heir, which suits me well. After all these years in America and after having fought on the rebel side, I'd make a sorry duke.

Decimus, I'm not certain I'll ever send these letters I've addressed to you and which have accumulated in my desk. For the present, at least, it is best if I stay dead and lost to the Dundas clan.

But I promise you this, my friend. Some day, I'll bring my family to England for a visit, and we'll crack a bottle or two or three—just like in the old days.

Chapter Twenty-eight

Some day, I'll bring my family to England for a visit . . .

A promise. But it could not be the promise that had driven her father to undertake the long journey just after his illness this past winter.

Jeannette tugged at one of the daisies brightening the hearth. The promise he mentioned aboard the *Merry Maiden* had been such a specific vow: to take her to England if she wasn't betrothed or married at eighteen. And to see her wed to an Englishman.

Only to *Maman* would he have made such a promise.

Her hands were unsteady when she gathered the sheets and folded them neatly. There was something about this letter, dated four days before her birth, that affected her deeply. She did not know whether her reaction was excitement, or fear, or something altogether different, unidentifiable.

Surely, it wasn't the date that made her breath shallow. Or confirmation that even then, almost twenty years ago, her father had been determined not to claim his birthright. Nor could it be the mention of Hugo, Cousin Cornelius's offspring, that made her tremble.

Cornelius was the man Papa had mentioned in the same breath as the rakish fourth duke and his scandals. Cornelius had died in a brawl somewhere. And Hugo was his son. He had visited her father. That was not so very strange, was it? Except that the family did not know that Papa was alive.

And why hadn't Hugo told anyone that he had seen Hugh?

Why did the letter affect her so strangely and set her trembling all over? Was it Simon's warning? The conviction in his voice when he said, "I do know he is not Hugh Dundas."

Nom de nom! Surely, she wasn't beginning to doubt her father again.

If only she could think straight. There was something of significance in the letter itself—and it wasn't the slash above the "i". It was something that caused a stir deep in her memory.

"Jeannette." Her father spoke so softly, she barely heard him. "You have read the letter?"

She rose. "Yes, Papa. Thank you for sharing it with me."

"Is that all you have to say?" He left his chair and came toward her. "No questions about Hugo, the illegitimate offspring of Cornelius Dundas?"

Nothing in the letter had indicated that Hugo was illegitimate, and it took her a moment to digest the notion. It made sense. An illegitimate son, more so than death in a brawl, put Cornelius in the same league as the rakish Augustus.

"Cornelius didn't give a damn about the brat," her father said. "It was your grandmother who saw to it that the boy and his mother lacked for nothing. Your grandmother paid for Hugo's education and later bought him a cornetcy in the 16th Light Dragoons."

Yes, that would be like her Grandmother Caroline,

who had taught the village children, tended the sick, and never turned her back on a poor girl "in trouble".

But at the moment her grandmother's generosity was of little interest. Jeannette was thinking of Hugo's arrival at the Plantation Vireilles at the height of the insurrection.

What was it that tugged at her memory? If only her mind weren't in such a turmoil.

"Papa, where is Hugo now? Could he help you put Malcolm's and Simon's doubts to rest?"

Even as she spoke, even before she saw her father shake his head, before she heard him tell her to think, to think back to the Plantation Vireilles, a small, long forgotten detail stirred in her memory. The "something" that had worried her.

And she knew that Hugo could not help.

She remembered herself as a child, accompanying her mother on All Saint's day to the old burial plot at the plantation. Neither she nor *Maman* had liked the place, so dark and silent within a circle of thick shrubbery and vines and tall mahogany trees. Usually a gardener had cared for the flowers blooming there. Every All Saint's day, though, *Maman* dutifully visited the graves.

Jeannette had gone only once or twice, but she remembered the wooden cross among the markers of polished stone. And carved into the wood, the name Hugo.

It was no wonder, then, that this letter telling about the intrepid, enterprising Hugo's arrival on Saint Domingue had affected her so strangely.

"Do you see it now?" asked her father, his voice tight. "Do you understand?"

"Yes, but how did he die? And when?"

"We did not know he was ill. There was no fever to alert him or your mother and me. Or even Nounou.

But it was the yellow fever. One of those 'masked' cases, without the febrile period when we could have administered a purgative or applied an ergot poultice."

Her father reached out and touched her shoulder.

"He simply collapsed, Jeannette. There was nothing we could do. Nounou even called on the *hungan* for a powerful *wanga*. But in vain."

Jeannette nodded. Poor Hugo must have been very sick indeed if Nounou with her vast knowledge of medicinal herbs and barks had admitted defeat and consulted a voodoo priest. Normally, Nounou would have crossed herself and looked the other way when she saw a *hungan*.

"My dear, nothing could save him. Two days after he collapsed, the day before you were born, Hugh was dead."

Hugh was dead.

She must have misheard.

But all of a sudden, she was shivering and trembling again.

The cross—it said *Hugo*. Even as a very small child, she had read and spelled faultlessly.

She looked at her father. In his eyes, as deep a blue as her own and filled with sorrow, pain, and fear, she saw the truth.

"Papa," she whispered. "You are Hugo."

"Hugo Winters!" exclaimed Lord Decimus, ensconced in the deepest and widest chair the study at Dundas House had to offer. "Stap me! But I never would have guessed it. Thought he went to India after he sold out."

"I went to America."

Their chairs forming a half circle, Hugo sat on Decimus's left, Malcolm on his right. Jeannette was perched on the arm of her father's chair. Mrs. Effington had taken a seat a little removed from the three gentlemen. She was armed with a vinaigrette in one hand and a fan in the other, but judging by the composed look on her face, she would have no need for either.

Lady Anne, restless as usual, paced along the shelf-lined walls. Frederick, relief and eagerness reflected on his open face, leaned against the massive desk behind him.

And Simon stood near the windows, a position that afforded him a clear view of everyone in the study. At least, to be able to observe everyone had been the purpose of stationing himself by the windows. But his mind and eyes were on Jeannette alone.

The disclosure that Hugh Dundas was Hugo Winters, nicknamed Hugo Fitzdundas by the village wisecracks, had not come as a surprise to Simon. An hour before the meeting, his father had summoned him and prepared him for the news he would hear. That the imposter was Hugo Winters, an illegitimate cousin, whom the late duchess had taken under her wing, and for whom Malcolm and Hugh had a fondness when they knew him as a boy.

But nothing his father told him had prepared Simon for the content of the last letter written by Hugh Dundas on Saint Domingue. That Hugh's wife Jeanne expected to be delivered of a child. Hugh's letter was dated the twenty-first of September, 1791. Jeannette was born on the twenty-fifth.

She was, indeed, Lady Caroline Dundas. Daughter of the Marquis of Luxton. Granddaughter of the Fifth Duke of Granby.

Above Simon's touch.

His family background on the Dundas side was impeccable. But there was no denying that his grandmother, first cousin to the late Fifth Duke of Granby, had made a *mésalliance* when she married his Grandfather Renshaw, founder of the law firm Renshaw and Renshaw. And neither could it be contested that his maternal grandfather, Silas Ashton, had made his fortune in the cotton and steel industry.

Cotton spinneries and steel mills, which Simon had inherited. Simon was, in fact, a man engaged in "trade," in the manufacturing business. And he had told Jeannette that, if she must marry an English fool, she would have to make do with him.

Indeed, a fool.

With some difficulty, Simon made himself listen as his father questioned Hugo Winters.

"Your regiment, the 16th Light Dragoons, was one of the first sent to America to quell the rebellion," said Malcolm. "Did you see Hugh during the war? In Philadelphia? Or, perhaps, in Savannah?"

"I didn't see Hugh, and I wasn't anywhere near Savannah. And I did not know until the spring of '90 that Hugh had been reported dead. It was Decimus who told me."

Lord Decimus nodded. "Remember it well. You had sold out and said you were off to make your fortune. That, I expect, is what made me think of India. Every Tom, Dick, and Harry was going to India and returning a nabob."

"Then it was pure coincidence that took you to New Orleans?" asked Malcolm.

"Coincidence had nothing to do with it. 'Twas fate. I almost bought land in North Carolina. I liked it there, but something drove me south." Hugo hesitated. "Malcolm, if you recognized me already the day you came to town, why the devil didn't you say so?"

"How could I be certain? I had my suspicions, but

all I knew for a fact was that you were *not* Hugh. You didn't have the scar."

"Ah, yes." Hugo opened his right hand and glanced at the palm. "I'd forgotten about the 'duel' you fought with him. Still, you should have spoken up."

"In Louisa's hearing? No, my friend. The late duchess would have turned in her grave if I had handed Louisa the ammunition to kick up more dust. Besides, I knew if you were Hugo, you'd eventually come clean. Hugo always did."

Lady Anne paused in her pacing. "What does it matter now? I want to know what happened on Saint Domingue, how long Hugh was ill. How you came to be Jeanne's husband, Caroline's father. Why you took Hugh's name."

Hugo sat stiff and silent.

Jeannette laid a hand on his arm and gave him an encouraging smile and, after a moment, Hugo relaxed.

He looked at Lady Anne. "Hugh collapsed just after the noon meal on the twenty-first of September. He had a lucid moment late that night. Jeanne and I were with him. He told me about the letters in a hidden drawer of his desk, and he asked me to look after his wife and the child she was about to bear."

Jeannette said, "Papa promised to take the child to England some day, and if the child was a girl and not married by the time she was eighteen, to see her wed to an Englishman."

Her gaze flicked to Simon, but so briefly that he wondered if he had imagined it.

"When Papa first told me about the promise, I believed it was made to *Maman* when she was dying."

Hugo said, "It was a solemn oath sworn before you were born. A promise given to your father."

Jeannette shook her head. "*You* are my father."

They looked at each other, and Jeannette remembered the pain and fear she had seen in his eyes when she understood that he was Hugo.

The fear of losing her and her love.

She had pushed aside the confusion, the bewilderment, the sensation of being lost after the startling news that her father was not her father. She would sort out her feelings later. At that moment it mattered only that he suffered, that he was afraid, and that she could reassure him.

She was glad to know she had succeeded. Glad to see his eyes light up in that special way, which all her life had meant, "Daughter, I love you and I am proud of you."

He might not be the father who had given her life, but he was the father who had given her love and care, who had rocked her, carried her, kissed away her tears. And she loved him.

Lady Anne said, "What about Jeanne? You promised to look after her, Hugo. Is that why you married her?"

Slowly, Hugo turned his head to meet Anne's frowning gaze.

"I loved Jeanne."

His voice was hoarse, and Simon, after a look at the sudden pallor of the older man's face, went to pour a glass of wine from the decanters set out on the desk.

The small act of courtesy earned him a smile from Jeannette, a smile that made him want to take her into his arms.

What a fool he was. What a damned presumptuous fool.

Hugo sipped gratefully while Frederick offered sherry and Madeira to the rest of the assembled company.

Color had returned to Hugo's face when he spoke again.

"Jeanne was devoted to Hugh. She was near her time, but those two days and nights of his illness she nursed him tirelessly despite the discomfort she must have been suffering. She would not admit that his condition was hopeless. When he died, she swooned. And by the time Nounou, her old nurse, had revived her, the pains set in. Jeanne was in labor for twenty hours before she gave birth on the evening of the twenty-fifth of September."

Hugo exchanged another look with Jeannette, still at his side, on the arm of his chair, and Simon could not doubt that Hugo loved Jeannette as deeply as only a father can love his daughter.

"When Jeannette was born, Nounou sent for me because Jeanne was asking for Hugh and refused to believe that he could not come to see her. My presence calmed her, and she fell asleep. We did not realize until later that Jeanne had convinced herself *I* was Hugh."

Lord Decimus, muttering something unintelligible, took recourse to his wine glass.

Frederick stared at the tips of his Hessian boots, and Lady Anne resumed her pacing.

Unexpectedly, Mrs. Effington spoke up.

"And that night, when you saw dear Lady Caroline for the first time, you turned into a devoted father."

"No girl could have been more fortunate than I," said Jeannette, hugging Hugo. "Papa, you're the best father in the world."

Lord Decimus cleared his throat. His cherub's face turning red, he said, "I agree that Hugh—or Hugo—is a dashed good fellow. Mustn't get maudlin, though."

Malcolm's brows knitted. "Jeanne never acknowledged Hugh's death? Never recognized you?"

There was a moment of silence before Hugo replied.

"I don't know."

"What do you mean, you don't know?" Briskly, Lady Anne crossed the room to perch on the edge of a chair. "She married you, didn't she? She *must* have known who you are."

"*Maman* did not marry Papa," Jeannette said quietly.

Lady Anne gasped. "Impossible! No lady would consider—"

"My dear Lady Anne, compose yourself." Mrs. Effington rose to offer her smelling salts. "I assure you, there is no reason for outrage or condemnation."

"You knew?" Lady Anne gasped again, this time from the fumes of the aromatic salts.

"Yes, indeed." Pink-faced but quite composed, Mrs. Effington resumed her seat. "Lord Luxton took me into his confidence yesterday."

Hugo said, "Anne, listen to me. When Jeanne could leave the lying-in chamber, Nounou and I took her to see Hugh's grave. With parts of the island still in unrest, I hadn't been able to commission a headstone. But there was a wooden cross with Hugh's name on it. Jeanne saw it."

In a quick, jerky gesture, he put both hands to his face. Just as abruptly, he dropped them.

"I never heard a woman scream as Jeanne screamed when she saw the cross. She became ill. She had a high fever and was often delirious. Nounou said it wasn't the yellow fever that had carried Hugh off, nor was it childbed fever. She said it was a fever of the brain, and she feared that Jeanne would die or—"

It did not matter that he could not bring himself to complete the sentence. The implication was clear. The old nurse had feared for her charge's sanity.

"I, too, feared Jeanne would die. And because I already loved her and the infant, I told Jeanne when she cried out for Hugh in delirium that Hugh was there, waiting for her to get well. And I ordered the carpenter to make a new cross—with my name on it."

"Gracious," said Lady Anne, looking helpless. "Frederick, I believe I will take a little sherry now."

She sipped from the glass Frederick brought her, then looked at Hugo.

"Dash it, Hugo! I cannot believe it. I was not yet four when Hugh left, and when you visited Granby and gave me the piggy-back rides Hugh used to give me, I often pretended you were he."

He nodded. "You even called me Hugh much of the time."

"So I did. But as young as I was, I *knew* it was pretense. How can a woman, after a marriage of eight years or more, *not know* when suddenly she lives in marriage with a different man?"

Malcolm said, "I agree, it is impossible. It would have been hard to swallow even if you and Hugh had been identical twins. I remember both of you well. You were what? Sixteen, when Hugh left?"

"Seventeen."

"And he was twenty. I admit there was a likeness, and I can believe that Jeanne's parents accepted you as Hugh when you returned to New Orleans in '03, twenty years after he left. But a switch on the plantation, where you had been seen together? Devil a bit! That's doing it too brown."

"The likeness between Hugh and me had increased with age. And you forget conditions on Saint Domingue at the time. None of Hugh's people were slaves. When the slave revolt broke out, they hid in the mountains and had only just started to return when Hugh died. They were glad to be home and asked no questions. And the neighbors—"

Looking weary, Hugo leaned back in his chair.

"None of the neighbors knew me. When the island was quiet again and visits could be resumed, we found that many of the plantations near us were deserted. And the families who had stayed—" Hugo shrugged. "If anyone doubted I was Jeanne's husband, they never said so to my face."

"About Jeanne," said Lady Anne.

Hugo sat up.

"I do not wish to discuss Jeanne. But I tell you this. If I could believe that Jeanne knew me as Hugo and not as an image of Hugh, I would be a happy man."

The pain in his voice silenced Lady Anne.

Jeannette laid a hand on his arm but did not speak.

After a moment, Hugo said, "I had no reason to wonder or worry about the ramifications of using another man's name until Jeanne conceived and I realized that any children we might have would be illegitimate."

Simon gave a start as, suddenly, he saw the situation through Hugo's eyes. Hugo was illegitimate, the son of a physician's daughter and Cornelius Dundas, a cad and a wastrel. Hugo knew what it meant to grow up under the stigma of bastard.

"I don't know whether I could have talked to Jeanne at that time," said Hugo. "I did not dare take the risk. But it was then that I made the final commitment *to be* Hugh Dundas. No child of mine would be called a bastard if I could help it."

"By golly, no!" Frederick, having spoken for the first time, colored but faced Hugo squarely. "I'd have done the same, sir."

"Thank you, my boy. Even though that child died, I never wavered in my decision. There was still Jeannette to be considered. She *is* Hugh's daughter, but I would not submit her to even the hint of a doubt."

Hugo looked from Lady Anne to Malcolm and Decimus. He looked at Frederick, then turned toward the windows to fix his eyes on Simon.

"Thus, I became Hugh Dundas. I am Hugh Dundas now and will remain Hugh Dundas until my death."

Chapter Twenty-nine

The challenging look Hugo Winters sent his way, stayed with Simon. A confession made, a gauntlet flung down. The old rogue was determined to retain the name Hugh Dundas.

Simon could not blame him. He, too, wanted to preclude even the slightest possibility that some sharp-tongued gossip would speculate on Jeannette's paternity or legitimacy. If Hugo's story were known to all and sundry, tongues would most certainly wag, and some, out of spite or just pure mischief, would not be kind.

When Simon broached the subject to Malcolm, his father agreed that it would be wise to let the matter drop.

"Hugo will return to New Orleans as Hugh Dundas, and Frederick will hold the title. It's for the best, considering the alternatives. And if you're thinking he doesn't deserve leniency or compromise, consider the twelve years he had with Jeanne. I'd say he suffered many moments of pure hell for his foolishness of taking on Hugh's identity."

Simon did not argue. He had seen Hugo's pain and knew the man had suffered. He believed that, on the whole, Hugo had good intentions when he assumed the name Hugh Dundas. He could not help wondering, though, about the manner of Hugh's death. So unexpected, so damned quick.

It was not a subject he discussed with his father, but it worried him sufficiently to want to seek medical counsel.

Several days after that third meeting at Dundas House, he saw his chance when the chief warden at the Old Bailey summoned him to meet with James Abernathy, the overworked young physician who not only kept infirmary hours every morning in a tavern in Castle Street near Seven Dials but also tended the sick at several hospitals and prisons.

The epidemic of gaol fever at the Old Bailey was stemmed. Simon's client was recovering and should be ready to stand trial within a day or two. No coddling of prisoners at the Old Bailey; no prolonged recuperation time. As soon as a prisoner was able to stand on his feet, he must face the Bench.

Simon thanked the physician and handed him a purse. As they left the warden's office, he described Hugh Dundas's sudden death and asked if yellow fever could have been the cause.

"Yellow fever?" The physician frowned. "Where did he live?"

"Haiti."

"Then, I suppose it's possible. Yellow fever has three marked stages. The febrile period, the period of remission or lull, and in severe cases the period of reaction. I won't bore you with a description of the symptoms since, in this case, most of them don't apply. In some rare instances, like the one you described, the febrile reaction does not come out, and the shock of the infection leads to sudden prostration of the yellow fever victim and almost certainly to death."

Stopping beside the physician's curricle, Simon shook James Abernathy's hand.

"Thank you. That's a great relief to me. I was entertaining the most horrid suspicions."

"Don't blame you." Dr. Abernathy thrust his bag into the curricle and swung himself onto the seat. "Mind you, I'm not saying it was definitely yellow fever. Just that it could have been. There are poisons, and I don't doubt Haiti has its share, that'll kill a man in a similar manner."

With a flick of the reins, Dr. Abernathy set his drooping pair in motion, leaving Simon to stare after him.

Devil a bit! He was back where he started.

Turning his back on the grim walls of the Old Bailey, Simon walked in the direction of St. Paul's. With Simpson recovering from the fever, it was time to pin down Bess. That was more important than speculating what happened to Hugh Dundas. If a murder had been committed twenty years ago on Haiti, it was best left alone.

Simon Renshaw, barrister, cringed at the thought. He would never be content until he knew for certain what happened to Hugh Dundas.

But Simon Renshaw, solicitor to the Dundas family, knew that it did not matter whether the truth was ever discovered. Hugo Winters, whether he continued as Hugh Dundas or not, was too close to the family to be brought to account for a twenty-year-old crime. If crime it was.

His mind churning, Simon walked past the cathedral. He thought of the power certain families held. The nobleman who died at the hands of the crossing sweep, Simpson, was of a powerful family. He had been a cad who forced himself on Simpson's young daughter. Simpson had heard the girl's screams . . .

Simon gave himself a mental shake. It did not matter

that the death of the brutish nobleman was an accident. Even if he could produce a witness. Bess. The nobleman's widow was entertaining the magistrate at tea and begging him with tears in her eyes to see justice done. The nobleman's sons openly demanded a hanging.

The best Simon could hope to gain for his client, even with Bess's testimony, was deportation.

It was not right. Simon knew it. Yet he also knew that if Hugo Winters killed Hugh Dundas, he would not be brought to account. Through Jeannette, Hugo had become a part of the Dundas family, and the family name must be protected at all cost.

Jeannette must be protected.

Jeannette.

He mustn't think of her. And yet, at times, he could not stop himself.

Simon walked faster, turned the corner into Watling Street so quickly that the watercress seller approaching from the other side could not save her basket of wares. Simon apologized and paid the woman twice what the watercress was worth.

He should not think of Jeannette. When he did, his mind raced ahead to the inevitable conclusion of her sojourn in town. Marriage to a sprig of the nobility.

An unbearable thought. A thought that tightened his gut until he felt physically ill.

She was a member of the Dundas family. He was the family solicitor.

He would advise her on the eligibility of a prospective suitor. He would make certain the marriage settlements were generous. He would attend the wedding. He would act with honor and integrity, and he would hate honor and hate integrity. He'd want to meet every one of her suitors with pistols at dawn. He'd want to tear up the settlements.

Bloody hell! He wanted to marry her himself, and damn the consequences.

Undoubtedly, she had on several occasions in the past quite thoroughly detested him. But their relationship had changed these past weeks. If he went to her and apologized for his caddish proposal—if proposal it could be called—the day he told her about her father's handwriting and the missing scar, if he took her in his arms and told her that he loved her, he stood a good chance that she'd accept him.

She would not have kissed him with such ardor if she still disliked him or was indifferent to him. She would not have shared her views and opinions with him if she did not trust him to respect her rather unorthodox ways of dealing with the plight of those less fortunate than she.

Indeed, she trusted him. All these weeks he had wanted to gain her trust, and he had not seen that he already held it. What a fool he was.

Was he a fool again when he told himself he must do the honorable thing and give up the goal he had so loftily set himself after only two meetings with her, the goal to make her his?

He thought of Hugo, loving Jeannette's mother so deeply that he had borne the pain of knowing she believed him to be another man. It was not something Simon could have done. Pride, a need for honesty in his dealings with another person would not have let him suffer a relationship as Hugo had with Jeanne.

If he won Jeannette's hand in marriage, would the need for honesty allow him to forget that he had taken advantage of her growing tenderness for him? That he had spoiled her chances of a more advantageous marriage?

And his pride . . . he doubted his pride would allow him to ignore those members of the *ton,* high in the instep and toplofty, who would consider him a grasping upstart. Rightfully so.

"Mr. Renshaw, sir! How's me da?"

With a start, Simon recognized one of the Simpson boys, Charlie, a gangly youth of about fifteen, who had taken over his father's crossing in Cheapside. Devil a bit! He had turned into Beggars Alley, walked the length of it, and turned into Cheapside without noticing what he was doing.

He gave the boy the good news of his father's recovery and a message for his mother that the trial might be as soon as the next day.

Charlie nodded. "Then, I 'spect, ye was talkin' to Bess?"

Simon reflected grimly that feeling a fool had become his lot in life.

"Not yet, Charlie. I'm afraid I wasn't paying attention and walked right past the print shop. Do you know if she's there?"

The boy had long ceased to be astonished by anything. Inattention was nothing new in adults, whether they came from Grosvenor Square or Beggars Alley.

Leaning on his broom, he said, "Aye, sir. She'll be with 'er aunt. Mrs. Hunter told 'er to stick around in case she be needed by ye."

"Mrs. Hunter did, did she? Thank you, Charlie."

Amelia Hunter had stubbornly opposed her niece's appearance in court but, apparently had relented enough to let him at least talk to the girl again. Hopeful that he might yet persuade Bess to speak up in court, Simon turned back into Beggars Alley.

Jeannette was certain that Simon would call. He must know that she needed to talk, that she felt . . . lost, a little confused.

She was not confused or uncertain about her feelings for her father. Whether he called himself Hugh Dundas or Hugo Winters, he was the same man she had loved all her life and would love always.

But who was she? All the traits, the characteristics she had assumed were inherited from her father—from Hugo—had been passed on by a man who had died before she was born. Even now, it was difficult to believe that this other man had ever existed.

She could not talk to Papa. Any mention of Hugh—that other man—or of *Maman* still brought a look of pain to his eyes.

But, surely, Simon would come to see her. Their last private meeting had been tense, angry even, and painful for her. Surely, he would call soon. Now that there was no doubt about her identity, they could once more share the warmth and intimacy they had known so briefly.

Several days had passed since the meeting at Dundas House, and he still had not called. Finally, she could bear it no longer and asked Mrs. Effington about Simon.

"Do you suppose he has been called out of town?"

Mrs. Effington hesitated. "It is possible."

She and Jeannette were enjoying a cup of tea in the front parlor after a visit to the lending library. Mrs. Effington, too, had wondered about Simon Renshaw, and she did not like the conclusion she had drawn from his continued absence. Perhaps, she ought to give Lady Caroline a hint.

She set down her cup. "My dear, I'm afraid I may have misjudged Mr. Renshaw."

In the act of pouring, Jeannette spilled into the saucer.

"What do you mean, Mrs. Effington?"

"Do you remember my saying that Mr. Renshaw

would make you an admirable husband once he got over the silly notion that you're an imposter?"

"Yes." Jeannette abandoned tea pot and cup. "You don't believe so any longer?"

"Oh, I do. You and he are well suited. What I fear is that Mr. Renshaw is one of those tiresome gentlemen who will withdraw the moment he realizes a woman is above his touch."

"Above . . . his touch?"

"Indeed. As long as he believed you to be Mademoiselle Jeannette something-or-other, he felt free to court you. And you cannot deny that he was courting you these past weeks!"

"Perhaps not exactly . . ." Jeannette's face grew warm under her chaperone's unwavering gaze. "Yes, ma'am. Simon was courting me. I'm as certain of it as I am of my own feelings."

Mrs. Effington gave a satisfied nod.

"But, you see, my dear, now that it has been proven you *are* the Lady Caroline Dundas, he no longer feels eligible to court you."

"Fudge! Simon wouldn't be so silly."

"Wouldn't he, dear? Now that he knows you can look as high as a duke for a husband?"

"Frederick, perhaps? All the other dukes are married. Unless—" Jeannette choked on a giggle. "Unless you think I should aim for one of the royal dukes?"

"I don't think you could, unless the Vireilles family is of noble stock. But I wouldn't suggest one of the royal dukes. All of them are dissolute, and they're quite old."

Gracious! The urge to giggle grew stronger. Mrs. Effington had taken her seriously!

"But there's Sophronia Aldrich's grandson, the Marquess of Wychford. You must have met him at the Venetian Breakfast. He'll be the Duke of Belmore some day, and he is only twenty-five or six."

"Mrs. Effington, I do not want to marry a duke or a marquess or an earl or anyone." Jeannette drew a deep breath. "I want to marry Simon."

"There you are, then. How will you get him to come up to scratch if he does not call? With everyone leaving town for the summer, there won't be any parties where you could meet."

Again, Mrs. Effington was serious. But this time, Jeannette had no desire to giggle.

If Simon was one of those "tiresome gentlemen" Mrs. Effington mentioned, a gentleman who withdrew if he thought a lady above his touch, then there was nothing she could do.

Nothing.

Stiffly, she rose.

"Pray excuse me, Mrs. Effington. Isabella was supposed to write her grandparents. I had best see if the letter is ready for posting."

Her legs acted strangely as she walked up the stairs. It was as if she were just learning to walk, and every step required concentration and effort.

But she could not concentrate. She felt hollowed out, empty. Only one thought occupied her mind. Simon had withdrawn.

When she reached the third floor, she sat down on the top step. She trembled all over, and when she put her head on her knees, she realized that her face was wet with tears.

Instantly, Jeannette straightened her back. This was intolerable. If *Grandmère* could see her, she would snap those dark eyes at her and order her to say three rosaries and count her blessings before even thinking of wallowing in despair. *Grandmère* firmly believed that nothing was ever so bad that it couldn't be borne with dignity.

Jeannette mopped her face and blew her nose. Madame Vireilles was correct insofar as Jeannette had too much pride to turn into a watering pot even if life was bleak, rotten, and unfair.

Once more, she blew her nose. She would never have started to cry in the first place if she weren't so disappointed that Simon didn't care enough to overcome a few little scruples. Surely he knew that *she,* at least, cared nothing for title or position.

But, then, she did not know for certain that he wouldn't call again, did she?

Mrs. Effington was a sensible lady and a good judge of character, but even sensible ladies could be wrong. In fact, Mrs. Effington must be wrong. Simon would not let a useless little thing like a courtesy title come between them.

Simon's kiss had not been mere flirtation, a polite response to her invitation. The way he looked at her, his eyes darkening and filling with warmth, was not the way a man looked at a woman to whom he was indifferent.

She rose, determined that somehow she would bring about a meeting with Simon. If he had changed his mind about courting her, he would have to say so to her face.

Another thought came, unbidden. She was Catholic. Would that be a deterrent?

She shook her head, angry with herself. Of course not, and lest she start moping again, she had better turn her attention to matters she had neglected far too long.

She collected Isabella's letter and asked the girl if she would be too afraid to accompany her on an errand in Beggars Alley, since she would rather not take her groom.

"I'd not be afraid anywhere with you, Lady Caroline.

And I'm very glad that there's finally something I can do for you."

"Thank you, Isabella. When you're ready, meet me downstairs."

Jeannette fetched her gloves and reticule, then went in search of Annie. She found her in the kitchen pantry, where the youngest maid was indulging in a fit of hysterics because, she swore, she had seen a spoon and a glass jar up and flying through the air.

Sweeping Annie along before her, Jeannette left the maid to the tender mercies of the housekeeper.

"Annie, how dare you," she whispered. "You'll have the maids too scared to work here."

"Never mind." Annie was dancing with excitement. "I've done it, Lady Caroline! The potion is perfect, and you can hardly taste it when mixed with Madeira."

"Very good. And now you can forget the potion for a while. We're going to see old Selina."

Chapter Thirty

The pale, drooping shadow that crept from Selina's sparsely furnished room while Jeannette thanked the old woman had nothing in common with the dancing little ghost who left the George Street house less than an hour earlier.

Jeannette caught up with Annie in the dark stair-well. The stench of poverty, of too many unwashed bodies, of stale or rancid food, the stink of grimy floors and walls permeated the whole tenement and made her gag. But she had to speak to Annie before they joined Isabella in the phaeton.

"Annie, I am so very sorry!"

Annie gave no sign of having heard but slunk down the second flight of stairs.

"Please stop a moment, Annie." Holding her skirts high, Jeannette followed. "I have a suggestion."

"And what good is a suggestion? There's nothing that can help me now."

Annie finally stopped on the first floor landing and faced Jeannette. "You heard her, Lady Caroline. The tenement burned. And every last one of my family with it!"

Indeed, more than half of Basket Lane, from Cheapside to the print shop, had burned to the ground forty years ago, and many of the tenants, including Annie's family, had died in the fire.

Old Selina had been fortunate. At the time, she lived in the building next to the print shop. It was the house ordered demolished by the owner of the tenements to stop the fire from spreading farther. But at least Selina and her family had time to get out.

"Why did it have to be a fire?" wailed Annie. "I was in a fire at Stenton Castle. I know how it feels. The heat! The choking! Gorblimey, Lady Caroline. Why did it have to be a fire?"

Hurting with compassion but utterly helpless, Jeannette could only repeat, "I am so sorry, Annie."

"Where are they, Lady Caroline? I'm still around, aren't I? Why can't they be?"

"I don't know. But I was taught when I was a little girl that people who die go to heaven."

"Or to hell," muttered Annie. "I was taught, too. But all I heard was stories of hellfire and brimstone."

"Well, the nuns taught me about heaven, and I'd rather believe in that than in hell."

For a long time, Annie said nothing, then, with a little sniff, she asked, "And what was your suggestion?"

"That you return to Stenton Castle."

The shadow that was Annie drooped even more. "Knew I'd be a nuisance to you."

"Not at all. But you've told me more than once that at Stenton you felt strong, that you could make yourself heard and seen by anyone you fancied."

"Aye."

"Which makes me think your destiny lies at Stenton."

"My destiny? The reason I'm still around instead of in heaven or hell?"

Jeannette nodded.

"Gorblimey! If you're right . . ."

Annie's shape grew denser. Jeannette saw the outline of the huge mobcap, the striped skirt, the dark blue overdress.

On one of the floors above, a door slammed. Footsteps pounded on the stairs.

Jeannette and Annie exchanged a look and hurried on, toward the ground floor.

"But how will I get there?" whispered Annie.

"Don't worry. I'll find someone. Lord Decimus, perhaps. He has missed you."

"I've missed him, too. I should have talked to him once in a while. Only it gets difficult at times. You see, he thinks I'm *human.*"

There was no time for more. They had reached the ground floor. Annie slipped outside. Jeannette was slower, since she must first open the door.

And then she stood motionless on the stoop as her gaze fell on the gentleman talking to Isabella, minding the horses.

Simon.

He came toward her.

"I see you found old Selina."

"Yes. Isabella knew of her."

Strangely breathless, she descended the two steps to the street.

Someone burst through the door behind her, clattered past, and hurried toward Cheapside—a butcher's lad, late for work, tying his striped apron as he ran.

She searched Simon's face, his eyes, for a sign of warmth—or even ire at her presence in Beggars Alley—but encountered only polite indifference, a most daunting sight.

"Simon, can we talk?"

He inclined his head. "I'm at your service, of course. But I am on my way to see Mrs. Hunter's niece. My client may go to trial as soon as tomorrow, and I need Bess to testify on his behalf."

"The man who had gaol fever? Who might be hanged?"

"Yes. He recovered and will stand trial."

She held out her hand.

"Then go. I'll say a rosary for your client."

A spark lit in his eyes then, but was ruthlessly extinguished with a quick lowering of his lids.

"Thank you, Lady Caroline. You're most gracious."

And he bowed and strode off toward the print shop, about nine or ten doors down the alley.

"He told me I could work as a clerk at one of his factories in Lancaster," said Isabella, her voice throbbing with suppressed excitement. "A cotton spinnery. He cleared it with the head clerk, and he'll be sending someone over with the details and the directions."

"What do you know!" Annie bounced into the phaeton. "Not only my problems are solved, but Isabella's as well."

But all Jeannette could think was that he hadn't even bothered to tell her.

He had called her Lady Caroline, gravely, and without the hint of mockery that accompanied the title while he believed her an imposter. And he had walked off without a promise to call after the trial.

That night, a messenger arrived with a letter from Simon, directing Mr. Neal Doolittle, head clerk of Ashton Spinnery, Lancaster, to employ Miss Isabella

Herder as junior clerk, employment to commence on the fifteenth of July.

"That's in two weeks!" Isabella snatched her gowns off the hook behind the door and flung them on the bed. She pulled a drawer from the chest below the window and dumped the contents on top of the gowns. "I must pack! I must get a stagecoach ticket!"

Jeannette laughed at the girl's excitement. "You're not going anywhere tonight. So clear off your bed again and look what's inside the box Mr. Renshaw also sent."

"It's a hat box."

Isabella frowned at the elegant silver and blue box from London's leading milliner dangling from Jeannette's hand. Her face drained of color. Her eyes, wide, horrified, flew to Jeannette's face.

"Lady Caroline! Surely he wouldn't—he couldn't expect—"

"No, Isabella." Jeannette's voice was crisp. "I'm sure Mr. Renshaw is not sending you a hat, and he is not expecting any favors in return for giving you employment. I suggest you open the box before you say anything else."

Isabella set the box on the bed and with trembling fingers pulled off the lid.

Inside, neatly folded, lay a pink lace gown.

Jeannette feared her heart would stop. But, of course, it did not. It had more sense than that.

But a gown! What could Simon be thinking of! A gown was worse than a hat.

"My wedding gown," whispered Isabella. "He went to Mrs. Pelham and fetched my things."

Jeannette found that, suddenly, breathing was easier. As if she had doubted Simon.

Reverently, Isabella lifted the lacy folds.

"There's something else," said Jeannette. "Wrapped in tissue."

"Mum's locket!"

Isabella tore the tissue in her haste to unwrap the locket. She snapped it open.

"My grandparents. Won't they be surprised when I get to Lancaster almost as soon as my letter? And I can tell them that I have employment at the spinnery—as a clerk! Oh, I'm so grateful to you and Mr. Renshaw, I could cry."

And Isabella did cry, but that was the following morning when Jeannette saw her safely into the stagecoach to Lancaster.

Neither her father nor Mrs. Effington was home when Jeannette returned to George Street. The footman disclosed that Lord Decimus had called, and a few minutes later all three, Lord Luxton, Lord Decimus, and Mrs. Effington had left together in a great hurry.

Jeannette did not enjoy being alone. Silence made it too tempting to think about Simon. She was determined not to give in to despair again, but it could not be denied that he had sent no personal message to her when he sent the letter for Isabella.

She had mulled over that brief meeting in Beggars Alley until her head started to throb. But she didn't mind the headache, for she had remembered that spark of warmth in his eyes when she told him she would pray for his client.

He had no reason to hide that warmth as quickly as he had done—unless he was indeed, as Mrs. Effington said, one of those tiresome men who would not court a lady he believed above his touch. Who would not send a personal note or call lest the gestures were misconstrued.

Truly, this time she would not despair. How could she, when above all she felt exasperated. She wanted to shake him but was denied the pleasure since he did not come near her.

What was a lady to do with an exasperating, tiresome man, who fetched a girl's wedding gown from a brothel and who defended those in court who could not pay for the services of a barrister?

The lady had no choice but to get into trouble. Or, at least, lead him to believe she'd be in trouble but for his intervention.

The answer was so simple, she couldn't understand why she hadn't thought of it before. Now, she only needed to figure out what sort of trouble would best suit her purpose. She did not want him to come dashing to the rescue in Beggars Alley or at the docks. She wanted him right here, in the front parlor, where they had met twice before.

She spent the day staging the scene in the front parlor. It did not worry her that she didn't immediately come up with a spot of trouble that would bring Simon hotfoot to George Street, but she did begin to worry when the afternoon progressed and her father had still not returned.

He could not have intended to be gone long, or he would have left word. But Mrs. Effington and Lord Decimus were with him. Even if he had been taken ill suddenly, she need not fret. Her chaperone was a sensible woman and would see to his care.

Finally, at five o'clock, her father's carriage stopped in front of the house. Her father, obviously in excellent trim and not a bit unwell, helped Mrs. Effington out. But there was no sign of Lord Decimus.

Drat! She wanted to talk to him about taking Annie to Stenton Castle.

Her father and Mrs. Effington stepped into the parlor.

Moving away from the window, Jeannette said, "Papa, I wish you had brought Lord Decimus with you! I particularly wanted to speak to him."

"I'm afraid you'll have to wait awhile, my dear. Decimus followed Prinny to Brighton. That's why he stopped by this morning. To take his leave."

"Oh."

Lord Decimus might be in Brighton all summer. She'd have to think of something else.

She noticed that her father and Mrs. Effington still stood just inside the door, Mrs. Effington's gloved hand resting lightly on his arm.

"Papa? Mrs. Effington? Is something wrong?"

Her father tugged at the collar of his shirt. Mrs. Effington's rosy face turned a shade darker.

Jeannette's eyes widened as she looked at the couple.

A couple. That was precisely the impression they gave.

"Papa?"

"Jeannette, my dear. Mrs. Effington has done me the honor of becoming my wife."

The room spun around her.

"Lady Caroline!"

A firm hand clasped her arm.

"Sit down, Lady Caroline. You mustn't swoon. Gracious! We should have broken the news more gently."

Jeannette protested, "I'm not the swooning type."

The spinning furniture settled. Her gaze focused on Mrs. Effington's plump, worried face close to hers.

She looked at her father, still near the door, his expression a mixture of anxiety and sheepishness.

"Papa, you eloped!"

"My dear, we didn't mean to do it this way. But I had no choice when Decimus said he was leaving town for the summer. He was to be our witness."

Mrs. Effington said, "I didn't think you'd mind. Not with your future being settled here in London and your dear Papa returning all alone to New Orleans."

Jeannette tried to retain composure but gave up the struggle as impossible. She burst out laughing.

"My *chaperone* and my father. Eloped!" She gave another choke of laughter. "Oh, this is precious! Something to tell my children, and my grandchildren, and my great-grandchildren."

She hugged Mrs. Effington, who beamed, and kissed her father, who looked vastly relieved.

Suddenly, all thought of laughter fled. "Papa, which name did you use for the marriage register?"

He raised a brow, sure of himself and in command of the situation.

"There's only one name I use. Hugh Dundas, Marquis of Luxton."

Jeannette glanced at Mrs. Effington, who smiled complacently. "It suits me to be a marchioness for the last years of my life."

"But—"

"There's no but, Lady Caroline. I know what I am doing, and I'm doing it with my eyes wide open. Your papa and I were both alone. He offered me the comforts and elegancies of life I've sorely missed, since my late husband neglected to provide for me. And I will give your father the care and companionship he needs, for he'll be lonely without you."

"Please, Mrs. Effington! You owe me no explanation. And believe me, I'm very happy for you both. It's just that . . ."

Helplessly, Jeannette looked at her chaperone, who fancied being a marchioness, yet couldn't possibly be one. Who might not even be married since the groom was using a false name.

"I understand, dear," Mrs. Effington said softly. A mischievous look flitted across the plump, comely face. "But who's to know? No one who would tell."

"No, indeed." Jeannette shook off doubts and concern. There was no need for anxiety. Mrs. Effington, the sensible chaperone, had much in common with Hugo Winters, alias Hugh Dundas.

"And what's more," said Hugh, echoing Jeannette's thoughts, ". . . we are very well suited."

"Down to the last card." Laughter danced in Jeannette's eyes. "The moment I learned Mrs. Effington is as much a gambler as you, Papa, I should have known you'd snatch her up."

Hugh rubbed his hands. "I feel like celebrating. Shall we have champagne?"

"Papa, when are you taking Mrs. E—your wife to New Orleans?"

"I'd like to be gone before autumn, but, of course, I'll stay as long as it takes to get you settled."

Jeannette's brow knitted as a scheme formed in her mind.

"Papa, my future is all but settled. Give me a day or two, and in the meantime, I want you to book your passage to New Orleans. Immediately."

It took some persuasion and several reminders that Dr. Moore had suggested more than once he should return to the warmth of New Orleans as soon as possible, but finally Hugh agreed to book cabins on the next available ship.

"And I'm sure," the new Marchioness of Luxton said helpfully, "Lady Anne would look after dear Lady Caroline if she cannot be married immediately."

"Please don't ask Aunt Anne! Or, at least," Jeannette amended hastily when she saw her father's frown, ". . . don't say anything to her just yet. There's no point, if I end up married long before you leave."

"Very well," said Hugh. "Though I'd like to know where this unexpected suitor will spring from, when throughout the Season you didn't look at any of the eligible young men."

Jeannette smiled, a secretive little smile, and one of relief.

Her suitor might be reluctant, but she could deal with that. Only Aunt Anne to the rescue had not fitted the scheme at all.

Chapter Thirty-one

The next morning, Jeannette sent Archer to the Court of Old Bailey to find out what had happened or would be happening to Simon's crossing sweep.

Archer returned just after luncheon. The trial had been held that very morning and sentence pronounced on Simpson, the crossing sweep. Ten years deportation.

"An' I dunno as justice was done, my lady." Archer twisted and untwisted his cap in his large hands. "Mr. Renshaw, he brought in a witness to swear the gentleman as was killed drew a knife on Simpson but stumbled over some rubbish an' killed hisself."

"Mr. Renshaw told me about the case, and I agree, the sentence is hardly fair."

"Still," said Archer, turning philosophical, ". . . could've been a hanging sentence or transportation fer life."

"Did Mr. Renshaw seem . . . angry? Upset?"

"Dunno how he felt about the trial, my lady. You know how he looks when he don't want ye ter know what he's thinkin'."

Yes, indeed, she did. No one could look as politely indifferent as Simon.

"But he seemed mighty interested ter see me.

Gave me one o' those sharp looks, he did. Then came over afterward an' asked if you sent me."

"He did, did he? Well, thank you Archer."

Jeannette handed the groom a coin and dismissed him. She rather thought Simon's interest in Archer was a good sign, but, of course, one could never be certain when it came to a tiresome, exasperating man like Simon.

Settling herself at the *escritoire,* she stared at the sheet of blank vellum that had been lying atop the blotter since the previous evening. It was simple to conceive a scheme, but rather more difficult to carry it out.

Scruples had to be overcome, the dictum that a lady did not cast herself at a gentleman.

She had not written her note to Simon the previous night. She had decided to wait for a more opportune moment, when the trial would be off his mind.

Well, the trial was over and done with. She had no further excuses for a postponement. In fact, if she did not act soon, her father was likely to cancel the passages he had booked that morning on the *Evening Star,* sailing in a week.

And the following morning would be perfect for a meeting since her father and Mrs. Effington planned to call on Lady Anne and tell her about the marriage. At ten o'clock.

A surge of excitement shot through her. She snatched up a pen, dipped it in the inkwell, and started to write.

The words flowed. It was quite easy after all. And to the dickens with the old-fashioned notion that a lady should not pursue a gentleman.

She sealed the note, then rang for the footman before she could change her mind.

Next, fetch the love potion from Annie.

But Annie had made her own plans, and she was not to be swayed. Annie wanted to add the measure of love potion to Simon's Madeira personally. Then, at ten-fifteen, she would leave for Stenton Castle. And since Lord Decimus was not available to take her, Annie had a suggestion that would work just as well.

Excitedly, she whispered in Jeannette's ear.

"Archer?" Jeannette sank onto the edge of her bed. "But, Annie! Have you considered? A drive to the coast will mean several stops. What if something happens? What if you get left behind somewhere?"

"I'll cling to him like a burr." Annie giggled. "Lady Caroline, I'm plain determined that Archer will hear me before we reach the castle. Perhaps even see me!"

"But what reason would I have to send Archer to Stenton? That's why I thought Lord Decimus would have been perfect. It's his nephew's castle, isn't it?"

"Just write a little note to Miss Elizabeth. Her grace, I should say. She'll be glad to have me back, and she'll see to it that Archer is put up for the night."

"Gorblimey! If this isn't the most harebrained scheme I've ever heard."

"Lady Caroline! For goodness' sake, mind your tongue. I told you gorblimey is not an expression a lady would use."

"But, then, I won't be a lady much longer."

Placing her hands on her hips, Annie cocked her head. "And what do you mean by that?"

"Never mind. But why should I worry about a harmless little expression when tomorrow morning I'll be tossing my cap over the windmill and do something utterly improper!"

It was a quarter to ten. Annie was alone in the front parlor. The drapes were flung wide to afford a view of the street and Archer when he drove up in the phaeton at ten-fifteen to fetch Lady Caroline's letter for her grace, the Duchess of Stenton.

A decanter of Madeira and glasses were set out on the credenza. Also on the credenza stood a round container of plaited straw. The lid did not fit quite properly but well enough to hide the small cork-stoppered bottle Annie had placed in the container.

The love potion.

In her hand, Annie held a second small bottle. Lady Caroline had balked at syrup of poppy as an ingredient for the love potion, but the recipe called for it. So Annie would add a drop or two of laudanum, which the housekeeper kept in a locked cabinet in her bedroom. Laudanum was made of poppy.

Annie took the love potion from its hiding place. She removed the corks from both small bottles. But as she was about to measure the laudanum into the potion, a picture of the nursery at Stenton Castle flashed through her mind. The nursery as it had been before the fire destroyed it.

She saw Old Nurse measuring a drop of laudanum into the children's warm milk at night, and later, when the children were asleep, several drops into the cup of chamomile tea Nurse herself drank before going to bed.

And she remembered the fire that had wakened her. She remembered racing to Old Nurse's room and to the children's rooms, and how long it took to rouse them. And then the nursery door had stuck and they were all trapped in the fire and the heat and the smoke.

Shaking, Annie stared at the bottle containing the love potion and at the bottle she had taken from the housekeeper's cabinet. Syrup of poppy. Laudanum.

Lady Caroline did not want it in the love potion.

Annie heard soft, quick steps on the stairs and knew that Lady Caroline would enter the parlor at any moment.

Again, she looked at the bottles. She must do it now. Immediately.

But she could not. Not with memories of the Stenton Castle nurseries tormenting her.

Recorking the bottles, she placed the potion in the straw container. The other bottle held tightly in her hand, she flitted off to put it back in the locked cabinet.

But, without this ingredient, would the love potion work?

Jeannette had checked the Madeira, she had checked the love potion in the straw container, and now she checked the clock on the mantel for the third time. And it still lacked five minutes to ten. Dash it! It wouldn't have hurt Simon if he had shown a bit of eagerness.

And where was Annie?

The door knocker rang out. Three sharp raps. Simon.

For an instant, she wavered. She couldn't do it. It was too brazen.

Rubbish.

She chose a chair and sat down as the front door opened. She heard Simon's deep voice and reminded herself that he had called her a brazen hussy in St. James's Park and that a smile had lit his eyes when he said it.

And then the footman showed him into the parlor. As she had anticipated, Simon's face was a thundercloud and he hardly waited until the door had closed before he gave annoyance rein.

"What the devil is this nonsense, Jeannette?"

He thrust a sheet of ivory vellum under her nose. A sheet, much creased as if it had been crunched by an angry fist, then straightened out again. A piece of writing she had no difficulty recognizing as her own note to him.

"Good morning, Simon. Won't you sit down?"

He shook the note. "You say your father married and is leaving you on your own. You demand that I find you a house in Grosvenor Square or some other fashionable place so you can set up your own establishment! Explain, if you please."

"But, Simon, I've said everything in the note. What else is there to explain?"

She met his stormy look warily. She had done her best to put him in a temper, for she had known that to try to sway him from his set course when he was smooth, in control, and persuasive, would have been a lost cause. But perhaps she had underestimated his reaction just a tiny bit.

"Devil a bit!" He sat down abruptly. "Your father cannot possibly have married."

From the corner of her eye, Jeannette saw Annie flit to the credenza.

"But he did. He married Mrs. Effington the day before yesterday. Lord Decimus witnessed the ceremony, and Papa is right now telling my Aunt Anne."

"Decimus! As if he hadn't done enough damage already. And now, I expect, we not only have a false Marquis of Luxton but a marchioness as well."

Jeannette saw Annie gesturing wildly and looked at the clock. It was five minutes past ten.

She rose. "Let me pour you a glass of Madeira, Simon."

Always a gentleman, he would not remain seated while she stood.

"No, thank you. Jeannette, are you certain they're married?"

"Gorblimey!" said Annie. "You *must* want a glass of wine.

"I don't." Simon raked a hand through his thick, dark hair. "And you shouldn't use an expression you picked up in Beggars Alley. It isn't suitable for a lady."

Jeannette sat down again. Simon wouldn't take wine. But he heard Annie. True, he believed it was *she* who had spoken. But the meeting was not going the way she had planned.

"Simon, I will need a house by next week when Papa and Mrs. Effington leave for New Orleans. There should be plenty of houses available now that everyone has left town. You must help me find one that will suit me."

"The devil I will! A young lady of nineteen does not set up her own establishment."

"I'll be twenty in September."

"You will be the talk of the town."

"I *have* been the cause of gossip practically since my arrival. Simon, I want a house. This one was leased for the Season. Any day Lord Decimus's niece could demand it back."

"If your father leaves, you must go to live with Lady Anne."

"No. I still want to open some kind of shop where young women can take refuge from the streets, where they will have honest employment and a home. That will cause more talk than setting up my own establishment. If I lived with Aunt Anne, it would reflect on her. And what do you think it would do to Agnes's chances of a good marriage?"

"Agnes's dowry will guarantee a good marriage." Again, he raked a hand through his hair. "But aren't you forgetting your own marriage? That, if you'll remember, was the purpose of your visit to London."

"It was Papa's goal. *He* made the promise. I would much rather not have a husband who will order my life and make me perfectly miserable."

He scowled. "A husband to order your life is precisely what you need. Though I don't doubt you'll lead the poor devil a merry dance."

"And don't you think he'll enjoy it?"

Abruptly, Simon turned from her. Twice before, they had faced each other in this suffocatingly small room. Twice before, the incredible number of chairs and tables crammed into the room had frustrated his urge to pace.

Devil a bit! He understood her desire to get out of this house. But setting up her own establishment! She might as well tie her garter in public.

There was nothing for it, but if she stayed in London without her father, she must be married.

"Jeannette—"

He turned to face her again, but she had left the chair and was pouring Madeira at the credenza. He'd take a glass now, by George.

He hadn't received her note until late the previous evening. After the trial, he had spent time with Simpson's family, a wife, a sister, and five children, who were disconsolate because Simpson had been taken straight from the courtroom to a transport ship. He had spent the afternoon and evening on the docks searching for a ship that would carry Simpson's family to Botany Bay.

That accomplished, he had gone to White's, had ordered dinner and a bottle of wine to wash down the acrid taste of "justice". It had been close to midnight when he arrived in Grosvenor Square where he had been staying since his father's arrival in town. Jeannette's note was propped against his shaving mirror.

He had ripped the seal and devoured every word—like a lovesick youth!—only to be recalled to sanity by her impossible demand for an establishment of her own.

Leaning a shoulder against the mantel of the fireplace, he watched her fill a second glass. Did she plan to join him, then? She preferred sherry or Madeira to ratafia, he remembered from her first visit to Lady Louisa's house, although her general preference was tea or coffee.

Simon frowned when, suddenly, he saw a second female at the credenza.

Great Scot! The mere thought of wine had gone to his head. He was drunk as a wheelbarrow.

The second female lifted the lid off a straw container and removed a small brown bottle. Jeannette pointed to one of the glasses, and the other girl, her face all but hidden by a huge mobcap, poured from the bottle into the glass.

Jeannette turned and saw him looking her way. For an instant, she looked guilty as hell.

Then she smiled. "I thought you might have changed your mind about the wine. I'll join you if you will take a glass."

While Jeannette's back was turned, the other female poured whatever it was in that small bottle into the second glass. He wanted to smash the ominous little bottle but did not dare shift from the fireplace lest he fall flat on his face, drunk as he was.

But, dammit, he wasn't drunk. He hadn't touched a drop of alcohol, save for the burgundy with his dinner the previous night. So what was it that he saw? The hallucinations of a fevered mind?

But the only sickness he suffered was love sickness.

Behind him, on the mantel shelf, a clock chimed the quarter hour past ten. Outside, a carriage drew up.

The mobcapped female dropped the little bottle into the straw container. She exchanged a look with Jeannette, then, suddenly, flitted across the room toward the windows.

"Good-bye, Lady Caroline!" the strange, waif-like

creature cried. "And remember! The love potion *will* work."

The *love* potion?

Simon cocked a brow. If this was hallucination, it was not without intrigue.

Bafflement was just changing to amusement when he saw the female with the ridiculous mobcap disappear through a window.

A closed window.

He shook his head, hoping to clear it of the strange imaginations, then stared in disbelief when next he saw the female on the seat of the phaeton, beside Archer.

The footman who had let him into the house approached Archer with a letter. Archer nodded, pocketed the letter, and drove off, apparently unaware of that strange little creature beside him.

Almost expecting to see yet more unknown females, Simon slowly faced the credenza again.

But Jeannette was alone. Carrying the two glasses of Madeira, she was coming toward him.

"Who was that?" he asked. "That girl in the impossible cap."

Jeannette gave a start, and a drop of wine ran down the sides of each glass.

"That was Annie." Her look dared him to laugh. "The ghost I told you about."

Chapter Thirty-two

A love potion and a ghost.

Hallucination or reality?

Simon went to the window and looked out. But the phaeton was gone, and what the devil did it matter!

"You didn't believe me when I first told you about Annie," said Jeannette. "You thought it was me, playing ghost."

Simon turned. Leaning against the window frame, he watched as she slowly came toward him. Not a ghost. A woman who had captured his heart.

She was wearing a gown of some ice-blue material, but it was the darker blue velvet ribbon marking the high waistline and decorating the short, puffed sleeves with tiny bows, that caught his attention. The color of the velvet matched her eyes. She wore the same color ribbon in her hair, and he noticed that the curls piled atop her head were once again askew.

"You need to let your maid go," he said. "She doesn't know how to dress your hair."

She handed him a glass. "I do not have a maid."

Simon looked at the wine, then at the straw container on the credenza.

He took a sip. A love potion, was it? Love potion be damned. He had imagined the whole.

Only this Madeira tasted dashed curious.

He frowned at Jeannette. She stood too close for comfort. How the deuce was he supposed to concentrate!

"Jeannette, we were talking about your marriage."

"Yes?" Her look challenged him. "Who do you think would marry me? Almost twenty years old. Picking quarrels with abbesses. Stealing girls from brothels."

He took another sip. Cinnamon. He definitely tasted cinnamon. Had she been real, then, the female of the quaintly old-fashioned look whom he had seen pouring something into the wine? Bloody hell! He had nothing to fear from a love potion. No man could be more in love than he was.

"I'm a Catholic," said Jeannette. "If I marry an English peer and I insist that our children must be raised in the Roman Catholic faith, wouldn't my husband's heir be barred from taking his seat in Parliament?"

His eyes narrowed. "What are you driving at?"

She reached past him and set her glass down on the window sill. Folding her arms beneath her bosom, she glared at him.

"That I don't want to marry a title, as you seem to believe!"

"Don't be silly. Of course you must marry a man of rank. It's why your father brought you to London. It's what he promised."

"Papa brought me here. The promise is fulfilled. Even Hugh Dundas—that other Hugh Dundas—cannot expect Papa to drag me to the altar. And besides, there was no mention of a nobleman in the promise. Only an *Englishman.*"

"You're quibbling—"

"I am not!" The glare in her eyes became more ferocious. "I would not mind marrying an Englishman. But I can hardly do so when no one has proposed to me, can I?"

She gave him no chance to reply. Arms akimbo, she continued ruthlessly, "Except for one overbearing solicitor who said that, if I must marry an English fool, I would have to make do with him. But even he has, apparently, thought better of his offer."

He flinched.

Pushing away from the window, he said, "Jeannette, that was no offer. It was an insult. And I beg your pardon."

"Well, I won't."

"Won't what?"

"I won't pardon you. I want you to find me a house, and I want you to arrange the lease of a business property."

Struggling for patience, he finished the wine.

"You don't know what you're saying." He set the glass beside hers on the sill. "Jeannette, you cannot—"

"Yes, I can. I have the means to do what I please. And it does not please me to marry some fancy nobleman who expects me to be an acquiescent wife and bear his children in the country while he amuses himself in town."

"No man in his right mind would amuse himself in town when he could be with you."

She took a step closer to him. Disturbingly close. Invitingly close. He need only reach out . . .

He walked around a chair, placing its solid form between them, and reminded himself that she was above his touch, that he was honor bound to guide and counsel her.

"How would you know, Simon?" She followed him around the chair. "Would you want to be with your wife instead of visiting your *chère amie?*"

"Yes," he said harshly. "But we're not discussing me."

"Why not?"

"Because we're discussing your hairbrained scheme of setting up your own establishment."

"It is not hairbrained. And you cannot stop me."

Something inside him snapped. Forgotten was the duty of a family solicitor. Forgotten were good intentions and resolve.

"Can I not? I'll prove you wrong."

He saw the gleam in her eyes just as his arms closed around her and he bent his head to claim her mouth. But nothing—not the knowledge that she was a brazen little hussy nor a renewed stirring of the voice of duty—could stop him from claiming that kiss.

It had been too long since he tasted the sweetness of her mouth. Too long since he felt her pliant body pressed against his. Ruthlessly, he drew her closer. Never again would he wait so long. He wanted to kiss her day after day, night after night. He wanted to hold and have her forever.

"Jeannette."

He kissed the corners of her mouth. He kissed her eyelids, brushed his mouth across her forehead and temples.

"Sweet, willful Jeannette."

Again, he tasted her lips, so eager and willing.

"I love you, Jeannette."

Her arms tightened around his neck. She opened her eyes.

"And I love you. But, Simon, if you love me, why won't you marry me?"

"Who says I won't?" Clasping her waist, he held her at a slight distance. "I told you, didn't I, that I'd stop you from setting up your own establishment."

She scowled but could not hide the blaze of happiness in her eyes.

"That, Mr. Renshaw, is the sorriest proposal of marriage I ever heard. But I suppose I had better accept, since it's doubtful I'll have a better one."

Gravely, he looked at her.

"You could have, Jeannette. You are one of the highest ranking women in the country. I am merely a solicitor and a factory owner."

"And I want to be Mrs. Simon Renshaw, wife of the solicitor and factory owner."

"But you'll be Lady Caroline. Always."

"No, I won't. I'll drop the title when we marry. Like the Dowager Lady Aldrich. She was Lady Sophronia, but when she married the baronet, she dropped her own title."

He crushed her to his breast.

"Sweet and willful," he murmured into the knot of curls from which the pins threatened to slip. "And a brazen hussy in desperate need of a lady's maid."

She drew back. "I don't need a maid. I like taking care of myself."

"You won't ever need to take care of yourself. Not when you're married to me."

Her eyes danced. "Are you offering to do my hair?"

"Baggage. But, yes, I'll do your hair. I'll button your gown. I'll assist with your bath."

A delicate pink suffused her cheeks.

"I'll do anything to see that blush again and again."

With the tip of a finger he traced her cheek, the long, delicate neck. He brushed over the creamy skin, the gentle swell of her breasts showing above the neckline.

His voice turned husky. "I'll wager my wig and gown that you blush all over."

"In that case, hadn't you better marry me soon?"

"As soon as I can get a special license. Will tomorrow do?"

"Yes." She flung herself into his arms. "Yes, let's get married tomorrow."

Tilting her head, she gave him a look of mischief mingled with eagerness. "Unless you could manage to find a license this afternoon?"

His gaze fell on the two glasses in the window sill. His, empty. Hers, untouched.

A love potion? A ghost?

Nothing but a flight of imagination. Neither he nor Jeannette stood in need of any potion. Certainly not he. Her kiss, the feel of her in his arms worked a magic more powerful than any aphrodisiac.

Epilogue

Late one afternoon toward the end of July, Mr. and Mrs. Simon Renshaw were taking tea in the sitting room on the first floor of the George Street house.

It was a daily ritual, a festive ceremony, this meeting in the one chamber not overstuffed with furniture, when Simon returned from his offices in Lincoln's Inn Fields and Jeannette from the dressmaker's and milliner's establishment she was planning in Oxford Street. Occasionally, Malcolm Renshaw joined the young couple. But most of the time they were alone, since the rest of the family had retreated into the country.

They were alone this afternoon. They'd had tea and scones and raspberry tarts, and Jeannette was sitting on the sofa beside Simon. Her feet were drawn up and tucked away beneath the folds of her sprigged-muslin gown. Her head nestled against her husband's shoulder.

She yawned delicately. It was hard work designing a shop elegant enough to draw the fastidious and demanding ladies of the *ton* when they returned to town for the Little Season. It was even harder planning the fitting rooms with their large mirrors, the work rooms which must have adequate light and ventilation, and comfortable living quarters above the shop for the seamstresses and milliners.

Living quarters . . . this reminded her of the letter delivered in the post that morning.

"Simon, we must make a push to find another house. Lord Decimus's niece wrote that she and her husband decided to live permanently in the country. They're coming to town in mid-August to consult an accoucheur and to arrange for the sale of this house."

"Hmm." Sliding an arm around her, he drew her close. "You must do as you deem fit, my love."

She liked the warmth of his hand on her bare arm, her neck, the tantalizing brush of his fingertips along the neckline of her gown and along the sapphire necklace her Aunt Louisa had sent at Malcolm Renshaw's command.

But she could not like the absentminded tone of her husband's voice or the distracting crackle of the papers he held in his free hand.

She straightened. "Simon, what are you reading? Is it so important that it cannot wait a few hours or until morning?"

"It's a report from Doolittle about trouble among the stockingers and cotton weavers in the Midlands. With exports of cotton goods falling and bread prices rising, Doolittle fears the unrest will turn to violence and eventually spread north."

"Will you have to go to Lancaster?"

"No. At the moment, the north is quiet. There's plenty of cotton to spin. But when we can no longer sell our—"

Simon dropped the reports from the factor and head accountant of the Ashton Spinnery in Lancaster. Placing the freed hand beneath his wife's chin, he gave her a look that made her pulse beat faster.

"It can wait," he said huskily before claiming her mouth.

There was nothing absentminded about his kiss or the way his hands awakened the yearnings which, perhaps, a proper lady should deny. But Jeannette had learned that those yearnings, if indulged, led to pure pleasure for both Simon and herself.

So wrapped up in their kiss were they that neither heard the front door knocker or the commotion in the foyer and, moments later, on the stairs.

It was the sound of the sitting room door bursting open that drove them apart.

"*Mon Dieu!* Jeannette, what are you doing? Have you no shame?"

"*Grandmère!*"

The stout, white-haired lady dressed in black from head to toe advanced on the sofa with her ebony walking stick raised threateningly.

"*Brute!* Cad! Unhand my granddaughter."

Hastily, Jeannette slid off the sofa and placed herself between her grandmother and Simon.

"*Grandmère,* I am married!"

"*Marié?*" Madame Vireilles stopped abruptly.

From the doorway came young Mr. Harte's voice, breathless from a scuffle with the footman who had unwisely attempted to deny the old lady access to the upper floor until he could enquire whether his master and mistress were at home.

"Madame, permit me to introduce Mr. Simon Renshaw, the gentleman who sent me to New Orleans."

Meanwhile, Simon had risen and firmly set Jeannette aside.

"Indeed, madame. I am Harte's employer. And I am also Jeannette's husband."

Snapping dark eyes darted from Simon to Jeannette. "Very well. You will explain in a moment how that came about. Now I want to know where is Hugh or Hugo or whatever his name may be. I have a crow to pluck with that gentleman."

Jeannette's eyes widened. "You know that Papa is Hugo Winters?"

"Of course I know. This young man—" Madame Vireilles stabbed her walking stick at Harte. "He went to the *boutique* and drove poor Nounou mad with his questions. She came to me and confessed the deception she and that Hugo perpetrated on my poor daughter at the plantation. And then she had the gall to demand that I arrange a passage to London for her!"

"Oh! Is Nounou with you?"

Jeannette would have dashed out the door, but her grandmother put out a detaining hand.

"Don't be ridiculous, child. Nounou is far too old to be jauntering around the world."

Jeannette blinked. Nounou too old? She was several years younger than *Grandmère,* to whom she had been recommended as wet nurse for Jeanne, the seventh and last child of her grandparents.

The ebony walking stick rapped sharply on the floor. "Now, where is he? Hugh . . . Hugo. Ah, bah! That worthless son-in-law of mine! Where is he?"

"On his way to New Orleans, *Grandmère.*"

There was a long moment of silence.

Although she knew her grandmother did not like overt affection or solicitude, Jeannette placed an arm around the older lady.

"*Grandmère,* Papa is still Hugh Dundas, Marquis of Luxton. And he is married."

"Hah! Didn't I always say he's an adventurer and

a gambler!" Madame Vireilles's voice turned gruff. "But I like him. And Nounou says he made my Jeanne happy."

"He did," Jeannette said softly. "And he has been a wonderful father to me."

Typically, her grandmother disguised any tender emotion with a scowl.

"Well, Jeannette? Aren't you going to show me to a room? Captain Wyllys will sail again in two weeks. I have much shopping to do before then. And you, child, have much explaining to do. But first I must have my rest."

When the door had closed behind the two ladies, Harte looked at his employer.

"Gad, sir! What a story! Do I understand that you already know all of it? That woman, Nounou, swore that Lady Caroline did not know about the Hugh-Hugo switch. But she seems to know now."

Simon poured two brandies at the sideboard.

"I know the full story as Dundas told it." He watched the amber liquid swirl against the sides of the glasses as he carried them to the table by the sofa. "There's just one question. How did Nounou explain the sudden death of Jeanne's husband?"

Harte accepted a glass. "Yellow fever, sir. It seems there are some rare cases when a sudden collapse is the only warning. And those cases inevitably result in death. Didn't Hugh Dundas—I mean, Hugo Winters, explain?"

"Call him Hugh Dundas, Harte. It's the name he bore for thirty years. It's the name he'll take to his grave."